W9-AUX-508

Easton glanced at her, then his gaze snapped back on the road.

The moment had been fleeting, but she'd caught something in that eye contact—something deep and warm.

"So you had a crush," she said, trying to sound normal. She still sounded breathy to her own ears. Bobbie started to whimper in the back seat, and Nora reached over to pop her pacifier back into her mouth.

"It was a weird thing to bond over," Easton admitted. "But I was the one guy who thought you were just as amazing as your dad did."

"I kind of knew you had a crush," she admitted.

"It was more."

Nora's heart sped up. She cast about for something to say but couldn't come up with anything. More than a crush... What was that? Love?

The Cowboy's Triplets

PATRICIA JOHNS
&
BRENDA HARLEN

2 Heartfelt Stories

The Triplets' Cowboy Daddy
and *Claiming the Cowboy's Heart*

If you purchased this book without a cover you should be aware
that this book is stolen property. It was reported as "unsold and
destroyed" to the publisher, and neither the author nor the
publisher has received any payment for this "stripped book."

Recycling programs
for this product may
not exist in your area.

ISBN-13: 978-1-335-47330-1

The Cowboy's Triplets

Copyright © 2022 by Harlequin Enterprises ULC

The Triplets' Cowboy Daddy
First published in 2017. This edition published in 2022.
Copyright © 2017 by Patty Froese Ntihemuka

Claiming the Cowboy's Heart
First published in 2019. This edition published in 2022.
Copyright © 2019 by Brenda Harlen

All rights reserved. No part of this book may be used or reproduced in
any manner whatsoever without written permission except in the case of
brief quotations embodied in critical articles and reviews.

This is a work of fiction. Names, characters, places and incidents
are either the product of the author's imagination or are used fictitiously.
Any resemblance to actual persons, living or dead, businesses,
companies, events or locales is entirely coincidental.

For questions and comments about the quality of this book,
please contact us at CustomerService@Harlequin.com.

Harlequin Enterprises ULC
22 Adelaide St. West, 41st Floor
Toronto, Ontario M5H 4E3, Canada
www.Harlequin.com

Printed in U.S.A.

CONTENTS

Patricia Johns is a *Publishers Weekly* bestselling author who writes from Alberta, Canada. She has her Hon. BA in English literature and currently writes for Harlequin's Love Inspired and Heartwarming lines. She also writes Amish romance for Kensington Books. You can find her at patriciajohns.com.

Books by Patricia Johns

Harlequin Heartwarming

The Second Chance Club

Their Mountain Reunion
Mountain Mistletoe Christmas
Rocky Mountain Baby
Snowbound with Her Mountain Cowboy

Love Inspired

Redemption's Amish Legacies

The Nanny's Amish Family
A Precious Christmas Gift
Wife on His Doorstep
Snowbound with the Amish Bachelor
Blended Amish Blessings

Visit the Author Profile page at
Harlequin.com for more titles.

The Triplets' Cowboy Daddy

PATRICIA JOHNS

To my husband and our son.
You are the best choices I ever made.
I love you!

Chapter 1

Nora Carpenter could have cared for one baby easily enough. She could somehow have juggled two. But three—she'd never imagined that accepting the role of godmother to her half sister's babies would actually put her into the position of raising those babies on her own. She was still in shock.

Nora stood in her mother's brilliantly clean farmhouse kitchen, more overwhelmed than she had ever felt in her life. The three infants were still in their car seats, eyes scrunched shut and mouths open in hiccoughing wails. She stood over them, her jeans already stained from spilled formula and her tank top stretched from…she wasn't even sure what. She unbuckled the first infant—Rosie—and scooped her up. Rosie's cries subsided as she wriggled up against Nora's neck, but anxiety still made Nora's heart race as she fumbled with Riley's buckle. She'd come back to Hope, Montana, that afternoon so that her mother could help her out, but even that was more complicated than anyone guessed. These babies weren't just orphans in need of care; they were three tiny reminders that Nora's father hadn't been the man they all believed him to be.

Everything had changed—everything but this kitchen. The counters were crumb-free, as they always were, and the room smelled comfortingly, and very faintly, of bleach. Hand-embroidered kitchen towels hung from the stove handle—two of them, one with Monday sewn across the bottom, and one with Thursday. Today was Friday. Unless Dina Carpenter was making jam or doing canning, this was the natural state—immaculate, with no care for properly labeled towels. The babies' cries echoed through the house.

Rosie, Riley and Roberta had finished their bottles just before Nora's mother had left for a quick trip to the store for some baby supplies.

"I'll be fine!" Nora had said. Famous last words. The minute the door shut, the cries had begun, and no amount of cooing or rocking of car seats made a bit of difference.

There was a knock on the back door, and Nora shouted, "Come in!" as she scooped up Riley in her other arm and cuddled both babies close. Riley's cries stopped almost immediately, too, and that left Roberta—Bobbie, as Nora had nicknamed her—still crying in her car seat, hands balled up into tiny fists.

Nora had no idea who was at the door, and she didn't care. Whoever walked through that door was about to be put to work. Served them right for dropping by.

"Need a hand?" The voice behind her was deep—

and familiar. Nora turned to see Easton Ross, the family's ranch manager, standing in the open door. He wore jeans and cowboy boots, his shirt pushed up his forearms to reveal ropy muscle. He'd changed a lot since their school days. Back then he'd been a skinny kid, perpetually shorter than she was. Not anymore. He was most definitely a grown man...and she was no longer the one with all the power. When her father died a few months ago, he'd left Easton a piece of property.

"Easton." She smiled tiredly. "Would you mind picking up Bobbie there? She needs a cuddle."

Her personal grudge against the man would have to wait.

"Yeah...okay..." He didn't sound certain, but he crossed the room and squatted in front of the car seat.

"You know how to pick up babies, don't you?" she asked.

"Uh...sort of." His face had hardened, his jawline now strong and masculine. He used to have acne as a teenager, but there was no sign of it now. Looking at him squatting there, she realized that she'd missed him more than she'd realized—and that wasn't just the fact that she didn't have enough hands right now. And yet, while she'd been away in the city, he'd been here with her dad, building a relationship that her father would reward him with her great-grandparents' homestead. Bile rose every time she thought about it.

"Support the head and the bottom," she instructed. "The rest will take care of itself."

Easton undid the buckle then cautiously scooped up the baby in his broad, calloused hands. Bobbie settled instantly as Easton pulled her against his chest. He looked down at the baby and then up at Nora.

"There," he said. "That worked."

"Thanks…" Nora heaved a sigh. The quiet was more than welcome.

"Bobbie?" he asked. The babies were all in pink sleepers.

"Her full name is Roberta. But she's my little Bobbie. It suits her."

Nora had only had the babies in her charge for a few days of her twelve-week parental leave from work, but she was already attached. They were so sweet, and so different from each other. Rosie was the quietest of the three, and Riley couldn't abide a wet diaper. Bobbie seemed to have the strongest personality, though, and Nora could already imagine their sisterly dynamic as they grew.

"Yeah, I guess so," he said. "Hi."

"Hi." She gave him a tight smile. "Nice to see you again."

Last time she saw him was at the reading of the will. She pushed back the unpleasant memory. Regardless, Easton was a fixture around here. They used to be good friends when they were younger, and they'd spent hours riding together, or just sitting on a fence and talking. When times were tough, Easton always seemed to materialize, and his solid presence made a difference. Apparently, her father had had equally warm memories.

Easton met her gaze, dark eyes softened by a smile. "You look good."

"Babies suit me, do they?" she joked.

"So the word around town—it's true, then?" he asked.

There it was—the beginning of the town's questions. There would be a lot of them, and the answers were complicated.

"What did you hear?" she asked warily. "How much do people know?"

"That you came back to town with triplets," he said. "That your dad had an affair, and you had a half sister…" He winced. "It that part true? I find it hard to believe of him. I knew your dad better than most—"

She chafed at that reminder. The homestead was an old farmhouse her great-grandparents had built with their own hands. Over the years, the Carpenters had maintained it and Nora's parents had used it as a guesthouse. It mattered, that old house. It was Nora's connection to her family's past and she'd loved that old place. For her father to have left it to someone else… that had stung. She only found out that he'd changed his will when he died. Her mother had been surprised because she said they'd talked about doing something for Easton, but hadn't landed on what exactly. Normally Cliff and Dina talked through everything. But it looked like even Easton had been in the dark about her father's biggest secret.

"Yes, it's true." Easton wouldn't be the only one to be disappointed in this town. "My half sister, Mia, introduced herself a couple of months ago. Her mom—the other woman—" those words tasted bitter "—passed away a few years ago, and Mia was looking for her dad's side of the family. When I met her, she was already pregnant. There was no dad—she'd gone to a sperm bank. She really wanted kids and hadn't met the right guy yet."

Mia had had no idea about the affair and she never got a chance to meet Cliff. She had introduced herself after he died. It had been an awkward meeting, but Nora and Mia had recognized something in each other. Maybe they felt the genetic link. They'd both been raised only children, and to find a sibling was like a childhood daydream come true. Except this was real life, and they'd both had to come to terms with their father's infidelity.

"And you're godmother," Easton concluded.

"Yes. When she asked me to be godmother, I swear, I thought it was just a kind gesture. I never imagined this…"

Mia had died from childbirth complications—triplets being a high risk pregnancy to begin with—and Nora had grieved more deeply than she thought possible for a sister she'd only known a couple of months, whose existence rocked her own world. Nora was certain they'd have been close.

"Wow." Easton cleared his throat. "So your mom… I mean, these babies…"

"Yes, these babies are my father's illegitimate grandchildren." Nora sighed. "And Mom isn't taking it well."

That was an understatement. Nora hadn't told her mother, Dina, about Mia for a few weeks, afraid of causing her mother more grief than she was already shouldering since her husband's death. So Dina Carpenter hadn't had long to adjust to this new information before Nora and the babies arrived on her doorstep.

And Dina *hadn't* adjusted. She was still coming to terms with her late husband's infidelity and learning to run the ranch on her own. The babies only seemed to fuel more heartbreak.

"So what are you going to do?" Easton asked.

Footsteps sounded on the wooden staircase outside; then the door opened and Dina came inside, dropping some shopping bags on the floor. She was plump, with graying blond hair pulled back into a ponytail. She shut the door behind her then looked up.

"You're back," Nora said.

"I got some baby clothes, diapers, formula, soothers, three bouncy chairs—they might help with…" Dina's voice trailed off. "Hi, Easton."

Nora recognized the trepidation in her mother's voice. The secret was out. She'd been holding this one close to her chest, and Nora knew how much her mother dreaded the whole town knowing the ugly truth about her husband's affair. So did Nora, for that matter. It was worse somehow that her father wasn't here to answer any questions, or take the brunt of this for them. He deserved to feel ashamed; they didn't. Nora and her mother hadn't been the ones to betray trust; he had. But he was dead, and they were left with the fallout of Cliff Carpenter's poor choices.

"Hi, Mrs. Carpenter." Easton stood awkwardly, the baby nestled against his chest, and seemed almost afraid to move. "Just lending a hand. I came by to tell you that we're rotating pastures for fence maintenance, and that will require a bit of overtime from the ranch hands."

"More overtime?" Dina sighed. "No, no, do it. The southwest fences, right? We put them off last year, so…" She sighed. "Is that all?"

"Yeah." Easton nodded. "I can get going." He looked down at the baby in his arms then at Dina as if he didn't know what to do.

If the homestead was still in the family, Nora would have moved in there with the babies to give her mother some space, but that was no longer an option. Nora and Dina would just have to deal with this together.

"I guess we'll have to get the babies settled in your

old bedroom," Dina said. She paused, put a hand over her eyes. "I still can't believe it's come to this."

"Mom, you know I can't take care of them alone—"

"And why did you agree to be godmother?" Her mother heaved a sigh. "I swear, your generation doesn't think!" She pressed her lips together. "I'm sorry, Nora. What's done is done."

Dina grabbed the bags and headed down the hallway toward Nora's old bedroom. Nora and Easton exchanged a look.

"She's not taking this well," Nora said, feeling like she had to explain somehow.

"I can see that." Easton glanced in the direction his boss had disappeared. "You going to be okay here?"

"Do I have a choice?" Nora failed to keep the chill from her tone. The guesthouse would have been the perfect solution, but Easton owned it now. That wouldn't be lost on him. No matter how big the ranch house, the five of them would be cramped. Her mother was right—she hadn't thought this through. If she'd imagined that she'd ever have to step in and raise these girls, she would have found a polite way to decline the honor. Mia must have had some close friends…maybe some relative on her mother's side that she could have named as godparent.

Dina came back into the kitchen, her eyes redder than before. Had her mother been crying in the other room?

"Okay, let's figure this out," Dina said, her voice wooden. "Where are they going to sleep?"

Nora was staring blankly, and she looked like she wanted to cry. Two of the babies were snuggled in her arms. It was a stupid time for Easton to be noticing, but she was just as gorgeous as she'd always been, with her honey-blond hair and long, slim legs. He'd been half-way in love with her since the sixth grade. She'd never returned his feelings—ever.

Bobbie took a deep breath in her sleep then scrunched her face. He felt a surge of panic and patted the little rump as if soothing the baby would fix all of this. He glanced toward the car seat then at Bobbie. He wanted out of here—to get some space of his own to think this through. Except Nora and Dina looked like they were ready to collapse into tears, and here he stood, the legal owner of the obvious solution.

Easton was a private man. He liked quiet and soli-tude, and he had that with his new home—Cliff had known exactly how much it would mean to him. But Cliff hadn't known that he'd have three granddaughters landing on his doorstep after his death...

Dina obviously needed some time to process all this, and Nora needed help—he could feel her desperation emanating from her like waves...

Guilt crept up inside him—a nagging certainty that he stood between Nora and her solution. He didn't want to go back to the way things were when they were teens, and he certainly didn't want to give up that house and land that his boss had given him, but he couldn't just stand here and watch them scramble for some sort of arrangement as if it didn't affect him, either. He felt responsible.

The words were coming out of his mouth before he had a chance to think better of them. "You can stay with me, Nora. It's not a problem."

Nora and Dina turned toward him, relief mingled with guilt written all over both faces. There had always been tension between mother and daughter, and the current situation hadn't improved things.

"You sure?" Nora asked.

"You bet. It'll be fine. There's lots of room. Just for a few days, until you and your mom figure this out." He was making this sound like a weekend away, not a complete invasion of his privacy, but he was already entangled in this family and had been for years. This was for old time's sake—for the friendship that used to mean so much to him. And maybe this was also a guilt offering for having inherited that house to begin with.

The next few minutes were spent gathering up baby supplies and getting the car seats back into Nora's four-door pickup truck. As Nora got into the driver's seat, Dina visibly deflated from where she stood at the side door. She'd been holding herself together for her daughter's sake, it seemed, and she suddenly looked small and older.

Cliff may have been many things, but he had been a good man at heart, and no one would convince Easton otherwise. A good husband? Perhaps not, given the recent revelation. But a man could be good at heart and lousy with relationships. At least Easton hoped so, because he seemed to fall into that category himself. If it weren't for Cliff, Easton's life would have turned out a whole lot differently. Loyalty might be in short supply, but Easton knew where his lay.

He got into his own rusted-out Ford and followed Nora down the familiar drive toward his little house. *His* house. Should he feel so territorial about the old place? He'd fixed it up a fair amount since taking ownership, and the work had brought him a lot of comfort. He'd grown up in a drafty old house in town filled with his dad's beer bottles and piles of dishes that never got washed. So when he found out that Cliff had left him the house and the land, something inside him had grown— like roots sinking down, giving more security than he'd ever had. He'd stared at that deed, awash in gratefulness. He'd never been a guy who let his feelings show, but he had no shame in the tears that misted his eyes when he shook the lawyer's hand.

I shouldn't have gotten attached. And that was the story of his life, learning not to get attached, because nothing really lasted.

The farmhouse was a small, two-story house with white wooden siding and a broad, covered front porch. He hadn't been expecting company when he'd headed out for his morning chores, and he hoped that he'd left it decently clean. But this was his home, and while the situation was emotionally complicated, the legalities wouldn't change. Mr. Carpenter had left it to him. The deed was in a safety deposit box at the bank.

After they'd parked, Easton hopped out of his truck and angled around to her vehicle, where she was already unbuckling car seats.

"Thanks," Nora said as she passed him the first baby in her seat. "I don't know how to balance three of them yet. I should probably call up Mackenzie Granger and see if she has any ideas. She's got the twins, after all."

He held the front door open for her with the heel of his boot and waited while she stepped inside. The sun was lowering in the sky, illuminating the simple interior. Nora paused as she looked around.

"It's different than I left it."

"Yeah…" He wasn't sure how apologetic he should

be here. "I got rid of the old furniture. It was pretty musty."

Easton hadn't put anything on the walls yet. He had a few pictures of his mother, but they didn't belong on the wall. She'd run off when he was eight—left a letter stuck to the fridge saying she couldn't handle it anymore, and that Easton was now his father's problem. He'd never seen her again. Considering the only family pictures he had were a few snapshots of his mom, the walls had stayed bare.

"Why did my dad leave this house to you?" Nora turned to face him. "I can't figure that part out. Why would he do that?"

Easton hadn't been the one to hurt her, but he was the one standing in front of her, regardless, and he felt an irrational wave of guilt. He was caught up in her pain, whether he meant to be or not.

"I don't know…" It had been a kind gesture—more than kind—and he'd wondered ever since if there were hidden strings. "A while ago, he said that he needed someone to take care of it, put some new life into it. I'd assumed that he wanted to rent it out or something. I didn't expect this."

"But this is my great-grandparents' home," she said. "I loved this place…"

She had… He remembered helping the family paint the old house one year when he was a teenager, and Nora had put fresh curtains in the windows in the kitchen—she'd sewn them in home economics class. She did love this old house, but then she'd gone to college and gotten a city job, and he'd just figured she'd moved on.

"You had your own life in the city. Maybe your dad thought—"

"That doesn't mean I don't have roots here in Hope!" she shot back. "This house is mine. It should have been mine... My father should *never* have done this." She had to point her anger at someone, and it was hard to tell off the dead.

"What he should have done is debatable," Easton said. "But he made a choice."

She didn't answer him, and he didn't expect her to. She hated this, but he couldn't change facts, and he wasn't about to be pushed around, either. They'd just have to try to sort out a truce over the next few days.

"I'm making some tea," he added. "You want some?"

They'd been friends back in the day, but a lot had changed. Easton grew up and filled out. Nora had gone to college and moved to the city. He was now legal owner of a house she was still attached to, and an old friendship wasn't going to be cushion enough for all of this.

"Yes, tea would be nice." Her tone was tight.

"Nora." He turned on the rattling faucet to fill up the kettle. "I don't know what you think I did, but I never asked for this house. And I never angled for it."

"You didn't turn it down, either."

No, he hadn't. He could have refused the inheritance, but it had been an answer to midnight prayers, a way to step out from under his past. Mr. Carpenter's gift had made him feel more like family and less like the messed-up kid who needed a job. Mr. Carpenter had seen him differently, but he suspected Nora still saw him the same way she always had—a skinny kid who would do pretty much anything she asked to make her happy.

And as dumb as it was, he also saw her the same way he always had—the beautiful girl whom he wished could see past his flaws and down to his core. He was a man now—not a boy, and most certainly not a charity case. Nora was a reminder of a time he didn't want to revisit—when he'd been in love with a girl who took what he had to offer and never once saw him as more than a buddy. It hadn't been only her…he'd been an isolated kid looking for acceptance anywhere he could get it, and he didn't like those memories. They were marinated in loneliness.

That wasn't who he was anymore. Everything had changed around here. Including him.

Chapter 2

Easton heard the soft beep of an alarm go off through a fog of sleep, and he blinked his eyes open, glancing at the clock beside him. It was 3 a.m., and it wasn't his alarm. The sound filtered through the wall from the bedroom next door. He had another hour before he had to be up for chores, and he was about to roll over when he heard the sound of footsteps going down the staircase.

Nora was up—though the babies were silent. It was strange to have her back…to have her here. She'd stayed away, made a life in the city where she had an office job of some sort. She would come back for a weekend home every now and then, but she'd spent her time with friends, cousins, aunts and uncles. Easton didn't fit into any category—not anymore. He was an employee. He'd worked his shifts, managed the ranch hands and if he got so much as a passing wave from her, he'd be lucky.

Now she was in his home. Her presence seemed to be a constant reminder of his status around here—employee. Even this house—legally his—felt less like his own. There was something about Nora Carpenter that put him right back into his place. For a while he'd been able to forget about his status around here, believe he could be more, but with her back—

He wasn't going to be able to sleep listening to the soft sounds of a woman moving around the house anyway. He swung his legs over the side of his bed, yawning. The footsteps came back up the narrow staircase again, and he rose to his feet, stretching as he did. He was in a white T-shirt and pajama bottoms, decent enough to see her. He crossed his bedroom and opened the door.

Nora stood in the hallway, three bottles of milk in her hands, and she froze at the sight of him. Her blond hair tumbled over her shoulders, and she stood there in a pair of pajamas—a tank top and pink, pin-striped cotton shorts.

She's cute.

She always had been, and no matter how distant or uninterested she got, he'd never stopped noticing.

"Sorry," she whispered. "I was trying to be quiet."

He hadn't actually been prepared to see her like this—her milky skin glowing in the dim light from her open bedroom door, her luminous eyes fixed on him apologetically. She was stunning, just as she'd always been, but she was more womanly now—rounder, softer, more sure of herself. They should both be sleeping right now, oblivious to each other. That was safer by far.

"The babies aren't crying," he pointed out.

"I'm following the advice of the social worker who

gave me the lowdown on caring for triplets. She said to feed them on a schedule. If I wait for them to wake up, we'll have three crying babies."

It made sense, actually. He'd never given infant care—let alone infant care for triplets—much thought before. He should leave her to it, go back to bed…maybe go downstairs and start breakfast if he really couldn't sleep.

"Need a hand?" he asked.

Where had that come from? Childcare wasn't his domain, and frankly, neither was Nora. He'd been through this before with her—he knew how it went. She batted her eyes in his general direction, he got attached, she waltzed off once her problems were solved, and he was left behind, wrung out. Letting her stay here was help enough. As was picking up the crib for the babies after he brought her to the house. He couldn't be accused of callous indifference, but he also couldn't go down that path again.

She smiled at his offer of help. "I wouldn't turn it down."

Well, that took care of that. He trailed after her into the bedroom. The crib sat on one side of the room, Nora's rumpled bed on the other side. A window, cracked open, was between the two, and a cool night breeze curled through the room. The babies lay side by side along the mattress of the crib. Rosie and Riley looked pretty similar to his untrained eye, but he could pick out Bobbie. She was considerably bigger than the other two. But "big" was relative; they all pretty tiny.

"I was hoping my mom would be able to help me with this stuff," Nora said as she picked up the first baby and passed her to him along with a bottle. "That's Rosie," she added.

She proceeded to pick up the other two and brought them to her unmade bed, where she propped them both up against her pillow. She wiggled the bottle nipples between their lips.

"Time to eat," she murmured.

The babies started to suck without any further prompting, and Easton looked down at the infant in his arms. He followed Nora's lead, teasing the bottle into Rosie's tiny mouth, and she immediately began to drink. It felt oddly satisfying.

"So this is how it's done," he said with a soft laugh.

"Apparently," Nora replied.

They were both silent for a few moments, the only sound babies slurping. He leaned an elbow against the crib, watching the tiny bubbles move up the bottle and turn into froth at the top of the milk. He'd done this with calves on a regular basis, but never with a baby.

"I don't blame your mom," Easton said.

"Me, neither," she replied quietly. "I just didn't know where else to go. When you feel lost, you find your mom."

Easton had never had that pleasure. His mom had abandoned them, and his dad...well, his dad could barely keep his own life together, let alone help Easton.

"Sorry..." She winced. "I forgot."

Yeah, yeah, his pathetic excuse for a family. Poor Easton. He was tired of that—the pity, the charitable thoughts. *Be thankful for what you have, because someone else thinks you're lucky.* It was a deep thought for the privileged as they considered how bad they could truly have it, before they breathed a sigh of relief that they still retained their good fortune.

"So why didn't you come back more often?" Easton asked, changing the subject.

"I was busy." She shot him a sidelong look. "Why?"

"It just seems to me that two weekends a year isn't much time with your family."

"We talked on the phone. What's it to you?"

He'd struck a nerve there, but she had a point. Who was he to lecture her about family bonds? He didn't have any of his own that counted for much. Besides, his complaint wasn't really about how much time she spent with her family. He'd missed her, too. His life kept going in Hope, Montana, and hers had moved on in the wider world. He resented her for that—for forgetting him.

"Mom and I—" Nora sighed. "We locked horns a lot."

"Yeah…" He hadn't expected her to open up. "I noticed it, but I never knew what it was about."

"Everything." She shook her head. "Politics, religion, current events…you name it, we land on opposite sides of it. When I left for college, it gave me a whole new freedom to be me, without arguing with Mom about it. So I stayed away a lot."

"Is that why you didn't tell her about your half sister?" he asked.

He was watching her as she sat on her bed facing the babies, one leg tucked under herself. Bobbie finished her bottle first, and Nora put it down, still feeding Riley with the other hand. She was oddly coordinated as she bottle-fed two infants. Maybe it came from bottle-feeding orphaned farm animals. If you could wrangle a lamb or a calf into taking a bottle, maybe it was a skill like riding a bike.

"I needed to sort it all out in my own head before I told her about it," Nora said, oblivious to his scrutiny. "It was like anything else. I thought I could have a sister—some semblance of a relationship with her—but I was pretty sure Mom would see that as a betrayal."

"I get it."

In fact, he understood both sides of it. It had to be hard for Dina to see her one and only daughter bonding with her late husband's love child. Yet he could understand Nora's desire to know her sister. The whole situation was a painful one—the sort of thing that made him mildly grateful for his lack of family coziness. At least he couldn't be let down any more than he already had been. Rock bottom was safe—there was no farther to fall.

Rosie was almost finished with her bottle, but she'd stopped drinking. He pulled it out of her mouth, leaving a little trail of milk dribbling down her chin.

"Is she done?" Nora asked.

"She stopped drinking." He held up the bottle.

"Okay. Just burp her, then."

Burp the baby. Of course. He knew the concept here—he wasn't a Neanderthal. He lifted Rosie to his shoulder, and she squirmed in her sleep, letting out a soft cry. Great, now he'd done it.

"Just pat her back," Nora said.

Easton gently tapped Rosie's back and she burped almost immediately, leaving a warm, wet sensation on his shoulder, dripping down toward his chest. He cranked his head to the side and could just make out the mess.

Nora chuckled. "Sorry."

Riley had finished her bottle, and Nora reached for Bobbie. It was an odd sort of assembly line as she burped them and he laid them back in the crib. He pulled the white T-shirt off over his head, getting the wet material away from his skin. He wadded up the shirt and gave his shoulder an extra scrub. It was then that he realized he was standing in front of Nora shirtless. Her gaze flickered over his muscular chest, and color rose in her cheeks.

"I'll just—" He pointed toward the door. He needed to get out of there. He'd fed and burped a baby—mission accomplished. He wasn't supposed to be hanging out with her, and he definitely wasn't supposed to be this casual with her, either.

"Okay. Sure—"

Nora's gaze moved over his torso once more, then she looked away quickly. She was uncomfortable, too. Soiled T-shirt in hand, he headed out of the room. That hadn't been the plan at all, and he felt stupid for not thinking ahead. Who knew what she thought now—that he was hitting on her, maybe? That couldn't be further from the truth.

Blast it, he was up now. He might as well go down and make some breakfast. An early start was better than a late one.

Nora hadn't ever seen Easton Ross looking quite so grown-up. And she hadn't imagined that under that shirt were defined muscles and a deep tan. He had a six-pack—that had been hard to miss—and it left her a little embarrassed, too. A good-looking man might be easy enough to appreciate in a picture or on TV, but when he stood in your bedroom in the moonlight...

She laid Bobbie next to Riley and Rosie in the crib and looked down at them for a moment, watching the soft rise and fall of their tiny chests.

It wasn't because she'd never seen a man without a shirt before. She'd always had a pretty healthy romantic life. But this was Easton—an old buddy, a quiet guy in the background. If he'd looked a little less impressive, she wouldn't have felt so flustered, but my goodness... When exactly had skinny, shy Easton turned into *that*?

She was awake now—she'd have to get used to going back to bed after the 3 a.m. feeding, but she could hear the soft clink of dishes downstairs, and she had a feeling that she and Easton needed to clear the air.

Grabbing a robe, Nora pulled it around herself and padded softly down the narrow, steep staircase. She paused at the bottom on a landing that separated the kitchen from the living room. Looking into the kitchen, she could see Easton at the stove, his back to her. He was in jeans and a fresh T-shirt now, his feet bare. The smell of percolating coffee filtered through the kitchen.

"Easton?" She stepped into the kitchen, tugging her robe a little tighter.

He turned, surprised. "Aren't you going to try to sleep some more?"

"I'm not used to the up and down thing yet. When I get tired enough, I'm sure I will."

He nodded and turned back to the pan. "You want breakfast?"

"Kind of early," she said with a small smile.

"Suit yourself." He dropped several strips of bacon into the pan.

"Look," she said, pulling out a kitchen chair with a scrape and sitting down. "I think I'm in the way here."

"Since when?"

"Since I woke you up at 3 a.m."

"I'll be fine." His tone was gruff and not exactly comforting. Was he doing this because she was the boss's daughter? It had to factor in somewhere.

"This is your home, Easton."

"You noticed." He cast her a wry smile then turned around fully, folding his arms across his chest. Yes, she had noticed. She didn't have to like it, but she was capable of facing facts.

"I should take the babies back to the house with my mom," she said. "I'm sorry. I hate that my dad left this place to you, but he did. So…"

She was sad about that—angry, even—but it wasn't Easton's fault. He could have turned it down, but who would turn down a house? She wouldn't have, either.

"You don't need to leave," he said.

"Oh." She'd thought he'd jump at any excuse to get her out of his home. If this night had proven anything, it was that this space was very much Easton's, and that felt awkward. This kitchen, where she remembered making cookies with her great-grandmother, was *his* kitchen now. She'd imagined she'd find peace here, but she'd been wrong. She shouldn't be surprised. A lot of her "perfect" memories hadn't been what she thought.

"You don't seem comfortable with me here, though," she countered. "And if I'm bound to make someone feel uncomfortable, it should be my own mother, don't you think?"

"I don't have a problem with you staying here," he replied, turning back to the pan. He flipped the bacon strips with a fork, his voice carrying over the sizzle.

"Do you realize that I've worked on this land since I was fourteen?"

"Yeah. It's been a while."

"That's sixteen years. And over those years, you and I became friends."

"I know."

"Real friends." He turned back, his dark gaze drilling into hers. "Do you remember when you broke up with Kevin Price? We talked for hours about that. I was there for you. I was there for you for Nathan Anderson, Brian Neville... I was there to listen, to offer advice. I mean, my advice was always the same—pick a better guy—but I was there."

Easton *had* been there for her, and she felt a blush rise at the memories. One rainy, soggy autumn day, they'd sat in the hayloft together, talking about a guy who wasn't treating her right. They'd sat for hours, just talking and talking, and she'd opened up more in that evening than she had with any guy she'd dated. But then her father had found them, ordered Easton back to work and told Nora to get inside. She could still remember the stormy look on her father's face. He hadn't liked it—probably assumed more was happening in the hayloft than a conversation.

Nora had talked too much back then. It had just felt so nice to have someone who listened like he did, but she might have led him on a little bit. She was a teenage girl, and her emotional world was vast and deep—in her own opinion, at least. She was mildly embarrassed about that now, but she wasn't any different than other girls. Easton was just a part-time ranch hand, and a guy. He hadn't been quite so in touch with his own "vast and deep" emotional life, and maybe he'd been a little in awe of her…maybe he'd nursed a mild crush. But she hadn't ever considered him as more than a buddy.

"I was an idiot," she said with a short laugh.

"And then you picked up and left for college, and that was it."

Well, that sure skipped a lot—like all the college applications, the arguments with her mother about living on campus or off and all the rest of the drama that came with starting a new phase of life. And since when was college a problem?

She frowned. "I went to college. You knew I was going."

"Thing is," he said, "you walked away, and life went on. For sixteen years I worked this land, drove the cattle, worked my way up. I'm ranch manager now because I know every job on this ranch and could do it myself if I had to. No one can get one over on me."

"You're good at what you do," she confirmed. "Dad always said so."

"And when you did come back to visit, you'd wave at me across the yard. That was it."

Admittedly, their relationship changed over the years. But having him here—that was the awkward part. If they'd just been school friends, then a change in the closeness they shared would have been natural—like the ebb and flow of any relationship. But he'd worked with her father, so unlike her school friends—where some of those old friendships could die a quiet death— she still saw Easton on a regular basis. From a distance, at least. He couldn't just slide into the past. When she did come home, she only had a few days, and she had to see a lot of people in that time.

"I was busy," she replied. "Friends and family—"

She heard it as it came out of her mouth. Friends—
and she hadn't meant him. She'd meant people like
Kaitlyn Mason, who she'd been close with since kinder-
garten. She winced. There was no recovering from that
one, but it didn't make it any less true. Easton hadn't
been high enough on her list of priorities when she'd
come back.

"Yeah," he said with a sad smile. "Anyway, I was
the worker, you were the daughter. Well, your dad saw
fit to give me a little patch of land. I *worked* for this. I
know that your great-grandparents built this house, and
I know it means a whole lot to you, but I'm not about
to sell it or tear it down. I actually think I might take
your dad's advice."

"Which was?" she asked.

"To get married, have a few kids."

That had been her father's advice to him? Her father's advice to her had always been "Wait a while.
No rush. Get your education and see the world." The
double standard there irritated her, but she couldn't put
her finger on why. Whoever Easton decided to marry
and whatever kids they'd have, they'd be no kin of the
people who built this house with their own hands. Her
family—the Carpenters—had been born here, had died
here... Easton might have worked for her father, but he
didn't *deserve* this house.

"Anyone special in mind?" she asked, trying to force
a smile.

"Nope."

There was no use arguing. The house was his. She
couldn't change it or fight it. Maybe one day she could
convince him to sell to her, but that was about as much
as she could do.

"If you ever want to sell this house," she said, "come to me first."

He nodded. "Deal."

Easton turned back to the stove and lifted the bacon from the pan with his tongs, letting it drip for a moment in sizzling drops before he transferred it to a plate. She had to admit—it smelled amazing. He grabbed a couple of eggs and cracked them into the pan. Was that it? Was that all she could ask from him—to sell to her if he ever felt like it? Probably, and he didn't look like he was about to back down, either.

He'd had a point, though. He'd spent more time with her dad than she had…he'd know things.

"Did you know about the other woman?" Nora asked.

He grabbed a couple thick slices of bread, dumped the bacon onto one of them, added the eggs sunny side up, and slapped the second piece on top. He turned toward her slowly and met her eyes.

"I get that you're mad at him," he said. "And you've got every right to be. But he wasn't my father, and what he did inside of marriage or outside of it wasn't my business."

Nora stared at him, shocked. Was that the kind of man Easton was? He was just talking about a marriage and family of his own. She'd thought he'd have a few more scruples than that.

"But did you know?" she demanded.

"I'm saying he was my boss," Easton retorted, fire flashing in his eyes. "His personal life wasn't my business. I had no idea about the other woman—how could I know? We were working cattle, not cozying up to women. I'm not going to bad-mouth him, even if that would make you feel better for a little while. He was good to me. He was honest and fair with me. He taught me everything I know and set me up with this house. If you're looking for someone to complain about him and pick him apart with, you'd better keep looking. I'm not that guy."

He dropped his plate on the table and squashed the sandwich down with the palm of his hand. Then he grabbed a few pieces of paper towel and wrapped it up.

"You're nothing if not loyal, Easton," she said bitterly. Loyal to the man who'd given him land. He should have been loyal to a few basic principles.

Easton tossed the wrapped sandwich into a plastic bread bag then headed to the mudroom.

"I'm sorry for what he did to you," he said, not raising his head as he plunged his feet into his boots. "I get that it was a betrayal. But I'm staff, and you're family. I know the line."

The line? What line? Was he mad that they'd grown apart over the years, that she'd moved away to Billings for a degree in accounting? What line was so precious that he couldn't stand up for the women who had been wronged?

"What does that mean?" she demanded. "Do you want me to go? Have I crossed a line with you?"

He grabbed his hat and dropped it on his head.

"No," he said quietly. "Stay."

He didn't look like he was going to expand upon that, and he pulled open the door, letting in a cool morning draft.

"You forgot your coffee," she said.

"I leave it on the stove to let it cool down a bit," he said. "I'll have it in an hour when I get back."

With that, he stepped outside into the predawn grayness. Then the door banged shut after him, leaving her alone with a freshly percolated pot of coffee and three sleeping babies.

Easton had made himself clear—his loyalty belonged to her dad. Well, her father had lost hers. Ironic, wasn't it, that the one person to stand by Cliff Carpenter's memory was the hired hand?

Chapter 3

Around midmorning, Nora heard a truck rumble to a stop outside the house. She looked out the window to see her mother hop out of the cab. She was wearing a pair of fitted jeans and boots, and when she saw Nora in the window, she waved. Nora hadn't realized how much she'd missed her mom until she saw her, then she felt a wave of relief. It reminded her of waiting to be picked up at Hope Elementary School. All the other kids got on the bus, and Nora had to sit on the curb, alone. Her heart would speed up with a strange joy when she finally saw her mom in the family truck. She felt that joy on that school curb for the same reason: sometimes a girl—no matter the age—just needed her mom's support.

The babies were all sleeping in their bouncy chairs, diapers changed and tummies full. Nora's ridiculously early morning was already feeling like a mistake. She was exhausted. Back in the city, she'd been working in the accounting office for a company that produced equestrian gear. She'd worked hard, put in overtime, but she'd never felt weariness quite like this. A work friend had told her that her twelve weeks of parental leave would be more work than the office, but she hadn't believed it until now.

Nora pulled open the side door and ambled out into the warm August sunshine.

"Morning," she called.

"Mackenzie Granger dropped this by," her mother said, pulling a collapsed stroller out of the bed of the truck. "She said she got the triplet stroller for the boys and the new baby, but hasn't used it as much as she thought she would."

Nora couldn't help the smile that came to her face. She'd been wondering how she'd ever leave the house again with three infants, but thank God for neighbors with twin toddlers and new babies.

"I'll have to call her and thank her," Nora said. "And thank you for bringing it by."

Her mother carried the stroller over and together they unfolded it and snapped it into its open position. It was an umbrella stroller with three seats lined up side by side. It was perfect. Not too big, not too heavy, and she could transport all three babies at once.

"I had an idea." Dina shot Nora a smile. "Let's load the babies into this and you can come pick the last of the strawberries with me."

They used to pick strawberries together every summer when Nora was young. They'd eat as they picked, and even with all the eating, they'd fill bucket after bucket. Dina would make jam with some of them, freeze a bunch more and then there would be fresh strawberries for everything from waffles to ice cream. Nora used to love strawberry-picking. Then she became a teenager, and she and her mother stopped getting along quite so well.

Nora met her mother's gaze, and she saw hope in Dina's eyes—the flimsy, vulnerable kind of hope that wavered, ready to evaporate. Maybe her mother was thinking of those sweet days, too, when they used to laugh together and Dina would let Nora whip up some cream for the berries.

"Yeah, okay," Nora said.

They transferred the babies to the stroller quickly enough, and the stroller rattled and jerked as Nora pushed it down the gravel road—the babies undisturbed. Maybe this was why Mack hadn't used it much. The wheels were quite small, so every rock could be felt underneath them. But Nora had gotten them all outside, and that was a feat in itself.

"So what are you going to do about the babies?" her mother asked as they walked.

"Would it be crazy to raise them?" Nora asked.

"Three infants on your own?" her mother asked.

"Three infants, you and me."

Her mother didn't answer right away, and sadness welled up inside Nora. It *was* crazy. And it was too much to ask of her mom right now. Maybe ever. Her mother reached over and put a hand on top of Nora's on the stroller handle.

"I've missed you," Dina said quietly. "It's nice to have you home."

It wasn't an answer—not directly, at least—but it was clear enough. They were still on opposite sides, it seemed, even with the babies. But Nora had always been stubborn, and she wasn't willing to let this go gracefully.

"I came home because I thought you'd help me," Nora pressed.

"And I will. As much as I can."

They all had limits to what they could give, and Nora had taken on more than she could possibly handle on her own. The problem was that she was already falling in love with these little girls. With every bottle, every diaper change, every snuggle and coo and cry, her heart was becoming more and more entwined with theirs. But was keeping them the right choice?

The strawberry patch was on the far side of the main house, and Nora parked the stroller in the shade of an apple tree then moved into the sunshine where Dina had the buckets waiting. Dina came back over to the stroller and squatted down in front of it. Sadness welled in her eyes as she looked at the sleeping infants.

"I get it," Dina said, glancing up at her daughter. "When I first held you, I fell in love, too. It couldn't be helped."

"They're sweet," Nora said, a catch in her voice.

"Adorable." Her mother rose to her feet again and sighed. "Your dad would have—" Dina's chin quivered and she turned away.

"Dad would probably have hidden them," Nora said bitterly. Mia had told her enough to be clear that Cliff had known about her existence, even if they'd never met. "He hid his daughter, why should his granddaughters be any different?"

That secrecy—the whole other family—stabbed at a tender place in Nora's heart. How was it possible for a man to have secrets that large and never let on? Didn't he feel guilty about it? Didn't something inside him jab just a little bit when he sat in church on Sunday? He had a reputation in this town, and this didn't line up with the way people saw him. She hoped that he did feel guilt—the kind to keep him up at night—because this wasn't just his private mistake; this had affected them all.

"Let's pick berries," her mother said.

But hidden or not, Nora's father would have fallen in love with these baby girls, too. He'd probably cherished a secret love for the daughter he'd never met. And hidden that love. So many lies by omission...

"Mom, if Dad had lived," Nora said, grabbing an ice cream pail and squatting at the start of a row, "what would you have done? I mean if Mia had suddenly dropped on our doorstep and announced herself, what then?"

"I'd have divorced him." There was steel in Dina's voice, and she grabbed a pail and crouched down next to Nora. They spread the leaves apart and began picking plump, red berries. "I had no idea he had someone else..."

"Mia said he wasn't in her life at all, though," Nora said. "Maybe the affair wasn't long-term."

Her mother shook her head. "I don't care how long it was. When your husband sleeps with someone else, there is nothing casual about it. It's no accident, either. He chose to do the one thing that would tear my heart in two. He chose it."

"Do you hate him now?"

Her mother's voice was quiet. "I do this morning."

The berries were plentiful, and they picked in silence for a few minutes. Nora's mind was moving over her plans. If she kept these babies, she'd need help. She'd taken her twelve weeks of parental leave from her bookkeeping job, but when she went back to work again, she'd be paying for three children in day care. She couldn't afford that...not on her middling salary, and certainly not as a single mom. Staying in Hope to raise the girls would be the smart choice, but she hadn't taken her mother's emotional state into the equation. She didn't have her mother's support in keeping the babies, and she didn't have that little homestead where she could have set up house. She didn't have a job here, either, besides the family ranch. So she'd come home, unsure what the next step should be, but certain that this was the place where she could make her decisions.

They were halfway down the second row, six buckets filled with ripe, plump berries, when a neighbor's truck pulled into the drive.

"It's Jennifer," Dina said, glancing up. Then she added with a dry tone, "Great."

The neighbor woman hopped out of her truck and waved, then headed across the lawn toward them. She wore a pair of jeans and a loose tank top, a pair of gardening gloves shoved into her back pocket. She was also Dina's second cousin twice removed or something to that effect.

"Morning!" Jennifer called. She was in her early fifties, and her hair was iron gray, pulled back with a couple of barrettes.

"Morning." Dina looked less enthusiastic, but she met Jennifer's gaze evenly. "What brings you by?"

"Curiosity." Jennifer peered behind them at the stroller. "I heard about the triplets."

Nora watched as her mother pushed herself to her

feet. It was already out there—their deepest pain being
bandied about by the local gossips.

"Well…" Dina seemed at a loss for words.

"They're sleeping right now," Nora said, and she led
Jennifer toward the stroller.

The older woman looked down at them then glanced
at Dina.

"I had no idea Cliff was that kind of man. To live
with a man for what—thirty-five years?—and you'd
think you knew him."

"You'd think," Dina replied drily.

"So what happened?" Jennifer asked, plucking a
berry from one of the filled buckets and tugging off the
stem. "Did you see the signs?" She popped the strawberry into her mouth.

"Of my husband fathering another child?" Dina
asked, anger sparking under the sadness. "What would
that look like exactly, Jen?"

Jennifer's ex-husband was a known philanderer,
while Nora's parents had always appeared to be the
most devoted couple. Nora had never seen her parents
fight—not once. Her father was a tough, unbending
man, but somehow he and Dina could look at each other
and come to a decision without saying a word. People
commented on the strength of that marriage. Jennifer
and Paul, however—everyone knew what Paul did on
the side. And Jennifer and Paul had very public arguments about it on a regular basis.

"Paul was obvious," Jennifer retorted. "Cliff wasn't.
I can normally point out a cheating man a mile away—
I mean, I'm kind enough not to tell the wife, but I can
spot it. Cliff didn't seem like the type."

Jennifer was enjoying this—there was a glimmer of

gaiety under the external show of concern, the cheeriness of not being the one in the crosshairs for a change. But this was Nora's father being torn apart…and Nora couldn't help feeling a strange combination of anger at her dad and protectiveness toward him at the same time. He deserved to be raked across the coals—by Dina and Nora, not the town. He was *theirs* to resent, to hate, to love, to be furious with. The town of Hope, for all its good intentions, could bloody well back off.

"I don't want to talk about it," Dina replied shortly.

"Oh, I get it, I get it…" Jennifer hunched down next to a row of strawberry plants and beckoned toward the pile of empty buckets. "Pass me one, would you? I'll give you a hand."

They wouldn't get rid of her easily, it seemed, and Nora exchanged a look with her mother. This wasn't just her mother's shame, it was Nora's, too. Cliff had left them in this strange position of being pitied, watched, gossiped over. And in spite of it all, he was still her dad. Besides, she couldn't help but feel a little bit responsible for bringing this gossip down onto her mother's head, because she'd been the one to bring the babies here. Without the babies, no one would have been the wiser.

"It's scary," Jennifer prattled on, accepting a bucket and starting to pick. "I mean, will it affect the will? Do you remember the exact wording? Because if the wording is about 'children' in general, it includes any children he's had outside of wedlock, too. But if he names Nora specifically…"

There wasn't much choice but to keep picking, and Nora realized with a rush that keeping these babies in the family wouldn't be as simple as winning her mother over. Dina wasn't the only one who would be thinking about Cliff's infidelity when she looked at those girls—the entire town would.

Those babies represented a man's fall from grace, a besmirched reputation and hearts mangled in collateral damage. It wasn't that this town was cruel, it was that a sordid scandal was interesting, and people couldn't help but enjoy it a little. Gossip fueled Hope, Montana, and these three innocent babies had just brought enough fuel to last for years.

"You know what, Jennifer?" Nora rose to her feet and wiped the dirt off her knees. "I think Mom and I have it from here. Thanks, though."

The older woman looked startled then mildly embarrassed.

"Oh…yes, of course."

Jennifer wiped her own knees off and took some long steps over the rows of strawberry plants until she was on the grass again. They had an awkward goodbye, and then Jennifer headed back toward her vehicle. The gossip would be less congenial now, but it would have spiraled down into something nastier sooner or later anyway.

"Let's go eat some strawberries, Mom," Nora said, turning toward her mother. "And I want to sit with you on the step and dip our strawberries in whipped cream. Like we used to."

She wanted that whipped cream so badly that she ached. She wanted to rewind those angst-filled teenage years and bring back the sunny, breezy days where she'd been oblivious to heartbreak—when both of them had been. She wanted her mom—that calming influence, the woman who always had an answer for everything, even if that answer was "Some things we don't need to know."

"Okay." Dina nodded, and tears came to her eyes.

Everything had changed on them, spun and tipped. But they could drag some of it back, like whipped cream and strawberries on a warm August day.

That afternoon Easton came back to the house, his body aching from a day of hard work. He'd ridden Scarlet over to the southwest pasture to check up on the fence that was being rebuilt. Scarlet was his favorite horse; he'd bought her from the Mason ranch five years ago, and he and that horse had a bond stronger than most people shared. Scarlet was a good listener—recently, Easton had started talking. Not to people, but letting the thoughts form words and then spill out of him was cathartic. He could see why Nora had relied on him to just listen for all those years.

Out at the southwest corner, one of the ranch hands had broken a finger, so Easton sent him back, called the medic and took his place for the afternoon with the pole driver. He'd have to fill out a pile of paperwork for the injury, but the fence was complete and all in all it had been a good day.

Now, as he ambled up the drive toward the house, he was ready for a quiet evening. But he had to admit, he'd been thinking of Nora all day. He'd gotten used to her hurried trips back to the ranch, that wave across the yard. He'd made his peace with the fact that their friendship was something from long ago when she needed someone to listen to her problems. It had never been a terribly reciprocal friendship. He'd been quiet by nature, and she'd never asked too many questions. Maybe she'd assumed all was fine in his world because he didn't feel the need to vent.

As he came closer to the house he could hear the chorus of baby wails. Wow—it sounded like all three of them were crying. He picked up his pace, concerned that something might be wrong, and when he emerged from the mudroom, he was met by Nora's frantic face.

She stood in the middle of the kitchen—two babies crying from their little reclined bouncy chairs on the floor, and Bobbie in Nora's arms, also wailing.

"Everything okay?" Easton asked, dropping his hat onto a hook.

"No!" Nora looked ready to cry herself. "They've been like this for an hour…more? What time is it?"

"Almost five," he said.

"I'm so tired…" She patted Bobbie's diapered bottom and looked helplessly at the other two.

He couldn't very well leave them like that, and seeing those little squished faces all wet with tears, tiny tongues quivering with the intensity of their sobs, made him want to do something. He didn't know how to soothe an infant, but he could pick one up. He bent and scooped up the baby closest—Riley, he thought. But he could be wrong. He tipped her forward onto his chest and patted her back.

"Hey, there…" he murmured, looking down at her. She didn't look any happier, and he followed Nora's example and bounced himself up and down a couple of times to see if that improved the situation.

Nada.

He hadn't meant to start singing, but a tune came into his head in the same rhythm of his movement— a song he hadn't heard in a long, long time. Brahms's

"Lullaby." He hummed it at first, and Riley stopped her hiccoughy sobs and listened, so he started to sing softly.

"Lullaby and good-night, hush my darling is sleeping.

On his sheets, white as cream, and his head full of dreams.

Lullaby and good-night..."

The baby lay her face against his chest and heaved in some shaky breaths. It was working—she liked the song...

He looked up to see Nora staring at him, an odd look on her face. She looked almost soothed, herself.

"I have an idea," she said, pointing to the couch in the living room. "Go sit there."

He did as she asked and sank into the couch. She deposited Bobbie next to her sister on his chest, and Bobbie had a similar reaction as Riley had, calming, blinking, listening as he sang. It was unexpectedly comfortable—the weight off his feet, two babies on his chest. Rosie still wailed from the kitchen, but when Nora scooped her up, she calmed down a little, and when Nora sank onto the cushion next to him, Rosie seemed to be lulled into quiet, too.

He sang the only verse he knew of that song a few times and the babies' eyes drooped heavier and heavier until they fell asleep, exhausted from their crying.

"I didn't know you could sing," Nora said softly.

"You never asked." He shot her a smile. "You know that cowboys sing. It soothes the herd."

"But they don't all sing well," she countered.

He chuckled softly. "I break it out when absolutely necessary."

There was an awful lot she didn't know about him.

He knew more about her—she'd opened up with him. He knew that she hated sappy songs but loved sappy books, that her first horse had been her best friend and that her dad had been her hero. She'd talked and talked... But as he sat here with her, the babies breathing in a gentle rhythm, he wished he'd said more back then. She'd taken more than she'd given, but that hadn't been her fault. He'd given and given, and never asked for anything in return. Ever. Maybe he should have asked.

"I heard that song on TV years ago," he said. "I was maybe ten or eleven. I thought it was so beautiful that I nearly cried. So I tried to remember the words to it but could only remember the one verse. I imagined that one day my mother would come back and sing that song to me."

"Did you ever hear from her?" Nora asked quietly.

He shook his head. "Nope."

His mother left when he was eight, and he didn't have a solid memory of her. He knew what she looked like from the pictures, a woman with curly hair and glasses, one crooked tooth in the front that made her smile look impish. Those photos replaced his memories of her somehow—maybe because he'd spent more time with the pictures than the woman herself. His father had destroyed the other photos. "She left us," he used to say. "Don't even bother trying to remember her. She sure isn't thinking about us."

Easton couldn't trust his memories of her. He'd made up so many stories about her, so many situations that had never really happened, that he almost believed them. In his imagination, she was gentle and soft, and she stroked his hair away from his face. In his imagination, she loved him so devoutly that she'd never leave. When he lay in his bed at night, his dad drinking in front of the TV, he used to close his eyes and pretend that his mother was sitting on the edge of his bed, asking about his day. He'd imagined that well into his teen years…longer than he should have needed it.

"Do you know why she left?" Nora asked.

"She and Dad both drank a lot. They fought pretty viciously. I don't know. She left a note that just said that she'd had enough. She was leaving, and we shouldn't try to find her."

"But she didn't take you with her," Nora pointed out.

Easton had questioned that over the years. If life was such hell here in Hope, why wouldn't she take her little boy along? Why would she leave him like that? She'd walked out, and he'd been left with an alcoholic father who could barely function. It was selfish. If she hadn't loved Dad, he could understand that. But why hadn't she loved *him*?

"Yeah…" He didn't have anything else to say to that. It was a fact—she'd left him behind.

"Do you remember her?" she asked.

"Not much," he admitted. "My dad dumped her stuff out into a pile and burned it. I guess that was cathartic for him. I managed to sneak off with one of her shirts— some discarded thing she didn't feel like bringing with her, I guess. I kept it under my mattress. It smelled like her cigarettes. I have that still."

"Why didn't I know about this?" Nora murmured.

A better question was, why had he told her now? Nora came from a loving home with parents who both adored her. Her family ran the ranch very successfully, and she'd had a bright future. He'd had none of those things, and yet he was still willing to be there for her, give her whatever support she needed. Why? Because he'd been in love with her, and maybe deep down he was afraid that if she knew the mess inside him, it would turn her off him.

"That's not how we worked, you and I," he said after a moment.

"Meaning I was self-involved." She winced. "I'm sorry. I must have been."

He shook his head. "I don't know. You were used to happier days than I was. You were more easily disappointed."

"I wish I'd been a better friend," she said.

But it wasn't friendship that would have soothed his teenage soul. If she'd been a more attentive friend, it might have made it harder. He might have actually held out hope that she'd see more in him. But being six inches shorter with a face full of acne had taken care of that.

"It's okay," he said. "It was a long time ago."

Easton needed to be careful, though, because not much had changed. She was still the heir to the ranch he worked, she was still the much loved daughter of the owner and she still needed his emotional support right now…except he wasn't so naive this time around. He knew how this ended. Nora would pull things together and she'd step out into that bright future of hers, leaving him right where he'd always been—on the ranch. She'd walk away again, and she wouldn't think to look back.

"You have the magic touch with the babies," she said, easing herself forward to stand up. "Thank you."

"No problem." What else was he supposed to do

when three tiny girls had taken over his home? She walked toward the stairs with Bobbie in her arms.

"Why didn't you call your mom when the babies wouldn't stop crying?" he asked, and she looked back.

"Because she isn't really on board with this. Getting my mom's help isn't as great a solution as I thought. If I'm going to raise these girls, I'll have to figure out a way to do it on my own."

He'd suspected as much. While she'd probably pitch in, it was a bit much to expect Dina to joyfully embrace raising her late husband's other family.

"I'll get them back up to the crib," she said. "I'll be back."

And she disappeared from the room. He wasn't a long-term solution, either. He never had been, not in her eyes, and he wasn't about to make the same mistake he'd made as a teen. He didn't cross oceans for someone who wouldn't jump a puddle for him. Not anymore.

Chapter 4

That night Nora had managed to feed the babies without waking Easton, and when she got up again for their 6 a.m. feeding, Easton was gone, leaving behind percolated coffee cooling on the stove while he did his chores. She'd gone back to bed—her theory had been right and exhaustion made sleep possible—and when she opened her eyes at eight and got dressed, she'd found another pot of coffee freshly percolated on the stove. He'd been back, it seemed. And he'd be back for this pot, too, but she took a cup of coffee anyway—she desperately needed the caffeine kick.

The house felt more familiar without Easton around, and she stood in the kitchen, soaking in the rays of sunlight that slanted through the kitchen window, warming her toes. She sipped the coffee from a mug that said Save a Cow, Eat a Vegetarian. That was a sample of

Easton's humor, apparently. She let her gaze flow over the details of this kitchen that she'd always loved...like the curtains that she'd sewn as a kid with the flying bluebird–patterned fabric. She'd made them in home ec, and she'd been so proud of them, despite the wandering hemline and the fact that one side was shorter than the other.

He kept those.

It was strange, because Easton hadn't kept much else of the original decor—not that she could blame him. The furniture and kitchenware had all been cast-offs from the main house. Anything of value—sentimental or otherwise—had been distributed amongst the extended family when Great-Granny passed away. Easton's furniture was all new, and the kitchen had gleaming pots and pans. The dishes in the cupboard were a simple set of four of each dish, but they had obviously been recently purchased except for a few well-worn mugs like the one she was using now. There had been some renovations, too—fresh paint, some added built-in benches in the mudroom. He'd taken pride in this place.

And yet the floor was the same—patches worn in the linoleum by the fridge and stove. Though freshly painted, the windowsills still had that worn dip in the centers from decades of elbows and scrubbing. Nora used to stand by those windows while her elderly great-grandmother baked in the sweltering kitchen. She used to scoot past the fridge, wondering if Granny would catch her if she snagged another creamsicle. This old place held so many childhood memories, so many family stories that started with "When Great-Granny and Great-Grandpa lived in the old house..."

It felt strangely right to come back to this place, or it would have if Easton didn't live here. If her father had just done the normal thing and left everything to his wife, then she would be settling in here on her own— her future much easier to handle because of this family touchstone. But it wasn't hers—it wasn't *theirs*. Instead she felt like an interloper. She still felt like she needed permission to open the fridge.

It was after eight in the morning now. She'd fed the babies and changed their diapers, and now she was antsy to get outside into the sunshine. She'd thought she wanted space and quiet, but the silence was getting heavy. Solitude wasn't going to cut it. She needed a plan for her future, how she'd take care of these girls by herself, and that didn't seem to be formulating on its own.

The day was hot, and Nora had dressed the triplets in matching yellow sundresses—clothes that Mia had lovingly purchased and set aside for her daughters. The babies squirmed a little as Nora transferred them into the stroller outside the door, but once in the stroller, they settled back into deep slumber, tiny legs curled up around their diapers. She brushed a wisp of chocolate-brown hair away from Bobbie's forehead, love welling up inside her. It was dangerous to be falling in love with these girls, but she was.

Nora shut the door behind her and pushed the stroller over the dusty path that led from the house to the dirt road. The morning was still cool, the sun bright and cheerful in a cloudless sky. Dew still clung to the grass in the shady patches of lawn that Easton seemed to keep mowed around the little house. Thatches of rosebushes grew unfettered beside the sagging fence that encircled it. She paused at one and fingered a lush, white bloom.

Her father had been wrong in giving this house away. More than wrong—cruel. And what he'd been thinking, she had no idea. Easton was treating the house well, but no amount of appreciation or hard work would make him family, and this house belonged with family.

Had Dad been angry that she'd created a life for herself in the city? Maybe there was unspoken resentment she'd never known about. Nora pushed the stroller on, bumping onto the dusty road. The ditch beside the road was filled with long grass and weeds, but beyond that ditch, and beyond the rusty barbed wire fence, green pasture rolled out. The old barn stood a hundred yards off, grass growing up around it. Every year it bowed a little lower, hunching closer to the ground that longed to swallow it up. Her father had never been able to bring himself to tear the structure down. Cliff was a practical man in every sense, but when it came to that old barn, he used to say, "Leave it. It makes a pretty picture."

And yet he'd given away the house. Blast it—why couldn't his sentimental streak have stretched long enough to keep the house in the family? If he'd willed it to a cousin, she'd still be upset, but at least the person living there would have a personal connection to the family history.

The road led around to the main barn—a large, modern building—and as she walked, her nerves seemed to untangle. There was something about the open country that soothed her right down to the soul. There had been countless times in the city when she'd considered coming back, but things were complicated here in Hope. She and her mother had always been at odds, and Nora loved having her own space. She'd never been able to spread her wings under her parents' roof, in the same tiny town that would always see her as a kid.

As she crested a low hill, she spotted Easton a stone's throw down the road. A rusted pickup truck was parked at the side of the road, and the cattle were nearby the fence, a steer trying to push through a sagging stretch to reach the lush weeds beyond. Easton shouted something at the steer and waved his arms.

He had toughened into a tall, muscular man over the years. How had she failed to notice? His shirt was rolled up to expose his forearms, and he moved with the ease of a man accustomed to physical labor. But under the muscular physique was the same old Easton she'd always known—an uncomfortable combination of hardened muscle and old friend. It almost made her feel shy watching him work, and she'd never felt that way around Easton before. She'd always been the one in control, the one with all the power. Somehow the years had tipped that balance.

Nora picked up her pace—that was a two-person job by the look of that steer, but she had the babies with her, too. There was no way she could leave him alone with this.

"Easton!" she called.

He turned and spotted her. He pushed his hat back on his head and gave her a wave, then returned his attention to the fence. If he could get the steer to back up, she could staple up the barbed wire and the problem would be solved. She put the brakes on the stroller, making sure it was well off the road, then jumped the ditch.

"Give me the staple gun," she said.

He passed it to her then took off his hat and swatted the steer with it. "Come on," he grunted. "Get going!"

The animal bawled out a moo of frustration and took a few steps in reverse. Nora grabbed the barbed wire, pulled it taut and stapled it in one deft movement. She could feel the tongs of the wire pressing into her hand, but she didn't have time to complain. Then she grabbed the next wire down, being more careful this time where she touched it, and stapled again.

"Done," she said, stepping back.

"Thanks." Easton took the staple gun back and shot her a grin. "You're handier than you look."

"Accounting is tougher than you'd think," she joked.

Easton bent down and eased through the space between the wires, emerging on her side of the fence. He was closer than she'd anticipated, close enough for her to smell his musky scent. Her breath caught in her throat as she looked up at him. He was tall and broad. While those eyes hadn't changed, the rest of him certainly had.

"Is it?" he asked teasingly. "All those numbers and cushy office chairs?"

"I fixed the fence," she shot back. "And I have the blood to prove it." She held up her palm where the scratch had started to bleed.

"You okay?" Was that sympathy she saw in his eyes?

"It's a scratch, Easton. I'll survive it. Give me a hand over, would you?"

He jumped the ditch first then took her hand as she jumped across. He followed and she bent over the stroller, checking on the babies, who were all still asleep.

"Let's see that hand," he said, and she straightened, holding it out.

His touch was gentle and warm. "You'll need some antiseptic on that."

Nora turned the stroller around. "Yeah, I'll take care of it. Where's the first-aid kit in the house?"

"Never mind," he said. "I'll come along. I'm ready for my coffee anyway."

"What about the truck?"

He shrugged. "Not going anywhere."

It was nice to have his company, and if she didn't look over at the new, taller, stronger Easton, it almost felt like old times. Except that it wasn't.

"I'm sorry about when we were teenagers," she said after a moment. "When I was only focused on my own issues, I mean. I feel bad about that."

"It's okay," he said. "It was a long time ago. We've both come a long way since then."

"Maybe not as long as you think," she said wryly. "I also had a cup of your coffee."

He glanced over at her, dark gaze drilling into her for a beat longer than was comfortable.

"Okay, that's it," he deadpanned. "That's where I draw the line." He paused. "You did leave me at least one mug, right?"

"Of course." She grinned.

Rosie woke up and squirmed, letting out a little whimper. Bobbie slept on, but Riley pushed out one tiny fist.

"Good morning, sleepyheads," Nora said.

The warm, low sunshine, these tiny girls, the sweet scent of grass carrying on the breeze, this good-looking cowboy walking next to her—it felt impossibly perfect, and the contentedness that rose up inside her was bittersweet. Staying in the old house—raising the girls here as would have been the plan if it weren't for her father's surprise will—wasn't an option. And having it so close, but just past her fingertips, made her ache for everything she couldn't keep.

She wanted to raise these girls, but she had to be realistic. She was an accountant, after all, and she knew how to look at a bottom line. And raising these girls alone didn't look possible.

Thanks a lot, Dad, she thought bitterly.

Back at the house, Easton rummaged up the first-aid kit from under the sink and pulled out some iodine and some bandages, tossing them onto the counter. His coffee sat on the stove, the smell warming the room. He'd get himself a mug in a minute.

He'd been impressed by her quick thinking out there with the steer at the fence. She'd been around the heavy work on the ranch, of course, but when the men were working, Cliff made sure she kept a more supervisory position—out of the way. She was family, not a hired hand, and there had always been a line there. After her time in Billings, and now with her focus on the babies, he hadn't expected her to be on her game when it came to ranch work.

"I can do it," she said, taking the bottle from him. She winced as the brown drops hit the torn skin.

Nora had always been that rare combination of vulnerable and stubbornly independent. She needed people, but she wouldn't stick around for long. She was like a wild deer, leaping to her feet and dashing off the moment she'd regained enough strength. But while she sat next to him, close enough to touch, opening up about her internal world, it was possible to forget that the leap for freedom was in her nature.

Easton peeled the backing off the bandage and put

it over the scrape. She smiled her thanks, ran her fingers over the bandage then moved toward the fridge.

Coffee. That was what he needed—his practical routine. He liked his coffee lukewarm—an oddity, he knew. But he liked what he liked, and his way of doing things provided for it. It had started when he was a young teenager, working part-time and trying to keep up with his schoolwork. He hated the taste of coffee back then, but it buzzed him enough that he could get everything done. And if he put enough cream in coffee, it ended up lukewarm. He preferred more coffee to cream now, but the lukewarm part remained oddly comforting.

And having Nora here was oddly comforting, too, as much as he hated to admit it.

"I'll get breakfast," Nora said, taking a mesh basket of eggs from the fridge. She paused to look down at the babies in their little bouncy chairs then glanced at her watch. "They'll need their bottles in an hour."

"I've already eaten." He put down his coffee on the counter and reached up for the slow cooker from the top of the cupboards. "But I'll start dinner."

Dinner was going to consist of pulled pork on some crusty rolls. The beauty of a slow cooker meant that the cooking could happen while he was out working. Single men had to suss up their dinner somehow, and he'd had a lot of practice in fending for himself. He had a whole lot less practice in providing for a family, though, even if they weren't his. He could have steeled himself to Nora again, but the babies complicated things. Or that was what he told himself. It was impossible to look down at a baby and refuse to feel something, and once he let in one feeling, the rest all tumbled in after it.

"You have Great-Granny's iron skillet!" Nora exclaimed, and he glanced over his shoulder.

"Your dad said I could have it if I wanted, and those iron skillets can go forever if you care for them right."

She looked like she was trying to hold back something between tears and anger, and he cleared his throat. Was that wrong to keep the skillet? He felt like he'd messed up somehow.

"Look, if you want it, take it," he said. "I can buy another one in town easy enough. It just seemed like a waste not to use it, that's all."

"I do want it," she said quickly.

"It's yours."

"Thank you."

Nora pulled a loaf of bread out of the bread box. She moved comfortably in this space—like she owned the place. But that didn't offend him this morning; it made him imagine doing this every day for the foreseeable future...her footsteps in the house, the scent of her perfume wafting through the place, navigating around her in the kitchen come breakfast time.

"Is that why you kept the curtains?" she asked as she cracked eggs into a bowl.

He glanced toward the window and shrugged. "I kept them for memory's sake. You told me how you'd made them to fit that exact window, and I—"

How to explain... He hadn't been able to take them down. They'd been something made by Nora, and she'd meant something to him. So he'd kept the curtains as a part of his own history—a piece of her.

"I guess I just thought they belonged. You can take them, too, if you want."

"No, that's okay." She kept her head down as she

whipped the eggs. "They belong there. I'm glad they made the cut, that's all."

She tossed some butter into the pan and it sizzled over the heat. It looked like she was having French toast.

Easton grabbed the pork roast from the fridge and deposited it into the crock pot. An upended bottle of barbecue sauce was as complicated as it got. They worked in silence for a few minutes, the sound of frying filling the kitchen in a comforting way. He hated how good this felt—a quiet domestic scene. He wished that having another person in his space were more irritating, because he didn't want to miss her when she was gone. It would be easier if he'd be relieved to see her go.

Cliff had suggested that he find "some nice girl" and get married, but "some nice girl" wasn't going to be enough to wash out his feelings for Nora. He suspected Cliff was trying to be helpful. He'd never told the older man how he felt about Nora, but Cliff wasn't stupid, and Easton wasn't that great of an actor. But it wasn't going to be quite as easy as hooking up with a "nice girl," nor would it be fair to the woman who ended up with him.

"My great-grandparents had seven kids in this house," Nora said, breaking the silence.

Easton glanced at the ceiling, toward the two bedrooms upstairs. There was another room that could have been used for a bedroom off the living room downstairs, though he used it for storage.

"That would have been cozy," he said wryly.

"Well, there was a bit of a gap between the eldest two and the youngest five. So by the time the youngest baby came along, the eldest were getting married and leaving home."

"And your dad—" Easton had never heard too many

details from Cliff. This was family land, accumulated over generations—he knew that much. Cliff had never expanded upon the story, though.

"My grandfather was the eldest, so he inherited the farm, and in turn left it to his eldest son, my dad," she said.

"And you'll inherit it next," he concluded.

"Yes." She pulled some French toast out of the pan and began soaking the next batch of bread.

"So why did you leave?" he asked.

Nora shot him an irritated look. "Did my dad complain about that?"

"No, I'm just curious," he replied. "You're next in line to run this place, and you take off for the city and get a degree in accounting. It doesn't make sense."

She was quiet for a moment then heaved a sigh. "Accounting is important for ranching these days. You need to know where the money is going and where it's coming from. If you don't have a handle on the numbers, it doesn't much matter how good you are with the cattle."

"Except that you didn't come back."

"Because I didn't want to," she snapped.

Easton was silent. She was ticked off now, and he wasn't quite sure which button he'd pushed. She was the one with all this family pride.

She sighed, and her expression softened. "I'm not living for a funeral," she said after a moment. "I've seen cousins doing that—constantly planning for the day they inherit, but my parents had me young. My mom is fifty-two. What am I going to do, spend the next twenty or thirty years living at home, trying to wrest the reins away from her? I could work with Dad really well, but you know exactly how well my mom and I get along. I had a choice—stay close to home and keep my thumb in the pie, or put some distance between us and have a life of my own. I chose to make my own life. I could always come back when they needed me, but coming back before then—"

She didn't have to finish the thought—he knew about the tensions between Nora and Dina. Nora had only ever visited for a few days at a time, and he knew that her stay in Hope would wear thin sooner or later. There had been a reason why she'd stayed away, and these babies didn't change the underlying problem.

"You won't be here for long, will you?" he asked.

"Probably not," she admitted. "I only have twelve weeks parental leave and I'll have to go back to my life in the city sooner or later."

"Okay." He wished his voice sounded more casual than it did, but he could hear the tension in it. He cleared his throat.

"Easton, I'm a grown woman."

"I know." He was painfully aware of that fact. "I just wanted to know what to expect. Thanks for telling me."

It suddenly occurred to him: she'd probably been counting on this house for when she did come back to stay. That would explain why she was so upset—her dad gave away her safety net. He didn't know how she planned to make this work with the babies, with the ranch, with her mom...but the old homestead would have been a convenient answer. Except he now owned the solution to her complicated situation, and he couldn't help but feel mildly guilty about that.

"I don't have a whole lot of options here in Hope," she said.

Her self-pity was irritating, though. She had actually

expected to waltz back into a life here at the ranch—at *her* convenience, not anyone else's.

"Not a lot of options?" He shot her an incredulous look. "You're the sole heir of six hundred acres. You have a university degree. Seriously, Nora. You're spoiled. You have every privilege and you don't even see it."

She blinked. "Did you just call me spoiled?"

Yeah, he had. If he was a little better rested, he might have rethought that one, but it was the truth. She always had been—her dad had mollycoddled her from the start. Nothing was too good for his little girl.

"Figure out what you're going to do," Easton said. "And for the record, I'm not pushing you out. I'm just not feeling as sorry for you as you'd like."

This was the thing—life was hard for everyone, not just Nora. In fact, life was arguably harder for pretty much everyone else. He could appreciate the position she was in, but she wasn't as stuck as she seemed to think.

"I didn't ask for your pity," she snapped. "And I *will* figure it out, but I'm not in any position to make promises about how long I'll be here."

Well, Easton wasn't in a position to make promises, either, and he had his own complications to sort out, without the benefit of a massive inheritance to come or a university degree to bolster him up. Cliff had left him this house for a reason, but the older man wasn't much of a talker. He'd told him that having someone living in the place full-time, someone with a stake in it, would take a load off his shoulders. Easton had even been considering renting the place from his boss, and then Cliff had passed away.

If he'd been a renter, would it still have been this awkward? Easton needed a few answers of his own if he was going to be able to go on living here, making a life out of this once-in-a-lifetime gift. He needed to know why Cliff Carpenter had given him this small patch of land, and ease his nagging conscience.

Chapter 5

The days here on the ranch were bleeding into each other. Maybe it was the lack of sleep or the constant feedings and diapers, but Nora was getting to the point where she wasn't even sure what day it was anymore. She'd had to check the date on her cell phone to be sure—it had been a full week now since she'd arrived. She had a doctor's appointment for the babies that she couldn't miss. She wasn't used to the blur of motherhood. It was exhausting in a whole different way than she was used to—no breaks, no turning off. At least in her bookkeeping job she could leave the office and turn off her phone. She could have silence, a bubble bath, let her mind wander. But with the babies, she was on constant alert, listening for cries or thinking ahead to feedings...

The last few days, she and Easton had been on egg

shells. He'd been out a lot, checking fences and cattle—more than was necessary, it seemed to her. And she'd been trying to stay as polite as possible, to keep her intrusion to a minimum. This wasn't going to last, and one of these days, she had a feeling one of them was going to snap again.

Today Nora could use another nap—the only way she seemed to get sleep these days—and she was about to try to lie down for ten minutes when her cell phone rang. She seriously considered ignoring it, but when she saw the name on her screen, she relented. It was Kaitlyn Mason, her oldest friend.

"Why didn't you let me know you were in town?" Kaitlyn asked when she picked up.

"It's complicated…" Nora confessed.

"Yeah, so I heard. Even more reason for a friend, right? You need coffee. I'm sure of it. And you need to vent."

"And you need to tell me about married life," Nora added. "I haven't seen you since the wedding. It's been like two years. Wow."

"See?" Nora could hear the smile in Kaitlyn's voice. "It's an absolute necessity. Now, do I come to you, or do we meet up in town?"

It would be nice to get out alone, if that was possible. Was it? Or was that selfish, like Easton has accused her of? Just then Riley started to whimper—very likely a wet diaper. She poked a finger into the top and felt dampness. Yep, wet diaper. Was it wrong to want some time to herself this badly? And was it normal to feel guilty about it?

"I'm going to call my mom and see if she can watch

the babies," Nora said. "I'd love to get out to see you for a couple of hours—alone. I'll call you back, okay?"

So Nora changed Riley's diaper, and then Bobbie's and Rosie's, too. Then she dialed her mother. Dina agreed to look after the girls for a couple of hours, and Nora felt a weight lift off her shoulders. Still, she felt that same nagging guilt—not only because she was getting some time off, but also because her mother was going to be looking after Mia's babies. Doing this alone was hard…really hard. And this was what grandmothers were for, right? Grandmas were on a whole different level than babysitters. If these weren't Mia's babies, but Nora's own, she wouldn't feel any guilt at all about having her mother babysit. Her own grandmother had watched her on a regular basis when she was young, and she'd treasured that relationship. Her grandma had played with her, told her stories and after a few hours together would look down into her face and say, "You are such a special girl, Nora." The triplets deserved to have a grandma who thought they were special girls, too.

When Nora arrived at the main house a few minutes later, her mother helped her to unload the babies from their car seats and get them settled inside. They were awake by then, and three pairs of brown eyes stared up solemnly from their bouncy chairs. Dina squatted next to the babies, her expression melancholy.

"They've all been fed and changed," Nora said. "Their next bottle is due at 2:30, but I find it helps to start about fifteen minutes early. I feed Rosie or Riley first and feed Bobbie last. She's able to wait a little more patiently than the other two. Riley can't stand a wet diaper, so if she cries, you can be pretty positive it's that. If you change Riley, it's a good idea to change the other two at the same time, otherwise it gets really overwhelming. Rosie is a snuggler, and she'd stay in your arms the whole time if you let her. I don't like Bobbie to be neglected, though, just because she's a little stronger—"

"Sweetheart." Dina stood up and put a hand on Nora's arm. "We'll be okay."

Would they? It wasn't really the babies she was worried about; it was her mother. This couldn't be an easy task for her. Dina regarded her with misty eyes. Suddenly, the strong, resilient woman who had strode through Nora's life with an answer for everything looked fragile.

"Mom, are you all right?"

Dina wiped an errant tear from her cheek.

"It's not what you think."

"Do they remind you—"

"No, no." Dina shook her head. "I mean, of course they do, but it's not that. It's just that I remember knowing you that well, once upon a time. You liked being on my hip every waking hour, and you'd toddle around in a wet diaper for hours. You hated being changed."

"I grew up," Nora said with a small smile. "It happens to the best of us."

"I know, but I could make anything better for you back then. I can't anymore." Dina sighed. "And while you grew up, I never stopped being your mom."

There had been a time when her mother had been able to predict every passing mood that Nora had, but that was in the days of strawberry-picking and whipped cream. If she raised these girls, would they drift away one day, too? Would she lose this ability to make things right for them?

Nora was tired, overwhelmed. She hadn't slept properly since the babies arrived almost two weeks ago, and every waking moment was taken up with diapers and bottles, crying and soothing…all times three.

"Mom, you doing this—taking care of the babies for a couple of hours—this is just what I need right now. And I really appreciate it."

And she meant that with every fiber of her being.

"Well." Dina cast her daughter a smile. "I'm glad."

Nora adjusted her purse on her shoulder and looked down at the babies. "I've been thinking about it lately… And I'm not sure that I'll be able to, but I want to keep these girls. And if I would be Mom to them, that will make you their grandmother…sort of. Right?"

Dina winced and swallowed hard. "I'm not their grandmother. Angela Hampton is their grandmother."

"Angela's dead," Nora replied. "And so is Mia."

"We're the *other* family." Dina's eyes glittered with tears. "It's not the same. I know you love them, sweetheart, but it's not the same at all."

If they were looking for *the same*, they could stop searching. Nothing would be the same again—Nora's father was gone, and his memory was tarnished. The security she'd had in her parents' marriage had been whipped out from under her. That was the thing—she was just recognizing it now: her father's affair had taken away her ability to trust. If she couldn't trust her own father, how could she trust anyone? Even an old friend like Easton suddenly became suspect.

"No, it's not the same as if I were the natural mother, but we're all the babies have," Nora countered.

"You're not the one who was cheated on," her mother replied. "It's easier for you. These girls are the grandchildren of the woman who slept with my husband behind my back. They belong to your idiot father and that woman—together. And I'm left out of that."

Did her mother think that Nora was unaffected by her father's infidelity? She'd been affected—very deeply—but she also had three innocent babies looking to her for love and comfort. She'd been thrown into the deep end of motherhood, and she didn't get the luxury of sifting through her feelings.

"This *isn't* easy for me," she retorted. "My dad cheated on my mom. That's not pretty. That's not pleasant. I had a half sister I never knew—a half sister I shouldn't have had. My role model for what to look for in a husband of my own turned out to be the wrong kind of man."

"I'm just suggesting that you think it through," her mother said, her tone tense. "Because I'm not Grandma. I can't be."

That felt like a rejection to Nora—of the babies, but also of her. "You actually could," Nora replied, emotion catching her throat. "If you chose to be. You're *my* mother."

"I can't…" Her mother shook her head, sorrow shining through her eyes.

Nora could see the truth in her mother's words. This wasn't about what should be or what could be…this was about what her mother could give and what she couldn't. She'd had her heart broken twice—first by her husband's death, and then by the revelation that he hadn't been faithful. Dina couldn't be the grandmother Nora needed her to be. She couldn't look down into these girls' faces and tell them how special they were …

"I'll cancel with Kaitlyn," Nora said.

"For crying out loud, Nora, I'm not a monster." Her mother tugged a hand through her hair in exasperation. "I can babysit."

Nora met her mother's misty gaze. Right now all Nora wanted was for her mother to become that strong, resilient font of all answers again. She wanted to hear her mother say that everything would be all right, and that they'd figure this out together. But that wasn't going to happen, because everything would not be all right. Everything was broken.

"Thanks, Mom," Nora said past the lump in her throat. "I won't be more than a couple of hours."

Nora shut the door and headed out to her truck. She'd come home because she couldn't imagine doing this alone, but it didn't look like she'd have much option. If she kept these babies, she'd be a single mom in every way.

That afternoon when Easton came back to the house for a coffee, he found a note on the fridge from Nora saying that she'd gone out for a few hours. It was strange, because coming back to the empty house had been all he'd wanted lately—to get back to normal—but it felt lonely, too. He'd started getting used to having her around, was almost tempted to call out "I'm home!" when he got back from working in the fields.

When he'd gotten back to the house after their argument, they'd both apologized for being too harsh and agreed that being both overtired and under the same roof was stressful for the both of them. So he'd been trying to be a more gracious host. He wasn't sure if it was working or not, because Nora was almost too nice to him lately, too—like someone who didn't know him well enough to be straight with him. And they had enough history to make that flat-out wrong. Regardless, there had been no more fights.

That afternoon he'd ridden out to the north field to check on the bulls, and on the way, he'd talked to Scarlet about the whole situation. Except that talking to Scarlet only made him realize all the things he wanted to say to Nora—if they weren't in the middle of this politeness standoff, that is.

Cliff had advised him to find a nice girl, and maybe he should do that. This time with Nora could be used to get her out of his system, and then he should look around next time he was at church and start thinking more seriously about filling up this house with a family of his own. Playing house wasn't going to suffice.

Easton had an hour or so before he needed to head out to the barn and check up on a sick cow, and without Nora here, he had a chance to do something he'd put off for too long. He gulped back some coffee then headed up the narrow staircase to the top floor. He paused, looking up at the attic door in the ceiling above.

Easton had seen a couple of boxes in the attic when he'd moved in. When he'd peeked inside, they looked like Cliff's things so he'd let them be. Maybe it was grief, or he'd simply been too tired to deal with the boxes then, but now that Nora had made him question why Cliff had left him the house, he'd been thinking about those boxes again. Maybe there'd be a few answers. And maybe not. Cliff had left these boxes in the homestead for a reason, and Easton suspected it was because he hadn't wanted his wife and daughter to know about them.

He pulled on the cord, and the attic stairs swung

slowly down. He unfolded them and they hit the wooden floor with a solid thunk. He climbed the narrow steps and ducked as he emerged into the A-frame room above. A single bulb hung nearby, and he clicked it on.

The attic was dusty but otherwise clean. An old single-width metal bed frame leaned against one side, half-rusted. A couple of cardboard liquor boxes were stacked next to it, and beside them some rat traps which were, thankfully, empty. There wasn't much else up here—probably cleaned out when the original owners died. He loved the feel of the attic—the warped panes of glass in the two square windows at either end of the room, the knot holes in the floorboards and the sense of lives lived for decade upon decade in this old house.

Easton had to duck to keep from hitting his head on the slanted roof, and he pulled the first box toward him and squatted next to it. He opened the flaps and peered inside. He found a worn denim jacket, a pair of old cowboy boots, a chipped coffee mug—nothing that looked terribly precious. Underneath the boots was nestled an old manila envelope. He took it out.

The envelope hadn't been sealed. Inside were what appeared to be a few old letters and a handful of photos. Easton sorted through the photos first. One was of a newborn, all bundled up, the date September 12, 1988 written on the bottom next to Mia's full name: *Mia Alexandra Sophia Hampton*. Angela hadn't used the Carpenter name for their daughter. There were a few pictures of a blonde toddler with her brown-haired mother. Angela was rounded, with a full bust and ample hips. She was attractive enough, and Easton paused, looking at the photo, trying to imagine Cliff Carpenter with this woman. Angela wore a little too much

makeup for Easton's taste, but he could see her love for
the little girl in her arms, and that was what mattered.
A few years of photos seemed to be missing, and then a
school picture of Mia as a blonde little girl with braces
and freckles, and then as a teenager without braces.
Mia had been quite lovely. Next was a snapshot of her
as a young woman in front of a Route 66 sign, squinting into the sunlight. She had her mother's full bust and
ample hips, but her face looked more like the Carpenters. There was something in her sparkling blue eyes
that reminded him of Nora.

Easton sighed, putting the photos aside. Mia had
grown up, and Cliff had known about his daughter, apparently. He looked at the address on the envelopes—a
PO box in town. Cliff had gone out of his way to keep
this hidden. There were about a dozen letters, and he
picked one at random.

These probably weren't his business. Cliff hadn't
meant them to be anyone's business. Still, Easton would
take a look and see what was here. If it was damning
enough, he would burn the lot and let Cliff keep some
posthumous privacy. But there was the chance that this
might give Nora and her mother a few answers.

The first letter he opened was dated May, 1998.

Dear Cliff,
Mia is doing well. She's getting As and Bs in
school, and the money you sent will go for her
summer camp. Her best friend is going and she's
been pleading to be allowed to go for months now,
so your money couldn't have arrived at a bet-
ter time. She still wants to play the violin, but I
can't afford the lessons, or the instrument. I've
looked into it, but it's just too much. Maybe you

could consider helping her with that if her interest doesn't change.

Thank you for your support. You should know that she's been asking more and more questions about why she doesn't have a dad. The other kids have dads, even if they aren't in their lives. It would mean a lot to her to know your name, at least. She wouldn't have to contact you. I know you have your family and we wouldn't interfere. Please reconsider letting me tell her.
Angela

The next letter was dated December, 2008.

Dear Cliff,
Thank you for the recent money. Mia is working two jobs to pay for her college tuition, and she's exhausted. She's switched majors, and now she's taking Education. She wants to teach elementary school. The money you sent will help to buy books next semester, and she's very grateful. She asked me to thank you.

I have some bad news. I've had back pain for a few months, and finally went to a doctor about it. It's cancer—stage 3. It's in my spine—quite treatable—and in my liver. There's hope, and I'll fight it, but my insurance will only go so far. I have no intention of dying yet—our daughter still needs me. I haven't told Mia yet, though. She needs to focus on her studies.

If the worst should happen, don't forget about your daughter.
Angela

It looked like Angela had told Mia about her father at some point. Easton knew from Nora that Angela had passed away, and he could only assume it was from the cancer.

He opened another envelope, and this one was different than the others—written in a child's hand. His breath caught in his throat as he scanned the printed words:

Dear Dad,
I only call you Dad because I don't know your name, because if I knew your name, I'd call you that. But Mom—Mom was underlined three times—says she'll mail this to you, and I can say anything I want to you. So here goes.

I hate you. I think you're awful. You don't even know me, and you don't want me. I'm a nice person. My friends say that I'm too good for a deadbeat dad like you. I don't care that you send money, because I don't want any of it. You can keep it and spend it on whatever stupid stuff you buy yourself.

My mom loves me and we do just fine on our own. We don't need you, and we don't need your money. So if you don't want to know me, and I'm a super-good person, you know, then you can get lost.

But if you wanted to know me, you'd find out that I'm pretty smart, and I'm nice to people, and I love animals, and my favorite color isn't purple like every girl in my class, it's green. And I'm going to be a marine biologist when I grow up. That's what you'd find out, and you'd probably

*like me, too. But you don't get to find out how nice
I am, because even if you wanted to meet me, I'd
say, "Sorry, I'm too busy being super-nice and
super-fun."
Without any love at all,
Mia Hampton*

There was a PS tagged at the end in Angela's hand-
writing: *I'm sorry about Mia. She's really angry right
now, but I promised I'd send this letter no matter what.
We do need the money. One day she'll understand how
much you provided. I promise you that.—A*

The poor kid. Her loneliness, her anger, her desperation to be wanted by her dad—it all just shone through
that letter, and Easton couldn't help but wonder how
Cliff had dealt with all of that. Obviously, he had never
told his wife and daughter about the other little girl out
there who hated him because she wanted to be loved
so badly.

Had Cliff ever written his daughter back? Or had
that letter gone unanswered? Easton wished he knew,
but everyone concerned had passed away.

Nothing else was in the box, and the one underneath
it held only an incomplete set of old encyclopedias.

This child hadn't been a secret from Cliff, obviously,
but it also didn't look like the affair was long-lived. Angela had never seemed to be pleading for anything, and
Easton wondered if that would be a relief to Nora on
some level. Maybe it was a one-time mistake and not
some lifetime of philandering.

This was an odd relief to Easton, he had to admit.
He'd always looked up to Cliff, and his fall from grace
had hit Easton, too. He knew what it was like to have a

disappointing father. He'd grown up with a father who embarrassed him constantly and hadn't been able to provide for him. But Cliff had been different—principled, successful, solid. Cliff had been the kind of man Easton would have wanted in a father, and he'd become a sort of father figure to him over the years. So finding out that Cliff had another child out there—that had hurt his sense of decency, even if Easton didn't have a right to feel it.

"You weren't my dad," he muttered.

But even with this mess, Nora was lucky. She still had more than she thought she did because while her father had been flawed, Cliff had at least been there for her. He'd raised her, provided for her, taught her what he could. Easton probably had more in common with Mia—standing on the outside of something they'd never have. So while Cliff's fall from grace was disappointing, it wasn't a betrayal to Easton. At least it wasn't supposed to be.

It hung heavy around his neck, but mostly he felt sorry for Cliff… In life, the man had been respected, admired, trusted. If Cliff had lived to see this, he'd have been crushed.

Maybe it was too late to offer, but this was one thing Easton could give his late boss: absolution, from him, at least. Because Cliff owed him nothing.

Chapter 6

Nora arrived at The Vanilla Bean coffee shop and parked in the angled parking out front. She could feel the pressure leaking out of her. She needed a break, and she still wasn't sure if that made her a bad mother. All she knew was that she felt lighter already for having driven by herself without three infants in the back of her truck.

"Kaitlyn!" Nora wrapped her arms around her friend and gave her a squeeze. "It's so good to see you!"

The Vanilla Bean hadn't changed a bit over the years. It still sported the same framed photos from decades past—Main Street before the murals had been painted, the old grain elevator in use, a grinning bull rider having won a ribbon in the 1957 county fair. There was also a bookshelf with a sign above that read "Lending Library—take a book, leave a book." Nora had read her first romance novel from that shelf—a scandalous secret that she hid from her parents and read out by the barn. This place held the town's history as well as their own, and no matter how long she stayed away, there was a part of her that counted on places like the Vanilla Bean to stay exactly the same.

Kaitlyn had put on a little weight since Nora had seen her last, but it suited her—adding some roundness to her figure. And she wore her hair in a bob now. Kaitlyn's eyes crinkled as she smiled. She motioned toward the table by the window where two coffees were already waiting. "I hope you aren't dieting, because I got you a mochaccino—for old time's sake."

They felt oh so grown up when they'd come here as teens. The last time they'd been here was just before Kaitlyn's Christmas wedding a couple of years earlier. Nora slid into the seat and pried the lid off the cup. This felt good to be out, away from it all for a little while. She watched as two pickup trucks going in opposite directions down the street stopped so that the drivers could talk through open windows.

"It's perfect," Nora said. "So how are you?"

"I'm good." She sipped her drink and licked her lips. "I'm not pregnant—that's what everyone asks. I swear, you gain a pound and everyone wants to be the first one to call it."

"They don't." Nora grimaced.

"They do." Kaitlyn nodded. "But it's okay. I survive it. Everyone is doing it to Nina, too, so I feel better."

"How is Nina?" Nora asked. Kaitlyn's sister had a bit of a scandalous past, having cheated on her fiancée who was fighting in Afghanistan and marrying his best friend while he was away.

"Their son is two now—smart as a whip, that kid. He already knows his alphabet. She's exhausted, but happy…but exhausted. So Brody and I wanted some time alone before we threw ourselves into that."

"I don't blame you," Nora agreed. Kaitlyn's husband came back to Hope when he was wounded in the war, and he was still recovering emotionally. "I'm exhausted, too, and it's only been a few days with the babies. It's harder than I thought."

"So what's going on?" Kaitlyn asked. "I heard a few rumors, but…"

Nora gave as brief an explanation as possible, and as the words came out, she felt relief. She'd been taking this one step at a time from discovering her half sister's existence to becoming the mother of three newborns overnight, and Kaitlyn's expression of sympathy and disbelief was comforting. Her life had turned upside down in a matter of weeks, and some sympathy helped.

"How are you and your mom dealing with all this?" Kaitlyn asked.

"We're—" Nora paused. Were they even dealing with it? They were stumbling through it, not exactly handling anything besides putting one foot in front of the other. "We're in shock still, I think," she concluded. "Thank God Mackenzie thought of us and sent a triplet stroller. I didn't even know where to start."

"Mackenzie is great," Kaitlyn agreed.

"The funny thing is, I keep seeing married couples having babies everywhere I go," Nora confessed. "Mack and Chet have three now, right? And here I am with three babies and no husband…or boyfriend. And the explanation is just so freaking complicated."

"Look, you'll feel like you have to explain yourself

no matter what. I'm married, and everyone is anxious for me to have a baby. If you're not married, everyone is anxious to find you someone. There's no point in worrying about public opinion, because you'll always be lacking in something. Those babies are lucky to have you."

"Are they?" Nora sighed. "The truth is, I can't afford them. Not alone. That's why I came home. I was hoping that I could sort something out with my mom so we could take care of them together. I could quit my job in the city and come back to Hope and find something part time in bookkeeping and put the rest of my time into the girls. But that's not really an option."

"And there's no help?" Kaitlyn asked.

"I'm a bookkeeper, Kate." Nora shook her head. "I work hard. I have a one-bedroom apartment in Billings. I can't afford day care, a bigger place in a decent part of town, clothes, formula, diapers... It's overwhelming. And if I can't sort something out—"

She didn't want to finish the thought out loud, because she hadn't actually admitted it to herself until now. She'd have to give the babies up to another family that could give them the life she couldn't provide herself.

The thought caught her heart in a stranglehold, and for a moment, she felt like she couldn't inhale. Give them up. That was the obvious solution that she'd been avoiding looking at all this time. She'd been hoping that something would present itself—some solution that would make it all come together.

"*Would* you give them up?" Kaitlyn asked quietly.

Nora shook her head. "I really don't want to, but I have to wonder what's best for them. My mom can't be a grandmother to them...they remind her of what my dad did to her. How do you explain that to your kids—this is my mother, but don't call her Grandma. It's not right. The girls would be the ones to suffer."

"I can understand that, though," Kaitlyn said. "If I found out that Brody had cheated on me—even that many years ago—and I was supposed to just accept his child by another woman, or his grandchild… That's a lot to ask."

"I know." It all felt so impossible. "I don't know what to do. Eventually, I'll have to figure something out."

"Maybe give it time?" Kaitlyn suggested.

Did time make it better or worse? That depended on whether her mom changed her mind about this. If she didn't, then Nora would have taken even more time to fall in love with the babies before she had to let them go.

"I'm not sure," she confessed. "But that's okay. I was hoping to hear all the news today, not wallow in my own self-pity. How are Dakota and Andy?"

Dakota had married Andy Granger just before Kaitlyn and Brody got married. Andy sold his half of the ranch he and his brother inherited and then left town. Everyone hated him at that point, because he'd sold out to some big city yahoos. But then he came back to help run a cattle drive for his brother, and Dakota had been hired onto the team. She'd hated him, but something happened on that drive that changed it all, because when they got back, they got engaged.

Tears misted Kaitlyn's eyes, and Nora felt a flash of alarm. What had she said? She reached out and took her hand. Kaitlyn swallowed a couple of times and blinked back tears. Something was wrong. Here she'd been so focused on her own life that she'd completely missed that something was deeply wrong in her friend's.

"What's going on, Kate?" Nora asked, leaning forward.

"Dakota's pregnant. Andy is over the moon—you've never seen a happier guy. He keeps trying to do things for her, and Dakota is all hormonal and wants to kill him." Kaitlyn forced a smile, although it didn't reach her eyes. "It's cute. If he survives this pregnancy, they'll make great parents."

"And yet you're crying," Nora said. Those hadn't been sympathetically happy tears.

Kaitlyn was silent for a moment, then she licked her lips. "I can't seem to get pregnant. Everyone else around me is either pregnant or a new mom… You aren't the only one noticing it. We've been trying since the honeymoon. I told you that we're just taking some time to be a couple, but that's not even true."

"Oh, Kate…"

"I was never the baby fever type. I just assumed that since we were…doing all the things it takes to make a baby…that it would just happen. Like with Nina. Like with Dakota. Like with every woman I seem to come across! This is supposed to be natural."

"It'll happen…" Nora said, but she knew she couldn't promise that any more than Kaitlyn could assure her that she'd find the man of her dreams. Sometimes life didn't pan out the way you wanted it to. Sometimes deeply devoted couples remained childless. Sometimes good women didn't find their guy.

"It'll happen when it happens," Kaitlyn agreed. "We're doing all the right things—on a daily basis."

A smile flickered across her face. "I shouldn't complain, should I?"

Nora laughed softly. Considering that Kaitlyn had a gorgeous husband to "do all the right things" with on a *daily* basis… She felt some heat in her cheeks. "They say the trying is the fun part, don't they?"

"They do say that." Kaitlyn smiled and wiped her eyes. "Sorry, I honestly didn't want to talk about this. I was supposed to be *your* supportive friend. So where are you staying? With your mom?"

"No, in the old farmhouse," Nora said. "With Easton, actually."

Kaitlyn's eyebrows rose, and she paused in the wiping of her eyes. "With Easton? How is that?"

"You know my father left him the homestead in his will, right?"

"I'd heard." Kaitlyn winced. "I'm sorry about that."

"Well, he has a guest bedroom so I'm using that with the babies. My mom can't deal with three newborns right now, and it's all so complicated, so this is a way to give her some breathing space. There isn't a huge amount of room in the homestead, but we're squeezing in."

"I'm not asking about sleeping arrangements," Kaitlyn replied with a quirky smile. "Unless I should be?"

"No!" Nora leaned back in her chair. "I haven't changed that much."

"But how is it with Easton?" Kaitlyn pressed. "I remember how crazy he was about you."

That was an exaggeration. Kaitlyn had always thought that Easton was in love with her, but Nora never believed it. They were friends, that was all. They talked about her boyfriends and sometimes went riding together. Easton had a bit of a crush for a while, but they'd moved past that.

"It wasn't as exciting as you think," Nora replied.

"You're wrong there." Her friend finished wiping her eyes. "What he felt for you was significantly more than friendship."

Had Easton really felt more for Nora? She'd thought that Easton got a lot from their friendship…like friendship. But maybe she'd been the naive one.

"I didn't think it was anything more than me hitting puberty first," she admitted.

"Do you remember that one birthday—I think you turned fifteen—when the girls snubbed you, and I was the only one to show up at your party?" Kaitlyn asked. "I think Easton had just started working at your place, and he brought you those wildflowers from the far pasture."

"That was sweet," Nora agreed. Easton had always been thoughtful that way, and she'd often thought that whatever girl he settled down with would be lucky to have him. He'd be a good boyfriend—to someone else. She just hadn't been attracted to him. And it wasn't because of his acne—that wasn't his fault, and she wasn't that shallow. He was a good friend, but she couldn't make the leap to something more.

"And when you broke up with whatever guy you were dating, who was there to talk you through it?"

"I get it, I get it." Nora shrugged weakly. "He was a decent guy—more than decent. I just wasn't interested back then."

"And now?" Kaitlyn asked.

"Now?" Nora shook head. "*He* isn't interested anymore, either. That's all in the past."

"Oh. That's too bad, because he most certainly grew up." She shot Nora a meaningful look.

Nora wasn't oblivious to how ruggedly good-looking Easton had turned out to be, but she chuckled. "He's not the same guy willing to do anything to make me happy anymore. So you can rest easy on that. He's willing to tell me what he really thinks of me now, and frankly… it's better this way."

Spoiled. That had been his descriptor. She'd been rather shocked to have Easton talk to her like that, but it was better than leading him on. The last thing she needed was to be pussyfooting around Easton's feelings. She had enough to worry about with the babies, with her mom…

"That *would* be better," Kaitlyn agreed. "For him, at least."

"Besides," Nora said. "He came out on top. He's walked away with three acres and my family's history."

"Did he know your father was changing his will?" Kaitlyn took a sip of her latte. "He was getting a lot of job offers at bigger ranches. He's good, you know. Your dad must have kept him around by putting him into the will."

That would actually make sense. Maybe her father hadn't signed it over because of tender feelings—it was possible he'd been negotiating with his ranch manager. That would make everything different…including her view of Easton. Her father had kept secrets—why not one more? Could it really come down to something as common as holding on to a skilled employee?

If that were the case, then Easton would be a whole lot less innocent than he appeared. Could he have actually been angling for that land? He'd said he wasn't, but he wouldn't be the first man to lie to her, either.

"You might be onto something," Nora said. "I've been going over this in my head repeatedly, trying to figure out why my dad would do that... It's like I never knew him."

"You know as well as I do that a good ranch manager is worth his weight in gold," Kaitlyn replied. "Easton is honest. He works like a horse. He's smart, too. My dad has said more than once that if he could afford Easton, he'd try to lure him over to our ranch."

"He wouldn't." Nora frowned.

"My dad?" Kaitlyn shrugged. "Maybe."

Mr. Harp was a jovial guy—but he was also a shrewd rancher. There was a strange balance with the Hope ranches—they were neighbors who supported each other and helped each other out, but they were also in competition for the best employees. The ranch would one day be hers, and it affected the way she'd looked at their land—including the three acres her father had left to Easton.

Easton could take another job if he wanted to. But another possibility made her stomach sink: maybe Easton was less of a nice guy than she'd always assumed. Just because he'd had a rough childhood didn't make him some kind of saint. Easton had some negotiation room, and he may have taken advantage of that.

"Who was trying to get Easton?" she asked.

"Not us," Kaitlyn said with a shake of her head. "But rumor around town was that some larger ranches out of state were putting their feelers out for experienced managers. A lot of people were mad. It's not nice to poach someone's manager after they've spent years grooming him."

Nora had no idea. Was it possible that she'd been duped by more than just her father?

Easton sat in the easy chair in the living room, listening to the sounds of Nora putting the babies to bed. Her voice was soft, the gentle tones carrying through the floorboards, but the words were muffled. It didn't matter what she was saying, of course. It was the comforting lilt that the babies would respond to.

His mom had never been that way—not that he could remember, and certainly not according to the stories his father had told him.

The stairs creaked as Nora made her way down and Easton looked away. He liked having her here, but he was getting increasingly aware of her presence. She was his guest and in his home, yet he still felt like he shouldn't be listening to the soft rustle of her moving around his home—like that was overstepping somehow. He certainly shouldn't be enjoying it.

"They're almost asleep," Nora said, emerging into the living room. She tapped her watch. "Three hours and counting."

She'd been distant all evening—polite, but closed off.

"You tired?" he asked.

"Always." She smiled wryly.

He'd been debating how much he should tell Nora, if anything, all afternoon. Was it his place? What would Cliff have wanted? And how could he possibly know? He shouldn't be in the middle of all this family drama—but maybe he should have seen complications coming.

"I went through the attic today," he said.

Nora sank into the recliner kitty corner to the couch and stifled a yawn. "Was there anything up there?"

He couldn't shoulder Cliff's secrets alone. He wasn't even sure it was fair of him to keep the letters to himself. Cliff wasn't his father, and Nora was the one who would live with a lifetime of questions.

"Your dad had put a box of personal effects up there," Easton said. "I saw it when I moved in but then forgot about it. I remembered it today, and I thought I'd take a look through it."

"My dad did?" She shot him a sharp look. "Why would he do that?"

Easton pushed himself to his feet and retrieved the box from the other side of the sofa. The contents would answer her questions better than he could.

"I don't know, exactly," he said. "But he did."

"That isn't true, though, is it?" She put a hand on top of the box but didn't look at it. Her gaze was fixed icily on him.

"What do you want from me?" he demanded. "Nora, this is awkward. I'm not supposed to be in the middle of your family issues. I found a box with your dad's things in it, and I'm handing it over."

"I had coffee with Kaitlyn Mason today."

That was supposed to mean something to him? Kaitlyn and Nora had been friends since school days. "Great. Glad you got out."

He was frustrated. He was a private man who had been sharing his personal space for a week now with a woman he used to love, and having her here with him, sleeping in the next room and sharing his living space... He was liable to start feeling things he shouldn't all over again if he let down his guard.

"She told me that you had job offers from bigger ranches," Nora went on. "And she suspected that you negotiated for this land in exchange for staying."

Easton blinked. She made it sound sordid, somehow, but it wasn't. "Why is it so surprising that I'd be in demand?" he asked. "I run a tight ship. I had offers, that's true. But I didn't strong-arm your dad into changing his will in exchange for sticking around."

"It didn't factor in at all?" Her tone made it clear she wasn't buying that.

"I was offered a position in Idaho for almost twice what I was making here," he said. "I mentioned it to your dad, but I hadn't even decided if the extra money would be worth it. But that had nothing to do with this house. He said that the house should be lived in, not just sitting there like a relic to days gone by."

"A relic. This is my great-grandparents' house!"

"I wasn't supposed to own it," he retorted. "He wanted me to live in it. I wasn't sure how I felt about that."

"And he decided to just leave it to you in the will?" She shook her head. "These three acres are more precious than the other five hundred ninety-seven. This is where it all started."

And this was the problem—family versus staff. She felt a connection to this land through blood, but for some reason that didn't evolve into actually doing anything. He was an employee here, and he could stay as long as he did his job. Family belonged in a whole different way, but ranches didn't run on sentimental feelings or rightful inheritances—they ran on hard work.

"If you cared about it so much, why didn't you tell him?" Easton retorted. "It isn't my fault you weren't helping out around here. If you showed the least bit of interest in your family's land—and this house—your dad might have done something differently."

"And you're just some innocent bystander who accidentally got some land." Her sarcasm was thick, and his patience was spent.

"All of a sudden I'm some thug, waiting to rob your family of three acres?" he demanded. "I'm the same guy I always was, Nora! You *knew* me! Have I ever been the kind of guy who would manipulate and lie? Cut me some slack!"

"I thought I knew my dad, too!" Her voice quivered and she shook her head, looking away. So that was it— she didn't know what to trust anymore, who was telling her truth. And he couldn't help her. Those were personal issues she'd have to sort out on her own.

"That's the box," he said instead. "I'm not hiding things from you, Nora."

A kind gesture from his boss had turned ugly fast. Her guess was as good as his when it came to why Cliff had done what he did, but he wasn't accepting the blame.

Nora sighed and pulled at the flaps. The boots were on top, and she put them on the floor.

"My mom kept trying to throw these out. They were worn through, and they had no more ankle support…"

She looked at the jacket and put it aside then pulled out the envelope. He knew this was the difficult part. She removed the letters one by one, fanned out the pictures on the floor in front of her. She opened the first letter, read it through, then the second. Easton just watched her.

"He knew about Mia," she said, looking up at Easton.

"Yeah." He wasn't sure what to say to that. This version of his boss—the secretive cheater—didn't sit right with him.

"It doesn't look like Dad and Angela were involved for long."

"That's good news, isn't it?"

"I think so." She pulled a hand through her hair. "I'm taking what I can get at this point. This is not the dad I remember."

"You'd know better than I would," he replied. He might have worked with Cliff, but the man had doted on his daughter. If anyone would have known that softer side of him, it would be Nora.

"He lied to me, too," she said woodenly.

He understood her anger at being lied to, but she didn't understand what utter honesty could get you. His mother had walked out and never once tried to contact him again—that had been honest. His dad had drunk himself into a stupor—that had been a pretty honest reaction, too. He'd have settled for some insincere security from his own parents any day, if it had meant that they'd actually stuck around and been there for him.

"Whatever the fallout," Easton said, "he made his choice—and you won."

Nora was silent for a couple of beats, then she sighed and began to gather the letters and photos back together into one stack.

"You're going to be okay," he said after a moment.

"Do you know that you're the first person to tell me that?" Her expression didn't look convinced. How could anyone comfort Nora in this? She'd lost her dad twice over, and nothing anyone said could make it better.

"And you can't forgive him?" Easton asked.

"I *believed* in him, Easton."

That seemed to be the part that cut her the deepest—she'd been fooled. And now she thought Easton had fooled her, too. But Easton knew he was the one man who hadn't been lying to her. He never had.

Nora pushed herself to her feet and stood there in the lamplight, her eyes clouded with sadness. He wished he could do something, say something, hold her, even, and make this hurt less. He could have been the teenage Easton again, looking at the girl he longed to comfort, knowing that she didn't really want what he had to offer. She wouldn't accept platitudes: *You deserve better.*

And she did deserve better—she always had. She deserved more than a sullied memory of the father she'd adored. She deserved more than the broken, scarred, albeit loyal heart of a man whose own mother hadn't wanted him.

"I'm going to go up to bed," she said after a moment of silence. "I have a doctor's appointment for the babies in the morning, so I'd better get some rest."

"Okay, sure."

She turned and left the room, and he watched her go. The scent of her perfume still hung in the air, as subtle as a memory. The creak of the stairs dissipated overhead. He had some evening chores to check up on, and he was grateful for the excuse to get out, plunge into the fresh air and get away from all of this for a little while. Work—it was cheaper than therapy.

Chapter 7

The next morning Nora sat in the driver's seat of her truck. The babies were all in their car seats behind her, diapers changed, tummies full. She felt like she'd achieved something, just getting this far. There had been two spit-ups just before leaving, one leaked diaper, Rosie had wanted nothing more than to be cuddled and Bobbie decided that she hated her car seat and didn't want to be strapped in. By the time Nora got them all into the truck, her nerves were frazzled. Now it felt good to just sit in relative silence—the soft sucking of pacifiers soothing her.

Nora had been angry the night before, and that hadn't exactly changed. He said he hadn't used his job offers as any kind of leverage with her dad...was she stupid to believe that? Apparently, she'd lived a lifetime of being altogether too trusting. And when she returned to Hope she'd trusted that Easton would be the same...to never be someone who would hurt her. Someone harmless.

He'd always been quiet, eager to please, willing to step aside for her. Now that she was an adult, she knew she didn't want him constantly giving in to her, but it was possible that she'd still expected it of him. But Easton had grown into a man—strong, resilient, with his own goals and objectives, and he was certainly not harmless anymore. She'd been comfortable feeling a little sorry for him, but she didn't like this new power he seemed to wield around here. And yet, mixed in with all that resentment, she missed him...or what they used to have...the guy who used to sit with her in haylofts and lean against fences as they talked.

Nora turned the key, and the engine moaned and coughed, but didn't turn over. She stopped, frowned then tried again. Nothing.

"Great!" she muttered. This was exactly what she needed. This doctor's appointment was important, and if she couldn't even manage this... She leaned her head against the headrest then heaved a sigh and tried to start the truck again. It ground for a few seconds but didn't start.

The rumble of an engine pulled up behind her, and she looked in the rearview mirror to see Easton. He must be done with his morning work and was back for some coffee. She'd been hoping to be gone by the time he returned. She unrolled her window as he hopped out of his truck and came up beside her.

"Morning," he said. "Everything all right?"

"Not really," she admitted. "I can't start the truck."

"Want me to take a look?"

Even if he got the truck to start, would she make the

appointment? She glanced at her watch. "I guess I'll call the doctor's office and say we can't make it."

It was like everything was against her succeeding in one small parenting task this morning. This was the goal for the entire day—go to an appointment. There was nothing else scheduled. Why did it have to be so hard? Was it like this for every mom, or just the wildly inexperienced ones?

Easton crossed his arms and looked away for a moment then nodded toward his vehicle. "Would you rather have a ride into town?"

Right now she didn't really feel like spending any extra time with Easton, but his offer would solve her problem.

"You probably need to eat, and I don't really have time, and if I'm not going to be late, we'd have to leave now," she rambled.

"Let me just clear out the backseat of my cab, and then we can get the car seats moved over," he said.

A kind offer wasn't going to make her trust him again. Regardless, she needed this favor, and she wasn't about to turn it down. Not this morning. If anything, he owed her after whatever he'd done to secure that land—this and so much more.

Ten minutes later they were bumping down the gravel road, past the barn and toward the main drive.

"Thank you," she said as they turned onto the highway. "I appreciate this."

"Sure," he said.

They fell into silence, the only sound the soft sucking of pacifiers from the backseat. It was a forty-minute drive into town, and Nora leaned her head back, watching the looping telephone wires zipping past outside the window.

"Remember that time we rode out past the fields and along the edge of the forest?" Easton asked.

Nora glanced at him. She did. It had been early spring, and she'd asked Easton to go with her. He hadn't wanted to at first because he still had work to do, but then she'd threatened to go alone, and he'd caved in.

"It was fun," she said. "Dad was furious when we got back."

"You were a terrible influence," he said with a teasing smile.

"Oh, I kept your life fun," she countered, chuckling. She'd always known she could convince Easton to do pretty much anything she wanted. All it took was a bat of her lashes. She felt bad about that now.

"You did." The teasing had evaporated from his tone. "Work kept me distracted from home, and you kept me distracted from work. You kept me sane. I ride out to check on fences and cattle, but I don't ride on my days off anymore."

"You should," she said.

"It's different without the company."

He didn't take his eyes off the road. Did he miss her, too? She could remember Easton with those sad eyes. He used to pause in the middle of a chore and look out into space, and she'd always been struck by the depth of sadness in his dark eyes. That had been part of why she liked to drag him away from his duties, because with her he'd laugh. She'd felt like she was rescuing him, saving him from whatever it was that was breaking his heart when he thought no one was looking...

"I was pretty mad last night," Nora said.

"Yeah, I got that."

She glanced over to catch a wry smile on his lips.

"You still mad?" he asked.

"Yes," she said. "I am, but not exclusively at you."

"That's something." He slowed as they came up behind a tractor, signaled and passed it.

"Here's what I want to know," she said. "And honestly. What was there between you and my dad that was so special? And don't say it was nothing, because obviously you were special to him."

Easton was silent for a few beats, then he said, "I didn't take him for granted."

"And I did?" She couldn't hide the irritation that rose at that.

Easton glanced at her and then back to the road. "Of course. He was your dad, and it was perfectly normal to take all that for granted. That's what kids do—they get used to a certain way of living, and they don't stop to think about all that goes into achieving it. That isn't a terrible thing, you know."

"But you were saintly and appreciative," she said, sarcasm edging her tone.

"I wasn't his kid," he retorted. "You're going to inherit all of that land, and I certainly won't. Cliff loved you heart and soul and always would. He was generally fond of me because I'd been around so long and I worked my tail off. There was a massive difference. I wasn't nosing in on your turf."

"That's ironic, because you ended up with my turf."

Easton smiled slightly. "Land isn't love, Nora. It was years of knowing my place. I wanted to learn from your dad, and he liked to teach me stuff. I would do anything extra he asked of me in order to learn. He made me into the professional I am today, and I never took that time with him for granted. Because he *wasn't* my dad."

"And that's why he liked you so much," she clarified.

"I think so," he said. "That and—" He stopped and color crept into his face. For a moment she could see the teenage boy in him again.

"And what?" she pressed.

"It's a little embarrassing," he said, "but he knew how I felt about you." He glanced at her, dark eyes meeting hers, then his gaze snapped back on the road. The moment had been fleeting, but she'd caught something in that eye contact—something deep and warm.

"So you had a crush," she said, trying to sound normal, but she still sounded breathy in her own ears. Bobbie started to whimper, and Nora reached behind her to pop her pacifier back into her mouth.

"It was a weird thing to bond over," Easton admitted. "But I was the one guy who thought you were just as amazing as your dad did."

"I always thought my dad hated the idea of us together," she said. "Anytime he caught us alone, like in the hayloft, he'd blow his top."

"That was then," he said. "After you left, he seemed to change his mind. He never liked the guys you dated, you know."

"They weren't so bad," she countered.

Easton chuckled but didn't answer. She'd known that her dad hated the guys she went out with in Billings. They were the kinds of guys whose boots had never seen mud.

"I kind of knew you had a crush," she admitted. "Kaitlyn thought it was more than that, but I told her it wasn't. You might have to reassure her."

"It was more."

Nora's heart sped up, and she cast about for something to say but couldn't come up with anything. More than a crush...what was that? Love?

"Anyway, after you left, your dad used to joke around that if he had to choose between one of those city slickers and me then he'd take me," Easton said.

"He never told me that." Not directly, at least. Her father had pointed out Easton's work ethic to her more than once. "He's the first one up, and the last one in," her dad had said. "He reminds me of myself when I was his age. You could do worse than finding a man who knows how to work hard, Nora." Was giving Easton the house her father's way of "handpicking" her husband? That wasn't really Cliff's style.

"Look, it was nice to have your dad's respect," Easton said. "But I wasn't the kind of guy who could be led to water, either. Regardless of how I felt about you. I respected your dad, and I appreciated all he did for me, but I make my own life choices."

"So you didn't really want anything more with me—" She didn't know what she was fishing for here— absolution, maybe?

"I didn't want to be the guy always chasing at your heels," he replied. "What I felt for you was considerably more than a crush, but I didn't want to chase you down and try to convince you I was worth your time. If you didn't know it yet, then that ship had sailed. I put my energy into getting over you instead."

"Pragmatic..." She swallowed.

"Always." He laughed softly, and her heart squeezed at the sound of it. He was every inch a man now, and it was a whole lot harder to ignore. But he'd made the right choice in getting over her.

"So you think Dad wanted us to get together," she clarified.

"I don't really think it matters what he wanted now," Easton said frankly. "He's gone."

Gone with her father were the days when Easton could be talked into horseback riding, and that was probably for the best.

"You're right," she admitted. "I might be able to pick that bone with him if he were still alive, but he's not."

Easton glanced toward her again, and she could see the warmth in his gaze—something that smoldered deeper. It wasn't the same shy look from years ago when he'd had a crush. This was the steady gaze of a man—unwavering, direct, knowledgeable.

He didn't say anything, though, and neither did she.

Easton parked in front of the two-story building that housed the doctor's office. It took a few minutes to get the babies out of the truck, and then Nora carried two car seats and he carried Rosie's into the waiting room. While Nora went to tell the receptionist that they'd arrived, Easton glanced around at the people seated in the chairs that edged the room. He nodded to two men he knew, and a couple of older ladies looked from the car seats to Nora and then up at Easton, their expressions filled with questions and dirty laundry, no doubt.

Easton glanced at his watch, wondering how long this appointment would take. They were getting low on calf formula. He could let Nora call him on his cell when she was done, and he could head down to the ranch and feed shop... Rosie started to fuss, and Nora glanced back at him. She looked overwhelmed by all of this, and he felt a tickle of sympathy.

"Do you mind?" she asked hopefully.

Easton unbuckled Rosie from her car seat and picked her up. That settled the infant immediately, and she snuggled into his arms, big brown eyes blinking up at him. Rosie definitely liked to be held. Bobbie and Riley were asleep in their seats, and Nora was rooting through her purse for something. He wasn't getting out of here anytime soon, was he?

"They're very cute," one of the older ladies said, putting down her copy of *Reader's Digest*. She had short, permed hair that was dyed something close to black. It made her face look pale and older than she probably was.

Easton used his boot to move the car seat toward a line of free chairs then sat down in one of them. The woman scooted over, peering into Rosie's tiny face.

"These are...the ones..." She looked at Easton meaningfully. Had gossip really gone around town so fast that people he didn't even recognize were asking about the situation? He decided to play dumb and hope she took the hint.

"They're cute all right," he said.

"But these are Cliff Carpenter's grandchildren, right?" she plowed on. "These are the babies with that poor, poor mother..."

He closed his eyes for a moment, looking for calm. "It's private," he said, trying to sound more polite than he felt right now.

"I never imagined," she went on. "My husband did some mechanic work for him on the tractors—you know, when it got beyond what they could handle on site—so I knew Cliff pretty well. And he just seemed so devoted to Dina. So devoted. Just…" She shook her head, searching for words.

"Devoted," Easton said drily. Why was he encouraging this?

"Yes!" she exclaimed. "He really was. He talked about her all the time, and he only ever mentioned his daughter—I mean the *local* daughter. He never, ever mentioned anyone *else*, if you know what I mean. If he had, I might have said something, but he never did. I wouldn't have guessed if those babies hadn't arrived."

She straightened, looking up guiltily as Nora came in their direction, a car seat in each hand. Nora sank into the chair next to Easton and nodded to the woman.

"Hi, Ethel," Nora said.

"Morning," Ethel murmured, but her gaze moved over the babies, her mouth drawn together in a little pucker of judgment.

"I never knew," Ethel said, leaning forward again. "Just so you know, Nora, I never knew."

Nora cast Ethel a withering look—apparently she was past polite at this point, and Easton had to choke back a smile.

"If I had, I would have said something, too," Ethel went on, not to be dissuaded. "I side with the women. How many times have we been tilled under by a man with a wandering eye? So I wouldn't have kept a secret like that. I'd have spoken up, and let him face the music. That's what I'd have done."

"It's a sensitive topic, ma'am," Easton said quietly.

"I'd say it is!" she retorted. "My sister married a man who couldn't keep it in his pants, so I know exactly how sensitive these things can be. It is amazing what some men do with their free time. My sister's husband didn't even try to be faithful. He slept with everyone within reach, and she knew it, but she wasn't about to give him his walking papers, either. It's all well and good to tell her that she should kick him out, but it was her life, and her marriage, and I couldn't interfere now, could I?"

"Hardly," Easton said wryly, but she didn't seem to read his tone, because she kept talking.

"Everyone in her town knew that her husband had fathered two other children. In fact, I attended the wedding of one of those girls. My sister's husband wasn't there, of course, because he was still pretending that he wasn't her daddy, but I was a friend of a friend, so I went to that wedding. I wasn't invited to the reception, but—"

"Ethel," Nora said, shooting a dangerously sweet smile in the older woman's direction. "Shut up."

Ethel blinked, color rising in her cheeks, and she opened her mouth to say something then shut it with a click.

"Ethel Carmichael," the receptionist called. "The doctor is ready for you now."

Ethel rose to her feet and stalked toward the hallway in time for Easton to overhear the nurse say something about taking her blood pressure. They might want to wait on that to get a normal reading, he thought, and when he glanced over at Nora, she sent him a scathing look.

"What?" he asked.

She rolled her eyes and looked away. This one wasn't his fault. Ethel was the storyteller. Women like Ethel had memories like elephants for juicy gossip, but looking down into Rosie's tiny face, the humor in the situation bled away.

This baby girl—and her sisters—would experience the kind of sympathetic tut-tutting that he had for most of his growing-up years. Easton had enough scandal surrounding his own parentage, and he knew what it felt like to have every woman in town look at him with sympathy because his mother had walked out on him. That kind of stigma clung like a skunk's spray.

When Easton was in the fifth grade, they were supposed to make key chains for their mothers for Mother's Day. Easton had dutifully made that key chain, braiding leather strips as they were instructed. All he'd wanted was to blend in with the class, but that never happened. The other kids whispered about him—he didn't have a mom to give the gift to—and the teacher was extra nice to him, which he'd pay for at recess time. So he'd finished his key chain and in the place where they were supposed to write "I love you, Mom," he'd written something profoundly dirty instead. He wanted to change that look of pity he saw into something else—anger, preferably.

It worked, and every Mother's Day afterward, he pulled the same trick, because things like Mother's Day couldn't be avoided. These girls would have the same problem, except for them it would be at the mention of grandparents, and everyone would clam up and look at them with high-handed sympathy. And they'd hate it—he could guarantee that. With any luck, they would find something better than profanity as a distraction.

Hang in there, kiddo, he thought as he looked down into Rosie's wide-eyed face. She flailed a small arm then yawned. He couldn't say it would get better, because it wouldn't. But she'd get used to it.

Chapter 8

That evening Easton stood over the open hood of Nora's truck where it had stalled out in front of his house. It needed a part—one he could swap out of another Chevy that was parked in a shed. The truck would be up and running in no time. He'd get the part tomorrow during his workday and fix her vehicle the next evening. Lickety-split.

The sun was sinking in the west, shadows lengthening and birds twittering their evening songs. He liked this time of day; after his work was done he had the satisfaction of having accomplished something. That was what he loved about this job—yeah, there was always more to do the next day, but a day's work meant something. He'd been thinking about that trip to the doctor's office with the babies earlier that afternoon, and he couldn't quite sort out his feelings. Truth was, he felt protective of those little tykes, but that didn't sit right with him. He wasn't supposed to be getting attached.

Their ride home from town had been quiet. He'd wanted to say something—he knew Nora was upset about Ethel Carmichael's attempt at conversation, but she'd probably be in for a whole lot more of that. People had known Cliff, loved him, which meant he'd left more than just Dina and Nora stunned by the truth. And in spite of it all, Easton still felt like he owed his late boss something more—a defense, maybe. He just didn't know how.

A cool breeze felt good against his face and arms. The bugs were out—he slapped a mosquito on his wrist. Easton wiped his hands on a rag then flicked off the light that hung from the hood of Nora's truck, unhooked it and banged the hood shut. Above him, a window scraped open and he looked up.

Nora stood, framed between billowing white curtains, and she lifted her hand in a silent wave. She looked so sweet up there, her skin bathed in golden sunlight, her sun-streaked hair tumbling down around her shoulders. Her nose and cheeks looked a little burned, and squinting up at her like that, he couldn't help but notice just how gorgeous she was.

"Hey," he said.

"I just got the babies to sleep," she said. "Are you fixing my truck?"

"Yup." He turned his attention to rubbing the last of the grease out of the lines in his palm. "But I won't be done until tomorrow."

"Thank you." She brushed her hair out of her face and leaned her elbows onto the windowsill. "You don't have to do that, you know."

"Yeah?" he retorted. "You gonna do it?"

It was a challenge. She'd never been one to tinker with an engine, and he'd fixed her ride more than once when they were teenagers.

"I'd call a garage."

A garage. Yeah, right. A garage was for quitters. Any cowboy with a lick of self-respect knew how to fix his truck, and only when it was halfway flattened did he lower himself to calling in a mechanic.

"You're going to be my boss one day," he said. "I might as well make nice now."

She rolled her eyes. "We'll be in our sixties by then."

She had a point. It'd likely be years before her mother grew too feeble to actually run this place. And she'd told him before that she wasn't living for a funeral. But if she settled down with her mom at the main house, he'd be fixing her truck for a long time to come as her employee. Did he mind that?

"You should stick around," he said, shooting her a grin. "You'd enjoy fighting with me more often."

"I thought you said you'd make nice," she countered.

"Yeah, how long can that last?" he asked with a low laugh. "I'm not sixteen anymore, Nora."

She raised an eyebrow. "Me, neither."

Then she disappeared from the window. He stood there, looking up at the billowing curtains for a moment before he smiled to himself and scrubbed his hand once more with the rag. Some things didn't change, like the way Nora could fix him to the spot with a single look... but she was no teen angel anymore. She was a grown woman, with a woman's body and a woman's direct gaze. He wasn't a kid anymore, either, and he wasn't at her beck and call. This had been about his job—a truck on this ranch that needed work. That was it.

The drive into town—okay that had been more than official duties around here, but he and Nora had some history. She'd always be special to him. Didn't they say that a first love was never fully erased? Something like that. She'd been part of his formative years.

Easton's cell phone rang, and he glanced at the number before picking it up.

"Dad?"

"Hi." His dad's voice sounded tight, and sober for a change. "What are you up to?"

"Working."

"Well...take a break. You need to come over."

"Why?" Easton looked at his watch. "It's not a good time, Dad. I have to get up early. You know that."

"You'll want to come by, son," his father said. "There's someone you'll want to see."

"Yeah?" He wasn't convinced. "Who?"

"Your mom."

Easton froze, the rag falling from his hand and landing in the gravel. He tried to swallow but couldn't. A cold sweat erupted on his forehead, and the breeze suddenly felt chilly.

"Ha," he said, forcing the word out. "Not funny. Actually, kind of mean."

"I'm not joking," his father said. "I'm looking at her right now. If you wanted to see her, now's the time."

"Okay," he said, his heart banging in his chest. "I'll be there in fifteen minutes."

Hanging up the phone, he fished his keys out of his pocket and headed for his own vehicle. Mom was back? Was Dad hallucinating? Maybe he'd widened his addictive repertoire to include some drug use. Easton scrubbed a hand through his hair and hauled open the door. He had to stop and suck in a few deep breaths because his hands were trembling. There was something in his dad's voice that told him this was no joke.

After twenty years' absence, what could she possibly want? After missing his childhood…after letting him grow up with a drunk of a father and a hole in his heart the size of Wisconsin, what brought her back to Hope?

Nora looked out the window in time to see Easton's truck back out of the drive then take off down the gravel road, leaving a billow of dust behind him.

That's weird, she thought. Where was he off to in such a hurry?

Maybe an evening to herself was better anyway. Flirting with Easton hadn't really been part of the plan, yet she kept finding herself doing it. Was it habit? A throwback from her teenage years? Or maybe she missed all the control she used to have—a boy following after her who'd do anything she asked.

"I'm not that shallow," she muttered to herself.

Her day had been tiring. The doctor's appointment itself had been routine. The babies had been weighed, measured and declared to be healthy. It was that encounter with Ethel Carmichael that had gotten to her. It was only an old woman's gossipy streak, she told herself. Nora shouldn't worry about it…but she did.

She sighed and rubbed her hands over her face. Hope, Montana, was a nice town—friendly, helpful, attractive—but it was also a town where not too much happened. Everybody knew everybody else, or just about, and half the town was related to each other by marriage. People remembered each other's stories because they were a part of each other's lives. And when people saw the girls in Beauty's Ice Cream Shop or saw them in church, they'd think of Cliff and the scandal around the triplets' arrival. These things didn't just go away.

Nora could handle some gossip. But these three little girls deserved a happy life. What options did Nora have? She could stay in Hope where the girls would have a distanced grandmother they weren't allowed to call "Grandma," and where the story of their grandfather's infidelity would follow them everywhere they went. That was assuming that Nora could make a life here—get a job, find a place that didn't cost too much... maybe with enough family about, she'd be able to pull together a decent life for the girls, financially, at least.

Or she could go back to Billings where she'd have to drop them off at day care every day...and maybe get a second job doing some contract bookkeeping to be able to afford that. They'd have a tired, overworked mom who did her best to keep up with everything. They wouldn't have many new clothes or the toys they wanted. There wouldn't be summer vacations, unless you counted coming back to Hope where everyone would look at them sideways and the girls still couldn't call their grandmother "Grandma."

Or—and this was the option that brought a lump to her throat—she could accept that she couldn't provide the kind of life that these babies deserved. She couldn't give them a comfortable home with a bedroom for each of them, or summer vacations, or new clothes. She couldn't even provide a stable family life to make up for those other things. She wasn't married. There would be no dad to give them that important male influence in their lives. There wouldn't even be a doting grandma to cuddle them and tell them stories about their family. And she'd never make this town look past the scandal the triplets' grandfather created...

Nora sank onto the side of her bed, her heart sodden with anxiety. That was what the visit to the doctor's office had shown her—she could provide the basics, but she couldn't shield them from the rest. And if there was a family out there that would adopt these girls together, love them and celebrate them, provide birthday parties and new shoes... If there were adoptive grandparents who would make cookies with them and read them stories, look them in the eye and tell them how loved and wanted they were... Could she really deny these little girls that kind of life?

Nora looked through the bars of the crib at the sleeping babies. Their lashes brushed their plump cheeks; their hair swirled across their heads in damp curls. Bobbie was making phantom sucking noises, her little tongue poked out of her mouth, and Riley let out a soft sigh in her sleep. Nora put a finger in Rosie's tiny hand, and she clamped down on it.

"I love you," she whispered.

It was true—she'd fallen in love with her girls, and if money didn't matter or if she could wave a magic wand and make everyone forget the pain associated with these children, she'd raise them herself and be their mom. But money did matter, and so did scandal. They were brand-new to this world, and already they were steeped in it. She was the one Mia had designated as their provider, and she had to do what was best for the babies.

A tear slipped down Nora's cheek, and she wiped it away with her free hand. She gently stroked Rosie's soft fingers, inhaling the delicate smell of sleeping infants. She'd remember this, cherish it always. She wasn't their mother—Mia was. Nora was an in-between person who had to give them her heart in order to take care of them. But she couldn't keep them, no matter how much her heart broke at the thought of letting go.

When she'd taken the babies from the hospital, they'd given her some business cards from social workers and adoption agencies. She'd shoved them into her wallet and forgotten about them, but she knew what she'd have to do.

Tomorrow. Not tonight. Tonight she had to let herself feel this pain and have a good cry. Then in the morning she'd call an adoption agency and see what kinds of options the girls might have.

Chapter 9

Easton's father, Mike Ross, lived at the end of Hunter Street. There were no shade trees, just brown lawns and old houses—several of which were empty. The Ross house was at the end of the road before asphalt simply evaporated into scrub grass. A couple of cars were on blocks in the front yard, and a chain and a massive dog bowl sat abandoned by the front door. The dog had died years ago, but the reminder of his presence seemed to help keep thieves and religious proselytizers at bay. Which was good when it came to thieves, but in Easton's humble opinion, a little religion wouldn't hurt his old man.

When Easton pulled into the driveway behind a red SUV, all those old feelings of anger and resentment settled back onto his shoulders, too. This was why he never came home—it reminded him of things he'd rather leave in the past. Like constantly feeling like a failure no matter what he did, and acting rough and angry to get away from the pity.

Except he'd longed for his mom every day since she'd left, imagined ways she might return, set scenes in his mind when she'd see him as a grown man and her heart would fill with pride. Those had been fantasies, because her actually coming back would solidify the fact that she'd been able to return all along and had chosen not to.

He sat in his truck for a couple of minutes, his hands on the steering wheel in a white-knuckled grip. That was probably her SUV, all new and shiny. So she had enough money for that. Maybe she'd stayed away for the same reasons he did now—because she didn't like to remember. He undid his seat belt and got out of the truck.

The front door was never used; in fact, his dad had a bunch of junk piled in front of it from the inside. Easton angled around to the side door. He didn't bother knocking, just opened it. The kitchen was smoky from his father's cigarettes, so Easton left the door open to let it clear a bit.

"Hello?" he called.

A woman emerged from the living room—slim, made up, wearing a pair of jeans and a light blouse. Her hair was dyed brown now, cut short but stylish. Her face was the same face he remembered, though. Even that one crooked tooth when she smiled hesitantly.

"Easton?" she whispered.

"Mom." Tears welled up in his eyes, and he stood there looking at her awkwardly.

"Oh, sweetheart—" She came forward as if to hug him, but he didn't move into it, so she ended up patting his arm a few times. She looked up into his face, and he could see that she'd aged. She was no longer the woman in her early twenties matching his dad drink for drink—she would be forty-seven this year. He'd done the math.

"So—" He cleared his throat. "Where've you been?"

"Can I hug you?" she asked softly.

"Not right now." If he let her hug him, the tears he'd been holding back for years would start, and he couldn't let that happen. He could cry later, alone, but not in front of her. He needed answers.

His father came into the room and scraped back a kitchen chair. He was thin and tall, lined and slightly yellowed from nicotine.

"Should we sit?" she asked cautiously. "Just come sit with me, son."

He followed her to the flier-strewn table and sat opposite her. She looked him over then reached out and put her hand on top of his.

"You look good," she said. "Really good."

"Thanks." He pulled his hand back as the tears started to rise inside his chest. "You look like you're not doing too badly for yourself. What took so long to come see how I was doing?"

"I wanted to—" She looked toward his father. "I talked to your dad on the phone a few times, and he said you were doing really well. He said if I came around I'd ruin things for you."

"What?" Easton darted a disgusted look at his old man. "And you believed that lying sack of—" He bit off the last word and sucked in a shaky breath. Profanity was a bit of a habit when he felt cornered. *"You left me."*

And suddenly, he was nothing more than an eight-year-old boy again, staring at the mom who was supposed to be better at this. In that note she'd left on the fridge, she hadn't said anything loving. Her last words had been "He's your problem now." She'd ditched him, left town, and while he'd squirmed his way around those words over the years, trying to apply different meaning to them that would still allow her to return for him, looking at his mother now brought the words back like a punch in the gut.

"I know…" She blinked a few times then licked her lips. "I was young when I had you—seventeen, if you remember. I didn't know how to deal with everything. I was so overwhelmed…"

"Except you weren't seventeen when you left. You were twenty-five. That's a solid adult."

"Yes." She didn't offer any excuses.

"And the note—"

"I wasn't in a good place when I scratched that out," she interrupted. "I don't remember exactly what I said."

"I do." Easton glanced at his old man. His dad would remember that note, too. "You said you were sick of this life and I was Dad's problem from then on."

She winced. "I didn't mean—"

"Sure you did. Or you would have come back."

She swallowed, glanced at his father. What was she looking for, some kind of united front?

"So you figured you'd leave me with him." Easton jutted a thumb toward his father. "He was a more suitable parent?"

"He had the house," she said. "I just drove away one day. I wasn't thinking about the future—just about getting some space." She was quiet for a moment. "And I knew I wasn't much of a mom."

Yeah, that was evident. With her sitting in front of him, he was able to separate the fantasies of the gentle mother stroking his hair from the reality of the emotionally distant mother who'd spent hours a day smoking in this very kitchen.

"I tried to see you," she added.

"When?" he demanded. He found that hard to believe.

"The summer you were fourteen. I was in the area and I called your dad. He said he got you a job at a local ranch and you were doing really well. He said you were happy, and you didn't remember me."

"*You* said that?" Easton glared at his father across the table. "I was happy, was I? I didn't need her?"

His father shrugged. "We did okay. She's the one who left."

That had been his father's mantra over the years—she was the one who left, as if all their problems had been caused by the one who walked away instead of the parents who hadn't done their job to begin with.

Easton turned back to his mother. "I was doing okay because Cliff Carpenter hired me and took over where Dad left off. I wasn't happy. I was making do. And Dad didn't get me anything. I waited outside the ranch and feed store and asked every single rancher that came and left if he'd hire me. Cliff was the only one to say yes. Dad didn't do squat for me. He drank every day, ran this house into the ground and smacked me around if I was within reach."

"Hey—" his father started.

"Shut up, Dad." Easton wasn't in any mood to argue about facts with his old man, and his father seemed to sense that, because he subsided back into a brooding silence.

"I—" His mother swallowed hard and dropped her gaze. "I didn't know all that."

"I'm a ranch manager now," he added. "I own my own home. I have a life, and I steer clear of this dump."

"Maybe I could—"

"No!" He knew what she was about to ask—to see the life he'd built for himself. And while he'd dreamed of that opportunity since he was eight years old, he realized that he didn't actually want it now. She didn't deserve to feel better about how he'd turned out. He wanted to hurt her back—make her feel the rejection he'd felt his entire life. "You aren't welcome in my home."

They fell into silence for a few beats. He could take all his pain and anguish out on her, or he could get some of those answers at last.

"So what have you been doing all these years?" Easton asked. "You're dressed pretty well."

"I'm—" She looked down at her hands splayed on the tabletop, and his eye followed hers to the wedding ring. "I'm married again. His name is Tom. He's very sweet. I'm a recovering alcoholic, so I don't drink. It took a few years of hard work, but I got there."

"So where'd you find... Tom...then?" The name tasted sour on his tongue.

"Church," she replied. "We've been married sixteen years now. He's a good man."

Sixteen years of marriage, and she'd stayed away from him. There had been a home she could have brought him to, a cupboard full of food... He did the mental math, and he'd been twelve when she'd gotten married—plenty of time to have given him some sort of childhood.

"What does Tom do?"

"He's an electrician."

Blast it—so normal and balanced. His mom walked

away and got to marry some utterly normal Tom, afford new clothes—something he'd never had growing up—and drive a new SUV... And he'd been left in addiction-induced poverty, dreaming of some fantasy mother.

"Where do you live?" he asked.

"Billings."

"Three hours away?" he asked incredulously. "I was here missing you, longing for my mom to come back for me, and all that time you were a mere three hours from here?"

Easton rubbed his hands over his face. He'd dreamed of a chance to see his mother again, to try to mend this jagged hole in his heart that she'd left behind. Some days he wanted answers, and other days he wanted comfort. Today he had the chance to hug her and he couldn't bring himself to do it. He was finally face-to-face with his mom again, and he felt something he'd never expected—he hated her.

"I'm so sorry—" Her voice shook and she wiped a tear from her cheek. "I thought you were doing well, that if I came back I'd ruin things for you. I was so ashamed of the woman I used to be. I was mean, drunk most of the time and just a shell of a person..." She shook her head. "I thought you'd remember all of that."

"Not really," he admitted. "A bit, I mean. But I was young. I think Dad remembered that more. I...uh... I kept your Led Zeppelin T-shirt under my mattress. I remembered the smell of your cigarettes in the morning, and the sound of your laughter."

"My T-shirt—" The look on her face was like he'd punched her with those words.

"It helped me sleep sometimes." Why was he telling her this? Blast it, his complaints made him sound like a whimpering puppy! He wasn't meaning to open up, but he'd been holding all of this in for so long…

"I wasn't sure you'd *want* me back."

"Not sure I do now, either," he snapped. That was half of a lie. He did want her back, but he also wanted her to pay for her absence. He wanted her to feel some of what she'd done to him. "So why now?"

"I don't know," she said quietly. "I got into my vehicle and started driving. I called Tom from the road and said I was coming to see my son. I need to go back tonight, but I had to see you again. I missed you so much."

"Not enough to drive the three hours before this," he pointed out.

"I wanted to…" She swallowed hard. "I couldn't shake the guilt of having left you like I did. Then Brandon had his eighth birthday…"

"Brandon?" he asked slowly. "Who's that?"

"My son—your half brother…" She grabbed her purse from the back of her chair and rummaged through it. She pulled out a school photo and pushed it across the table toward him. Easton didn't touch it, but he looked at the smiling face of a kid with dirty-blond hair and a lopsided grin. *Her son.*

Easton's stomach dropped as the reality of this moment settled into his gut. She'd gotten married, had another little boy and she'd been the mom she should have been to Easton to this other kid.

"So…" Easton's voice shook. "I have a half brother."

"Yes." She nodded, a tentative smile coming to her lips. "And he's a sweet boy. I know you'd like him. He's got such a big heart."

"And you've been there for him," Easton clarified, his voice firming up as rage coursed through him.

"You've taken him to soccer practice and given him birthday parties...hell, even birthday presents?"

"He likes chess, actually, but—" She stopped, sensing where he was going with this. "I was older. I was wiser. There's enough money now—"

Easton let out a string of expletives and rose to his feet, the chair underneath him clattering to the floor.

"You were my *mother*!" he roared.

She sat in stunned silence, and his father shuffled his feet against the crumb-laden floor. Easton stared down at the parents who'd brought him into this world and then failed to provide for him. He couldn't stop the tears anymore—he was blinded by them. His shoulders shook and he turned away, trying to get some sort of control over himself, but now that it had started, he couldn't seem to dam it up. He slammed a hand against the wall then leaned there as he sobbed.

He felt his mother's arms wrap around him from behind, and she shook with tears, too.

"Damn it, Mom, I hate you," he wept.

"I know," she whispered. "I know..."

Then he turned around, and for the first time since he was eight years old, he wrapped his arms around his mom and hugged her. He hugged her tighter than was probably comfortable, but she didn't complain, and he didn't dare let go.

She'd learned how to be a mother after all, but she'd learned with somebody else. And that didn't do a thing for Easton. He'd already grown up, and he'd done it without a mom.

Nora stood in the kitchen mixing baby formula at the counter. She shook up the third bottle, watching the bubbles form. She was getting used to this hour, and she woke up before her cell phone alarm now. It was midnight, and she was in her white cotton nightgown, the cool night air winding around her bare legs. It was strange, but this house, which had always been so firmly *hers* in her heart, felt empty without Easton in it. He'd driven off that evening, and he hadn't come back.

Earlier that evening, her mother had asked if she'd come for lunch at the house. She was having Nora's aunt and uncle come over, and she needed some moral support. This was Cliff's sister and her husband—both of whom had been close with Cliff.

"They'll want to meet the babies, too, I'm sure," her mother had said. "They're Cliff's grandkids, after all."

There weren't going to be any easy explanations, no simple family relationships for these girls. And they needed family—the supportive, loving kind, not the backbiting, gossiping kind. Nora needed to know now if that was even a possibility after what her father had done. She was willing to look into adoptive options for the girls, but she hadn't fully committed to it—not yet. Other single mothers managed it—pulled it all together on their own—but *how*?

Normally at this time of year, the Carpenters hosted a corn roast and barbecue for family and friends, also as a way to thank the staff for their hard work over the summer. She'd asked her mother if she wanted to go ahead with it this year, but with Cliff's death and the subsequent drama, it hardly seemed like a priority.

Standing in the kitchen at midnight, Nora put down the last bottle of formula. She'd considered calling Easton's cell phone a couple of times, but hadn't. This was her problem to untangle on her own, and while a listening ear might be comforting, no one else could give her the answer. Besides, it wasn't Easton's job to listen to her go on about her problems. He had problems of his own. But would it be too much to ask of a friend?

As she gathered up the bottles, a truck's engine rumbled up the drive. She felt a wave of relief. Why she should feel this way, she didn't know, but perhaps it was just old habits dying hard—tough times nudging her toward Easton. She really wanted to talk to him about the girls—but more than that, she wanted to hear what he had to say about them. It would help her hammer out her own feelings out loud with another person who wouldn't judge her, because Heaven knew she was judging herself pretty harshly right now.

The back door opened and Easton stepped inside. His shoulders were slumped, and his face looked puffy and haggard. If she didn't know him better, she'd think he'd been crying. He didn't look up at her as he kicked off his boots and hung his hat on the peg.

"Easton? Oh my goodness, are you all right?"

He scrubbed a hand through his hair. "Yeah, I'm fine."

"No, you're not!" She crossed the kitchen and caught his arm on his way past. "Look at me."

He turned toward her and she could see the red rims of his eyes, the same old sadness welling up in his dark gaze. "My mom came back."

Nora stared at him. A slew of questions cascaded through her mind, but they swept past as she saw the pain etched in Easton's features.

"She was at my dad's place."

Nora's breath came out in a rush and she looked from Easton to the bottles and then back at her friend again.

His mom—she knew what this meant…or at the very least she knew how heavily this would have hit him.

"I need to feed the babies," she said quietly. "You want to help? We could talk…"

He was silent for a beat, and she half expected him to say no, that he was fine, and to go up and lock himself into his bedroom.

"Sure," he said.

She picked up the bottles from the counter and they moved together toward the stairs.

"What happened, exactly?" she asked as they climbed the narrow staircase. "Is she still here?"

"She's left already—for Billings. She's been there this whole time. She's remarried with another kid."

His voice was low and wooden as he went over what had happened tonight. Nora picked up Riley and passed her to Easton. He was more practiced now in handling babies, and he took the infant easily. His expression softened as he looked down into the sleeping face.

"They're so little," he said quietly. He teased the bottle's nipple between her lips. Nora scooped up Rosie and let Bobbie sleep for another few minutes. "Can you imagine anyone just walking away?"

Tears misted her eyes. Wasn't that exactly what she was considering with the triplets? Was she just as bad as Easton's mother? Or had Easton's mother done the best that she could under the circumstances? Maybe she just wanted to excuse Easton's mom because it would make her look infinitely better by comparison.

"How do you feel now that you've seen her again?" Nora asked quietly.

"Conflicted," he admitted. "I've wanted this for

years—a chance to see her, to hug her again—and now that I have it, I'm filled with rage."

"You're probably in shock," she said.

"I spent years loving her in spite of her faults." He heaved a sigh. "But she figured out how to be a decent parent when she had her second child—Brandon. I saw a picture. Cute kid. And all I could feel was anger. That's awful, isn't it? He's just some kid. Do I really want him to suffer like I did?"

She didn't respond, and the only sound in the room was that of the babies drinking their bottles.

"She wants me to meet him," Easton said after a moment.

"Do you want to?" Nora asked.

"I don't know. Not really. Yes." He shook his head. "You know what I want? I want to go back in time and have her be there for me, too. She takes Brandon to chess club three times a week, and she drives him to birthday parties. She's a stay-at-home mom." He muttered an oath then looked sheepishly at Nora. "Riley'll never remember that."

Nora smiled. "She'll be fine."

Easton jiggled the bottle to get Riley drinking again and adjusted her position, then he continued, "My mom said she wanted to be home for Brandon, because her husband works long hours, and he needs someone to talk about his school day with. Talk about his school day! What I would've given for my mom to just sit and listen to me for a few minutes."

"Will you see her again?" she asked.

"She'll come back again on Saturday afternoon. She'll text me the details."

Nora tipped Rosie up against her shoulder and patted her back. Easton did the same with Riley. From the crib, Bobbie was starting to squirm in her sleep, probably feeling hungry. Riley burped, and Easton wiped her mouth with a cloth, then laid her back down in the crib. He picked up Bobbie next. When had he gotten so good at this?

"Should I feed her?" he asked.

Rosie hadn't burped yet, and Nora nodded. Easton grabbed the third bottle and Bobbie immediately started slurping it back.

"It's funny—I have her cell number. I could call her if I wanted to… I could text my mom. How many times have I wished I could contact her—say something to her? Now I could…with a text." A smile creased his tired face. "That's something, isn't it?"

And in those shining eyes, she saw the boy she used to know, who would sit next to her in the hayloft, listening to her go on about her small and insignificant problems. He hadn't mentioned his mother often back then, but she could remember one time when he'd said, "When my mom comes back, I'm going to buy her a house."

"A house?" she'd asked. "How will you do that? Houses cost more than you've got."

"In three years I'll be eighteen. I'll drop out of school and work full-time," he'd replied. "And then we'll live in that house together, and my dad can rot by himself. I'll take care of her."

He'd always planned for his mother's return. Somehow he'd been convinced that she'd come back, and he'd been right. Except when they were kids, he'd been certain that she'd need him.

They resettled the babies into the crib, but they

stayed there in the darkness, standing close enough together that she could feel the warmth of his body radiating against hers.

"The one thing she didn't tell me—" His voice broke. "She never said why she left me behind."

She couldn't see him well enough in the dim light, but she could hear that rasp of deep emotion against his iron reserve. That was a wound that wouldn't heal.

"Easton…"

She wrapped her arms around his waist and leaned her cheek against his broad chest. He slipped his muscular arms around her and she could feel his cheek rest on the top of her head. He smelled good—musky, with a hint of hay. His body was roped with muscle, and he leaned into her, his body warming her in a way that felt intimate and pleading.

Neither of them spoke, and he leaned down farther, wrapping his arms around her a little more closely, tugging her against him more firmly. She could feel the thud of his heartbeat against her chest, and she closed her eyes, breathing in his manly scent. Somehow all either of them seemed to want was to be closer, to absorb all of each other's pain into their bodies and share it.

Easton pulled back and she found her face inches from his, and his dark eyes moved over her face. She could see the faint freckles across his cheekbones, the soft shadow of his stubble veiling a few acne scars. He was the same old Easton, all grown up, and while she could still see the sweet boy in those dark eyes, she could also see the rugged man—the survivor, the cowboy—and the intensity of that gaze also reminded her that he was very capable of being so much more than that…

"I missed you," he whispered.

"Me, too." And standing there in his arms, his muscular thighs pressed against hers, she still missed him. Pushed up against each other wasn't close enough to touch the longing for whatever it was that they'd lost over the years.

His dark gaze met hers and her breath caught in her throat. She couldn't have looked away if she'd wanted to. His mouth hovered close to hers, a whisper of breath tickling her lips. He hesitated, and before she could think better of it, Nora closed the distance between them, standing on her tiptoes so that her lips met his. He took it from there, dipping his head down and sliding a hand through her hair. His other hand pressed against the small of her back, nudging her closer, closer against his muscular body, her bare legs against his jeans, her hands clutching the sides of his shirt. His lips moved over hers, confident and hungry, and when he finally pulled back, she was left weak-kneed and breathless.

"Been wanting to do that for a while," he said, running the pad of his thumb over her plumped lips.

She laughed softly. "Oh..."

"Don't worry," he said, his voice a husky growl. "We can chalk that up to an emotional evening, and tomorrow you won't have to think about it again."

Easton's gaze moved down to her lips again, then he smiled roguishly and took a step back, cool air rushing over her body. She didn't know what she thought, or what she wanted, but he wasn't asking for anything. He moved to the doorway and looked back.

"Good night," he said and then disappeared into the dark hallway.

Nora stood there, her fingers lightly touching her

lips. He'd *kissed* her just now, and she realized that the attraction he felt for her was very, very mutual.

Nora went to close her bedroom door, and she paused, looking out into the hallway. All was quiet, except for the soft rustle of movement coming from the room next door. He was probably getting ready for bed, and she pulled her mind firmly away from that precipice.

If only she'd seen deeper into Easton's heart when they were younger…she might have been a bigger comfort to him, a better listener. If she'd realized then the man he'd mature into in a few years—but all of that was too late. If there was one thing the discovery of her father's unfaithfulness had taught her, it was that a man could be as loving and doting as her father had been, and he could still cheat, lie and hide his tracks. Nora needed to be able to count on a man for better or for worse, or those vows were pointless. She'd been lonely for what she and Easton had experienced together in that innocent adolescent friendship, but she'd been hungry for something more just now—something that hadn't existed before. She'd wanted security—she'd wanted kisses in the moonlight that didn't have to end, that could be hers and only hers…

Nora shut the door and slid back into her bed. Two and a half more hours until the girls needed another bottle. She'd best get some sleep.

Chapter 10

The next afternoon Easton wrapped the starter in a clean rag then used another one to wipe the grease off his hands. He'd have Nora's truck up and running tonight as promised.

He'd left early that morning, not wanting to run into her after the kiss last night. He still carried that image of her in a knee-length nightgown—totally chaste by all accounts, but still... What was it about Nora that could make a granny nightgown alluring? If he hadn't left when he did, he wouldn't have stopped at holding her close, and he wouldn't have stopped at the kiss, either. Her bed had been right there—yeah, he'd noticed—and if he'd been listening to the thrum of the impulses surging through him, he would have nudged her over to those rumpled sheets and pulled her as close as two bodies could get.

Except he wasn't just a horny teenager; he was a grown man, and for the most part he didn't do stupid things he'd regret the next morning. He knew where this led—the same place it had led when they were teenagers. She was vulnerable right now, her life was upside down and she needed someone to lean on. His shoulders were broad enough for the weight of her burdens, and that was all she really wanted deep down—he was convinced of it. She'd been there for him, too, and he was grateful for that. But a moment of mutual comfort wouldn't turn into anything that would last. He knew better. He could try to convince himself that she was interested in a real relationship with him, but had she been, she'd have shown that interest long before now. When things got tough for Nora, she came to him. Then she left again. It was their pattern.

Easton didn't have the emotional strength right now to deal with yet another rejection from the one girl he'd always pined for. Pining didn't do a thing—even as a boy, longing for his mom to come home. Now she had, but it wasn't what he'd imagined. It hadn't smoothed things over—and it certainly wouldn't fix the past. He was a grown man now, and he wasn't willing to set himself up for more heartbreak. So he'd kissed Nora, and while he didn't regret it, he wasn't about to do it again. He'd been serious when he said he was chalking it up to an emotional night. He was letting them both off the hook.

He heard the scrape of boots on the cement floor, and Easton turned to see Dale Young, Cliff's brother-in-law. He was an older guy, skinny and tall with a prominent nose and gray brush of a mustache.

"Hey, Dale," Easton said. "What brings you here?"

He crossed the garage and shook the other man's hand.

"Just checking up on things," Dale said. "I told Dina I'd come say howdy. One of your ranch hands told me where I could find you."

"Just getting a part for Nora's truck." Easton held it up. "So how've you been?"

"Not bad…" Dale winced. "The gossip around this place has been something fierce. My wife has been taking it personal."

Easton shrugged his assent to that. Nora and Dina were taking it hard, too.

"Did you know about the other woman?" Dale asked.

"Before my time," Easton said. "And from what I gather, it wasn't a lengthy affair. Just a mistake."

"Hmm." Dale grunted.

"I don't like how people are talking," Easton admitted. "Cliff was a good man—a solid neighbor, a helping hand. How many times did he help with a cattle drive or with hay baling when someone was sick?"

"Preaching to the choir," Dale replied. "I know you two were close. He was good to you, too."

The two men walked out of the garage into the sunlight, and Easton adjusted his hat to shade his eyes. Cliff had been good to him, and it wasn't just about the three acres and the old house. That land came complicated, and it had been rubbing at his conscience ever since Nora's return.

"Dale, I was wondering about that," Easton said, pausing. "The land he gave me, that is."

"Yeah?"

"It's your wife's grandparents' house," Easton said. "Does that rankle her at all, me having it? I'm not family."

Dale sucked in a deep breath then let it out slowly and shrugged. "A little, truthfully."

Easton expected as much.

"She'd never say nothing about it," Dale went on. "Cliff owned that house, and could do what he wanted with it. None of us expected that he'd just give it away like that, though."

"And you?" Easton pressed. "Do you have an issue with me living there?"

"Nah." Dale smoothed his fingers over his mustache. "It's a house, and Cliff wasn't a man to do something like that lightly. He gave it to you for a reason. He wanted you to have it."

A reason—that was what Easton needed to nail down. Why had Cliff done that—written over a piece of his family history?

"Before he died, he wanted me to move into that house and live there. He said he wanted someone to take care of the place for him. Thing is, I can't rest easy knowing that I'm sitting on land that means this much to the Carpenters. I mean, it's a godsend for me, but that's because I come from a hard place. I was just a cowboy who respected his boss. Nothing more and nothing less. Was I really worth that kind of gift? If I knew what made him do it, it might make it easier to carry on as he intended."

Because if Cliff had only been trying to keep him as an employee, he'd feel really bad about that. He didn't need to be bought off, especially with something that meant so much to the rest of the family. Now that Cliff was gone, Dina might be okay with replacing him eventually.

Dale nodded slowly. "I think Cliff had a big heart."

Was that it? Was this emotional?

"What do you mean by that?" Easton pressed.

"Meaning you weren't just an employee to him. He cared for you—and while you think you weren't family to him, there's three acres of land that begs to differ." Dale shrugged. "You mattered to him, and he made sure you were taken care of. God knows your own dad wasn't going to leave you nothing. People are gonna talk—and that's not gonna change. They'll talk about Cliff's affair, and about your land… It's what people do. If you really can't rest easy there, then sell it to Nora. You'd have some money to start fresh somewhere else, and she'd have that precious house back."

Nora's problem seemed to be that she had nowhere to call home in Hope anymore—nowhere truly hers. If she had that house back, the seat of her family's memories, then maybe she could have what she wanted most. And a fresh start for him…it gave him a little hopeful rush to even consider it right now.

"It's a good idea," Easton said with a nod. "Thanks."

"Not a problem." Dale eyed Easton for a moment. "Or marry her. That could take care of the family issue pretty quick."

Easton smiled wryly. "I've known Nora for a long time, Dale. I've been friend-zoned since we were fourteen."

Dale barked out a laugh and shook his head. "Those Carpenter women are a handful."

And Dale would know—he'd been married to Cliff Carpenter's sister for the last thirty-five years. But he had a point. Selling the house to Nora would take care of things right quick. She'd get the house she loved; he'd get a new start somewhere else. And if his mom

could have a fresh start—all clean and respectable—
then why not him? She'd left him behind in that hole
with his father, but that didn't mean he had to stay here
in Hope. What was holding him here now, after all?
Cliff had passed on, his father had never had much right
to Easton's loyalty and his mother was raising another
son with her electrician husband, *Tom.*

This was a big country—heck even the state of Montana was pretty large. He'd had some job offers before;
he'd be able to find another position without too much
trouble—a new life where no one knew the skeletons in
his closet. Everyone had issues—that wasn't the problem. It was having everyone know you well enough to
be able to point out your issues plain as day. That was
the aggravating part. But a chance at a life where no
one else knew the things that stabbed him deepest?
Well, that was a whole new kind of freedom that he
longed to taste.

But still—that took walking away, and just leaving
Nora and the babies. While it would solve everything, it
would be hard. He wasn't a part of that family—wasn't
that what he'd been acknowledging all along, that he
wasn't really family? But still, while he may want a
fresh start, a small and stupid part of him stayed the
hopeful teenager, and saw Nora by his side.

His phone blipped and he looked down to see a text
from his mom.

Hi Easton—how about Saturday at 11 at Beauty's Ice
Cream? Brandon wants to meet you.

He stood, frozen for a moment, his mind spinning.
She'd done it. She'd gotten that fresh start, and the

thing he hated most about it was how blasted happy she looked now. A husband, another kid, a comfortable life... If his mom could do it, then why not him?

He texted back:

Sure. See you then.

Nora, Dina and Aunt Audrey sat around the kitchen table in the main house, mugs of coffee in front of them. Dale had left after lunch to go take a look at the ranch. With Cliff gone, Dale had taken it upon himself to make sure things didn't slump while Dina grappled with her grief. People could get taken advantage of during times of tragedy, and it took a family pulling together to make sure that didn't happen.

Lunch dishes were piled on the countertop, mugs of coffee replaced them on the scratched table and the women sat together, sipping their coffee, waiting for Dale to get back. Audrey bore a striking resemblance to her late brother. She had his mix of blond and white hair, the same stalky build, the same short fingers.

Audrey held sleeping Bobbie in her arms. Nora was snuggling Riley, and Rosie lay in her car seat. Dina's arms were empty. She leaned her elbows on the table, a half-finished mug of coffee in front of her.

"They look like Carpenters," Audrey said. "I can see it in the shape of their faces. All the Carpenter babies have these little chins."

Dina glanced at Audrey, her expression blank.

"They're here now," Audrey said pointedly. "You might want to accept it, Dina."

"And if Dale had another family somewhere?" Dina

retorted. "You'd just open your arms to all of his grand-children?"

Audrey smoothed a hand over Bobbie's downy head. "Dale isn't the type—"

"And Cliff was?" Dina demanded. "You're telling me you saw that coming?"

"I told myself I wouldn't mention it, but is it possible that you were a tad too controlling with Cliff?" Audrey's voice stayed quiet, but her tone hardened. "He had to come home and ask you before he did *anything*. Maybe he had a small revolt—an inappropriate one, obviously, but—" She paused and put her attention back into the baby.

Dina's eyes flashed, but her chin quivered with repressed tears. She pushed her mug away and stood up, turning her back on them and stalking toward the kitchen window.

"What do you know about my parents' marriage?" Nora snapped.

"He was my brother," Audrey replied. "I knew *him*."

"Dad wasn't whipped," Nora retorted. "He respected her opinion. And what did he come home and discuss with her—lending you and Dale money? Has it ever occurred to you that he wanted to say no to giving you more cash, and needed some distance to do it?"

The room hummed with tension, and Nora looked at her mother's rigid back. This was what Dina was facing now—judgment from women who didn't want to believe it could just as easily have happened to them. Dina would be the one to blame, because if it was her fault, then the others could avoid her fate. Heaven knew no one would want to cheat on a woman like Audrey—

always so virtuous and right all the time. Nora suppressed the urge to roll her eyes.

"All I'm trying to say," Audrey said at last, "is that these children are here, and they are my relatives, too. If you can't be a granny to them, Dina, then I'll step in."

Was that a solution? Audrey was a blood relative to these baby girls, and if she'd be "Grandma," then perhaps it would let her own mother off the hook. Audrey lovingly stroked Bobbie's hand with one finger, but Nora caught the look of stricken grief on her mother's face as she turned back to face them.

Dina would be pushed out. Nora could see how this would unfold. The girls would be loved and spoiled by Audrey and Dale, but that wouldn't stop gossip about their grandfather, and it would only put Dina, the loving wife of their grandfather, on the sidelines where she would still be blamed for her husband's cheating. Because if there was one thing about Audrey, it was her utter conviction that she was right.

Nora didn't want Dina to be Grandma because of her relationship to Cliff; she'd wanted Dina because of her relationship to *her*. Audrey's offer wasn't a solution so much as a threat—step up as grandparent, or live forever in the shadows.

Dale's boots echoed on the side steps, and the door opened. He took off his hat as he came in.

"Howdy," he said, then he stopped short. "Everything okay in here?"

"Just snuggling babies," Audrey said, a shade too chipper. "Why don't you come hold this little angel, Dale?"

Dale's gaze moved to Dina then back to his wife. He seemed to do the math pretty quickly, because his mustache twitched a couple of times, then he said, "We'd better get back, Aud."

"Seriously, Dale, come and see these little treasures…" Audrey leaned down and breathed in next to Bobbie's head. "They smell so good."

"Aud." He didn't say anything else—his tone was enough, and he stared at his wife flatly until she sighed, rose to her feet and brought Bobbie over to Nora.

"You remember what I said, Nora," she said quietly. "There's more than one way to be family."

Dale waited by the door until Audrey had collected her purse and said her goodbyes. Before shutting the door, Dale cast Nora an apologetic look.

"Take care now, Nora," he said with that usual flat tone of his. "And take care of your mom, too, okay?"

"Bye, Uncle Dale." She smiled, but she wasn't sure she pulled it off.

Then they were gone.

Nora sat with her mother in silence. The two babies slept on in Nora's arms and she looked at their peaceful faces. The clock ticked audibly from the wall, and Nora felt like her heart was filled with water. This was a mess. Audrey would make her mother miserable for the rest of her life if she was given the chance. Dina and Audrey had respected each other, but there had always been a little bit of a chilly distance there—history that Nora didn't know about, no doubt.

"Was I controlling?" Dina asked hollowly.

"Not with Dad," Nora said. "You were the toughie with me, though."

"I was the toughie because your dad wouldn't discipline you," Dina said with a sigh. "He wanted to be the good guy all the time, so he'd leave getting you back into line for me. Do you know how badly I wanted to be the good guy every once in a while?"

"Really?" Perhaps their marriage had been more complicated than Nora realized. She blinked back sudden tears. Her dad had been the quiet strength in her life, the one who would nod slowly and say, "Your mother isn't as wrong as you think..." But still, someone had to draw lines and give lectures. Just not Cliff.

"Dad just did things differently." That was probably an understatement. They were only finding out now how differently he'd been doing things.

"Yeah." Dina rubbed a hand over her eyes.

Nora hadn't told her mother about the letters Easton had found yet—she hadn't been sure it was a good idea, but now she reconsidered. Audrey would love nothing more than to pass around that Cliff had been keeping up a long-term romance with Angela, but that wasn't the case.

"Easton found some letters that Angela wrote to Dad," Nora said. "They didn't seem to have any kind of ongoing affair. But she kept Dad up-to-date on Mia, it seems."

Dina frowned. "What—did he have a secret post office box or something?"

"Yes."

Dina shook her head but didn't say anything. Another betrayal. Another secret. How many would they unearth before this was over?

"Mia really hated him as a kid," Nora said. "She wrote him a letter telling him how much she hated him for not being a part of her life."

"I hate him right now, too," Dina said, and a tear escaped and trickled down her cheek. She wiped it away then sucked in a breath, visibly rallying herself again. "It's just as well we've canceled the corn roast."

"Is that what you really want?" Nora asked.

"What I want is to have my husband back," Dina retorted. "And for his sister to go jump in a lake."

"Yeah, she's not my favorite, either."

Nora looked out the kitchen window, her mind going back over all those other Carpenter corn roasts—the fun times, the laughter... Her dad had always been the center of it all, barbecuing up burgers for everyone. They could abandon the tradition, or they could face it.

"Will it help to skip it?" Nora asked after a moment. "I mean—they'll talk anyway, but if we call off the corn roast and keep to ourselves, will they talk more?"

"That corn roast turned into tradition over the years," Dina said thoughtfully. "What if... I mean, it might be our last one, but I think you're right. Let them come and see us in our complicated mess. The less they see of us, the more they'll talk. And with any luck at all, Audrey will get food poisoning."

Nora barked out a laugh. "Okay. Sure. In Dad's honor."

Rosie started to fuss from her car seat, squirming and letting out a whine. She hated being out of arms, that little girl, but Nora had both Riley and Bobbie in her arms and she couldn't pick up a third. Nora glanced pleadingly at her mother. "Help me?"

Dina slowly undid the buckles and lifted Rosie into her arms. She stood there, looking down into the baby's tiny face, her expression softening.

"They do look like Carpenters," she said. "Your idiot father would have been so proud..."

Nora felt laughter bubbling up inside her. "Are you

going to call him my idiot father for the rest of your life?"

"Yes." Dina smiled wryly. "I think I will. He's certainly earned it."

Rosie immediately settled now that she was in Dina's arms, letting out a soft sigh of contentment. It was impossible not to fall for these babies, and Nora could see that reality in her mother's face as she gently patted the diapered rump.

"You were this small once," Dina said. "And it was easier then. So much less complicated."

"Are you saying it'll only get worse—this mess, I mean—as the girls get older?"

Dina nodded slowly. "I'm afraid that's the case, but I can't make those calls for you, Nora. You're a grown woman now, and these are your choices."

They were her choices, but some choices had very little wiggle room.

"I've been looking into adoption for the girls," Nora said. "Another family, I mean. It's all so messed up here, and I can't do this without you. I'm certainly not doing it with Audrey as my go-to support, either."

Her mother met her gaze sadly. "You'd give them up?"

"I don't think this situation is good for them," Nora said. "We could hope that things would get easier, but what if they don't?"

Dina didn't answer. Nora knew that her mother couldn't help her to make this choice. She was the only one who could decide what she could live with. Easton's mother had left him, and he resented her so much because she hadn't been thinking about Easton and what was best for him—she'd only been thinking of her own escape. Nora didn't want to make that mistake. She needed to do what was best for the girls, regardless of what it did to her.

"I emailed an adoption agent," Nora went on. "We went back and forth a little bit, and she'll come by and see us next week, give us some more information."

She tried to blink back the tears that welled up in her eyes, but they slipped down her cheeks. She hated this—she loved these girls so much that she was willing to give them up. But it hurt so much more than she'd thought it would. Dina came over to Nora, and Nora leaned her face into her mother's side. She could feel her mother's fingers smoothing over the top of her head, just like when she was little.

"I'm so sorry, baby," Dina whispered. "I'm so, so sorry…"

They both were—everyone was. It seemed that pain was the price paid for having loved.

Chapter 11

Saturday morning Easton pulled up in front of Beauty's Ice Cream. His mom had brought him here once that he could recall—after some massive fight she and Dad had had, and she'd bought him an ice cream cone and stared at him morosely while he ate it. Treats didn't come often, so he'd scarfed it down, but he could still remember offering her a bite. She'd said no. Funny the things that stuck.

He parked next to the red SUV—she was here already, apparently. Glancing in her window, he saw a kid's hoodie in the backseat, next to an empty chip bag. This was it. He was about to meet his brother for the first time, and he honestly couldn't say he was looking forward to it.

Beauty's Ice Cream was a quaint little shop with a red and white awning. Windows lined the front, and he could see the back of a woman's head in a booth. Was that Mom? He assumed so. Most guys could pinpoint the backs of their own mothers' heads easily, but his mom had changed a lot over the last twenty years.

Mom... He still felt a well of emotion at the thought of her, and he hated that. It would be easier to just be angry, or to resent her, but his true feelings were more complicated—so much more difficult to separate.

He opened the front door and entered the air-conditioned interior. Trent, the owner, stood behind the counter. He wore a heavy metal shirt, partially covered by a white apron, and he gave Easton a nod.

"Morning," Trent said. "What can I get for you?"

"Uh—" Easton glanced toward his mom, his gaze landing on the sandy-haired boy. He had a sundae in front of him, chocolate sauce in the corners of his mouth, and Easton found all of his thoughts suddenly drain from his head. "Nothing right now," he said, then angled over to the booth.

"Easton." His mother smiled up at him then scooted over. "Come sit."

Brandon stared at Easton wide-eyed then took a bite of ice cream as if on autopilot. Easton scooted into the semicircular booth so that his mom sat at the bottom of the curve between both sons.

"Brandon, this is your brother," she said.

"Hey," Easton said. "Nice to meet you."

"He's a *man*," Brandon whispered, eyeing his mother questioningly.

"Yes. He's grown-up."

Brandon's clothes looked new, and he had an iPad on the table next to him, a set of headphones draped around his neck. The kid had stuff to entertain him, that was for sure. Easton had never had a Game Boy or decent headphones. His headphones had always been taped together where they broke so that they wouldn't fit right.

They were silent for a few beats, and Easton searched his mind for something to say.

"Easton is a ranch manager," his mother said at last. "He runs someone's ranch for them—he's very good."

"Oh." Brandon frowned slightly. "I'm in grade three."

"Yeah…" Could this get any more awkward? This kid didn't care about meeting his mom's adult son. If anything, Easton's existence was confusing.

"Brandon loves horses," his mother tried again. "He draws them all the time."

"Not anymore," Brandon replied. "I draw monster trucks now."

Easton wondered if this had been a mistake. What had his mother been expecting from this little get-together—warmth and coziness? She hadn't provided that when she'd been in his life, and it wasn't going to suddenly materialize because they all shared some DNA.

"Mom brought me here once when I was your age," Easton said.

Brandon looked around. "Here?"

"Yeah. She used to live in this town with me and my dad."

"She lives in Billings now," Brandon said, and Easton caught the flicker of fear in the boy's eyes. He was eight years old, and he was scared of losing his mom. That was something Easton could sympathize with. Eight was too young to worry about those things, and this kid had all the security that Easton had lacked growing up. He had the clothes, the toys, the stay-at-home mom who drove him to chess practice.

"I know," Easton said quietly. "I'm grown-up, so I don't need our mom to take care of me anymore. She belongs with you. So don't worry about me trying to keep her here."

His mother's eyes filled with tears, and she put a hand out, tentatively touching Easton's arm. What, did she suddenly want to be needed in his life?

"Dad was right about me being okay," Easton said, turning to his mom.

"I'm glad," she said. "I'd hoped so… I made mistakes, son. I wasn't sure if I'd want to do this in front of Brandon, but I think it's better for him to see his mother acknowledge her mistakes than to wonder about them for the rest of his life."

"Were you a little kid when Mom left?" Brandon asked.

"Yeah." The same age as Brandon, but he wouldn't torment the boy with that. "I was. I had my dad, but he drank a lot, so…" He sucked in a breath. He didn't exactly want to horrify the boy. "You know, I got a job, and my boss was a really decent guy. He helped me figure things out, and he taught me how to work a ranch. So I was okay, actually."

"Didn't you miss her?" The kid was connecting the dots here. He was thinking about what it would be like to face his young existence without his mom by his side.

"I did," Easton nodded, a lump rising in his throat. "I missed her a whole lot."

Mom reached out and brushed Brandon's hair off his forehead, and Easton saw it—his fantasy of a loving mother being played out in the life of his half brother. He'd longed for a hand to brush his hair off his forehead just like that…

Easton cleared his throat. "So tell me about your dad."

"Dad works a lot," Brandon said. "But when he's home, he plays LEGO with me. I've got the whole cops and robbers setup, and I play cops and Dad plays robbers. Have you seen the new prison?"

Brandon scooped up his iPad and turned it on. "I'll find it for you—Mom, is there Wi-Fi here?"

For the next few minutes they talked about Brandon's love of LEGO, they discovered that Beauty's Ice Cream did not, in fact, have Wi-Fi and Easton ordered himself a chocolate cone. Brandon was a sweet kid—an untarnished version of himself at that age. Easton had grown up with substance abuse, poverty, neglect, and he'd raised himself. He'd been tougher than other kids his age, and while he used to think of himself as resilient, he wondered now if he'd merely been damaged.

Brandon was smart, intuitive, passionate about his interests. But he wasn't tough—his emotions swam over his face and he didn't hide behind a mask of indifference. Easton was willing to bet that this kid didn't know half the curse words he did at that age. Maybe this was what he'd have been like if he'd been raised in a safer environment.

"Do you have a girlfriend?" Brandon asked him.

"No—" Easton paused and looked into the face of this boy who was finally relaxing a little bit. His little brother. Whatever happened all those years ago, this kid was related to him, and he'd probably want to be in his life somewhat as the years went on. He could close off and keep this impersonal, or he could share something. He decided on the latter.

"There's a woman I care about a lot," Easton said.

"Who is she?" Brandon asked.

"Her name is Nora, and I've had a crush on her since I was a bit older than you. Do you like girls yet?"

Brandon shook his head. "But they like me. Isabel T. said that Olivia liked me last year. I think she did. She was really annoying."

So it began. Easton shot his mother a rueful smile.

"Does Nora like you back?" Brandon asked. "Because if she likes you back, then she's your girlfriend."

"It's a little more complicated when you get older," Easton said.

Life was pretty simple if you were a kid—especially a protected kid like Brandon. But life had a way of getting difficult when you least expected it; of kicking your expectations out from under you. Easton needed a woman who would face the hard times with him, be the shoulder he needed once in a while. Love wasn't enough to make a relationship last, and Easton had been let down in life too many times to take a risk when it came to a life partner. And Nora was a risk. A beautiful, passionate, intoxicating risk. She could be there for him when he needed some emotional support—like that kiss in her bedroom in the moonlight—but Nora also had a pattern of taking off again once her own problems were solved. Had she changed now that she had the babies to care for? Or was he just hoping?

An image rose in his mind of that morning he'd woken up to find his mother gone. His father was drinking already at the kitchen table, and he'd pointed to the note on the fridge.

"Your mom took off," his father said, words slightly slurred.

"What?" Easton hadn't believed it. She wouldn't just

leave *him*. He was her kid, and moms didn't walk out on their kids. He'd searched around, looking for the things that cemented her in their home—her nightgown, her jewelry, the hairbrush that always had hair stuck in it like a small animal. They were gone. Her clothes—the nicer ones—were gone, too. There was an empty space in his parents' closet. Her purse—that sagging bag he was forbidden to touch—was gone from its place on the back of a kitchen chair.

He could still remember what it felt like as the truth dawned on him—Mom was gone. He'd headed up to his room and sobbed his heart out. He wasn't safe alone with Dad—he knew that well enough. He'd have to fend for himself now, because his father sure wouldn't be doing his laundry or cooking him meals. Dad didn't make school lunches.

And when he crawled into his bed that night, the house silent except for the sound of the TV downstairs, he'd closed his eyes and imagined that his mother was stroking his hair away from his face…

"Will you come visit us?" Brandon asked, and Easton pushed the memories back.

His mother looked at him, her brow furrowed, and she clutched at the handle of a new purse—something expensive by the look of it.

"We would really like that," his mom said. "Tom wants to meet you, too. You'll like him, I think."

Had she ever wondered how he went to sleep at night without her there to say good-night? Or if he was eating properly, or if he was embarrassed at school because his dad had drunk away the money for bigger clothes? Did she ever wonder if she'd broken his heart beyond repair?

"Okay. Sure. One of these days."

His mom was back. As weird as this felt. She looked so successful now, so put together. Her hair was nicely done, her makeup making her look a little younger. And he was glad that she was doing it right with her second-born. That was something, wasn't it?

Even if it had all started with an escape...from him.

That evening Nora sat on the front steps of the homestead, her arms wrapped around her knees. She'd found an old framed photo up in the bedroom closet, and she sat outside in the lowering light, looking at it. She hadn't seen this one before. There were a certain number of photos that everyone had a copy of—her great-grandparents' wedding portrait, a picture at some family member's funeral with all the extended family present, grouped around the coffin. There were a few others of her great-grandparents and their children seated on kitchen chairs stuck out in the yard—their equivalent of a family portrait. But this photo was different than the others.

The photo was a small rectangle, not even filling up the entire frame. It depicted her great-grandparents standing alone, likely in their first years of marriage because there were no children about. They were in front of a large tractor—the kind that would be in a museum these days. Her great-grandmother was wearing a pair of overalls, her light hair swept back by the wind, and she leaned against a tractor tire. Her great-grandfather was in a pair of patched jeans, looking at his young wife with adoration. His shirt was open a few buttons, and his sleeves were rolled up to reveal tanned forearms. It was such a perfect moment, and Nora could understand why someone had framed it.

Tomorrow they'd have the corn roast, and somehow she thought her great-grandmother might have made the same choice she and Dina had, to face it head-on. There was something brave and almost defiant in her eyes, and when Nora looked closer at the photo, she noticed something she hadn't seen before in the other, more formal pictures.

Mia looked an awful lot like their great-grandmother. Wow. Funny how DNA worked. Nora didn't take after their great-grandmother physically. She looked more like her mother's side of the family, but she'd still felt a great connection to the Carpenter lineage. Yet Mia, who was the accidental love child conceived during some tryst, was the spitting image of their ancestor. Genetics certainly didn't take legitimacy into account. Mia would have liked to know this, Nora realized sadly. She might have even taken some pride in knowing where her looks came from.

Easton's rusty truck rumbled up the drive, and she watched as he parked and got out. He slammed the door behind him and came toward her. He paused before he reached her then took off his hat.

"Hey," he said. "Care for some company?"

"Sure." She moved over and he sat down next to her, tossing his hat onto the step beside them. His hair was disheveled, an errant piece of hay stuck into one of his flattered curls. He was dusty, and he smelled like hard work and sunshine.

"How was your day?" she asked.

"Not bad." He nodded slowly. "I met my half brother."

"Really?" She shot him a look of surprise. "What's he like?"

"A nice kid," he said. "He's got the whole package—

parents who love each other, financial security, all the attention that he needs."

"That's a good thing," she said. "Right?"

"Yup." He smiled wanly. "At least Mom figured it all out eventually."

"Will you see them again?" she asked.

"Probably," he said. "But I'm not ready to hammer out Christmas plans or anything. I'm taking it slow."

That was fair. Still, she could see how much this had hurt him. Sometimes when a person's deepest longing was fulfilled, it hurt as much as it healed. Mia might have discovered the same thing if she'd ever met their father. To Nora, her dad was a superhero. To Mia, he was the selfish jerk who missed her childhood. It might have hurt a lot to see the parenting he was capable of.

Easton nodded toward the photo in her hands. "What's that?"

"My great-grandparents," she said. "I found it up in the closet in your guest bedroom."

He leaned closer to look, slipping a hand behind her as he did so, but it didn't seem intentional. Without really thinking about it, she leaned back against his arm. He looked startled, then he nodded back to the photo.

"He loves her," Easton said, his voice low and next to her ear.

"They were the great Carpenter love story," she said. Easton straightened, pulled away. She swallowed, trying not to let her discomfiture show. "She came from a moderately wealthy family in the city. She and my great-grandpa met at a dance, I think. I don't know how that worked out exactly, but she ended up eloping with him. It took years for her family to forgive her. Even then, she never got a penny from them."

Easton smiled then shrugged. "I'd say she made the right choice."

"They ended up having seven children together," Nora said. "But that picture—I've never seen it before."

"No?"

He leaned forward, his elbows on his knees, and she found herself so tempted to slip her arm through the gap and take his hand. Why was her mind constantly going there with him?

"It makes you wonder," she said quietly, "if he was faithful."

"Why wouldn't he be?" Easton asked. "He had a beautiful wife."

"So did my father."

That was the problem all along—there had been no good reason for her father's cheating. Not that there ever was when someone did that kind of thing. Had he loved Angela? Had it been meaningless sex, or had he fallen for her on some level? And if it was love, how could he claim to love his wife at the same time? She'd believed that her father was above that kind of ugliness, but she'd seen that he wasn't.

"I saw my aunt today," she said after a moment of silence. "She blamed Mom for Dad's affair."

"What?" Easton straightened and shot her an incredulous look. "How'd she figure?"

"She said Mom was too bossy and she implied that it was understandable that Dad would use cheating as a way to gain a bit of freedom from her."

"That's BS."

"Yeah, well… I always thought my parents had a marriage of steel. My dad would come and talk to my mom before he made any decision. I mean, *any* decision. He wouldn't buy a cow without her input, and it wasn't because she demanded it. He just really wanted to know what she thought first. But Audrey said that Mom was too controlling. Was I wrong about it? Did I see a strong marriage, where really my father was suffocating?"

Easton was silent—probably the smart choice, she realized wryly. He wouldn't know any more about their marriage than she did.

"Because I'm just like my mom in a lot of ways, Easton."

That was what scared her. She and her mother were both strong personalities with their own way of doing things. So if Dina wasn't woman enough to deserve fidelity…if Nora's mother was too controlling or too opinionated…if there was something innately unworthy about Dina that made Cliff feel like cheating was an option for him…what about Nora?

"Your dad talked about your mom a lot," Easton said. "He said he was lucky to have her. He said he wouldn't have been half as successful without her, so his advice to me was to find a good woman with a head on her shoulders and get married. He said two were better than one. I saw your mom consulting with your dad just as often. They relied on each other. He loved her… I don't know what happened when he cheated, but I do know that he loved her."

"And yet, he did cheat." She'd never make her peace with this. How could someone claim to love a woman and then step out on her? How could he see how much she added to his life and then betray her?

"Maybe he lived to regret it," Easton said. "Sometimes that's all you've got to hang your hat on—that the person who wronged you regretted it."

"Did your mom regret leaving you like she did?" Nora asked.

"I think so," he said.

"And is that enough for you?" She arched an eyebrow and caught his gaze.

"No," he admitted. "But it's a start."

"They were no better than we are…just the generation before us. So what makes us so different? We have their DNA, we come from the same genetic line and our formative years were under their care."

Easton reached over and moved a hair out of her eyes. His fingers lingered against her cheek, and those dark eyes met hers tenderly. He didn't seem to have an answer for her, but he leaned in and kissed her lips gently. He pulled back then moved in again, sliding an arm around her and slipping a hand across her thigh as his warm lips met hers.

From the open window above, a baby's cry filtered down to them. Nora pulled back, heat rising in her cheeks. Why did she keep falling into kissing this man? She swallowed hard and rose to her feet. She was supposed to know better, and the minute her pulse slowed down, she'd remember why.

"I'd better go see what the trouble is," she said and headed into the house.

Chapter 12

The next morning was Sunday, the day of the corn roast, and Nora's cell phone rang while she was feeding Bobbie. She fumbled with the phone and picked it up, pinching the handset between her shoulder and ear. Bobbie's big brown eyes were fixed on Nora's face as she drank.

"Hello?"

"Hi, is this Nora Carpenter?"

"Speaking." A dribble of milk dripped down Bobbie's chin, disappearing into the cloth Nora had waiting on the baby's chest. She was getting better at this—anticipating burps and dribbles like a pro.

"This is Tina Finlayson from the adoption agency. Do you have time to talk?"

After a few brief pleasantries, Tina got down to business. "I've just had a home visit with some new clients this morning, and I have a feeling this is something that would interest you."

Nora looked at the clock on the wall. It was nine in the morning on a weekend. "That's early."

"They have a toddler who is an early riser. In my line of work, I make a point of being flexible."

She felt a wave of regret. Emails were one thing, but a phone call made all of this feel a lot more real. Was she absolutely certain about this?

"I haven't made my decision yet about whether I'll be finding another home for them," Nora qualified. "I know we've been emailing—"

"I don't mean for this to pressure you, but it might help to have some concrete information to work with. Are you interested in knowing a bit about them?"

Nora adjusted Bobbie in her arms, and the infant stretched out a leg. This wasn't a decision—it was only getting some facts. Right? That was what she'd been telling herself all along.

"All right," she agreed.

"These are people in a suburb of Billings," Tina went on. "He's a children's psychologist and she's a stay-at-home mom. They live in a large home, are financially secure and they're looking to expand their family. They have one adopted son who is three right now, and they are looking to adopt siblings. They'd love newborns, but they know that isn't always possible."

Nora realized she'd been holding her breath and she released it. They sounded perfect, actually.

"Would they be able to deal with triplets?" she asked.

"The mother has two sisters living in the same neighborhood," Tina went on. "And his parents live on a nearby acreage where they have horses and a hobby farm. So they'd have plenty of support in baby care."

A family that could offer the girls everything from cousins and grandparents to horseback riding on weekends. A father who was trained in child psychology would be an excellent support as they grew up, and a mom at home with them, too. They'd even have an older brother to grow up with.

What could Nora offer? She had a job in Billings—so she couldn't stay home with them. There would be day care, a single mom struggling to make ends meet and little extended family if Nora wanted to protect the girls from all the talk. But they would be loved. The most valuable thing she could offer was her heart, and right now that hardly seemed enough.

"Do they know about the girls?" Nora asked.

"I told them only the basics," Tina said. "That you weren't positive about what you wanted to do yet, but there was the possibility of three newborns becoming available. They were very eager to hear about them."

Of course. For another family, these three babies would be an answered prayer, a dream come true. Didn't the girls deserve to be wanted that desperately?

"Maybe I could meet them," Nora said.

"That would be wonderful," Tina agreed. "Don't feel pressured, but we could set up a little meeting where you could see them in person, get a feel for the type of family they are and you could see where you stand then. They might even be willing to have an open adoption where you could receive updates on how the girls are doing and perhaps be included in some major life events."

Not a complete goodbye…that might be something.

Nora's parental leave wouldn't last forever, and right now she was getting a fraction of her normal pay. Maybe it was better to meet this family before she got so attached to the triplets that she couldn't possibly change her mind.

"Are they free today?" she asked.

"Let me call them and see if we can set something up. I'm sure they'd be very happy to meet with you."

As it turned out, the family was more than happy to meet with her that day. Dina agreed to watch the babies, and Nora drove the three hours into Billings. Her GPS led her down the wide streets of a new subdivision, large houses on either side of the road. It was picturesque, idyllic city life. This was the kind of neighborhood that Nora couldn't hope to afford.

She found the house, and when she parked in the driveway, the front door opened and the dad came out, a toddler in his arms.

"Hi," he said, holding out his hand to shake hers as she slammed the driver's side door shut behind her. "I'm Mike. This here is Bryce."

Nora shook his hand then smiled at the toddler. He was clean with blond curls and new clothes.

"Nice to meet you both," she said. "I didn't bring the girls—my mom is watching them right now." Why did she feel the need to explain to these people?

"Totally understandable," Mike said and as she came around the truck she saw his wife, Sarah. She was pretty—brunette waves framing her face, big eyes and plump lips. She looked like she'd give good hugs. Blast it—why did she have to be so perfect?

But this wasn't a competition. This was about a situation beyond her control, and what would be better for the girls. Yet somehow, Nora didn't much like this motherly looking woman. They shook hands, too.

Tina had arrived before Nora had, so they had some professional guidance for their meeting. And over the course of the next hour, Nora toured their home, which had two extra bedrooms that weren't being used, a hot tub out back and a large vegetable garden that Sarah apparently had time to keep up. The kitchen was covered in little drawings that Bryce had done—scratching on paper with a fisted crayon, by the looks of it.

The house was clean, and the couple was affectionate and seemed to be in a secure and happy marriage. They even showed her some family photo albums from their wedding onward. They seemed to travel a lot.

"What are you looking for in a family for the girls?" Sarah asked once they were all seated in the living room. Nora had an untouched iced tea in front of her. Tina was smiling encouragingly at all of them.

"I don't know exactly," Nora said. Was there anything this family was missing? "A loving home, enough money to raise them well, a supportive extended family…"

Sarah and Mike exchanged a hopeful smile.

"Do you have any questions for us?" Mike asked.

"Have you considered an open adoption?" Nora asked. "It's going to be so hard to let go of them, and…" She didn't even know how to finish that.

"I had mentioned that it was a possibility," Tina said, her tone professional.

"We'd be willing to talk about that," Mike said with a nod. "They used to think that just closing all those doors was best for the children, but not anymore. It's good for kids to know that it was hard for their families to give them up. And if they can have contact with their birth family—limited, of course, without drama and stress—it's thought to be better for the kids overall."

"And we're interested in what's best for the children," Sarah added. "Children aren't owned, they're lent to us by God. And that's not an honor we take lightly."

"How much contact with the girls would you want?" Mike asked, and Nora didn't miss the caution that entered his tone.

"I don't even know." Nora swallowed then heaved a sigh. She felt like she was failing here—sitting in the living room of a "better" family, interviewing a couple that would be a stronger support to the babies she adored.

"Do you have any pictures of them?" Sarah asked.

Nora shook her head, and she suddenly felt protective. She didn't want to share photos of the girls. She didn't want to get this couple's hopes up, either. Knowing that a couple was interested in adopting the babies was one thing, but seeing that interest shining in their eyes hit Nora in a whole new place. This was real—too real. But she was here to see who they were—what they had to offer.

"They're two weeks old now," Nora said. "Their names are Riley, Rosie and Roberta."

"My grandmother's name was Rosie," Sarah said with an encouraging smile.

Would they even get to keep their names? Or would Bobbie turn into a Tiffany or an Elsa? All things that Nora hadn't thought about until this moment. And she'd have no control over that. This couple could rename them, and who would Nora be to complain? This room was suddenly feeling very small, and Nora glanced toward the door.

"To be honest," Nora said, "I haven't made up my mind. I'm pretty sure Tina told you that."

"Yes, it was clear," Mike said. "We aren't trying to pressure you."

Of course not. They were trying to impress her, show her the beautiful home they could give to the girls, if only Nora could find it in her to walk away from them.

"I love these girls." Tears misted Nora's eyes. "If I could provide for them, I'd keep them in a heartbeat. I don't want to do this. At all. I hate this, as a matter of fact."

"We understand." Sarah leaned forward. "It can't be easy."

Why did this woman have to be sympathetic, too? Couldn't she just show a crack already? Reveal some imperfection?

Bryce sidled up to his mother and she scooped him into her arms. He settled into his mother's lap, and she smoothed his hair with one porcelain hand. One day in the not-too-distant future, the girls would be toddlers like Bryce, and they'd be coming for hugs and attention—reminders that they mattered. Did Nora want to give that up? Or did she want to be the one who got to scoop them into her lap and cuddle them close? Could she really let another woman do that?

This wasn't about what she wanted…this was about her financial and emotional reality. If she'd given birth to them herself, she might feel better about dragging them through hard times in her wake, but she wasn't their biological mother. And they deserved better than what she could offer.

She looked at her watch. It was only one-thirty, but it was a three-hour drive back, and they still had the corn roast today. She'd seen enough of this couple to know what they could offer, and it wasn't Mike and Sarah who were the problem.

"Thank you for meeting with me." Nora stood up abruptly. "I have a lot to think over."

Everyone else stood, too, and Nora looked around herself for a moment. She held all the power right now, and they were all being incredibly nice about it… What was the polite way to get out of here?

"If you'd like to talk further, Mike and Sarah, you can give me a call and I'll contact Nora on your behalf. And the same goes for you, Nora." Tina was handing out business cards. "Sometimes after everyone has had a chance to think things through, choices are a little easier. This has been a very good start."

Tina made it all sound so normal, but nothing about this felt normal. Mike and Sarah were a lovely couple, and she hoped they managed to adopt a whole heap of kids, because they had a lot to offer. But *her* girls…

Nora said her goodbyes—shook hands, thanked people for their time—and then escaped to her truck. She needed to call her mom and see how the babies were doing, and then she needed to get back. This was the longest she'd been away from the girls since their birth, and instead of a welcome break the way coffee with Kaitlyn had been, this felt like guilt-ridden abandonment.

Was it possible that she'd already passed the point of no return—that she was selfish enough to put her needs before what was best for the girls?

Easton looked forward to the corn roast every year—light duties, good food and a chance to relax. This year was the first one without Cliff. In a way, today would be goodbye to the boss they'd all loved.

The day started out like any other with general ranching duties, but when those were complete, he and some other ranch hands started the fire pits that would be used to boil corn and bake potatoes. Several barbecues would cook up everything from sausages to steaks. Then they'd indulge in a veritable feast.

"Tony, carry that tub of ice over to the table," Easton said, and the ranch hand in question gave a nod and headed in that direction.

Trucks were arriving in a steady flow now—family giving hugs and waving to each other. Dale and Audrey arrived, and Dale spotted him across the yard and tapped his hat in a salute. Audrey made straight for the babies, but there were already a few ladies who'd beat her there.

He found himself watching the hubbub around the babies more closely than he needed to. Nora was there—she had it well in hand. He had no reason to supervise, but he made note of where the girls were. Audrey had Rosie, Nora held Bobbie and another aunt held Riley, but then there was a trade off and someone else had Bobbie—why on earth was he bothering about this?

Easton pulled his attention away and noticed Dina coming in his direction.

"Easton!" she called. "We need to bring one more table out to where the barbecues are—do you mind?"

"Yes, ma'am," he replied, touching the rim of his hat.

Easton gestured for another ranch hand to help him, and they headed around the side of the barn to the shed where folding tables and chairs were stored. They returned a few minutes later, carrying the large table between them, and that was when he spotted it...

Tony was moving a box of unshucked corn, and as he turned, he swung the box past a woman who had Riley in her arms. The box came within a breath of the baby. Easton's temper snapped and he dropped his end of the table and marched in Tony's direction.

"What was that?" he bellowed.

"What?" Tony looked around.

"Did you see her?" Easton demanded. "You came within an inch of the baby!"

"There was lots of space," Tony retorted. "It's fine."

"It's not fine," Easton said. "Get over here!"

Tony complied, and Easton couldn't quite explain this level of rage. He normally operated on a "no harm, no foul" philosophy, but there was something about those babies that sparked a protective instinct in him.

"The corner of a box connecting with a baby's head would be fatal," Easton said, keeping his voice low and his glowering gaze firmly on the ranch hand in front of him. "There are three newborns and numerous kids around. You walk carefully and look where you're going."

Tony seemed annoyed, but he nodded anyway, and Easton let him get on with his work. Another ranch hand helped get the table over to the barbecues, and Easton looked around. It was all running smoothly. One of the large cauldrons of water had already come to a boil and two uncles were feeding corn into it. A couple of ranch hands were checking the temperature of the barbecues. The food was starting, the setup was virtually complete and now they'd all cook and eat. Mission accomplished. He still felt irritable and unsettled. What was his problem?

Nora stood with a group of family. Kaitlyn was there, too—and across the yard her husband, Brody, was chatting with some other men. But it wasn't Kaitlyn who drew his eye—it never had been. Nora's hair shone golden in the smattering of sunlight, and his heart sped up a little at the sight of her. His irritation wasn't rational. Nora was being friendly, but there was still a gulf between them—family and staff were in different ranks around here. And he wanted more. Blast it, that was the problem—he'd been happy enough over on this side of things when Cliff was around. He'd been grateful for the opportunity to work here, grateful for a boss who was willing to help him mature as a rancher. But now it wasn't that he wasn't grateful...he wasn't satisfied.

Easton was respected, liked, trusted by the family... He was relied upon, irreplaceable in their eyes, but he was still hired help, and looking across the ranch yard at Nora, he realized what he wanted—to be next to her. Not as a friend. Not as the ranch manager. Not as a secret, either. He wanted to be with her, the man by her side.

There was work to be done, and he was the manager around here, so he turned away to check on the barbecues. Cliff wasn't here anymore to keep everything running smoothly. That responsibility was Easton's now.

From across the yard, he heard Rosie's soft cry. Strange that he should be able to pick out which baby was crying, but he could. The last little while with the girls in his house had attuned him to their schedules and the sound of their whimpers and wails. He glanced over to see Audrey trying to shush the little thing. Nora was feeding Bobbie her bottle, and Riley was with a younger cousin who looked absolutely thrilled to be holding a baby. Kaitlyn took Rosie from Audrey's arms, but Rosie wouldn't be soothed, and she wouldn't take the bottle, either.

"Everything okay, boss?" Tony asked, following the direction of Easton's gaze.

"Yeah, of course."

Easton turned away. This wasn't his job, and he tried to ignore that plaintive cry. She was in good hands—most of the women there had raised babies of their own. But he couldn't cut himself off from Rosie's wail. It wasn't just "some baby," it was Rosie, who normally was happy as long as she was being cuddled.

Why couldn't he just tune this out? It was like Rosie's cry was tugging at him.

Tony had the barbecues under control. He turned and strode across the yard.

Rosie's face was red with the effort of her cries. Her tiny fists pumped the air, and while all logic said that he shouldn't have any more success than Audrey did, he had a feeling that he might.

"Howdy," he said, giving Audrey a disarming smile. "Let me try."

"What?" Audrey looked surprised to be spoken to, let alone that Easton would offer to take the baby from her. "No, I'm fine. Thank you." She turned bodily away from him as if he was some stranger instead of the man who'd been helping to care for these babies for the last couple of weeks.

"Audrey, let him," Nora said from a few paces away.

The older woman reluctantly passed the infant over, and Easton gathered her up in his arms, flipped her onto her back and patted her diapered rump with a few firm pats. Rosie's wails stopped, and she opened her eyes, looking up at him in mild surprise.

"Hey, there," he said quietly. "Miss me?"

Rosie blinked a couple of times and opened her mouth in a tiny yawn.

"Well, I'll be—" Audrey said, her tone chilly. "I don't think he's washed his hands, Nora."

"He's fine," Nora replied. "Rosie likes him."

And she didn't like Audrey—that much was clear. It was a strange relief to have this little girl in his arms again, and to know that she wasn't crying her heart out anymore, either. That irritating tug at his heartstrings had relaxed, and he heaved a sigh.

"That did the trick," Nora said, coming up beside him. "Thanks."

"Yeah, sure." He smiled slightly then put Rosie up on his shoulder. She snuggled into his neck. "Not sure how I'm going to do anything else around here, though."

"Supervise." Nora shot him a grin. "I'm sure Rosie would love the walk around."

So he'd be a cowboy trotting around with a baby in his arms. Somehow that didn't seem so bad. He might not be family, but he was the answer to Rosie's cries, and that resonated deep inside him in a way that he knew would only hurt all the more when this was over.

And his time here at the Carpenter ranch was coming to an end. He'd known that Cliff's death had changed things, but Nora's return home had solidified that in his mind. Easton reached out and tucked a tendril of hair behind Nora's ear. He'd miss her—oh, how he'd miss her. He'd miss these girls, too. But any more time spent at the Carpenter ranch, and he'd never be able to disentangle his heart.

Sometimes a man had to put his future first.

Nora let one of her cousins take Bobbie from her arms, and she glanced back toward Easton. He was walking Rosie around the fence and appeared to be pointing out horses to her. She had foggy memories of being held in her own father's strong arms, her dad sitting her on the top rail of the fence and pointing out the horses. She'd have been three or four at the time, but the similarity still made her heart ache.

Why was it that a man could make an excellent father, and still not be capable of fidelity? What was it her dad had said about Easton? "He's a younger version of myself, Nora. You could do worse."

Daddy, you ruined him for me...

Her father had ruined a lot of things for her, now that his secret was out. He'd broken a part of her foundation.

"He loves the babies," Kaitlyn said, coming up next to her.

"Yeah..." Nora nodded. "They took to him."

She shouldn't have agreed to stay with Easton. She'd been thinking of giving her mother space, but instead she'd gotten herself into an impossible situation—playing house, almost. They weren't a couple, but sharing a bathroom and a kitchen made imagining herself as part of a couple that much easier...

Kaitlyn looked pale and she slid a hand over her stomach.

"You okay?" Nora asked.

"I think the corn's not sitting right."

Was the corn off? That wouldn't be good. But Nora

could see several other people munching on butter-drenched corn on the cob, and no one else looked sick.

"Do you want a drink?" Nora asked. "There are cans of ginger ale on the table."

Kaitlyn nodded. "Yeah, I think I'll get one."

Her husband, Brody, was already at the drink table, and Nora watched as her friend tipped her head against Brody's shoulder. He slid an arm around her waist, and Nora couldn't help but feel a stab of envy. Brody handed his wife a can of ginger ale, and Nora didn't miss the way he looked at her. Kaitlyn had it all—the doting husband, the supportive extended family, a home that was ready for kids.

Like the adoptive family in Billings who were anxiously awaiting her decision, she realized bitterly. They were ready for more children. They had it all, too—the home, the marriage, the money, the career... Everything that Nora lacked, that family could give. And family most definitely mattered.

Nora turned back toward her own milling family and ranch hands, who were starting to line up for freshly barbecued sausages and burgers. A family was more than support, it was a library of personal histories. Family never forgot the details, even if you'd rather they did. Rewriting history wasn't possible with a family this size—there was no avoiding the truth.

It was one thing to embrace who you were, but it was that very history that would plague these girls for the rest of their lives in this town. Did she want to raise them and have them move away from her as quickly as possible to get away from the dysfunctional family tensions?

Rosie seemed to have fallen asleep on Easton's shoulder, and he patted her back idly, chatting with one of the ranch hands.

Babies were simple—diapers, bottles, hugs. It was raising the older versions of these triplets that truly intimidated her. And she couldn't do it alone. Sometimes true love meant hanging on through thick and thin, and other times it meant backing off to allow happiness to come from someone else. As much as she hated to consider it, giving the girls up might be the best choice.

Chapter 13

Rosie slept for a while propped up on Easton's shoulder. The other ranch hands showed him an odd amount of respect with a baby in his arms, and when a couple of guys were getting too noisy, one look from him silenced them.

Clouds had been gathering again after a clear afternoon, and the wind had cooled noticeably. People were gathered around various tables of food, some sitting in lawn chairs and others lounging on blankets. A few ranch hands were sitting on upended firewood as they ate their burgers. The day might stay fair yet, though a smudge of cloud could be seen a few miles west.

"Looks like rain," Tony said, biting into a burger and talking past his food.

"Yeah, maybe," Easton agreed, although for the sake of the corn roast, he hoped not. Rosie pulled her knees up and wriggled. A smell mingled with the scent of bar-becued meat. Was that what he thought it was?

Tony looked at the baby in Easton's arms and made a face. "Baby's leaking," he announced.

Easton pulled Rosie away from his chest and gave her a once-over. The ranch hand was right. A smear had formed by the edge of her diaper, corresponding with that suspicious smell.

"Wow, Rosie," Easton said, and Rosie opened her eyes enough to blink at him before shutting them again. "I'd better bring her back to Nora."

"Good call," Tony agreed.

Easton headed back through the yard where Nora had been earlier, but she was nowhere to be seen now. Neither were the other two babies.

"Nora's inside," Kaitlyn called. She was sipping from a can of pop. He smiled his thanks and headed in the direction of the side door.

He stepped inside and the screen door banged shut behind him. The house was silent, everyone outside with the food, and he paused in the entryway to the kitchen, unsure of what to do.

"Nora?" he called.

Nora looked around the doorway to the living room, and he stopped short when he saw her face. Her eyes were red, and she wiped at her cheek with one hand. She'd been crying.

"You okay?" he asked.

His boots thunked across the kitchen floor, and he emerged into the living room. She wiped at her face again as if trying to hide the evidence.

"Fine," she said quickly. "Just working on diapers."

She wasn't fine—he wasn't blind. Nora had the babies laid out on towels on the floor. She added a third towel when she saw Rosie, and he laid the baby next to her sisters.

"Hey," he said softly. "Nora—"

"I'm fine!" Her voice rose, and he could tell she was fighting back tears. Something had happened—had someone said something? Was there more flack about her dad? Protectiveness simmered deep inside him—he'd deal personally with whoever had caused this. But she didn't say anything else.

Nora unsnapped Riley's onesie and peeled back the tabs on the diaper. He could stand there, or he could help. Easton knelt next to her and started with Rosie's diaper. If nothing else, he could do this. He'd seen Nora do enough diapers that he knew the drill—theoretically, at least.

"Wipes," he said, and she passed them over.

They worked silently for a couple of minutes, and Nora passed him a new sleeper for Rosie.

"I need help with this one," he said. He had Rosie diapered, but the sleeper was going to be tricky. Nora smiled feebly, and gave him a hand with tiny arms and legs that just kept curling back as if she were inside an egg. When the babies were all changed and dressed, Easton and Nora sat on the floor and leaned against the couch. The babies were snuggled up together in front of them. They looked so peaceful—Riley's little fist resting on Bobbie's face, and Rosie making sucking noises as she dozed. These girls had the life right now—anything could be fixed with a diaper change and a nap.

"So what's going on?" Easton asked.

Nora looked toward him for a moment then sighed. "I visited a family that wants to adopt the babies."

The information took a moment to sink in, and when it did, Easton's stomach sank. "You did? When?"

She shrugged weakly. "This morning. They live in Billings—the father is a child psychologist..." She licked her lips. "They can give the girls so much. Financial security, love, good schools, a stay-at-home mom—" Tears misted her eyes again. "More than I can." The last words came out in a whisper.

The thought of these babies going to another family felt wrong—like a betrayal, although he had no right to feel that way. He knew it—this wasn't about him.

"And you're really considering this?" he asked.

"I can't do it alone, Easton. Mom is so hurt by Dad's affair that she can't face doing this with me, and I don't even blame her. You know people are talking about it. It's one thing to deal with what he did, and quite another to face the questions and pitying looks that she'd get constantly with the girls living with her..."

Easton understood, but was that really the end of it? Was there no other way for Nora to keep the girls with her? He knew firsthand how much she loved these babies, and he knew exactly what it would do to her to give them to another family. If he left Hope, at least he'd hold on to the mental image of Nora and these triplets together. Separating them...

"The homestead," he said. "If your father hadn't left it to me, you'd have been able to stay there."

Was he the one standing between her and keeping these girls?

"What if you bought me out?" Easton asked. "Dale suggested that. You could have that house again. It belongs with family anyway. I know your dad was trying to do something nice for me, but if he knew what it would do to you and his granddaughters, he wouldn't have willed it to me. I know that for a fact."

"I can't buy you out." Her voice was tight and she swallowed hard. "If I stay here, I won't be working right away. I can't get into a mortgage."

"Then stay with me." The words surprised him, but this was a solution. He didn't have to leave Hope, did he? They were already staying together quite successfully. He could continue helping out with the girls, and she wouldn't have to worry about rent or anything like that. He could rethink that escape he'd been planning— if she needed him.

"How would that work?" she asked, shaking her head.

"Like it has been." He turned to face her and slipped his arm behind her. "We've been working it so far. I could get used to this. Couldn't you?"

"No." There was a tremor in her voice.

Did she mean that? Was she already finished taking what she needed from him?

"Why not?" he asked, irritated. They'd better just get this out into the open. If she was done with his help, he needed to hear it, because that was the only way he was going to accept this—if she told him straight.

"Because it doesn't solve *us*!" Nora's voice shook and she blinked back tears. "What are we going to do, keep cuddling on the couch, kissing on the porch and live together like a couple? That's *not* a solution, Easton. That's a shortcut to heartbreak, and I'm not doing it. You're a lot like my dad, you know." She swallowed hard. "He said it over and over again—that you're just like he was when he was young. You know what that means to me. It's so hard to trust—"

Yeah, he understood all of that, but in spite of it all, they'd been taking care of those girls together. He wished she could trust him, see deep inside him and recognize the man in there—but apparently some things would never change between them.

Easton leaned closer as her words trailed off, and she met his gaze, her breath catching as he took her lips with his. Her eyes drifted closed and she leaned into his kiss. She was warm and soft, and he moved closer, tugging her into his arms. Why couldn't this work? He'd had reasons of his own up until this moment, but he couldn't seem to think straight when he was with her, and certainly not with his lips moving over hers.

She pulled back and shook her head, her fingers fluttering up to her lips. "We've got to stop that," she breathed.

"Do we?" he asked, catching her gaze and holding it. "Really?"

Because he sure didn't want to. She looked ready to reconsider, and given a chance he'd move in for another kiss, but she moved back.

"Easton, stop it."

That was clear enough. He pulled his hand back.

"I'm not starting something I can't finish." She whispered. "Love you or not—"

And maybe he should appreciate that she wouldn't start up with him if she could foresee herself walking away…but she'd mentioned love and his heart skipped a hopeful beat.

"*Do* you love me?" His voice dropped and he swallowed.

Tears rose in her eyes. "Against my better judgment."

He felt the smile tug at his lips. How long had he

waited to hear that confession? How many years had he dreamed of her finally seeing the man he was at heart?

"Because I've loved you for years." He remembered all those years of loving her from afar, being there for her in her tough times and watching her walk away when she pulled it all together again. He could push those memories aside and ignore it in a heated moment when he was so focused on getting closer to her...but what about after the conquest? What about after he had her, and they settled into a routine? She'd never wanted what he could offer before—not for the long-term. His own mother hadn't wanted him, either. He knew better than to start expecting things.

She was vulnerable. He was pushing this, and pressure wouldn't change the end result.

"But I know what you mean," he said gruffly. "I want to short-cut this so badly, but you're right. We should stop."

Tears glistened in her eyes, and he leaned forward and pressed his lips against her forehead. How he longed to kiss those lips again, to forget all the logic and clear thinking, and just melt into her arms. But she was right. Trust was the problem here—she was afraid he'd turn out just like her dad, and he was afraid that she'd walk away when things got tough. There was no point in starting something that would end in him staring at an empty spot in the closet...again. There were only so many times a man could have his heart torn apart in one lifetime, and he was pretty sure he'd already reached his limit.

"So I'm right." Nora swallowed hard. This would be a first—a man admitting that he would likely be unfaithful. But what was she wanting him to do—try to change her mind? She wasn't that easily swayed.

"Not about me cheating," he said, "but I understand why you're scared. I doubt I could convince you that I'm any different. That's an argument I can't win."

Nora's chest felt tight. "It shouldn't be an argument, should it?"

"Probably not." He rubbed a hand over his face, and the gesture brought back memories of the teenage Easton in a flood. He was no kid anymore, and he'd proven that over the last two weeks. This was a man in front of her—a man just like her father.

"Thing is, Nora, I can't offer you the world. I don't have it to give. You're used to a better life than I am, and I'm pretty sure I can't match what you're used to. You're afraid of me turning out like your dad, and you couldn't face that kind of heartbreak. Well, I can't face being walked out on by another woman I love."

Another woman like his mom? For years Nora had watched that sadness swirl inside Easton, and only recently did she discover what had caused it. Now, she blamed his mother, resented her, even. Easton deserved better…and he thought she'd be no different? That hurt.

"Do you really worry about that?"

"Life gets hard," he said quietly. "Really hard. I don't think my mom imagined herself leaving, either, until she did it." He scrubbed a hand through his hair. "And maybe I'm a little bit like her, too. She got out of this town—started fresh where no one knew her past. I get why she'd want that so badly. I've been thinking seriously about doing the same thing."

Easton's words hit her like a blow to the stomach. He would leave? Somehow that hadn't occurred to her as even a possibility, even though she knew other ranchers had been trying to woo him. Easton had been a constant around here. The ranch ran like clockwork because of his professional skills. But he was more than an employee at the ranch—her dad had made sure of that. It was impossible to imagine this place without him. It would be empty here—lonely.

"But you *live* here." It sounded so trite, but she couldn't articulate the depth of her feelings about this. This was his home—over the years he'd become an integral part of *her* home, and she'd taken his presence here entirely for granted. Could he really just walk away?

She rose to her feet, walked toward the window then turned back. He stood up, too, and they stared at each other for a few beats. Easton nodded a few times as if coming to a conclusion.

"I wanted to sell you the house—it would give me money for a new start—but I'm used to roughing it. I'll sign the house back over to you. I'll give your mom my written notice tomorrow."

Anger writhed against the wall of sadness, and she strode back over and punched him solidly in the chest. "You're seriously just going to leave?" she demanded. "Just like that?"

"I can't do this!" His voice raised and he stopped, shutting his eyes for a moment. Then he moderated his tone. "Nora, I'm *not* doing this anymore. I'm not sitting here, loving you, and not having anything more. We both know why it can't work, and you're right—playing house isn't going to take the place of a real, honest commitment. I don't want to just see what happens—I want a family that I can claim as mine. Call that old-fashioned if you want, but it's what I want. And I know myself—I'm not going to get over you that easily. You don't love a girl for over a decade and just bounce back." He swallowed hard. "I never have."

He was right—just like when they were teens, she wanted too much. She wanted him to be there, her support, her confidant. If the last couple of weeks had taught her anything, it was that skirting that line between friendship and more was harder than she'd imagined. He wasn't the only one who sailed past "just friends" in a vulnerable moment. It wasn't fair to expect him to keep trying to toe the line, and she knew that, but the thought of losing him completely...well, that tore at her heart. Their balance wasn't a long-term solution.

He deserved a full life. He deserved a family of his own. Who was she to stand between him and his happiness?

"I'm going to miss you." Her chin trembled, and she struggled to maintain control.

"Me, too. But at least I'll have made it possible for you to keep the girls. I think it's what your dad would have wanted."

Outside, lightning flashed and there was a boom overhead. Rain spattered against the living room window. Easton put his hat on just as the kitchen door opened and people came pouring inside. He held her gaze for a moment, those dark eyes swimming with regret. Then he turned and walked away as the first wave of aunts and cousins flooded, laughing, into the living room.

He'd sign the house back over to her. All would be balanced again, and she'd have a home to raise the girls. She'd have the homestead in her name—her family's history back where it belonged. It wouldn't solve everything, but it was a good start. Yet despite all she would gain, she was losing the man she'd loved against all her better judgment. Pain was the cost of having loved, but the price of saying goodbye to Easton was almost more than her heart could bear.

Chapter 14

Easton stood in his kitchen, the coffeepot percolating on the stove next to him. He felt gutted, scraped out. His throat felt as raw as if he'd cried, although he hadn't shed any tears. He'd been trying to avoid this kind of pain by not starting up with her, but that hadn't exactly worked, had it? He was alone—Nora had stayed at her mother's house to weather out the storm, but he didn't get that luxury. He still had a job to do, and it only got harder during inclement weather.

Even with Nora gone, there were reminders of her, from the baby chairs lined up across the kitchen table, to the soft feminine scent that lingered. What was that— soap, shampoo, just her? He couldn't tell, but he liked it. He'd never had a woman living with him before. Not since his mother, at least, and he wished he didn't know how soothing a voice filtering through the floorboards could be, or how nice a hallway could smell while the steam from a shower seeped through the crack under the door.

Easton had been serious when he said he'd sign the house over to her. He couldn't keep this land and still like himself. He could let Nora live in this house and keep it in his name, but even that felt wrong. It should be hers—completely hers.

The bird-patterned curtains billowed in the wind that whistled through the open window, and he heaved it shut. From the very beginning he'd known that she belonged here, and that was why he'd never been able to take down those curtains. The house had a soul, and it was time for him to stop making another family his own, and start fresh.

The coffee was done percolating, and he flicked off the stove. He'd let his brew sit until he got back. He needed to double-check that all the horses were inside the barn, check the locks for the night and then he could call it a day. Tomorrow he'd give his notice. It was probably better to do this as quickly as possible.

Thunder crashed outside, and it shook the house hard enough for some silverware to rattle in the sink. He headed to the mudroom and grabbed his hat and an oil slicker.

He'd miss this house, this family and its connection to the only woman he'd ever loved. Until he left, however, he had a job to do, and they could count on him to be professional. It was all he had left.

Nora stood by the window, watching the rain come down in sheets. The storm had raged for hours now without any respite—the savagery of the weather matching her mood. Wind whipped through the trees, tearing at the leaves and whistling ominously. A crack, a boom and then a flash of lightning lit up the sky. She glanced back to the couch where the babies lay in their usual row, sound asleep and oblivious to nature's tantrum. Dina sat in a rocking chair next to the couch, and when the lightning flashed, she'd instinctively put a hand out toward them.

"Why don't you look happier, Nora?" her mother asked quietly.

Nora came back to the couch and bent down to push a soother back into Bobbie's mouth.

"I told you—he's leaving."

"But you said that he's signing the house back over to you," her mother said. "You can raise the girls. You wanted that..."

"I'm still wondering if that's the right choice." Nora ran a finger down Bobbie's silken cheek. "I want it, but with all of the gossip here..." She pulled her hand back and straightened. "I came home for you, Mom. Not for Aunt Audrey, or Uncle Dale, or anyone else. I came for *you*."

"I know. And that was the right thing to do—"

"Except in this—" Nora bit back the rest. It was wrong to push this—to plead for more. But when she came home, it was because it was the only way she could handle all of this. She needed her mother's support, and if raising the girls meant she'd be isolated in that little house, trying to explain away people's attitudes to little girls with tender hearts, then keeping them would still be a mistake.

"It's all been a shock to me," Dina said quietly. "The love of my life cheated on me, and I didn't even get the chance to scream at him." Tears misted her eyes, and she sighed. "That's the thing that I'm angriest about— he didn't give me the chance. I needed to deal with this whole mess with him, not *after* him." She reached out and touched Rosie's tiny, bare foot. "I just needed some time, sweetheart."

"Has anything changed?" Nora asked cautiously.

"I suppose," her mother said. "You have no idea how much I appreciate you giving me space in my own house, Nora. I did some crying and screaming into my pillow. I've had my time to argue with your dad in my head, play out on all the different scenarios, but at the end of it all, I come to one thing—I love him. Not past tense. I still do. I always will. I just don't think I can be Grandma."

Anything less than Grandma wasn't good enough— it was too distant to be any use. They were back to where they'd been all along—

"I think I'd be Nana," Dina said. "I've always thought I'd be a good Nana."

Nora blinked, her heart speeding up. "Nana?"

"Does it suit me?" her mother asked uncertainly. "Or is that too old-sounding?"

Nora wrapped her arms around her mom and swallowed against the emotion in her throat.

"It's perfect, Mom."

Dina squeezed Nora's hand and looked up into her daughter's face. "If your dad had been brave enough to tell me the truth, I'd have been angry—that's true. I'd have screamed and cried and stomped out for as long as I needed to. But after we worked through all of that, I'd have stood by him." Her chin trembled with emotion. "I'd have been a stepmom to Mia. He didn't give me the chance."

And how different Nora's childhood would have been! She'd have had a sister—but whether or not they'd have been able to like each other at that stage was up for debate. She'd have known the worst, and that would have been easier in some ways. But it wouldn't change the fact that she'd never quite trust that a man could stay faithful.

"I don't think I'd be that noble myself," Nora said. "When Dad cheated on you, he broke more than your trust, he broke *mine*. I thought he was the world, Mom. I really did. I thought if I could find a man like my dad, I'd be happy ever after. But that's no guarantee, is it? Because even Dad couldn't stay faithful."

"And you're afraid that Easton wouldn't be faithful, either," her mother concluded.

Nora was silent, and her mother shot her a rueful smile.

"I still know you better than you think. You love him."

Nora tried to swallow the lump in her throat. "It's so stupid…"

"No, it isn't," her mother replied. "He's loved you for years. In the last few years your dad hoped that you'd—"

"My dad doesn't get a vote!" Nora snapped.

Her mother rose to her feet and went to the sideboard. She picked up the small framed photo that Nora had brought from the old farmhouse. She looked at the photo for a few moments then handed it over to Nora.

"Did you ever hear the story about that tractor?" Dina asked.

"No, I don't think so."

"This picture reminded me of it because it probably happened at about this point in their marriage, before the kids. This picture is in the summer, but the winters could be really harsh. One winter, your great-grandfather had gone out to check on the cows. Their breath could freeze over their noses, even in the barn. So he went out in a blizzard to do his check. Anyway, he didn't come back, and your great-grandmother waited and waited. She got worried—her husband had his routines and she knew something had gone wrong. So she bundled up and went after him. She found him in the barn, but he was knocked out cold underneath the tractor. No one knows what happened exactly, but he must have slipped on some ice, the tractor had rolled and he was pinned. You see the size of her in that photo—"

Nora looked down at the slim, light-haired woman, leaning up against the wheel of that tractor.

"The story goes," her mother went on, "that she picked up that tractor herself, hoisted it off her husband and carried him from the barn back to the house. She saved his life that day."

"Is it true?" Nora asked. She hardly looked big enough for those kinds of heroics.

Her mother shrugged. "It's family lore. You can decide if you believe it. But the point I'm trying to make is that when you choose a man, you're not trusting in his strength alone. You bring strength to the table, too. Your great-grandfather couldn't have run that dairy without her, and he'd surely have died that night if she hadn't gone after him. So yes, men can make mistakes. They can let you down. They can break your heart. Heck, they can even die on you. But you aren't passive in all of this, and you aren't putting your faith in him alone." Her mother fiddled with the wedding ring on her finger. "You're strong, Nora. And you're smart. You're a force to be reckoned with. You aren't trusting in a fallible man, you're trusting in what the two of you are together. Don't underestimate what you bring to the relationship."

Nora turned back to the window, her heart hammering in her chest. She had no control over the future, and she had no guarantee against heartbreak. But she knew what she felt for Easton, and she knew what he felt for her. She'd felt the strength of his feelings when he held her in his arms, and if she was only trusting emotion alone...

Easton had told her that he wasn't sure she could handle a life with him—the ups and downs, the uncertainties. But she knew in the depth of her heart that she could. She could weather any storm with Easton, if she knew that they were weathering it together. She could be his strength, just as much as he could be hers.

But he was leaving—and that realization shook her to the core.

"Mom, I need to talk to him," Nora said, turning to face her mother. She looked toward the babies then back out at the storm.

"I'll stay with the girls," her mother said. "Go."

Nora went through the kitchen to the mudroom, grabbed a hat from a peg and snatched up her mother's oil slicker. She needed to talk to him...there was more to say. He might still leave, but at least she'd have said it all before he did.

Chapter 15

Nora slammed the door to the old homestead behind her and shook off her rain slicker. She'd barely been able to make out the road through the deluge on her windshield, and she'd nearly gone off the road a few times, but she'd made it all right. There were lights on in the kitchen.

"Easton?" she called.

Silence. She glanced around the kitchen and saw nothing amiss. She went over to the stove and lifted the lid of the coffeepot—it was completely full, but only barely warm. She knew his routine. He percolated his coffee then left it to cool a little while he did his last rounds, checking locks and whatnot. If the coffee was nearly cold, then he'd been gone a long time.

Thunder rumbled again, a pause then a mighty crack as the room lit up in a momentary blinding display. She looked out the window as the realization dawned on her. Easton was out there somewhere, and if there wasn't a problem, he'd have been back long ago. The other ranch hands were supposed to have done the last of the work, and he was only doing the last check. Even in a winter storm, it shouldn't take this long.

Nora pulled her cell phone out of her pocket and dialed his number. It rang, but there was no reply. Obviously not—he'd be crazy to pick up a call in that downpour, if he even heard it. Should she stay a little longer and wait? Accidents happened in storms, and a mental image of that tractor in the black-and-white photo rose in her mind. It was silly, maybe, but she'd feel better if she found him.

She slipped back into the rain slicker and pushed her hat back onto her head. She opened the door and had to shoulder it to beat back the wind. Rain swamped her as she pushed through the blinding torrent. It took twice as long to get to her truck, and when she was finally creeping down the road toward the barn, she could barely see a thing past her swishing wipers. She knew his circuit ended with the barn, so she'd try there.

The wind changed direction momentarily, and she could see movement in the horse corral. Horses couldn't possibly still be outside, could they? She pulled up next to the barn and tried to see through the downpour, but couldn't make anything out. She'd have to check in person. She pulled her coat up around her neck—it wasn't going to do much good, but it was something—then hopped back out into the driving rain.

"He's fine," she muttered to herself, preparing to come across him dry and safe in the barn, but through the howl of the wind, she caught the terrified whinny of a horse.

Had she heard that right? Her boots slipped in the mud as she made her way around the side of the barn, rain pounding against her so that she had to keep her eyes shut until she made it to the gate to the corral. She shielded her eyes, and in a flash of lightning, she saw him. He was holding a lead rope, and Scarlet had reared up on her hind legs, pawing the air in fright. As the mare came down, she didn't see the point of contact, but Easton crumpled.

Nora fumbled with the latch, but soon she was through. She slipped and slid through the mud, and grabbed the lead rope again, pulling Scarlet closer.

"Easton!" she gasped.

He crawled farther away, one arm tucked around his side. He'd need medical attention tonight after that kick, but first the horse had to be calmed. She fumbled with the buttons of her coat, and as she tried to take it off, Scarlet reared again. Nora jumped back and tore the coat from her body at the same time. A blast of cold rain hit her, but she was too focused to shiver. She caught the lead rope again, and when the horse came down, she whipped the coat over the mare's head. The horse whinnied in fear, but didn't rear again. Without the lightning to spook her, she'd be able to find her calm again.

Nora gulped in deep breaths of humid air and murmured softly as she led Scarlet toward the barn door. Easton pushed himself to his feet and followed. His face was ashen as he came into the light of the barn, and he hunched forward with a grimace.

"You okay?" she asked.

"Sure." That was a lie, because he leaned back against the wall, wincing. "Just let me rest a second."

Every breath lanced through Easton's side, and he breathed as shallowly as possible as he watched Nora get Scarlet settled in her stall. He'd been impressed—she'd known exactly what to do. If she hadn't shown up when she did, Scarlet might have been seriously hurt. Let alone him...

Nora locked the stall and headed in his direction. He tried to straighten a little more, look slightly less pathetic, but he wasn't sure it worked. She hauled a stool over to him and helped him sink down onto it. That made things easier, but he still didn't like being the winded one.

"Let me see." She eased his slicker off his shoulders and he grimaced as he straightened. Then her fingers deftly undid the front buttons of his shirt and she pulled it aside to reveal purple and red welts across his side. She ran cool fingers over his skin and when she reached his ribs, he let out a grunt of pain.

"Broken," she confirmed.

"Why were you out here?" he breathed.

"Your coffee was cold," she said irritably. "You never let your coffee get cold."

She knew him better than he thought, and he was grateful that she'd come after him. She wasn't calming down, though. Her eyes snapped fire and she took a step back.

"You know as well as I do that you're not supposed to be working with spooked animals alone. That's a safety issue! You could have been killed, you know! A good kick to the head, and it could have been over for you!"

"Had to make a choice," he said, pushing himself up against the pain. He caught her hand as she went to touch the spot again. "Nora, I'm fine."

"You are *not* fine!" Tears welled up in her eyes, and the blood drained from her face. He squeezed her hand and felt her trembling.

"Stop." He tugged her against his other side, but the pain was nearly unbearable.

"I'm hurting you." She pulled back.

"Just a bit." But yeah, maybe less squeezing. He attempted to adjust his position. She was watching him, and it was more than sympathy in those cloudy eyes. "What?" he asked.

She pushed a wet strand of hair out of her face. "I had to ask you to stay."

This only made it harder. They'd been over this already.

"Nora, I can't just be your—"

She moved in closer, her mouth a breath away from his, and the words evaporated on his tongue. Then she closed the distance. His body immediately responded to her, but when he leaned into the kiss, he was stopped by that slice of pain.

"Nora, you gotta stop doing that to me," he said with a low laugh. "A guy's liable to get the wrong idea."

"Please stay," she whispered.

"I thought we talked about this." Did they have to rehash this again to convince themselves that this was folly? It wasn't a matter of not wanting her—he wanted her so much it would probably scandalize her. But if he let himself go, really let himself love her with all the passion that he kept sealed away inside him, he wouldn't be able to turn it off when she couldn't face the hard stuff. That would be a heartbreak that would never heal. What man walked into that willingly?

"My mom told me something tonight that made a whole lot of sense. She said that when you choose a man, you aren't just putting your faith in his strength and his character, you're choosing what the two of you are together. I'm scared, I'll admit that, but I'm no wall-flower, either. Together, you and I are pretty tough, Easton. It isn't just you—it's who you are when you're with me. And who I am when I'm with you. And I think—" She blushed slightly then looked down. "I think we're something special when we're together."

He reached out and caught her hand, easing her closer until he could put his arm around her waist. He held her there, his mind spinning. She'd just braved the worst storm in a decade because his coffee was cold. Obviously, he'd misjudged how tough she was. She'd come after him and hauled a spooked horse away from him, to boot.

"I'm not staying here for friendship," he clarified. "I'll lay it out for you. If I stay, I want to get married and raise those girls together. I want the whole pack-age, Nora. Three kids. Mr. and Mrs. Maybe-More-Kids-Later-On."

Her gaze flicked up to meet his—steady, constant.

"And I can't offer much money. Heck, I work for your mom. I might move on to another ranch—depends on the future. If you take me, you take me in the good times and the bad. But I'll work my hardest to keep those times good…" His voice caught. Would she ac-cept him when she really thought it through? He was putting it all on the line—everything he had to offer. He wasn't holding anything up his sleeve.

"You want to raise the girls with me?" she asked. "You really do? Because there is no halfway with three kids, Easton."

"I'm not offering halfway," he said, running his work-roughened hands over her smooth ones. "I know what it's like to grow up under a shadow. My family has a stigma around here, so I get it. I don't ever want those girls to feel like they were less than wanted. I want to raise them together, love them like crazy and teach them how to let stupid comments roll off their backs. I love you, Nora. I want to marry you, and I want to be the only daddy those girls ever know. So if you're serious about this—if you're willing to be something with me, then I want to be married. What do you say?"

"I say yes." Her eyes sparkled with unshed tears and she nodded.

It took him a moment to register her words, but when he did, he pulled her into a kiss until he couldn't take the pain anymore. He let out a soft moan and she eased out of his arms.

"Let's go," she said, helping him to stand. "You need a doctor."

"I'll be fine," he muttered.

"Are you going to try to fight me?" she asked incredulously. "Because if you can stand up straight, I'll let you be."

He smiled ruefully. "Never mind." He allowed her to guide him to the door. The wind had died down and it was just rain now, thunder rumbling in the distance.

"I want to marry you just as soon as you can find a dress you like," he said with a low laugh. "I hope you shop fast."

After all these years of holding himself back, he was

never going to get tired of pulling that beautiful woman into his arms. She was right—they were better together, they were tougher together and they were just what those girls needed around here. The triplets might have been born Hamptons, but they'd be the Ross kids, and no one would ever make them feel less than the beautiful gifts that they were. Their dad would make sure of it.

Epilogue

On a chilly autumn morning, as rain pattered down on the little church in downtown Hope, Nora stood in front of a full-length mirror willing her heartbeat to calm. The veil blurred her vision as she regarded her reflection. She wore a dress of clinging satin cream that spread into a rippling train behind her. The veil was simple, attached to a jeweled tiara that sat on her golden waves. She spread her hands over her fluttering stomach, the engagement ring glittering in the low light.

She was getting married this morning... She'd become Mrs. Nora Ross.

The door opened and Kaitlyn slipped inside the room. She wore an empire waist bridesmaid dress of mint green, and Nora was glad she'd chosen such a forgiving cut now that Kaitlyn's belly had started to grow. After the nausea at the corn roast, Kaitlyn had disbelievingly taken another pregnancy test... She was five months along now and glowing with the new life she carried.

"Are the girls okay?" Nora asked.

"They're all asleep," Kaitlyn reassured her. "And the bottles are ready. They'll be fine. Are you ready?"

"I think so." Nora shot her friend a nervous smile.

"Easton told me to give you this—" Kaitlyn handed her a black velvet box, and Nora looked down at it in surprise.

"Was I supposed to buy him something?" she whispered.

"Oh, stop," Kaitlyn laughed. "Just open it."

Nora pried open the clamshell. Inside was a white gold charm bracelet. She lifted it out of the box, running her fingers over the delicate charms. There were three pink crystal pairs of booties, and on either side of them were two silver halves of a heart. A lump rose in her throat.

"It's us..." she whispered.

At the clasp there was a tiny silver horseshoe—luck. But she didn't need luck. Today they'd confirm their promises in front of friends and family, but these were words Easton had already murmured to her that morning.

I'm going to love you every day, Nora. I'm going to tell you the truth always. I'm going to stand by your side whatever comes at us. I'm yours.

Kaitlyn helped her to put the bracelet on, and as she looked down at the sparkle on her wrist, the old organ's music swelled from the sanctuary where everyone was waiting. Easton was at the front of that church, and imagining him up there, all her nervous jitters melted away.

I'm going to love you every day, Easton. I'm going to tell you the truth always...

These weren't hard promises to keep—they were simply putting into words what was already there. Today she was marrying her best friend.

"Okay," Nora said, gathering up her train. "I'm ready."

* * * * *

Brenda Harlen is a former attorney who once had the privilege of appearing before the Supreme Court of Canada. The practice of law taught her a lot about the world and reinforced her determination to become a writer—because in fiction, she could promise a happy ending! Now she is an award-winning, RITA® Award–nominated nationally bestselling author of more than fifty titles for Harlequin. You can keep up-to-date with Brenda on Facebook and Twitter, or through her website, brendaharlen.com.

Books by Brenda Harlen

Match Made in Haven

The Sheriff's Nine-Month Surprise
Her Seven-Day Fiancé
Six Weeks to Catch a Cowboy
Claiming the Cowboy's Heart
Double Duty for the Cowboy
One Night with the Cowboy

Those Engaging Garretts!

The Single Dad's Second Chance
A Wife for One Year
The Daddy Wish
A Forever Kind of Family
The Bachelor Takes a Bride

Visit the Author Profile page at
Harlequin.com for more titles.

Claiming the Cowboy's Heart

BRENDA HARLEN

For Neill—with love and gratitude. xo

Chapter 1

"Oh, no," Liam Gilmore said, shaking his head for emphasis when he saw his sister Katelyn walk through the front doors of the inn with her briefcase in one hand and a rectangular object that he knew to be her daughter's portable playpen in the other. The baby was strapped against Katelyn's body and an overstuffed diaper bag was draped over one of her shoulders. Loaded down with the kid's stuff, she looked like a Sherpa ready to embark on a mountain trek.

"I've got an emergency hearing at the courthouse in half an hour," she explained, as she dropped the diaper bag next to his makeshift desk and set her briefcase beside it.

"And I've got interviews scheduled for this afternoon," he told her.

"You've got a manager, a weekend housekeeper and a

breakfast chef—what more does a boutique hotel need?" she asked, as she unzipped the carrying case of the playpen.

Because he couldn't sit there and watch his sister struggle, he took the portable enclosure from her and opened it up, then clicked to lock each of the sides, pushed down the center support and slid the mattress pad into place. "Andrew decided to take a job in Los Angeles, so I no longer have a manager," Liam admitted.

"I'm sorry," Kate said sincerely, as she unbuckled the baby carrier and carefully extracted the sleeping baby.

He shrugged. "Not your problem," he said. "Just as your requirement for a last-minute babysitter—*again*— isn't my problem."

"And yet I'm willing to help you out, because that's what siblings do," she told him.

"Tell me how you're going to help me," he suggested.

She pressed her lips to Tessa's forehead, then carefully laid the sleeping baby down in the playpen.

And maybe his heart did soften a bit as he watched his sister with her little girl, and maybe that same heart had been known to turn to mush when his adorable niece smiled at him, but he had no intention of admitting any of that to Kate, who already took advantage of him at every opportunity.

"By giving you the name of your new manager," she said.

"Please do. Then I can cancel the interviews I've scheduled."

"Your sarcasm is unnecessary and unappreciated, and if I didn't have to be in court in—" Kate glanced at the slim silver bangle on her wrist "—sixteen minutes, I'd make you not just apologize but grovel. Since I do have to be in court, I'll just say *Macy Clayton*."

Liam recognized the name. In fact, Macy was scheduled for an interview at two thirty, but he didn't share that information with his sister, either. "And why should I hire her?" he prompted.

"Because she's perfect for the job," Kate said. "She's been working in the hotel industry in Las Vegas for the past eight years, including several as a desk clerk and concierge before she was promoted to assistant to the manager at the Courtland Hotel & Casino."

"If she had such a great career in Las Vegas, what is she doing in Haven?" he wondered aloud.

"That's something you'll have to ask her," she told him.

He hated when his sister was right.

And as he looked through the applications on his desk after Kate had gone, Liam couldn't deny that she was right about the woman she'd recommended for the managerial position.

Macy Clayton was, at least on paper, perfect for the job. Then again, he'd thought Andrew would be perfect, too—and so had the Beverly Hills Vista. Not surprisingly, Andrew had chosen the possibility of celebrity sighting on the West Coast over the probability of boredom in northern Nevada.

Most of the locals had expressed skepticism about his plan; opening a boutique hotel in a sleepy town off the beaten path was a risky venture. David Gilmore had been less kind in his assessment, referring to his oldest son as both a disappointment and a fool.

"Gilmores are ranchers" had been his refrain every

time Liam tried to talk to him about the inn. And while it was true that the family had been raising cattle on the Circle G for more than a hundred and fifty years, Liam had been chafing to get away from the ranch for more than fifteen years.

Not that he'd had any specific plans. Not until he'd seen JJ Green affixing a New Price sticker to the faded For Sale sign stuck in the untended front yard of the Stagecoach Inn.

The old, abandoned hotel had been falling apart when Hershel Livingston bought it for a song nearly a decade earlier. The Nevada native had made his fortune in casinos and brothels, but he'd planned to make his home in Haven, one of only a few places in the state where those vices were illegal.

Hershel had spent millions of dollars on the rehab, then abandoned the project just as it was nearing completion. No one knew why, although the rumors were plenty. One of the more credible stories was that his wife had visited Haven during the renovation process and immediately hated the small town. A different version of the story suggested that his wife had caught the billionaire dallying with a local girl.

There were as many variations of this claim as there were single women in town. The only indisputable truth was that Hershel had abruptly ordered his construction crew to vacate the premises, and then he called Jack Green to put a For Sale sign on the narrow patch of grass in front of the wide porch.

The real estate agent got a lot of calls about the property in the first few weeks, but they were mostly local people who wanted to walk through and take a gander at the work that had been done. None of them was seriously interested in buying the inn, because they didn't believe a fancy hotel could survive in Haven. As a result, interest had faded more quickly than the paint on the sign.

Then, nearly two years ago, JJ Green—now working in the real estate business with his father—slapped that New Price sticker across the weathered sign. More out of curiosity than anything else, Liam had called the agent to inquire and learned that the price had been drastically reduced.

Without any prompting, JJ confided that the elusive Mrs. Livingston had filed for divorce from her cheating husband and was going after half of everything. To retaliate, Hershel was selling off his assets at a loss to decrease the amount of the settlement he would have to pay to her.

Kate had pointed out that the wife could argue fraud and claim half of the fair market value rather than half of the sale price. On the other hand, the property was only worth what someone was willing to pay, and the fact that the old hotel had been on the market for years without anyone making an offer might support Hershel's decision to slash the price. Either way, Liam wasn't going to protest the lower number. In fact, after securing the necessary financing, he managed to negotiate an even further reduction before he signed on the dotted line.

Now he was only weeks away from opening, still waiting on deliveries and attempting to schedule the final inspections—and trying to fill unexpected vacancies in his staff.

If Macy Clayton had responded to the original posting, he might have hired her rather than Andrew and not been feeling so panicked right now. Of course, he was making this assumption on the basis of her résumé and his sister's recommendation without even having met the woman. So while he agreed that she seemed to have all the necessary qualifications for the job, he was going to reserve judgment.

Then she walked in—and his body stirred with a purely sexual awareness he hadn't experienced in a long while. And in that first moment, even before the introductions, he knew there was no way he could hire her. He also knew that he had to at least go through the motions of the interview.

When she accepted his proffered hand, he felt a jolt straight through his middle as their palms joined. Her skin was soft but her grasp was firm, and he caught a flicker of something that might have been a mixture of surprise and awareness in her espresso-colored eyes when they met his. Her hair was also dark, with highlights of gold and copper, and tied away from her face in the messy-bun style made famous by the Duchess of Sussex before she was royalty.

He guessed Macy's height at around five feet five inches, though her heeled boots added a couple of inches to that number, and her build was on the slender side, but with distinctly feminine curves. The long coat she wore in deference to the season had been unbuttoned to reveal a slim-fitting black skirt that fell just below her knees and a matching single-breasted jacket over a bright blue shell.

"It's a pleasure to meet you, Ms. Clayton." He resisted the temptation to brush his thumb over the pulse point at her wrist to see if it was racing; instead, he let his hand drop away.

"Likewise," she said.

"Can I take your coat for you?"

"No need." She shrugged it off her shoulders and draped it over the back of the chair before perching on the edge of the seat. "I have to tell you, I was skeptical when I'd heard that the old Stagecoach Hotel was being renovated and reopened, but based on what I've seen so far, you've really done a wonderful job with this place."

"Most of the major renovations were done by the previous owner—I just hired the right people to pick up where he left off," Liam admitted.

"Well, the actual coach at the back of the lobby is a nice touch," she noted.

"I thought so, too," he said. A simple idea that had been a lot more complicated to execute, as the antique carriage had to be taken apart to get it through the doorway and then reassembled inside.

"You're planning to open in three weeks?" she prompted.

He nodded. "Valentine's Day."

Her smile was warm and natural. Friendly. He imagined she'd make the guests feel welcome—which was, of course, what he wanted, but didn't alleviate his other concerns.

Sexual harassment in the workplace was a serious issue, and Liam had been raised to be respectful of all women. Still, he suspected it would be a mistake to hire a woman who, upon their first meeting, made him think all kinds of inappropriately tempting thoughts.

"Your résumé shows that you spent the last four years working at the Courtland Hotel in Las Vegas," he noted, forcing himself to refocus on the matter at hand.

"That's correct."

"So why did you leave Las Vegas and move to Haven?"

"I moved *back* to Haven," she clarified. "I grew up in this town and my parents still live here and—" Her words stopped abruptly, as if she'd caught herself saying more than she wanted to.

"And?" he prompted.

She offered another easy smile and a quick shrug. "And I was ready to come home."

It seemed like a reasonable response, but he doubted it was what she'd initially intended to say.

He looked at her résumé again, skimming through the pages that attested to a wealth and breadth of experience. She'd worked a lot of different jobs on her way up to her most recent position as assistant to the manager of the Courtland Hotel & Casino in Las Vegas: she'd served drinks in a hotel casino, worked as a hostess in the restaurant and even done a stint cleaning rooms.

"Your experience is impressive," he told her.

"Thank you."

"But why do you want to work here?"

"Because there are no openings at the Dusty Boots Motel."

His brows lifted. "Is that a joke?"

The corners of her mouth tipped up at the corners. "Yes, Mr. Gilmore."

"Liam," he said.

"I'm not sure it's appropriate to call my boss by his given name."

"I'm not your boss," he pointed out.

"Yet," she clarified, and smiled again.

Before he could reply to that, he heard a rustling sound in the playpen behind him, followed by a tiny, plaintive voice asking for, "Ma-ma?"

Macy leaned forward in her seat, looking past him to the little girl who'd pulled herself up into a standing position, holding onto the top rail.

"Mama's going to be back soon," Liam promised. *Hoped*.

"You have a beautiful daughter," Macy said.

"What? *No*," he responded quickly. Firmly. "She's not my daughter—she's my niece."

"Then you have a beautiful niece," she amended.

He looked at the child in question and felt a familiar tug in the vicinity of his heart. "Yeah, she is kinda cute."

Tessa lifted her arms, a wordless request.

Liam glanced at his watch and tried to remember if Kate had told him when she expected to be finished in court. Out of the corner of his eye, he saw Tessa's arms drop back down and her lower lip thrust forward in a pout.

He sighed and reached for her. "I'm conducting an interview here," he said, as he settled his niece on his hip. "So let's try to keep things professional, okay?"

She responded by leaning forward and pressing her puckered lips to his cheek.

"Not really a good start," he noted dryly.

But his potential innkeeper smiled, clearly charmed by the little girl.

"And if your diaper needs changing, that's going to have to wait until your mom gets back," he warned his niece.

"You don't do diapers?" Macy guessed.

"Not if I can help it. And Kate promised she'd be back from court before Tessa woke up so that I wouldn't have to."

"Either Kate was delayed or Tessa woke up early—

maybe because she was wet," she suggested. "Did your sister leave a diaper bag?"

"If you can call something that would likely be tagged 'oversized' by an airport luggage handler a *bag*," he remarked, gesturing to the multipocketed behemoth.

Macy reached for the bag and, after rifling through its contents, pulled out a change pad, clean diaper and package of wipes, which she set on the table in front of him.

Still, Liam hesitated. "I'm sure she can wait until we've finished our interview."

"Maybe she can, but she shouldn't have to be uncomfortable," Macy said. "I can step out of the room, if you want privacy."

"Do you have much experience with babies and diapers?"

The corners of her mouth tipped up again. "Some."

He unfolded the changing pad and laid his niece on top of it. "Then you should probably stay, because I might need some pointers—or an extra set of hands," he said, as Tessa started to roll away from him.

While Macy seemed willing and able to help, he managed to unsnap his niece's corduroy overalls with one hand and hold her in place with the other.

"Give me some specific examples of guest complaints you've heard and tell me how you dealt with them," he suggested, as he pulled a wipe from the dispenser.

Macy shared anecdotes from her work experience while also jiggling a plastic ring of colorful keys she'd found in the diaper bag to hold the little girl's attention while he focused on changing the diaper.

Her stories proved that she was creative and clever,

and by the time he'd slid the clean diaper under his niece's bottom, he didn't doubt that the Courtland Hotel had been sorry to lose her when she left Las Vegas.

"Usually I fasten the diaper tabs before I do up the pants," she remarked, as he began to pinch the snaps that lined the inseam of Tessa's overalls together.

"What?"

"You didn't secure the diaper."

"Of course I did." He finished his task and let Tessa roll over. She immediately pushed herself to her feet and clapped her hands. Since she'd learned to stand and, more recently, walk, she'd become accustomed to her every effort being applauded.

His own efforts were hardly cause for celebration, because the awkward bulging in her pants confirmed that Macy was right. He sighed. "Apparently I didn't."

So he scooped up Tessa again. "Uncle Liam messed up," he said. "And now we need to fix it."

But Tessa didn't want to be reasoned with—she wanted to be free. And she kicked and screamed in protest.

"What's this?" Macy said, offering the little girl a sippy cup filled with juice that she'd found in the bag.

Tessa stopped kicking and reached out with both hands. "Joosh!"

"Do you want your juice?"

The little girl nodded.

Macy gave her the cup and Liam unsnapped her overalls again—only to realize that the diaper tabs were stuck to her pants. He tried to peel them away from the fabric, determined to salvage the diaper—but his fingers felt too big and clumsy for the task.

"I think I need some help," he admitted.

Macy didn't hesitate to brush his hands aside, unstick the tabs from the little girl's pants, reposition the diaper and deftly fasten it in place. Though the woman kept her gaze focused on the child, she spoke to Liam as she completed the task. "I trust you know that a good employee is one who steps up to do a job that needs doing, even if it falls outside of her job description."

"You can't expect me to hire you just because you helped change my niece's diaper," he remarked—*after* the task was completed.

"Of course not," she agreed, passing the clean and happy little girl to him. "I expect you to hire me because I'm the best person for the job."

Chapter 2

In retrospect, Macy acknowledged that she should have taken a change of clothes when she left home for her interview. Whenever she headed out with Ava, Max and Sam, she triple-checked to ensure she was prepared for every possible contingency. But when it came to making plans for herself, she couldn't seem to think two steps ahead.

Her friend Stacia called it "pregnancy brain" and confessed that she'd experienced similar bouts of absentmindedness during both of her pregnancies. But that title suggested to Macy a temporary condition that would correct itself after she'd given birth. Instead, it had transitioned to "momnesia."

Apparently there was scientific proof that the hormonal changes designed to help a new mother bond with her baby could interfere with the brain's ability to process other information. This explained why Macy could jolt from a deep sleep to wide awake when any of her babies stirred in the night but the cook at Diggers' had to repeat her name three times before she realized that an order was up. And even though the triplets were close to eight months old now, her brain apparently hadn't gotten the memo that she'd bonded with them and could, perhaps, start to focus on other things again.

So she was feeling a little bit guilty about boasting to Liam Gilmore that she was the best person for the manager's job—because what if she wasn't? What if she'd forgotten everything she'd ever learned about the hospitality industry? Maybe her only real talent now was being able to diaper three squirming babies in less than a minute.

But she wanted the job. She'd been excited about the possibility as soon as she'd learned that the new owner of the Stagecoach Inn was looking for a manager, and even more so when she'd walked through the front door and breathed in the history and grandeur of the old building.

Her only hesitation derived from the frisson of *something* she'd experienced when Liam Gilmore clasped her hand in his. It had been so long since she'd felt *anything* in response to a man's touch that she hadn't been sure how to respond. Thankfully, her brain had kicked back into gear and reminded her that the handsome cowboy was her potential boss and not a man she should ever contemplate seeing naked. Which was a shame, because the breadth of his shoulders—

No, she wasn't going there.

The admonishment from her brain had helped refocus her attention on the interview. She could only hope he hadn't sensed her distraction, because she really wanted the job.

Macy had started working at Diggers' Bar & Grill because she'd wanted—needed—to do something to help support her family. But she missed the hospitality business more than she'd anticipated. Working at the inn wouldn't just be a job, it would be a pleasure. For now, though, she was still a waitress—and if she didn't hurry up, she was going to be late for her shift.

She took a few minutes to play with Ava, Max and Sam, though, because they weren't just the reason for everything she did but the center of her world. Yes, she'd been stunned—and terrified—when she'd discovered that she was pregnant with triplets, but after only eight months, she couldn't imagine her life without her three precious and unique babies.

Ava, perhaps because she was the only girl, was already accustomed to being the center of attention. Of course, it helped that she had a sweet disposition and was usually quicker to smiles than tears. She also had big blue eyes with long dark lashes and silky dark hair that had finally grown enough that Macy no longer felt the need to put decorative bands on her head to broadcast that she was a girl.

Max was her introspective child—usually content to sit back and watch the world around him. His eyes were green, his hair dark, and his happy place was in his mother's arms.

Sam looked so much like his brother that it was often assumed they were identical twins, though the doctor had assured Macy they were not. Sam was the last born and smallest of her babies. He was also the fussiest, and

Macy felt a special bond with the little guy who seemed to need her more than either his brother or sister did.

When she could delay her departure no longer, Macy headed out again, entrusting her precious babies to the care of their doting grandparents.

Bev and Norm had been shocked to learn of their unmarried daughter's pregnancy—and even more so when she confided the how and why it had happened. To say that they disapproved would be a gross understatement, but they'd put aside their concerns about the circumstances of conception to focus on helping their daughter prepare for the life-changing event.

And having triplets *was* life changing. Macy's apartment in Vegas had been far too small for three babies, but she couldn't afford anything bigger. And she'd budgeted for the expense of daycare for one baby, but triplets meant that cost would be multiplied threefold. So when she was five months pregnant and already waddling like a penguin—another perk of carrying three babies—she did the only thing she could do: resigned her position at the Courtland Hotel, packed up everything she owned and moved herself and all of her not-so-worldly possessions to her parents' house in Haven, Nevada.

At least she hadn't had to move back into her childhood bedroom, instead taking up residence in the in-law suite downstairs. The apartment was originally designed for her maternal grandmother, so that Shirley Haskell could live independently but close to family, and she'd occupied the space for almost six years before her dementia advanced to a stage where she needed round-the-clock nursing care. After that, Bev and Norm had occasionally offered the apartment for rent, most recently to Reid Davidson, who'd come to town to finish out Jed Traynor's term when the former sheriff retired. Almost two years later, most people still referred to Reid as the new sheriff—and would likely do so until he was ready to retire.

The apartment had remained vacant for a long time after the sheriff moved out, and Macy suspected it was because the rooms were in dire need of redecorating. The sofa and chairs in the living room were covered in bold floral fabrics that attested to their outdatedness, and the coffee table, end tables and lamps all bore witness to the tole painting class Bev had taken while her mother was in residence.

When Macy moved in, the first thing she did was buy covers for the furniture and strip away all evidence of cabbage roses and daisies and tulips. If Beverly was disappointed that her art wasn't appreciated by her daughter, she never said so. Instead, she focused her energy on getting ready for the arrival of three new grandbabies.

For the first few months after Ava, Max and Sam were born, Macy had done nothing but learn how to be a mother. It was a bigger adjustment than she'd anticipated. With three babies, she felt as if she was constantly feeding, burping, changing, bathing or rocking one or more of them. Bev helped as much as she could, and Macy knew there was no way she would have made it through those early days without her mother.

Norm had done his part, too. Although he occasionally made excuses to avoid diaper duty—not unlike Liam Gilmore had attempted to do earlier that afternoon—Macy's dad was the first to volunteer to take the babies for a walk in their stroller or rock a restless infant to sleep. And he never once complained about the fact that the presence of his only daughter and her three children had completely upended his life—as she knew they had done.

Life was busy but good, so Macy had been a little surprised when, shortly before the triplets' six-month birthday, Beverly suggested that her daughter think about getting a job. Macy had assured her mom that she had savings and could increase the amount of rent she paid—because she'd refused to move into their home without contributing at least something to the cost of the roof over her head.

Of course, they'd argued about that, with her parents recommending that her savings should remain that, as there was no way to know what unexpected expenses might arise in the future. But Macy had insisted, and her parents had finally relented—then promptly started education savings plans for Ava, Max and Sam with the money Macy paid to them.

"We don't need you to pay more rent," Bev had assured her. "But you need a reason to get out of the house and interact with other people."

"I do get out of the house."

"Taking Ava, Max and Sam to the pediatrician doesn't count."

"But…if I got a job—who would look after the kids?"

"Oh, well." Bev tapped a finger against her chin, as if searching for an answer to a particularly difficult question. "Hmm…that *is* a tough one."

"I can't ask you to do it," Macy explained. "You already do so much for us."

"You don't have to ask, I'm offering. In fact, I'm insisting."

And that was how Macy found herself replying to the Help Wanted ad in the window at Diggers' Bar & Grill.

At first she'd only worked the lunch shift two days a week. But after a couple of weeks on the job, Duke had added dinner shifts to her schedule—and dinner occasionally extended to late night. Usually she worked the restaurant side, but she was sometimes tagged to help out in the bar when it was particularly busy.

Tonight she was scheduled to work 6 p.m. to midnight in the bar. It was six-oh-seven when she parked her car and six-oh-eight when Duke found her in the staff lounge—really not much more than a closet where employees hung their coats and stashed their personal belongings—tying her apron around her waist.

Her boss folded his beefy arms over his chest and pinned her with his gaze. "You're late."

"I'm sorry." Macy's apology was automatic but sincere. "Max was fussing and I wanted to help settle him down before I left."

"I've got kids," Duke said. "Of course, mine are grown now, but I remember the early days and can empathize with your situation. However, your customers don't care if Sam's cutting teeth or Ava's got a fever—they just want to order food and drink from a waitress who's on time."

"You're right. I'm sorry," she said again.

"You were bussing tables here while you were still in high school. We both know you're overqualified for this job, but as long as you're working here, I need you to do the job you were hired to do."

She nodded.

"Of course, if you were to get another job more suited

to your interests, then I could hire someone who is more interested in waiting tables," he remarked.

"I had an interview with Liam Gilmore today," she told him.

"Good. Because I interviewed Courtney Morgan for your job here."

"Hey," she said, because she felt compelled to make at least a token protest. Though it wasn't her lifelong dream to wait tables, she usually enjoyed working at Diggers'—the hub of most social activity in Haven. Of course, the town only boasted two other restaurants: the Sunnyside Diner and Jo's Pizzeria, so if residents wanted anything other than all-day breakfast or pizza, they inevitably headed to Diggers'.

Early in the week, business wasn't nearly as brisk as it was on weekends, but Macy didn't mind the slower pace because it meant that she had more time to chat with the customers she served.

"Somebody was hungry," she commented, as she picked up the now-empty plate that had contained a six-ounce bison burger on a pretzel bun, a scoop of creamy coleslaw and a mountain of curly fries when she'd delivered it to Connor Neal.

"Yeah, me and the sheriff got caught up with a case and worked right through lunch," the deputy told her.

Macy hadn't really known Connor while she was growing up in Haven. He was a few years younger than she was and, even as a kid, he'd been known around town as "that no-good Neal boy."

She'd never been sure if he'd earned his bad-boy reputation or simply had the misfortune of living on the wrong side of the tracks with his unwed mother and younger half brother, but notwithstanding this difficult start, he'd managed to turn his life around. Not only was he a deputy in the sheriff's office now, he'd recently married Regan Channing, whose family had made their substantial fortune in mining.

"Do you want dessert?" Macy asked him now.

"No, thanks. But I do need an order to go." He scrolled through the messages in his phone, then read aloud: "Buffalo chicken wrap with extra hot sauce, fries and onion rings, and one of those big pickles."

"It sounds like your wife might have worked through lunch, too," she noted. "Or it might just be that she's eating for two."

"Three actually," Connor confided.

"Three?" Macy echoed.

The deputy nodded. "She's having twins. *We're* having twins," he hastily amended.

"I hadn't heard," she said. "That's wonderful news—congratulations."

He smiled weakly. "Two babies are twice the fun, right?"

"For sure," she agreed. And twice the diapers and midnight feedings, but she kept *that* to herself. The reality would hit him quickly enough when the babies were born. "Do you know if you're going to have two sons or daughters or one of each?"

"Daughters. They're both girls. Although I've been told that sometimes the techs make mistakes," he added.

She couldn't help but laugh at the obvious hopefulness in his tone. "Sometimes they do," she agreed. "And sometimes expectant mothers get cranky when they have to wait too long for their food, so I'll get this order in for you right away."

"Thanks," Connor said.

Aside from being freaked out by the idea of two girls, it was obvious to Macy that the deputy was looking forward to the family he was going to have with his wife. And as she made her way to the kitchen, Macy found herself envying Regan that.

It was what she'd always wanted—not just a child, but a husband who was her partner in every aspect of life and a father for her children.

She'd given up on that dream and opted to go it alone. And though she wouldn't give up her babies for anything in the world, there were moments when she regretted that she hadn't been able to give them more.

A family.

It was almost eight o'clock when Liam left the inn. His booted feet pounded on the recently stained wooden slats of the porch that wrapped around three sides of the building. In the spring, there would be an assortment of benches and chairs to entice guests to rest and relax, interspersed with enormous pots of flowers to provide both privacy and color. But now there was only a light dusting of snow on the steps and the rail.

It had been snowing when Kate came back after court to pick up her daughter, he recalled. He'd noted the flakes melting in his sister's hair and on the shoulders of her coat when she walked into his office—while he was meeting with another applicant for the manager's job. He'd pretended to be annoyed by the interruption, but the truth was, he'd been grateful for an excuse to cut the interview short.

Having left his gloves in the truck earlier, he shoved his hands deep into the pockets of his jacket now and hunched his shoulders against the bitter wind as he considered his next move. He had an apartment on the third level, so that he'd be onsite overnight if his guests needed anything. But since there were no guests to worry about just yet, he'd postponed his move to continue helping with morning chores at the Circle G. If he was smart, he'd head back to the ranch, grab a bite to eat and hit the hay for a few hours before he had to be up again to help with those chores. Apparently he wasn't very smart, because he turned toward Diggers' instead.

The double doors opened into an enclosed foyer and two other doorways—one clearly marked Bar and the other designated Grill. Once inside, patrons could easily move from one side to the other as there was only a partial wall dividing the two sections, but the division ensured a more family-friendly entrance to the restaurant side. The interior was rustic: the floors were unpainted, weathered wood slats, scuffed and scarred from the pounding of countless pairs of boots; framed newspaper headlines trumpeting the discovery of gold and silver hung on the walls alongside tools of the mining trade—coils of rope, shovels, pickaxes, hammers and chisels.

"You look like you've had a long day," Skylar remarked when he straddled a stool at the bar. The regular bartender at the town's favorite watering hole was also a master's candidate in psychology—and Liam's younger sister.

"You have no idea."

"So tell me about it," she suggested, already tipping a glass beneath the tap bearing the label of his favorite brew.

"You heard that Andrew took a job in California?"

"I did," she confirmed.

"Well, that leaves me without a manager three weeks before opening," he told her.

"Macy Clayton," she said without hesitation, and set the pint glass on a paper coaster in front of him.

He shook his head. "Not you, too."

Sky's brows disappeared beneath her bangs. "Too?"

"Kate mentioned her name earlier," he explained.

"Maybe because Macy's the only person in Haven who has the kind of experience you need."

"How does everyone seem to know so much about her?" he wondered aloud.

"It's Haven," his sister pointed out unnecessarily. "Everyone knows everything about everyone in this town—unless they've been living under a rock…or buried in the details of a property renovation."

"Well, I interviewed her today," he admitted, and lifted his glass to his mouth.

"And?" she prompted.

"And…she's got the kind of experience I need," he agreed.

Sky set a bowl of mixed nuts on the bar beside his glass. "So why haven't you hired her?"

He nibbled on a cashew. "I don't know."

"You're attracted to her," Sky guessed.

He scowled, not because it was untrue but because he was uncomfortable with the accuracy of his sister's insights. "Where is that coming from?"

"The fact that I know you. And the fact that she's an attractive woman, *but* not at all your type," she cautioned.

"You've always said I don't have a type," he reminded her.

"You might not show any preference between

blondes, brunettes and redheads, but since your one failed attempt at a grown-up relationship—"

"I've had several grown-up relationships," he interjected.

"I'm not talking about sex," she said dryly. "I'm talking about meaningful interactions that happen with your clothes on."

"Now you've lost me."

She sighed. "And that's Isabella's fault. When you were with her, you actually seemed to be growing into a mature and responsible human being. But since she broke your heart—"

"She didn't break my heart," he denied.

"—you've been all about having a good time," she continued, ignoring his interruption. "And Macy is all about responsibility."

"I can't remember the last time I had a good time," he lamented.

"At Carrie and Matt's wedding—with Heather," she surmised.

"Oh, yeah." He smiled. "That was a good time." Until Heather decided that one night meant they were back together again. "It was also seven months ago."

"Working for a living really sucks, huh?" she teased.

"You know I'm not just putting in a few hours at the hotel every day. I'm helping out at the ranch every morning, too."

"Why is that?" she prompted, because she got her kicks out of digging into other people's psyches and prying into their motivations. "You've made no secret of the fact that you want a life away from the ranch, but you keep going back."

"Because there are chores that need to be done."

"You don't think there are enough hands to manage without you?" she asked.

He shrugged. "Okay, so maybe I don't want the old man to forget that he's got two sons."

"He's not going to forget you," Sky assured him. "He's also not going to get over being pissed off any quicker just because you're mucking out stalls every morning."

"I know. But at least when I'm there, he has to talk to me."

His sister's sigh was filled with exasperation. "He's reverted to the silent treatment again?"

"He's barely spoken a dozen words to me since January 2," Liam confided. Because the holidays had officially ended then and, with them, the détente Katelyn had imposed on her family. During the period of eight days between Christmas Eve and New Year's Day, she'd forced her father and brother to play nice, threatening to celebrate Tessa's first Christmas without them if they couldn't get along. But now the holidays were over and so, too, was the father-son ceasefire.

"I'm sorry," Sky said. "Obviously Dad's going to need some time to accept that the hotel is more than a whim to you...assuming it is more than a whim."

He scowled at the implication. "You think I'd invest all my money—and a fair amount of our grandparents'—on a whim?"

"Maybe not," she allowed.

"Not to mention that the whole town will benefit from the reopening of the hotel," he assured her.

"Everyone except the owner of the Dusty Boots," she remarked dryly.

"No doubt there's a specific type of clientele that will still opt to pay the hourly rate at the budget motel."

Sky chuckled at that. "No doubt," she agreed. "And in addition to being an opportunity for the community, the hotel is an opportunity for you to finally escape the ranch you've hated since—"

"I've been thinking the hotel should have a bar," Liam said, deliberately cutting his sister off. "It would be nice to have a place to grab a beer without being psychoanalyzed by the bartender."

"A bar isn't a bad idea," she said. "A restaurant would be even better."

"Have you been talking to Grams?"

"Occasionally, since she happens to be my grandmother, too. But yes, she told me about The Home Station."

He shook his head. "We don't have a restaurant, only a solarium where we're going to serve breakfast. I don't know where she got it in her head that we should offer an upscale dining option, but you shouldn't encourage her."

"It's not a bad idea," Sky mused.

"It's not happening," he assured her.

Then a movement in the corner of his eye snagged his attention and he turned his head for a better view of the waitress delivering a tray of drinks to a nearby table. His gaze skimmed slowly up her long, slender legs to a nicely rounded bottom, trim waist and—

Sky interrupted his perusal by reaching across the bar to dab at the corner of his mouth with a cocktail napkin, as if he was drooling. He swatted her hand away and resumed his perusal.

Between the ranch and the inn, he'd had little time

for anything else since the wedding his sister had referred to—and even less interest. But somehow, after months had passed without anyone snagging his attention, he'd felt his body unexpectedly stir in response to two different women in the same day. Obviously it was a sign that he needed to readjust his priorities and find the time—and a willing woman—to help him end this unintended period of celibacy.

Then the waitress turned from the table, and his jaw nearly dropped. Because the female he'd been eyeing wasn't different at all—she was Macy Clayton.

Chapter 3

"You didn't know she worked here?" Sky guessed, her tone tinged with amusement.

Liam shook his head. "This job wasn't on her résumé."

"She's only been here a couple weeks. Or maybe I should say *back* here, because apparently she worked for Duke when she was in high school."

"Is she a good waitress?"

"Why? Do you want to hire her to work in your restaurant?" his sister teased.

"There is no restaurant," he said firmly. "And I'm asking you because you have an opinion about everything."

"Then I'll tell you that she's got great people skills. She's friendly without being flirty, and she knows when and how to placate an unhappy customer but she's not a pushover. Definite management material."

"I'll keep that in mind," he said dryly.

"And I'll go put in your food order."

"I haven't told you what I want."

"Steak sandwich with mushrooms, onions and pepper jack cheese with fries."

"Yeah, that sounds good," he admitted.

With a smug smile, she turned toward the kitchen.

And he shifted his attention back to the waitress who'd caught his eye. "Macy."

She pivoted, her eyes widening with surprise and recognition. "Mr. Gilmore."

"Liam," he reminded her.

"Liam," she echoed dutifully.

"You didn't mention that you had a job here."

"It's a temporary gig," she said, then smiled. "Just until I start my job at the Stagecoach Inn."

He couldn't help but smile back. "Confident, aren't you?"

"Qualified," she clarified.

"So why is a former assistant to the manager of a Las Vegas hotel working at a bar and grill in Haven?"

"I needed a job and Duke needed a waitress."

It sounded like a simple enough explanation, but he couldn't shake the feeling that he was missing a major piece of the puzzle that was Macy Clayton. And though he knew he was treading dangerously close to a line that should not be crossed, he was intrigued enough by the woman to want to know more.

"I didn't give you a tour of the hotel today," he noted.

"And I was so hoping for one," she confessed.

"Stop by tomorrow, if you want," he said. "As long as I haven't had a kid dropped in my lap, I should be free to show you around."

"I want," she immediately agreed. "Anytime in particular?"

"Whenever it's convenient for you."

"Okay. I'll see you tomorrow."

He watched her move away, making her way toward a table of six that had just sat down. Regulars, he guessed, as they didn't seem to need to look at the menus that were tucked beneath the tray of condiments on the table.

"It's my fault," Sky lamented, as she set a plate of food and his cutlery on the bar in front of him.

"What's your fault?" he asked.

"I should have realized that saying Macy wasn't your type would compel you to prove otherwise."

"Maybe you should tell me why you're so sure she's not my type," he suggested, lifting his sandwich from the plate.

"And maybe you should trust me for once," his sister countered.

His gaze shifted to Macy again. "Yeah, I'm having a little trouble with that."

"Then keep in mind that she's going to be working for you."

He wanted to argue that point, but after interviewing three other candidates for the job, he'd been forced to acknowledge that none of them was even remotely qualified.

Darren, currently a bouncer at a honky-tonk bar in Elko, was looking for a day job so he could go to night school. When Liam, simply out of curiosity, asked him why he wasn't choosing to study during the day and continuing to work nights, it was immediately apparent that Darren hadn't considered the possibility—an oversight that didn't bode well for success in his future studies.

Felix's résumé indicated that he was already college educated and had a master's degree in English literature. Unfortunately, he had absolutely no experience in the hospitality business and even less interest. During the interview, he confided that service industries were tedious and boring and acknowledged that he'd only applied for the job because employment opportunities in the town were limited.

And then there was Lissa, a college dropout who claimed that her life experience made her uniquely qualified for the job. When Liam asked her to give him an example, she explained that she'd lived with her in-laws for eighteen months without killing either of them— though she confessed that she'd given the idea more than a passing thought on a few occasions.

Which meant that, for the sake of the business, there really was only one choice for Liam to make.

He was going to have to hire Macy Clayton.

As he chewed on his sandwich, he accepted that whether she was or wasn't his type, hiring Macy Clayton would definitely put her off-limits for any romantic overtures.

And that was a damn shame.

Macy showed up just as the delivery truck was pulling away from the inn the following afternoon. Liam had kept himself busy directing the unloading and placement of the furniture so that he could pretend he wasn't watching and waiting for her to arrive for the promised tour of the property. At the same time, he reassured himself that his response to her couldn't possibly have been as powerful as he remembered.

Then he saw her, and the awareness hit him again, like a sucker punch in the gut.

It wasn't just that she was beautiful, though she was undoubtedly that. Even dressed casually, as she was today, in slim-fitting jeans and a cowl-neck sweater beneath a charcoal-grey wool coat belted at her waist, she was stunning. But he'd crossed paths with plenty of attractive women in his twenty-nine years without ever experiencing such an immediate and intense reaction, and he couldn't deny that it worried him a little.

"Good timing," he said, in lieu of a greeting as she walked up the steps.

"Was that the delivery truck just leaving?" she asked. He nodded.

"I recognized the logo," she said. "You're obviously a man of exquisite taste."

"Garrett Furniture has a great collection of pieces that coordinate without being exactly the same," he told her. "The idea is that every room will offer the same level of luxury but in a distinctly individual setting, so that guests who enjoyed their stay in the Doc Holliday Suite might want to come back to experience the Charles Goodnight Suite—or upgrade to the Wild Bill Getaway Suite."

"Are all of the rooms named after famous people?"

"They are," he confirmed. "It was my grandmother's idea, and she did the research, from Annie Oakley to Wild Bill. Interesting details about their lives are engraved on plaques in each room—but instead of telling you about them, why don't I show you?"

"Sounds good to me." She reached toward the door

before he could, but instead of grasping the handle, her fingers traced the outline of the raised panel on which was carved an intricate and detailed image of a horse-drawn stagecoach. "This is amazing."

"The previous owner wanted to acknowledge the building's origins," Liam told her. "There's a series of paintings in the library—original oils by local artists—that also pay tribute to the town's history."

Since the door opened into the lobby on the main level, that's where they started the tour.

Macy had come in the same way when she'd arrived for her interview the day before, but the folding table and cheap plastic chairs that had created an ad hoc interview space had been replaced by an elegant double pedestal executive desk with dentil molding and antique brass hardware. The high-back chair behind the desk was covered in butter-soft leather that coordinated with the sofa and oversized chairs that faced the stone fireplace.

"You should have a lamp for that table," she suggested, pointing. "And a focal point for the coffee table. Maybe a copper bowl—wide and shallow. Have you ever been to the antique and craft market out by the highway?"

"I don't think so."

"You should go," she told him. "There's a local artist who sells his pieces there. I bet you could find all kinds of unique things to add not just visual interest but local flavor."

"I'll keep that in mind," he said, as he directed her toward the library.

The room had the potential to live up to its name, with two walls of built-in floor-to-ceiling bookcases—

currently completely empty of books. She thought about the fun she could have stocking those shelves to provide guests with a variety of reading materials. Maybe she'd even throw in some board games, lay out a chess set on the square table between the two silk-upholstered wing chairs.

She took a moment to study and admire the paintings he'd told her about, appreciating not just the talent but the subjects represented in every brush stroke and color.

"Basque linens," she said, as they moved down the hall to the main floor guest rooms.

"What?"

She chuckled. "Sorry—I'm sure that seemed to come out of nowhere, but I was just thinking about other ways to highlight the history of not just this building but the local area."

"I know about the Basques but nothing about their linen."

"It was originally made from flax grown in the fields and woven with colorful stripes, traditionally seven, which was the number of Basque provinces in France and Spain. The source of the fabric and the process has evolved over the years, but the colorful stripes remain a defining feature."

"How do you know this?"

"In high school, I did a research paper on how the Basque people and culture have influenced our local community, which is just one more reason—" she offered a hopeful smile "—I'd be an asset at your front desk."

"I'll keep that in mind," he promised, leading her down the hall to the Annie Oakley Room.

She wondered if he'd chosen the color palette and

furnishings, or if his grandmother had taken the lead in that, too. Either way, the overall impression of the room was warmth and comfort, and she could imagine herself contentedly curling up in the middle of the half-tester and dreaming sweet dreams. That tempting fantasy was followed closely by one of sinking into the claw-footed tub filled with scented bubbles when she peeked into the bath.

Appropriately, Bonnie & Clyde were adjoining rooms—the former with a single queen-size sleigh bed, the latter with two double beds of the same style.

"A, B, C," she realized. "I assume you did that on purpose?"

"Yeah, although it kind of fell apart upstairs where we jump from D to F."

"What's beyond those doors?" she asked.

"Serenity Spa."

She sighed, a little wistfully. "When I heard you were looking for a manager, I knew I wanted the job," Macy told him. "Because it's what I've trained to do—and what I'm good at. But that was before I'd seen what you've done here, and now that I have, I want it even more."

"You haven't seen half of what we've done here," he said, leading the way to the second floor.

He was right. And with every door she walked through, she fell more and more in love. The rooms were all spacious and inviting, with natural light pouring through the windows, spilling across the glossy floors. She'd often thought hardwood was cold, but the rugs that had been added provided warmth, color and texture. There were crown moldings in one room, window seats in another, elaborate wardrobes and antique dressing screens, padded benches and hope chests. The en suite baths boasted natural stone tiles and heated towel bars, waterfall showerheads inside glass enclosures and freestanding soaker tubs.

Each room was unique in its style and substance, and Macy honestly couldn't have said which one was her favorite—until they reached the third floor and Liam opened the door to Wild Bill's Getaway Suite.

Everything about the space screamed luxury, from the intricate mosaic pattern in the floor tile to the elegant chesterfield sofa and forty-two-inch flat-screen TV mounted above the white marble fireplace. Beyond the parlor was the bath, with more white marble, lots of glass and even an enormous crystal chandelier. There was a second fireplace in the bedroom, along with a king-size pediment poster bed flanked by matching end tables, a wide wardrobe and even a makeup vanity set.

"Well, it's not the Dusty Boots Motel," she remarked dryly when they'd made their way back down to the main level—and the solarium where he told her breakfast would be served.

Liam chuckled. "The idea was to give visitors to Haven another option."

"I'd say you succeeded."

The solarium had two sets of French doors that opened onto the deck, where additional bistro tables and chairs would be set up for guests to enjoy their breakfast in the warm weather.

"Did you have another space in mind for more formal, evening dining?"

He shook his head. "We're limiting our service to breakfast-slash-brunch, with an afternoon wine and cheese in the library on Fridays and Saturdays."

"I like the wine and cheese idea," she said. "But if you're not offering an evening meal, you're missing out on the opportunity for guests to spend more of their money right here."

"There are other places people can go for dinner," he pointed out.

"There's no place in town that offers an upscale dining experience. When my parents celebrated their fortieth anniversary last year, they drove all the way to Reno because they wanted candlelight and a wine list that wasn't printed on the bottom of a laminated page below the kids' menu."

He smiled at that. "I can see your point, but I know nothing about the restaurant business."

"Which is why you hire people who do," she said.

"Like you?" he guessed.

She immediately shook her head. "No. That's not my area of expertise. But Kyle Landry studied at the School of Artisan Food in England."

"I'm sure his mother could have taught him everything he needed to know about making pizza."

"Except that Kyle doesn't want to make pizza. He wants to run his own kitchen in a real restaurant."

Liam winced. "Don't let Jo hear you say that."

"His words, not mine," Macy explained.

"Maybe that's why he's not working in her kitchen right now," he suggested.

"Yeah, she's not happy that Duke gave him a job. But Kyle's not really happy, either, because Duke won't even contemplate any changes to the menu. Kyle added chili-dusted pumpkin seeds to the coleslaw to give it a little bit of crunch and zing, and three customers sent it back. They grudgingly acknowledged that it was good but complained that it 'didn't taste right.'"

"People want what they want, and local people don't want fancy food."

But Macy disagreed. "They might not want fancy food in a familiar setting," she allowed. "But a new restaurant would open up a world of new possibilities. Not to mention that a restaurant would create another revenue stream for your business."

"Have you been talking to my grandmother?"

She laughed. "No, but I'm guessing she said the same thing."

"Yeah," he admitted. "And maybe it is something to think about."

"You might think about talking to Kyle, too" Macy suggested.

"I might," he agreed.

She didn't ask him about the job.

Macy figured there was a fine line between eager and pushy and she didn't want to cross it. Besides, Liam had promised to make a decision by the end of the week, so she would hold on to her patience a while longer.

But by Friday afternoon, with another long and late shift at Diggers' looming ahead, her patience was running out. She was grateful that she had a job, but it was hard to keep a smile on her face when she was working on less than five hours of frequently interrupted sleep.

Her babies, now eight months old, had started sleeping a lot better, more consistently and—maybe even more important—concurrently, which allowed Macy to get more sleep. But the past couple of weeks had been rough as two of the three were cutting teeth. Two tiny buds had poked through Ava's bottom gum almost a week earlier with minimal fuss, but her brothers were struggling and miserable.

And despite Macy's optimism after she'd completed her tour of the Stagecoach Inn—and Liam Gilmore's promise to be in touch by the end of the week—she still hadn't heard anything from him about the job. So she left a little early for her shift at Diggers' and stopped by the hotel on her way. There was no one in the main lobby when she arrived, so she peeked inside the library, but that was empty, too. She wandered a little further and finally found Liam in the kitchen, muttering to himself as he opened and inspected a stack of boxes on the island.

"Is this a bad time?" she asked.

He held up a dinner plate. "Does this look like white to you?"

"Only if tangerines are white," she noted.

He set the plate on the counter and selected a bowl from another box. "How about this? Is this—" he glanced at the notation on what she guessed was an itemized list of his order "—dove?"

"Um, no. I'd say that's lemon," she said.

"And this?" He showed her a salad plate.

"Lime."

"Great," he said dryly. "I ordered tableware and they sent me fruit salad." He held up a mug.

"I'm tempted to say blueberry." She fought a smile. "But it's actually closer to turquoise."

He shook his head, obviously not amused.

"I'm guessing you got someone else's order."

He scrubbed his hands over his face. "An order that I've been waiting on for three months."

She moved to the island and set the salad plate on top of the dinner plate, then the bowl in the center of the salad plate and the mug beside it. "I like it," she decided.

He lifted a brow. "You're kidding."

She shook her head. "White and grey are basic, boring. This tableware makes a statement that's more reflective of what you're doing with the distinctive décor in each of the guestrooms—providing your visitors with a unique experience."

"I wanted basic and boring," he said stubbornly.

"So you can send this back and find basic and boring tableware somewhere else, or you can keep this and negotiate a price reduction from the supplier."

He looked dubious. "You really think I should keep it?"

"I do, but it's not my decision to make. Unless that kind of thing falls under managerial duties," she added hopefully.

"Someone once told me that a good employee is someone who steps up to do what needs to be done, even if it isn't in her job description."

"Touché."

"And I'm guessing that's why you're here," he realized.

"Well, you did say you'd make a decision by the end of the week, and it's the end of the week."

"So it is," he agreed. "And there's no doubt you're the most qualified of the applicants I've interviewed."

"Why do I get the feeling there's a *but*?" she asked warily.

"But I have some reservations about hiring you," he admitted.

"What kind of reservations? Did Duke complain

about me being late? Because that was once. Okay, maybe twice, but—"

"Duke gave you a glowing recommendation," he interjected to assure her.

She frowned. "Then why don't you want to hire me?"

"Because you're an incredibly attractive woman and… I find myself incredibly attracted to you."

His reply wasn't at all what she'd expected, and it took Macy a moment to wrap her head around it and decide how to respond to it—and him.

She was undeniably flattered. Liam Gilmore wasn't at all hard to look at, and he was built like the rancher she knew he'd been before he bought the old Stagecoach Inn. And she admittedly felt a stir of something unexpected whenever she was near him, but she hadn't let that dissuade her from going after the job she wanted, because she knew that a man like Liam Gilmore would never be interested in a woman whose first, second and third priorities were her children.

"I fail to see how that's relevant to my ability to do the job you need done," she finally said.

"You don't think the attraction might make our working relationship a little…uncomfortable?"

"Not at all," she assured him. "Because I have no doubt that you want this venture to succeed, and that requires hiring the right person for the right job. Aside from that, an initial feeling of attraction is always based on superficial criteria, and once you get to know me, you'll realize I'm not your type."

He scowled. "Why does everyone keep saying that?"

"While I must admit to some curiosity about the 'everyone' else who might have said the same thing, the reason is simple," she said. "Because I'd guess that someone known around town as 'Love 'em and Leave 'em Liam' is only looking for a good time and—"

"That nickname isn't just ridiculous, it's completely inaccurate," he interjected.

She ignored his interruption to finish making her point: "And, as a single mom, I don't have time for extracurricular activities of any kind right now."

Liam took an actual physical step backward, a subconscious retreat.

"You have a kid?"

Macy's lips curved in a wry smile. "Yeah, I figured my revelation would have that effect."

"I'm sorry," he said. "I just… I didn't know."

"Like I said—not your type," she reminded him.

And she was right.

Everyone was right.

Because as much as he adored his niece—and he did—he wasn't willing to play father to some other guy's kid.

Not again.

He looked at Macy, dressed for another shift at Diggers' in a different short skirt and low-cut top, and couldn't help but remark, "You sure as heck don't look like anyone's mother."

She smiled at that. "Thanks, I think. But I don't want platitudes—I want a job. I want the manager's job," she clarified. "I don't mind waiting tables at Diggers', but the late hours mean that I miss the bedtime routine with my kids almost every night."

"Kid*s*?" he echoed, surprised to learn that she had more than one.

She nodded.

"How many?"

"Three," she admitted. "They're eight months old."

He waited for her to provide the ages of her other two children, then comprehension dawned. *"Triplets?"*

She nodded again.

"Wow."

"Yeah, that was pretty much my reaction when the doctor told me—although I might have added a few NSFW adjectives."

"And the dad?" he wondered. "I imagine he was shocked, too."

"I'm not sure it's appropriate to ask a prospective employee about her personal relationships," she noted. "But since there are no secrets in this town, I'll tell you that he's not in the picture."

"You're right—it was an inappropriate question," he acknowledged.

Also, Macy's relationship with the father of her babies was irrelevant. She might be the sexiest single mom he'd ever met, but he had less than zero interest in being the "dad" who transformed the equation of "mom plus three kids" into "family."

"I guess the only question left to ask is—when can you start?"

Chapter 4

The smile that curved Macy's lips illuminated her whole face. "I've got the job?"

Liam nodded, though he worried that his heart seemed to fill with joy just to know that she was happy. Clearly the wayward organ hadn't received the message from his brain that his new manager was a single mom or it would be erecting impenetrable shields.

"I'd have to be a fool to hire anyone else," he said.

And from a business perspective, it was absolutely true.

From a personal perspective, it might turn out that he was just as big a fool to hire her.

During their tour of the inn a few days earlier, he'd been driven to distraction by her nearness. And he'd wanted to move nearer, so that he was close enough to touch her—or even kiss her. Would her skin feel as soft as it looked? Would her lips taste as sweet as he imagined?

"A lot of people think you're foolish to reopen the hotel," she noted.

Her comment dragged him out of his fantasy and back to the present.

"I guess it's lucky for you that I didn't listen to those people."

"I guess it is," she agreed. "But in response to your earlier question, I can start whenever you need me."

"Two weeks ago?"

She chuckled softly. "Are you running behind schedule on a few things?"

"A few," he acknowledged.

"Since I have to go so I'm not running behind schedule for my shift at Diggers' tonight, why don't you fill me in on Monday morning?"

He nodded. "That works for me."

After a late Friday night at Diggers', Macy usually struggled to drag herself out of bed on Saturday mornings. But knowing that this was her last such morning after her last late night, she was able to greet the day with a little more enthusiasm.

"What are you doing up so early?" Bev asked, when Macy tracked down the triplets—and her mother—in the upstairs kitchen.

Ava, Max and Sam were in their high chairs, set up side-by-side at the table where their grandmother could keep a close eye on them while she fried bacon on the stove.

Sam spotted his mama first, and he gleefully banged his sippy cup on the tray of his high chair. Ava, not to be outdone by her brother, stretched her arms out and called "Ma!" Max just smiled—a sweet, toothless grin that never failed to melt her heart.

"I wanted to get breakfast for Ava, Max and Sam today." And though caffeine was required to ensure that she could function, she paused on her way to the coffee pot to kiss each of her precious babies.

"Because you don't think I can handle it?" her mother queried, transferring the cooked bacon onto paper towels to drain the grease.

"Because you handle it all the time," Macy clarified, reaching into the cupboard for a mug that she filled from the carafe.

After a couple of sips, she found the box of baby oatmeal cereal in the pantry. She spooned the dry mix into each of three bowls, then stirred in the requisite amount of formula. Ava, Max and Sam avidly watched her every move.

"You guys look like you're hungry," Macy noted, as she peeled a ripe banana and cut it into thirds. She dropped a piece of fruit into each of the bowls and mashed it into the cereal.

"Ma!" Ava said again, because it wasn't just her first but also her only word.

She chuckled softly as she continued to mash and stir.

"While you're taking care of that, I'll make pancakes for us," Bev said, as she gathered the necessary ingredients together.

Macy had given up asking her mother not to cook for her, because the protests had fallen on deaf ears—and because it was a nice treat to have a hot breakfast prepared for her on a Saturday morning. Especially pancakes.

"You always made pancakes as part of a celebration," she noted, with a smile. "Whether it was a birthday or a clean room or an 'A' on a spelling test."

"Which is why you got them more often than your brothers," her mother remarked, as she cracked eggs into a glass bowl.

It wasn't true, of course. If Bev made pancakes, the whole family got to eat pancakes, but she always acknowledged when one of her kids did something special to warrant a breakfast celebration.

"Well, we've got something to celebrate today, too," Macy said.

Her mother looked up from the batter she was whisking. "You got the job?"

Macy grinned and nodded. "You are looking at the new manager-slash-concierge of the Stagecoach Inn."

Bev set down the whisk to hug her daughter. "Oh, honey, I'm so proud of you."

"I'll work Monday through Friday for the next few weeks, and then, when the hotel is open, Wednesday through Sunday, eight a.m. until two p.m."

"That's perfect," her mom said. "You'll have more time with your kids and be able to work at a job you enjoy."

Macy carried the bowls of oatmeal to the table. "I'm already looking forward to getting started," she confided. "This is exactly what I've always wanted."

Her mother sprinkled a few drops of water on the griddle, testing its readiness. "Except that it's in Haven," she pointed out.

Macy scooped up some oatmeal and moved the

spoon toward Max's open mouth. "You don't want me to stay in Haven?"

"Of course, *I* want you here," Bev said, ladling batter onto the hot pan. "But I know that was never your first choice."

"Where are you getting that from?" Macy shifted her attention to the next bowl, but she was sincerely baffled by the statement.

"Maybe the fact that you were on your way out of town practically before the ink was dry on your high school diploma."

Macy used the spoon to catch the cereal that Sam pushed out of his mouth with his tongue. "I graduated in June and I moved in August—three days before the start of classes at UNLV."

"Well, you've hardly been home since," her mom remarked.

"I came home every chance I got, which wasn't a lot because I was juggling two part-time jobs along with my studies." Ava swallowed her first mouthful of cereal, and Macy gave her a second before making her way backwards down the line again.

"We could have helped you a little more," Bev said.

"You offered," Macy assured her. "But the experience of those jobs was even more valuable than the paycheck."

"I know you've always wanted to work in the hospitality industry—ever since we visited your aunt at The Gatestone in Washington when you were a little girl," her mother noted, as she began to turn the pancakes. "And, of course, the best career opportunities are probably in Las Vegas."

"There were *zero* career opportunities for me in

Haven when I left," Macy pointed out, as she continued to feed her babies. "The only place around that offered any kind of temporary accommodations was the Dusty Boots Motel, and they weren't hiring.

"I came back to Haven because I knew I couldn't handle—or afford to raise—three kids on my own in Vegas. Maybe I was a little disappointed to give up my career, but I was happy to be home and happier still to know that my babies would grow up close to their extended family.

"I might not have envisioned an arrangement quite this close," she said. "But it works. And if I haven't mentioned it lately, I'm incredibly grateful to you and Dad for everything you've done for all of us."

"You tell us every day," Bev said. "And we're happy to help."

"Still, I should probably look into making other arrangements for part-time childcare, don't you think?"

"What?" Her mom turned around so fast, the pancake on her spatula dropped to the floor. "Why?"

Macy got up to retrieve the broken cake and toss it into the sink. "Because I feel as if I'm taking advantage of you and Dad."

"That's ridiculous," Bev said. "Your father and I aren't doing anything that we don't want to do."

"You're also not doing things that you *would* like to do," Macy pointed out. "Like last Saturday, when Dad had to cancel his fishing trip with Oscar Weston because I was working a double shift and you were in bed with a migraine."

"Well, he's fishing with Oscar today."

"And you gave up your pottery classes because I worked almost every Wednesday night."

"I was happy to have an excuse to quit—I couldn't ever make a lump of clay look like anything else."

"I don't believe it." Macy scraped the last of the cereal from the bottom of Ava's bowl. "But I appreciate you saying so."

"And since you won't be working nights anymore, I can join Frieda's book club."

She wiped Ava's mouth with her bib, then offered the little girl her sippy cup of juice. "Mrs. Zimmerman has a book club?"

Her mother nodded. "She started it last summer, after she saw the movie."

"*The* movie?" Macy echoed, because she was pretty sure that the local movie theater would have shown more than one movie the previous summer.

"*Book Club.*"

"Ahh, that makes sense," she said, helping Max finish his breakfast.

Bev stacked three pancakes on a plate, added four strips of bacon, then set it on the table. "Eat while it's hot," she instructed her daughter.

Macy picked up a slice of crisp bacon, nipped off the end. "I'm glad the pediatrician finally approved the introduction of solid foods for Ava, Max and Sam," she said, pouring maple syrup over her pancakes. "They're definitely sleeping for longer stretches now and waking up happier."

"You're grumpy, too, when you're hungry," her mom noted, bringing her own plate and mug to the table to eat with her daughter.

"Is that why you always have breakfast ready for me when I get up on a Saturday morning?"

"One of the reasons," Bev acknowledged. "Another is that I really do enjoy having someone to cook for."

"You cook for Dad," she pointed out.

"Bacon and eggs. That's what it's been every Saturday morning for forty years."

"That doesn't mean *you* have to eat bacon and eggs."

Her mother shrugged. "It seems like too much bother to make something different just for myself, but it's a pleasure to make it for you."

"Maybe I'll make breakfast for you tomorrow," Macy offered impulsively.

"You've got enough to do with three babies without worrying about cooking for anyone else," Bev protested. "Plus, you've got to get ready for your first day at your new job on Monday."

"There's nothing to get ready for. And you managed to raise three kids and put meals on the table while also working outside the home."

"My kids weren't all in diapers at the same time."

"On the plus side, they'll hopefully all be out of diapers around the same time," she said.

"There is that," her mom agreed.

Macy glanced over at Sam, who'd started banging his cup on his tray again to get her attention. When he had her attention, he smiled.

"What's that in your mouth, Sam?" She pulled his high chair closer to the table for a better look. "Have you got a tooth in there?"

He grinned again, giving her another glimpse of a tiny white bud barely poking through a red and swollen gum.

Macy felt her eyes sting. "My youngest baby has his first tooth."

"It had to come sooner or later," her mother pointed out with unerring logic.

"I know," she agreed, as she lifted a hand to ruffle his wispy curls. "But he's been miserable for so long, I was starting to wonder."

She turned her attention to his brother, gnawing on the spout of his cup, drool dripping down his chin. "What about you, Max? Do you have a smile for Mommy?"

He did, of course, but he had no new teeth—or any teeth at all—to show off to her.

"Yours will come," she promised. "Probably just another day or two."

"Don't be in a hurry for them to grow up," Bev cautioned her daughter. "I know it seems like they're making slow progress now, but before you know it, your babies will have babies of their own."

Macy was up early Monday morning, because today she had something to look forward to besides feeding her babies their breakfast.

She was excited about starting her new job at the Stagecoach Inn. Although the boutique hotel wasn't scheduled to open for another two weeks, she knew there would be a lot of last-minute details to take care of in advance of the big event, and she was happy to help. Liam had agreed that 8 a.m. was an acceptable time for her to start, but she was there by 7:30. In fact, she pulled into the parking lot beside the inn at the same time as her boss.

"You're early," he noted, as he fell into step beside her.

"I've got three babies who are up by five every morning," she confided. "Plus I'm eager to hear all about your plans for this place."

"Compared to Las Vegas, they're not very grand," he warned.

"Since this isn't Vegas, it would be silly to make such a comparison. And while Haven isn't ever likely to be a tourist mecca, there are people who visit Nevada for reasons other than gambling and quickie weddings," she noted.

"And weddings are really just a different kind of gambling, aren't they?" he remarked.

Her brows lifted. "Spoken like a man who has some experience in the matter."

"Just one close call," he said, as he slid his key into the lock of the front door.

Not wanting to pursue what she sensed was a touchy subject, she instead shifted the direction of their conversation. "When I was growing up in Haven, no one locked their doors."

"A lot of people still don't," he told her. "And with this property being centrally located, I'm not really worried about theft or vandalism, but I don't want people sneaking in after hours to nose around.

"There will be pictures on the website, of course, but I'm hoping that residents who are curious enough to want an up close and personal look at the rooms will book a stay."

"You'll get some of those," she assured him. "And when they tell their friends what an amazing job you've done with the renovations, you'll get more."

"Fingers crossed."

She grinned. "You don't need luck when you've got a fabulous property and a savvy manager."

* * *

Macy threw herself into assisting with the preparations for the opening, willing to tackle any task Liam assigned to her. She also seemed determined to make him buy more stuff.

When he'd given her the tour, he'd thought the rooms were ready for the arrival of guests. But while Macy approved of the furnishings and linens, she thought there should be a ladder shelf in the corner of one room, perhaps a quilt rack in another room, a fabric bench at the foot of this bed, more pillows on those window seats.

He balked at her suggestions, reluctant to spend more money on a property that wasn't yet generating any income.

"Let me show you," she urged, and dragged him out to the antique and craft market.

Her first find was a wooden wash-basin stand with ceramic pitcher and bowl and a swivel vanity mirror.

"This will fit perfectly in that empty corner in the Charles Goodnight Suite," she told him.

Aside from the fact that he didn't believe every corner needed to be filled, he had to ask, "Isn't one of the benefits of having running water the ability to turn on the tap to access that running water?"

"Your point?" she challenged.

"In the era of indoor plumbing, an antique wash-basin set has no practical purpose."

"In the beginning, you're going to draw guests for one primary reason," she explained, in the same patient tone he imagined she'd use to reason with a stubborn child. "Either they're visiting Haven or just passing through town and looking for a place to sleep that has a little more ambience than the Dusty Boots Motel.

Sure, you'll get some locals booking a room or suite for a night, to celebrate a special occasion or score points with a special someone. But for the most part, your early guests will show up more by accident than design."

"So far this explanation is doing nothing to convince me that I need to fork over—" he looked at the tag affixed to the back of the mirror and winced "—a lot of money that is unlikely to give me any kind of return on my investment."

"But it will," she insisted. "Because it's part of your brand. And I know you know what I'm talking about— it's why you invested in quality furniture and pillow-top mattresses over cheap laminate and economy sleep sets."

He did know what she was talking about. In his business courses at college, they'd discussed image and branding as a way of making a company or product stand out from the rest. And as she'd noted, he'd already distinguished his property from the Dusty Boots Motel, which represented the total sum of the rest of the over-night accommodations available in town.

"So why do you think this other stuff is necessary?" he asked her.

"Because there aren't enough people just passing through town to keep you in business. You need to make the Stagecoach Inn a destination—not just a place for guests to lay their heads on their way to somewhere else, but a place they want to come to and stay at."

"And a wash basin and pitcher are going to do that?" he asked dubiously.

"It's the details that make a lasting impression. It's the reason guests post online reviews to share their experiences with other potential guests. Almost better

than reviews are the pictures. And people don't take pictures of empty corners—they take pictures of antique wash stands and Arts and Crafts andirons."

"Andirons?" he echoed.

"We'll get to those next," she promised. "The point is, you don't want to give your guests a room, you want to provide them with an experience. One that they'll want to enjoy again and again and tell their friends and family about, enticing those friends and family to book a room—no, an experience," she immediately corrected herself. "To see for themselves what all the fuss is about.

"Which leads me to another idea I wanted to discuss with you."

"How much is it going to cost me?" he wondered aloud.

She ignored his question. "Spa packages."

"The spa isn't really part of the hotel."

"I know. I was talking to Andria yesterday," she said, naming the woman who owned and operated Serenity Spa. "And I won't tell you that you missed out on a terrific opportunity there, but I will suggest that you could partner with her to offer special rates and packages for guests of the hotel.

"There could be a separate page on the website," she said. "The word *indulge* in a flowy script at the top of a page, maybe with an image of a woman wrapped in a plush robe, her feet in a warm bath. Or a man facedown on a massage table with a woman's hands sliding over his strongly muscled back. Or both. And the copy could read something like—pamper your body and your soul, from head to toe, with a unique package of exclusive services offered by Serenity Spa at the Stagecoach Inn."

He could picture it, exactly as she described, and he

couldn't deny the appeal. "You really are good at this," he acknowledged.

"Told you." Her smile was more than a little enticing.

And if she'd been anyone else—not an employee and not a single mom—he might have lowered his head to taste those sweetly curved lips.

But she wasn't anyone else. She was the manager of the inn, and he had to respect that professional relationship and keep his hands off.

She also had three babies at home, a fact that should have destroyed the last vestiges of temptation. But when he was with Macy, it was an effort to remember all the reasons he shouldn't be attracted to her. Because he couldn't deny that he was.

She, however, gave absolutely no indication that she felt the same way, and he knew that was probably for the best. His unrequited attraction might be the cause of physical frustration, but at least it wasn't going to lead to a broken heart.

While he was mulling over these thoughts, she was chatting with the vendor. Haggling over the price on the tag, he realized, but in such a way that the seller looked pleased to be able to negotiate a sale with her. She waved as she walked away, with a smile on her face and his business card in hand, and Liam following with the much more cumbersome wash-basin stand.

"And now the andirons," she said.

He just sighed. "Can I put this in the truck first?"

She nodded. "That's probably a good idea."

Liam had never been a fan of shopping, but he couldn't deny that he had fun exploring the market with Macy. And the happiness that lit up her face whenever she spotted what she referred to as a hidden gem was almost worth the price of the trio of brass oil lamps she talked him into buying.

And when they got back to the inn and she'd arranged his purchases as she'd envisioned them, he couldn't deny that she had a good eye.

Actually, she had gorgeous eyes. Deep and clear and dark.

And a temptingly shaped mouth with a sexy dip at the center.

And he really needed to stop focusing on all the parts that appealed to him and remember that she was off-limits.

On Wednesday morning during her second week on the job, he got a pointed reminder when he found her in the kitchen, arranging spices and seasonings. She moved with her usual brisk efficiency, but he noticed that she was wearing something a little different than her usual business casual attire.

"Is that part of the uniform in Vegas?" he asked, gesturing to the baby carrier strapped to her body.

"So much for thinking you wouldn't notice," she remarked. "But a stylish accessory, don't you agree?"

He eyed the contraption dubiously as he took a few steps closer to peek at the baby snuggled up against her mother's chest. "Cute kid," he noted.

She smiled. "This is Ava."

"Eight months?" He seemed to recall that was a number she'd mentioned.

"Eight months, two weeks and four days now," she clarified. "I hope you don't mind that I brought her with me, but my mom had an appointment this afternoon and my dad would struggle on his own with three babies."

"I don't mind," he said.

In fact, he was kind of glad she'd brought Ava with her today, because the more time he'd spent with Macy over the past several days, the harder it had been to remember all the reasons she wasn't his type. Now one of those three reasons was strapped to her chest, and he refused to acknowledge that he found the sight of his new manager and her infant daughter at all appealing.

But the baby really was a cutie, with her adorably chubby cheeks, little button nose and big blue eyes fringed with ridiculously long lashes. She was also surprisingly content to be hauled around in the carrier, those big eyes taking in every detail of her surroundings.

When she shoved her fist into her mouth and began sucking on her knuckles, Macy took a bottle out of the fridge. She didn't miss a beat in her telephone conversation but switched the phone to speaker mode and set it on the counter so that her hands were free to unhook the carrier and lift out the baby.

She expertly cradled her child in the crook of one arm, and Ava's little hands helped hold the bottle as her mouth worked the nipple. Liam was so preoccupied watching the baby that he didn't realize Macy was wrapping up the call until she pressed a button to terminate the connection.

"Fifteen percent," she said.

"What?"

"That was your dinnerware supplier. He'll be emailing you a revised invoice with the amount due reduced by fifteen percent."

"I'm impressed."

She smiled. "Impressed enough to add a fifteen percent bonus to my paycheck?"

"Not this week," he said. "But we'll discuss your salary at your performance review after six months."

"You're going to give me a raise," she said confidently.

He didn't doubt it was true. If he'd learned nothing else during their trip to the antique and craft market, he'd learned that his new manager knew how to get what she wanted.

She gently pried the nipple of the now-empty bottle from her daughter's mouth, then lifted her to her shoulder and rubbed her back. The baby emitted a shockingly loud burp for such a little thing, then yawned hugely and closed her eyes.

"She'll sleep now for at least an hour," Macy told him. "Is it okay if I put her down in the library for her nap while I meet with the wine merchant?"

She'd set up the baby's playpen in that room earlier, so he knew she was informing him as a courtesy more than asking permission, but he nodded anyway.

While she was in her meeting, he signed for a delivery and carted the boxes from the bookstore into the library. Four boxes of books—and each one weighed as much as a sack of grain.

He'd just torn open the flaps on the first box when Ava woke up.

She didn't make any sound at first. It was the movement he noticed, as she rolled herself over from her back to her belly. She lifted her head, a happy smile on her face as she looked up, no doubt expecting to see her mama—and finding a strange man instead.

The smile disappeared, and her big blue eyes filled with distress.

Chapter 5

Macy lost track of time while she was with the local wine merchant, selecting options for the daily wine and cheese hour Liam had proposed and negotiating quantities and prices. When she finally signed the order and glanced at her watch, she hurried to the library and her daughter.

Any concerns she'd harbored about momnesia interfering with her job performance had, so far, proven to be unfounded. In fact, with each day that passed, she felt more and more confident in her role.

And increasingly unnerved by the unexpected—and unwanted—attraction to her boss.

The revelation that she had three infants seemed to have effectively killed any romantic interest on his part, for which she knew she should be grateful. Instead, being in close proximity to the sexy cowboy-turned-innkeeper only made her feel churned up.

And that was before she stopped in the doorway of the library and saw him cuddling her baby girl in his arms.

"You really are just a little bitty thing, aren't you?" he mused aloud. "Of course, you're a few months younger than Tessa, but I don't think my niece was ever such a lightweight."

Ava's gaze was focused on his face, as if trying to decide if he was a friend or foe. She didn't have a lot of experience with strangers, and the furrow in her tiny brow along with the quiver of her lower lip warned Macy that the little girl was close to tears.

She started to take another step forward but paused when Liam spoke again, obviously reading the same signals and wanting to soothe the baby's distress.

"I know I'm not your mama," he said. "But your mama's busy right now, so we're just going to hang together until she finishes her meeting. She shouldn't be too much longer, and if you give me a chance, you might discover that I'm not such a bad guy, really.

"And when I say 'give me a chance,' I mean no crying, okay? Because I'm at a complete loss when it comes to tears."

What was it about a strong man showing his gentle side that arrowed directly to her heart? Macy wondered.

Or was it specifically this man?

Or maybe the fact that her baby was the beneficiary of the tender demonstration?

Regardless of the rationale, she suddenly realized that she was in trouble.

Prior to this exact moment, she'd been so focused on her excitement over the job that she hadn't let herself worry that working in close proximity to a sexy man would be a problem.

Obviously she'd been wrong.

"Some people might say I'm clueless about a lot of things when it comes to women," Liam continued his confession. "And they'd be right, but tears are probably my biggest weakness. Thankfully you're too young to understand what I'm saying—so this will be our little secret, okay?"

"My lips are sealed," Macy promised.

Liam started and turned toward the doorway, then spoke to Ava again, "See? I said your mama wouldn't be too long."

The baby squirmed in his arms, stretching her own out toward her mother.

"Your books were delivered," Liam said, as Macy took Ava from him. "And when I came in to unpack the shipment, I discovered that she was awake. I hope you don't mind that I picked her up. She seemed to be looking for you, and getting distressed when she couldn't find you, so I tried to distract her."

"Of course I don't mind," she said. "I'm grateful you were here." She patted Ava's bottom, then reached for the tote bag beside the playpen. "But I do wonder—if my meeting had gone five minutes longer, would she be wearing a clean diaper?"

"Not likely," he said.

She laughed softly. "At least you're honest."

"I've found that's the best way to eliminate misunderstandings."

"In which case—" she unfolded the portable change pad and laid Ava on top of it "—there's something I should tell you."

"What's that?" he asked, wariness evident in his tone.

"This probably won't be the last time I have to bring one or more of my kids to work with me."

"You don't have an unsuspecting brother you could leave them with?" he asked dryly.

She smiled as she unsnapped Ava's pants. "Actually, I have two brothers, but neither of them lives in town."

"I was only joking, anyway," he assured her. "I've grown to appreciate the juggling act that is required of a working mom, and I don't have a problem with you bringing your kids to work on occasion. But if I have a choice, I don't do diapers."

"I'll keep that in mind," she promised, sliding a dry one under her daughter's bottom.

"And since you're busy with that…do you want me to shelve these books? Or will you just rearrange everything when I'm done?"

"Can you group them by genre then alphabetize them by author?"

"I can take them out of the box and put them on the shelves."

She shook her head as she refastened the snaps on Ava's pants. "I'll do it."

And she'd be grateful for a task that required her focus and attention, keeping her mind busy so it wouldn't spin any romantic fairy tales about handsome cowboys and single moms and sweet babies.

"Okay," Liam agreed readily. "I was planning to head out to the Circle G after the staff meeting to show my grandparents the new brochures this afternoon, anyway."

While they were at the antique and craft market, he'd confided that his grandparents had helped him with the down payment on the property, allowing him to move ahead with his plan to purchase the Stagecoach Inn.

But it was the first part of his statement that snagged her attention. "Staff meeting?"

"'Meeting' sounds more official than 'greeting,'" he explained. "But it really is just a chance for the employees to get acquainted with one another."

The total number of employees was six—including Liam and Macy. Rose was a part-time desk clerk who would be called upon to fill any gaps in the schedule, Camille would help out with the housekeeping on weekends, Emily would cook breakfast for the inn's guests and her grandson Nathan would serve it. Macy was pleased that Liam had thought to bring them together to make the introductions and, after that was done, she was looking forward to working with all of them.

"How was work today?" Beverly asked, when Macy sat down for dinner with her parents later that day. "Did you manage okay with Ava?"

"Ava wasn't a problem at all," she said. "And work was good. Of course, the inn isn't officially open yet, but I've loved helping with all the little details. Folding sheets and fluffing pillows, cutting flower stems and arranging decorative soaps. With every task, I feel more invested in the inn and its success."

"You always did love playing house as a kid," Norm recalled. "You would push that pretend vacuum around with one hand, carrying a doll in the other."

"Multitasking," she said.

"Fake multitasking," her mother pointed out. "You were never as eager to push around a real vacuum."

"I learned, though," Macy said. "I vacuumed more

guest rooms than I could count when I worked in house-keeping."

"And now you're the manager of Haven's own up-scale hotel," Bev said proudly.

"Which sounds good but doesn't get me out of folding sheets and fluffing pillows."

"I've thought about stopping by, to sneak a peek into one of those fancy guest rooms," her mother confided.

"You should do more than sneak a peek," Macy said. "You and Dad should spend a couple of nights."

"Why would I pay to sleep in a hotel less than five miles away from the perfectly good bed I have here?" Norm wanted to know.

"You wouldn't have to pay—it would be my treat," Macy said, knowing it was the least she could do to thank her parents for everything they'd done for her. "As for the why…it might add a little romance to your marriage."

Her father scoffed at the notion. "I don't think we need to be taking romantic advice from our unmarried daughter."

He was teasing, of course, but it still stung when the barb struck home.

Because her dad was right—compared to her parents, who had been married for almost forty-one years, Macy knew less than nothing about romance. And when she'd become disillusioned with the whole dating scene, she'd given up hope of ever finding love.

Except that wasn't really true. Even while she'd moved forward with her plan to have a baby, she hadn't completely written off the possibility that she might someday meet a special someone. A man whose eyes would meet hers across a crowded room and be drawn to close that distance by the instant sparks he felt. Then they'd meet and they'd talk, they'd kiss and fall in love, and he'd love her baby, too, and want nothing more than to marry her so they could be together forever—a family.

It was, admittedly, a romantic dream.

When she'd realized she was going to have three babies, that romantic dream shot straight into the realm of fantasy.

Because only in the pages of a novel could she imagine a man wanting to take on the responsibility of three kids who weren't his own.

"This was not a good idea," Macy muttered, as she juggled the baby while rifling through the diaper bag for the tube of homeopathic teething gel she was certain she'd tucked inside—to no avail.

Sam continued to cry, deep, wracking sobs that shook his whole body. She offered a teething ring, which he immediately threw to the ground.

"I'm sorry," she said. "But I can't give you what's not here."

He wailed louder.

"Shh." She jiggled him gently, swaying and swirling, trying to take his mind off his obvious distress. "It's going to be okay, I promise. But you need to pipe down a little so that Mama's boss doesn't fire her."

"Do you really think your boss would be that callous?" Liam asked.

"No," she said, turning to face him. "But I think he'd be justified in feeling irritated that there's a screaming baby in the lobby of his fancy hotel."

"A fancy hotel that is, at the moment, empty of guests

who might complain about the screaming baby." He took a few steps closer to peer at the infant in her arms. "Who's this big guy?"

Sam looked back at Liam through tear-drenched eyes, then he drew in a deep, shuddery breath and stretched his arms out.

"Benedict Arnold," Macy muttered.

Liam chuckled. "Do you want me to hold him while you pack all that stuff back up?"

"Please," she said, and willingly passed him the baby.

Sam sniffled...then offered his new friend a droolly smile as Macy began to shove diapers and toys and various paraphernalia into the bag.

"I didn't think there existed, anywhere in the world, a diaper bag bigger than the one my sister hauls around," he noted. "But I think hers would fit inside of yours."

"I have three babies," she reminded him, then shook her head as she looked at the one currently snuggled contentedly in her boss's arms. "And that one was crying for forty minutes before you showed up. Nothing I said or did would make him stop. Now suddenly he's all smiles and cuddles."

"Kate says that babies sense when their mothers are stressed," he said. "And that mothers with babies are almost always stressed."

"I won't argue with that," Macy told him. "And I promise, this won't be a regular occurrence, but my mom was going to Battle Mountain with Frieda Zimmerman today and, as great as my dad is with his grandbabies, I couldn't leave all three of them with him for the whole day."

"Is Frieda having her surgery today?"

She shouldn't have been surprised by the question.

After all, this was Haven, where everyone knew everyone else's business, and her mother's best friend hadn't been shy about telling people that she was having a double mastectomy—a preventative measure after two of her sisters were diagnosed with breast cancer in the past year.

Macy nodded.

"Well, there's nothing urgent happening here today, if you want to take Ben home."

"Sam," she corrected automatically, then smiled when she realized that he'd derived the name from her comment about her traitorous son—whose gaze was riveted on the face of the man who was holding him. "And it might not be urgent, but I'm meeting with Emily to go over the breakfast menus."

"Breakfast menus?" Liam echoed blankly.

"We talked about this yesterday."

"When?"

"First thing in the morning. You did seem a little distracted," she noted. "But when I suggested that cook-to-order breakfasts had more appeal than a buffet—and would result in less waste—you said you'd defer to my expertise."

"I was distracted," he acknowledged. "My dad refuses to listen to anything I say about the ranch, because obviously I don't care enough about the ranch to stick around and help run it."

"And yet, you're there every morning," she remarked.

"Ranching isn't a part-time job," he said, in what she suspected was an echo of words his father had spoken to him.

"Neither is owning and operating a hotel," she pointed out.

"Or parenthood," he commented, as Sam dropped his head down on Liam's shoulder.

Macy felt her heart swell inside her chest as she watched her baby curl his hand into a fist and lift his thumb to his mouth, totally content and secure in the cowboy's arms. "You know, you're much better with kids than you think you are."

"So it would seem," he agreed.

"Sam doesn't usually take to strangers."

"Well, maybe I'm not as strange as you think I am."

She smiled at that. "Actually, I think you're pretty great. If you could keep an eye on Sam while I meet with Emily, I'd bump 'pretty great' up to 'awesome.'"

For the first few months after her babies were born, Macy stuck close to home. Worried about their premature immune systems, she'd tried to shield them—as much as possible—from the potentially hazardous germs carried by those who might want to pinch their cheeks or tickle their toes.

Maybe she was a little paranoid, but she'd seen how people gravitated toward babies. Twins drew twice as much attention, and triplets—adorable times three—were an even bigger draw.

She got a little braver after Ava, Max and Sam had had their six-month immunizations. She'd even taken them to the mall in Battle Mountain to see Santa before Christmas, though she'd questioned the wisdom of that decision the whole time they'd waited in line with countless runny-nosed kids and likely would have bolted if her mother hadn't been there to stop her.

Now she was more willing to venture out with them, but their outings were restricted to venues that could be navigated with the triple tandem stroller. The Trading Post was one of those places—if she was picking up a limited number of items that would fit in the basket beneath the stroller. For a major shopping excursion, she usually took only one of her babies.

This week, it was Max's turn to go, but her sweet baby boy had woken up with a bit of a fever, so she let him stay home under the watchful eyes of his grandparents and took Ava instead. Her little girl already thought herself a princess and accepted it as her due when strangers oohed and ahhed over her.

On her way to the grocery store, Macy popped in to Diggers' to say "hi" to her former boss. After a brief visit that included lots of fussing over Ava, she headed out—just as Liam and an older woman were on their way in.

He introduced his companion as his grandmother, Evelyn Gilmore, and Macy and Ava as his innkeeper and her adorable baby girl.

"I've been meaning to stop by the inn to meet you," Evelyn said, shaking Macy's hand warmly.

"Now you don't have to," Liam told her.

"My grandson doesn't like me poking around in his business," Evelyn confided to Macy.

"Because my grandmother has trouble with the *silent* part of our silent partnership," he said.

The older woman waved a hand, dismissing his comment. "Have you had your lunch already?" she asked Macy.

"No, we just stopped in to see Duke for a minute on our way to the Trading Post."

"Then you can join us," Evelyn decided.

"Thanks, but we really need to get to the store—"

"The store will still be there after you've had a bite to eat," Evelyn said reasonably. "Besides, I want to talk to you about The Home Station."

Macy sent a quizzical glance in Liam's direction.

"That's the name Grams has chosen for the restaurant we don't have," he explained.

"Yet," Evelyn clarified.

And that was how Macy ended up having lunch with her boss and his grandmother—and Ava ended up wrapping another new acquaintance around her tiny finger.

As opening day drew nearer, Liam had to admit that hiring Macy Clayton was the smartest decision he could have made for the business—even when she brought one or more of her kids in to work with her. Truthfully, he didn't mind having the babies around and was sometimes disappointed when she showed up alone.

He'd thought the little ones would act as a buffer between them, but the more time he spent with her, the more his attraction continued to grow. However, she gave him no reason to suspect that his feelings might be reciprocated—until the day before Valentine's Day, when they were doing a final check in preparation of the grand opening.

"Tomorrow's the big day," she said, practically bubbling with enthusiasm.

"So it is," he agreed, unwilling to admit that he was probably more apprehensive than he was excited. The family and friends who'd stopped by over the past few weeks had raved about everything, so he had no concerns about the adequacy of the accommodations. And he'd taken Macy's suggestion and partnered with the spa to offer special weekend packages, but he still worried that no one would show up.

"Another two reservations came in today," Macy said, and that information eased a little of his worry.

"How many is that now?" He asked her because he knew she'd be able to answer the question more quickly than he could look it up in the reservation system.

"Five," she immediately replied. "Two rooms are booked for single nights, but three more are occupied through the weekend."

"Out-of-towners?" he guessed.

She nodded.

"I can't imagine how they're going to keep busy for three days and two nights."

"They're in town for a company retreat, participating in team-building exercises at Adventure Village," she told him, naming the local family-friendly activity center that was primarily responsible for the modest rise of tourism in the northern Nevada town.

"Team building exercises?" he echoed dubiously. "Is that really a thing?"

"A very popular thing," she assured him.

"Who would've guessed?"

"Anyone who picked up one of the brochures in the rack by the front desk," she told him.

"You were right," he admitted. "The rack was a good idea. Partnering with local businesses was a good idea."

"The partnerships were a *great* idea," she amended.

But it had been an uphill battle to convince Liam of the benefits of working with Jason Channing, the owner and operator of Adventure Village. Because Jason's mother was a Blake, and the Gilmore–Blake feud was deeply entrenched in Haven's history, dating back to the settlement of the area more than a hundred and fifty years earlier. Both Everett Gilmore and Samuel Blake had been sold deeds for the same parcel of land and, unwilling to admit that they'd been duped, they decided to split the property down the middle.

As Everett Gilmore had arrived first and already started to build his homestead on the west side of the river, he got the prime grazing land for his cattle, leaving Samuel Blake with the less hospitable terrain on the east side. While the Circle G grew into one of the most prosperous cattle ranches in the whole state, the Crooked Creek Ranch struggled for a lot of years—until gold and silver were discovered in the hills. But the change in their fortunes did not change the bad blood between the families.

"And don't you think it's long past time the Blake–Gilmore Feud was put to rest?" she asked him.

"It's hardly up to me," Liam said.

"Well, I'm glad you and Jason were able to overlook the history between your families for the benefit of both of your businesses."

"Did I have a choice?" he asked.

His dry tone made her smile. "You made your choice when you hired me."

"Probably the smartest decision I've made since buying this building," he said.

Grateful for his comment—and the job she already loved—she impulsively hugged him. "Thank you."

The gesture was intended as a simple and sincere expression of appreciation. The heat generated by the contact between their bodies was *un*intended and *un*expected. And undeniably arousing.

His arms went around her, as if to prevent her retreat.

And though she knew she should draw away, she didn't want to. She didn't want to continue pretending she was unaware of the chemistry that hummed between them. She didn't want to ignore her growing feelings for him.

So instead of drawing away, she pressed closer and lifted her mouth to his.

Chapter 6

It was a casual kiss—a whisper from her lips to his, tentative, testing.

Liam's response wasn't at all tentative.

He didn't just kiss her back, he took control of the kiss. One hand traced its way up Macy's spine to cup the back of her head, tipping it back a little more so that he could deepen the kiss. His tongue slid between her lips, stroked the roof of her mouth, making her shiver and yearn.

His scent, clean and masculine, teased her senses. His hands, strong and skilled, tempted her body. His mouth, clever and talented, clouded her mind.

Had her brain not completely clicked off, she might have realized that she was treading on very dangerous ground. But she was no longer capable of rational thought. She could only feel and wish and want.

And she wanted more.

So much more.

He gave her more, kissing her deeply and oh-so-very thoroughly. Only when they were both desperate for breath did he ease his mouth from hers so they could fill their lungs with air. But even then, he continued to hold her close, his forehead tipped against hers.

"This is why I didn't want to hire you," he reminded her. "I knew it would be a struggle to keep my hands off you."

"This was my fault," she said, because it was true. And though she knew she should be ashamed of her actions, she didn't regret kissing him. She only regretted that it was over, because she knew it couldn't happen again. "*I* kissed *you*."

"I wasn't looking to assign blame," he said, sounding amused. "If anything, I'd like to express my appreciation."

"That's what I was trying to do," she admitted.

"And then the chemistry took over."

That chemistry continued to spark and sizzle between them, but she ignored it. Or tried to. She finally pulled out of his arms, putting some much-needed space between them. "It won't happen again."

"Do you really believe that?" he challenged.

The heat in his gaze warmed her all over. "I'm not your type."

"You sure felt like my type when you were in my arms."

"Single mom," she reminded him, gesturing to herself with her thumb. "Three kids. *Babies*."

And that quickly, the heat in his gaze cooled. "Yeah, I guess I shouldn't forget about them, should I?" he asked. "A guy would have to be crazy to get caught up with all that."

His response dashed any tentative hope she might have harbored about a romance developing between them. But it was his blatant disregard of her children—the center of her world—that made her angry.

"And a woman with all that would have to be crazy to get caught up with a guy like you," she retorted.

He held up his hands, a gesture of surrender. "I didn't mean to upset you. It's just that…kids aren't really my thing."

"Yeah, you've made that point quite clear."

And yet, she couldn't help but note that his words were in marked contrast to his actions.

The man who claimed kids weren't his thing was the same man his sister trusted with her little girl when she needed a babysitter on short notice. Of course, family usually stepped up to help family in a pinch.

But he'd stepped up for Ava, too. The day Macy had run late dealing with the wine merchant, he'd been there for her daughter when she'd awakened from her nap. He'd also been there for Sam, when her little guy was distressed by his sore gums. And he hadn't appeared to be the least bit reluctant or uncomfortable in either of those situations. But Macy wasn't going to waste her time trying to figure him out. The whole point of taking this job was to spend more time with her children, who were waiting at home for her right now.

"Good night, Mr. Gilmore," she said, and made a hasty retreat before she said something that might jeopardize her employment.

But her lips tingled all the way home, because the

kiss she'd shared with Liam was, without a doubt, the most amazingly incredible first kiss of her life.

If she'd ever known another man who'd made her feel half as much with a single kiss, she might not have been so eager to mate her eggs with the sperm of Donor 6243. But she hadn't and so she did, and now she had three beautiful babies as a result—and no business kissing a man who wasn't just her boss but who had made it clear that he was absolutely not interested in a relationship with a single mother.

"You better not be here with some kind of lame excuse about why you can't be at the party," Kate said, when Liam stepped into her office a short while later.

He halted in midstride. "Party?" he echoed, as if he had no idea what she might be talking about.

His sister's gaze narrowed. "You better be joking."

He grinned. "I have not forgotten my favorite niece's first birthday party," he assured her. "I even have a present for her."

"Is it wrapped?"

"With a big pink bow on top."

"You had it done at the store, didn't you?"

"Of course," he agreed unapologetically.

Apparently satisfied now that he wasn't trying to get out of attending her daughter's party, Kate turned her attention to other matters. "So why are you here?"

"Because I'm an idiot," he said.

"That's hardly a news bulletin," she remarked.

"But this is," he began. Then, realizing her office door was still open, he pushed it closed before continuing. He trusted that Kate's legal assistant-slash-receptionist understood the concept of client confidentiality, but he still didn't want anyone else to know what he was about to confide to his sister. "I kissed Macy."

"Yep. Idiot," Kate agreed, shaking her head despairingly. "Do you listen to *nothing* I tell you?"

"I always listen," he assured her.

"You just don't heed my advice," she surmised.

"Actually, the truth is that *she* kissed *me*," he told her.

"So you're here to file a sexual harassment suit?"

He scowled at that. "Of course not."

"Then you want me to tell you all the reasons that it was a bad idea to kiss a woman who works for you?" she suggested as an alternative. "In which case, you should have a seat, because I promise you, the list is long."

"I know all the reasons it was a bad idea," he admitted. "Except that it sure seemed like a good idea at the time."

"You are the boss. She is the employee." She spelled out the facts, clearly and concisely. "That's a lawsuit waiting to happen."

"*She* kissed *me*," he said again.

"It doesn't matter."

"You're right," he acknowledged. "I know you're right. But… I think I really like her, Kate."

"No, you don't," she denied. "You want to have sex with her."

"Well, yeah," he agreed.

"Well, you can't," she said. "There are lots of other women in this town who don't work for you. Go have sex with one of them."

"I don't want one of them. I want Macy."

"Lawsuit. Waiting. To. Happen."

"You're so cynical," he chided.

"I'm a lawyer," she reminded him. "That's part of

my job description." Then both her expression and her voice softened. "But I'm also your sister, and I don't want to see you hurt again."

"I don't think you need to worry about that. Macy was none too happy with me when she left."

"Hmm…maybe your technique needs some work?"

"It had nothing to do with the kiss," he assured her. "It was after the kiss—when I told her that I didn't want to get involved with a woman with kids."

"Maybe you're not such an idiot, after all."

"Except that what I feel for Macy, even after only knowing her a few weeks, isn't like anything I've ever felt before," he confided.

She shook her head. "Why can't you fall for a woman who isn't carrying child-sized baggage?"

"Everyone's got baggage," he pointed out.

"It's like kids are your kryptonite."

"You're mixing your metaphors."

"I'm trying to knock some sense into your thick head," she told him. "Do you not remember Isabella?"

"Of course I remember Isabella." And he remembered Simon, the little boy who'd asked Liam to be his dad. But that was before Izzy decided to reconcile with Simon's real father.

"You were devastated when she cut you out of her son's life."

"That was four years ago," he pointed out. "And yeah, it sucked for me, but—"

"It sucked for you?" she echoed in a disbelieving tone. "You were gutted."

She was right. In the years that had passed since, he'd managed to put most of the heartache behind him. But when memories of Simon occasionally surfaced, they were always bittersweet.

Isabella's son had been three years old when she started dating Liam, about six months after separating from her husband. It hadn't taken him long to become attached to the little guy who enjoyed building blocks and piggyback rides. Then Izzy had decided to give her husband—and her marriage—another chance.

Liam had been devasted. He hadn't been in love with Izzy, but he'd fallen hook, line and sinker for her kid. With a little time and distance, he'd come to accept that she'd done the right thing for her child. Nevertheless, he'd vowed that he wouldn't ever set himself up for that kind of heartache again.

So yeah, Macy Clayton, mom of eight-month-old triplets, was definitely not his type.

Because if he let down his guard and fell head over heels for Macy and her three children and then she got back together with their father, it would be three times as devastating.

And that was a chance he wasn't willing to take.

He should have stayed in town.

With the grand opening scheduled for the following day, Liam had any number of reasons not to make the trek out to the Circle G when he left Katelyn's office. He made the trek, anyway.

Three hours later, his extremities were so numb he had to look to be sure they were still attached. After parking the ATV in the garage, he stomped his feet on the hard ground to restore circulation and headed to the barn to feed the horses.

He found them already chowing down, proof that

someone else had taken care of the chore, so Liam moved to the office for the pot of coffee that was always on the warmer. At this time of day, it would undoubtedly be stale, but right now, he only cared that it was hot.

"Where've you been?" Caleb demanded, when Liam walked through the door of the enclosed space.

David was there, too, inputting some data into the computer, but he said nothing to acknowledge the appearance of his eldest son.

Liam shoved his gloves into the pockets of his jacket and reached for a mug. "Up in the northeast pasture, retrieving a lost steer."

That got his father's attention—and earned a frown. "One of ours?"

"According to the brand on his flank," Liam said.

"How the hell did one of ours get away from the herd and all the way out to the northeast pasture?" Caleb wondered aloud.

Liam shrugged, because the how didn't matter as much as the fact that the steer had got away—and been brought back home again.

David shook his head. "Some things will do anything to escape a life they don't want."

Caleb snorted. "I doubt the stupid steer was—oh." His gaze shifted between his dad and his brother. "You weren't really talking about the cow," he realized. "And now that the horses have been fed, I'm going to head up to the house to see if our dinner's ready."

When his brother had gone, Liam turned to his father. "Do you have something you want to say to me?"

"It seems that I do," David acknowledged.

Liam folded his arms over his chest. "Go ahead and say it then."

"You should know better than to ride that far out on your own and without telling anyone where you're going."

And for just a second, Liam thought his dad was worried about him.

David's follow-up remark quickly disabused him of that notion. "The last thing I need is to send out more men and horses on a rescue mission because you did something foolish."

"I took an ATV and Wade knew where I was," Liam said, naming the ranch's foreman. "He was going to ride out himself, but I said I'd go because his wife's just getting over the flu and he wanted to get home to check on her."

"Well, alright, then," David said.

"That's it?"

His father shrugged his broad shoulders. "What more do you want me to say?"

"I don't know—maybe thanks for showing the initiative and retrieving valuable stock."

"A rancher doesn't do his job for thanks—he does it because ranching is in his blood."

"And that brings us full circle now, doesn't it?"

"I guess it does," David agreed. "And I guess, since you're supposedly a hotelier now, I should say 'thanks.'"

Liam sipped the hot, bitter coffee. "As you've pointed out on numerous occasions, you don't need me around here. So why are you so opposed to me having a life and a career away from the ranch?"

"Because you're running away."

"If I was running away, I would have gone farther than town," he pointed out.

"Are the snow drifts deep in Horseshoe Valley?"

Liam puzzled over the abrupt shift in topic as he lifted his mug to his lips again. "I didn't go through the valley," he admitted. "I followed the western boundary."

"Would've been quicker to go through the valley."

"Maybe," he allowed.

"No maybe about it," David said. "But you ride around the valley rather than through it whenever you can, don't you?"

It was true, though Liam hadn't realized it himself until just now. Because the valley was where his mother had been riding the day she was thrown from her horse. She'd broken her neck as a result of the fall and died a few hours later. "I got where I needed to be to bring back the damn steer, didn't I?"

His father nodded. "But until you deal with your grief, you're always going to be running."

"Thanks for your concern, but it's seventeen years too late."

"You're right. I didn't do anything to help you and your brother and sisters at the time, because I was grieving, too."

"I know," Liam said, not unsympathetically.

"And it took me a long time to realize it, but I understand now that that's when and why you started to hate the ranch."

"I don't hate the ranch," he denied.

"That's good," David said. "Because your mother loved it. And she loved to ride. And though she would never have chosen to leave her kids without a mother,

I've found some solace in the fact that she died doing something that she loved."

"That's great for you," Liam said.

David shut down the computer and pushed his chair away from the desk. "We should head up to the house. Martina will be eager to get dinner on the table."

"Actually, I'm going to go back into town tonight," Liam decided.

His father frowned. "Why?"

"The grand opening's tomorrow, and I need to do a final check to ensure everything's in place."

"You should have something to eat first."

Liam knew the words were the verbal equivalent of an olive branch, but there were too many emotions churning inside him right now to allow him to take it. "I've got food at the inn."

David shrugged. "Your call."

"You could stop by tomorrow," he suggested. "See what all the fuss is about."

"I've got enough fuss here to worry about."

As Liam headed back to town, he understood what it meant to be caught between a rock—his father's stubborn refusal to see any viewpoint but his own—and a hard place, which was the inn, where every room held the echo of Macy's laughter.

Macy knew that kissing her boss had been impulsive—and completely unprofessional—but since that one very steamy lip-lock, she tried to convince herself that at least her curiosity had been satisfied. Now she needed to forget about her sexy boss and his toe-curling kisses and focus on the job he'd hired her to do.

But that was easier said than done, because even if

she could pretend that her curiosity had been satisfied by the kiss, all her female parts remained dissatisfied. Thankfully, she had plenty to do to keep herself busy on Valentine's Day—the day Liam had chosen for the grand opening of the Stagecoach Inn.

To her mind, February 14 was no more or less significant than any other day of the year, but that opinion hadn't prevented her from capitalizing on the date to push Sweetheart Deals at the inn. The upgraded room packages included bubbly wine and chocolate-covered strawberries from Sweet Caroline's Sweets and/or bouquets of roses from Blossom's Flower Shop, and they'd proved to be popular options with several of the guests who'd booked rooms for that night.

Although Blossom's offered delivery, the florist had warned that she couldn't guarantee the arrangements would arrive by a specific time—especially on Valentine's Day. So Macy texted Liam—a completely legitimate and totally casual message—asking him to pick up the order so they could ensure they were in the appropriate rooms prior to the arrival of their guests. There would be red roses in each of Doc Holliday, Charles Goodnight and Wild Bill (three dozen! Of course, she figured anyone who could afford the luxury suite could afford three dozen roses—and the champagne and chocolates, too), pink in Annie Oakley and Clark Foss.

When she returned to the lobby after delivering the flowers and double-checking that everything else was as it should be for their expected guests, she found Liam sitting in the chair behind her desk with a single long-stemmed red rose in hand.

"Where did that come from?" she asked, when he offered it to her. "Did it fall out of one of the vases?" And since she hadn't thought to count when she'd tweaked the arrangements of the flowers, she would have to go back now and—

"No, it didn't fall out of one of the arrangements," he assured her. "It's for you."

"But…why?"

"Because it's Valentine's Day," he said simply.

She couldn't remember the last time anyone had given her flowers on February 14—or any other day of the year—and she was absurdly touched by the gesture. And maybe a little wary.

"Thank you," she said, taking the stem he offered.

"And before you start wondering and worrying, it's not an overture—it's just a flower…and maybe an apology."

"It's beautiful," she said, gently tracing the velvety edge of a deep red petal with her fingertip. "And you're forgiven."

"I meant what I said yesterday, but I didn't mean it the way I said it," he explained.

"No need to say anything more," she assured him.

And then there was no time to say anything more, because the inn's first guests had arrived.

Clint and Dawna MacDowell were long-time Haven residents celebrating not only Valentine's Day but their thirty-fifth wedding anniversary. They'd been encouraged by their daughter, Hayley, to splurge on a night at the inn, and they walked slowly through the reception area after Macy gave them their key, marveling at all the little details.

Liam led the way, carrying their luggage. And Macy knew exactly when they spotted the antique stagecoach by the doors leading to the courtyard, because she heard

Dawna gasp, and Liam patiently answered some questions about the age and origins of the conveyance before nudging them on toward their suite.

There was a steady flow of people in and out throughout the afternoon. Though there were only seven rooms in the hotel—and they were all booked—a lot of locals stopped in to congratulate Liam on his endeavor and wish him success. Having anticipated exactly this, Macy had arranged for complimentary refreshments to be set up in the solarium—coffee, tea and lemonade, along with a variety of cookies and pastries from The Daily Grind. Among the well-wishers were other business owners, friends and family, including Liam's grandparents and both his sisters—Sky on her way into work at Diggers', and Kate on her way home from the office.

Liam mingled with the visitors while Macy covered the front desk, checking in guests, taking reservations for future bookings and answering inquiries.

"I know it's short notice," Kate said, stopping by the desk on her way out again. "But we're having a party at the Circle G to celebrate Tessa's first birthday on Sunday afternoon."

"That sounds like fun," Macy said.

"I'm glad you think so, because I'd like you to come."

"Me?"

"And Ava, Max and Sam, of course," Kate clarified.

"That's very kind of you," Macy said. "But the triplets can be a real handful...are you sure you want them at your daughter's party?"

The other woman laughed. "Of course, I'm sure. I know first birthday parties are usually more about the parents, but I really want Tessa to meet and make friends with other little ones. Reid has been encouraging me to get her into daycare so we're not constantly juggling our professional responsibilities along with our daughter, but since I haven't done that yet, I'm relying on playdates and parties to develop her social skills."

Macy didn't really have to worry about that, because Ava, Max and Sam were always together. In addition, her mom had recently conscripted her neighbor and friend, Frieda Zimmerman, to accompany them to a story-time group at the library. Beverly had said it was a good opportunity to get them out of the house so they could interact with other babies; Macy suspected it was also an opportunity for her mother to get out of the house and interact with the parents of other babies—to which, of course, she had absolutely zero objection.

"And there will be cake," Kate said, adding further incentive for Macy to accept the invitation.

"Who could say no to cake?" Macy wondered.

The other woman grinned. "Great. I'll see you at the Circle G around two. Best wishes only."

As Kate made her way out the door, Macy told herself it would be a good experience for the kids—and a chance for her to maybe get some ideas for the triplets' first birthday, which was now only a few months away. She refused to admit, even to herself, that her boss's guaranteed presence at the party had been a factor in her decision, even if she was curious to know more about the man who'd hired her to help manage his hotel.

Of course, aside from the curiosity, there was the attraction. And what was wrong with her that she could want a man who'd made it clear that he considered her children a burden rather than a bonus? Obviously the attraction was purely physical. And maybe that wasn't so surprising, considering the sheltered life she'd led through her pregnancy and the first six months that followed the triplets' birth. When she'd finally ventured away from home to work the occasional shift at Diggers', she'd still been preoccupied and sleep-deprived. It was only in the past few weeks, since her babies had started eating cereal and sleeping through the night, that she'd started to feel human again.

So it was reasonable, she decided, that an increased awareness of the outside world might also allow her to experience sexual awareness, too. Of course, she had no intention of abandoning her self-respect and indulging her hormones, and giving in to her attraction to a man who'd made it clear he had no interest in a relationship with a single mother would be doing exactly that.

But as her gaze shifted to the single red rose on her desk, she acknowledged that her resolve didn't prevent her body from continuing to yearn whenever he was near.

Chapter 7

At the end of the day, she took the rose home with her.

Liam had said that it was just a flower—and maybe an apology. She appreciated both.

Not that saying "I'm sorry" changed anything, but it did clear the air between them. And although his harsh words had stung, they'd also opened her eyes—forcing her to accept that the attraction between them wasn't ever going to develop into anything more.

So she put the flower on the little table beside her bed, then went upstairs to get her babies.

Macy wasn't surprised to see the cut-crystal vase in the middle of the dining room table filled with a dozen long-stemmed red roses. It was her dad's traditional Valentine's Day gift to his wife. He would have grumbled as he placed the order and paid the florist, lamenting—as he always did—that the cost of flowers skyrocketed on the fourteenth of February "every single goddamned year." But he always ordered them anyway, and his wife's eyes always got a little misty when she read the card that was simply signed *Love, Norm.* Because after forty years, those words weren't just a complimentary closing but a testament to the deep and abiding love they continued to share.

Macy knew she was fortunate to have grown up in a home with two parents who loved one another. Bev and Norm weren't overtly demonstrative and they occasionally argued, but she'd never had cause to doubt that they were committed to each other, their marriage and their family.

And she'd taken for granted that, when she was ready to get married and have a family, she'd find the right person and fall in love, just as her parents had done. She'd thrown herself into the task of meeting that future husband and father of her children. She'd accepted every invitation to dinner, every set-up arranged by her friends and colleagues, even when she was skeptical. And when none of those dates had led to anything further, she'd tried online dating.

She'd dated so many guys she'd lost track of the number, ever hopeful that one of them would be The One. After four years, she'd met some interesting men, but none with whom she wanted to establish a relationship. Obviously this was a major snag in her plan for a husband and a family, but she refused to let it get in the way of her determination to have a baby.

It had never occurred to her that she would end up with more than one. As far as she knew, there was no history of multiples on either side of her family. Apparently she was just lucky.

And she knew that she was. She had the children she'd always wanted, but she hadn't considered—couldn't have imagined—how much of a struggle it would be to raise them on her own. Thankfully, she didn't have to. She had her parents to help. But it wasn't the same as having a partner to share not just all the milestones in the lives of their children but all the moments of their own. "For better, for worse, for richer, for poorer…"

Not that she needed a man to complete her life, but she was admittedly a little worried that the choices she'd made might not have been the best choices for her children. She'd decided to have a baby because it was what *she* wanted and, in retrospect, she had to acknowledge that it might have been a selfish decision. She hadn't given a lot of thought to what was best for her babies, or what it would be like for them to grow up without a father. She'd been so determined to prove that she could do it on her own she hadn't considered that maybe she shouldn't.

She knew a lot of women who weren't just single moms but proof that a woman could do it all. But none of those single moms had triplets. Of course, it was far too late to make a different choice now. And when she entered her parents' living room and saw them with her babies, she was reminded once again that although she was technically a single parent, she wasn't doing it alone. Ava, Max and Sam might not have a father, but they had amazing grandparents who would—and did—do anything for them.

"Look who's home," Bev announced.

Three little heads turned, three smiles beamed and Macy's heart filled to overflowing, assuring her again that she didn't need a man to make her life complete. She had everything she needed right here.

But when she went to sleep that night, she dreamed of being snuggled in Liam's embrace.

Macy could understand why Tessa's parents had planned a big bash for her first birthday, and even why Katelyn had invited her and Ava, Max and Sam. But when she'd accepted the invitation, Macy obviously hadn't been thinking about the logistics of taking three babies out on her own, in the middle of winter, when she would have to haul not just the kids but all their essential paraphernalia through snow, up the long drive—already packed with vehicles—to the house.

"Why did I agree to this?" She muttered the question to herself as she unbuckled Sam from his car seat.

"Because there will be cake."

Macy jolted at the unexpected response and turned, her cheeks flushing, to face the amused birthday girl's mom.

"I was talking to myself," she confessed.

"I do that all the time," Katelyn told her.

"She does," her husband—the sheriff—confirmed.

"Because my husband doesn't listen," his wife said pointedly. "But he does have two strong arms, which is why we came out to give you a hand."

"I appreciate it," Macy said, as Reid took the baby from her. "I don't often venture out on my own with all three of them, so I sometimes forget how much stuff they need."

"Liam claims that I look like a Sherpa when I'm hauling Tessa's gear—and she's only one kid," Kate noted, reaching into the vehicle to unbuckle Ava from the middle baby seat.

After she transferred the little girl to her husband's

other arm, she moved around the vehicle to get Max while Macy opened the back of her SUV.

"You won't need your playpen," Reid told her. "We've got an enclosure set up inside that's big enough for all the little ones."

"That simplifies things," Macy agreed, sliding the diaper bag onto her shoulder.

"And what is that?" Katelyn demanded, when Macy reached for the gift bag stuffed with pink tissue.

"Just a little something for the birthday girl."

"Did I forget to say *best wishes only*?"

"You didn't," Macy admitted. "But Ava, Max and Sam wanted to bring a little something."

"So they're responsible, are they?" the hostess asked, clearly skeptical of this claim.

"You're not going to scold my babies, are you?"

Kate shook her head. "I might, but they're just too cute." She looked at the little boy in her arms. "I guess the boys get their green eyes from their dad?"

Macy was used to fielding questions about her babies' paternity—and often much less subtle ones—so she responded easily, "Well, there's no green on my side of the family."

"And since we don't want them turning blue from the cold, we should get them inside," Reid interjected.

As they moved toward the house, Macy thanked them again for their help with Ava, Max and Sam. Once inside, it was fairly quick work—with Kate and Reid's assistance—to get the triplets out of their snowsuits and into the secure enclosure with the other little ones in attendance. Macy recognized Tessa, of course, but the little boy with her didn't look familiar.

Before she could ask, the parents of the birthday girl

went off in different directions, but a moment later another woman approached, a baby girl in her arms.

Noting the arrival of three new babies, she said, "You must be Macy," and shifted her baby to offer a hand.

"I guess being the mom of triplets has made me infamous."

"Katelyn described you as Wonder Woman without the sword and shield."

Macy laughed. "A flattering—if completely inaccurate—description."

"I'm Emerson," the other woman said. "Kate's oldest and best friend, and mom to Keegan—" she gestured to the boy with Tessa "—almost two-and-a-half, and Karlee, eight months."

"Mine are eight months, too," Macy told her.

"I know," Emerson said. "They're in the same story-time group as Karlee at the library."

"I didn't know that. I don't make it to story-time with them."

"You shouldn't feel guilty. Your mom and Frieda seem to enjoy it as much as the kids. And Kate says you've been a godsend to Liam and the inn."

"I know it's early days yet, but I love working there."

"I've been bugging Mark to book a room for our anniversary," Emerson confided. "Usually we go out of town, but with Karlee being so young, I don't want to be too far away. Not to mention that I've been dying to see the place."

"You don't have to book a room to get a tour," Macy said. "Stop by anytime that I'm there and I'd be happy to show you around. Although I promise, you'll be even more eager to stay there after the tour."

"Then I'm definitely going to come for the tour—and to book the room," Emerson promised.

Another mom came over to talk to Emerson then, and Macy excused herself to get a drink. The non-alcoholic punch was pink—no doubt to coordinate with the other decorations in the oversized family room that had been designated as the party spot. There were bouquets of balloons and streamers and banners and paper lanterns and floral centerpieces. Macy made mental notes of what she liked (everything!) and the variations she might consider for her triplets (2:1 ratio of blue and pink decorations).

She sipped her punch and smiled to see Tessa plucked out of the enclosure by a man she recognized as Caleb Gilmore. Liam's younger brother was as tall—and nearly as handsome—with light brown hair, hazel eyes and the powerful build of a rancher, which Macy knew him to be. Skylar was there, too, of course, as were Tessa's great-grandparents. Jack and Evelyn Gilmore were still involved with the daily operation of the ranch as well as contributing to the larger community.

"Me-um! Me-um!" Tessa called, toddling across the floor toward her uncle when Liam finally arrived.

"There's the birthday girl." He scooped her into his arms and planted a noisy kiss on her cheek.

Tessa giggled.

The interaction made Macy smile—and marvel again at the man's inherent contradictions. How could he claim that he didn't really like kids when it was obvious he adored his niece—and that she adored him right back?

Regardless of the answer to that question, Macy wasn't going to let herself adore the man. She had other priorities right now—and Ava, Max and Sam were at the top of the list—so she turned back to the punch bowl to refill her cup and found David Gilmore with the ladle in his hand.

"Can I top you up?" he offered.

"Yes, please." She held her cup toward him.

"You're Bev and Norm's daughter Macy, aren't you?" he asked her.

"I am," she confirmed. It wasn't uncommon in Haven for people who hadn't been introduced to at least share acquaintances. As a result, she was accustomed to being referred to in connection with her parents—or as the sister of her brothers. Since returning to Haven, she'd frequently been referred to as "the triplets' mother," but now she was also known as "the manager of the inn"— a title she wore proudly.

"How are your folks doing?" David wondered.

"They should be enjoying their retirement," she acknowledged. "Instead, they've taken on new careers as daycare providers to those three." Macy gestured to the enclosure where the triplets—and a few other little ones—were confined.

"Being a grandparent is the best job in the world," he said, and sounded as if he meant it. "I know Tessa's just a year old, but I almost can't wait for Katelyn and Reid to give her a little brother or sister."

"Well, you're going to have to," Kate said, obviously having overheard her father's remark. "Because I'd like to get my first kid out of diapers before I have a second one."

"Macy seems to manage well enough and she's got three in diapers," David pointed out, with a conspiratorial wink in her direction.

"I only manage well enough because I've got so much help at home," she was quick to clarify.

"And if you're so eager for another grandchild, you've got three other kids who could help you out," Kate suggested.

"Caleb isn't ready to settle down, Sky would rather poke into a man's brain than win his heart, and Liam's too busy playing at being an innkeeper to make any effort to find a suitable wife."

Macy sipped her punch and wished she was anywhere but in the middle of what she sensed was a family argument brewing—especially when Liam drew nearer. Maybe she could slip away on the pretext of checking on her babies, but they were currently being fussed over by Liam's grandparents and basking in the attention.

"And what kind of woman do you think would make a suitable wife?" Liam wondered, joining the conversation. "No, wait. Let me guess—a woman who would convince me to sell the inn and come back to live and work on the ranch?"

"Gilmores are ranchers," David said, his tone growing steely.

Kate exhaled a weary sigh. "Can we please not do this at my daughter's birthday party?"

"We're just having a conversation," her father said.

"A conversation that's quickly going to turn into an argument," she predicted.

"No, it's not," Liam promised.

And then, to be sure, he set his glass on the table and walked out of the room.

Macy didn't want to interfere in something that was clearly none of her business. But during the brief exchange between her boss and his father, she couldn't help but notice that Liam had been gripping his glass so tight his knuckles had gone white. So when he set that glass down and slipped away from the gathering, she double-checked that Ava, Max and Sam were in capable hands and then followed.

She saw him disappear through the back door, and quickly grabbed her coat and shoved her feet into her boots. He was already halfway to the barn while she was still pushing her arms into her sleeves.

When she muscled open the door of the barn, her senses were immediately assailed by the scents of fresh hay, oiled leather and horses. She hadn't grown up on a ranch, but she'd always loved horses and had learned to ride at a young age. Of course, it had been years since she'd been on the back of a horse, but the familiar setting brought the memories—and an unexpected longing to climb into the saddle—rushing back.

She closed the door again and took a moment to allow her eyes to adjust to the dim light. As she made her way down the concrete aisle, she noted the shiny nameplates on the stall doors and the glossy coats of the equines within. The Gilmores obviously took pride in and care of their animals—of course, they could afford to do so as the Circle G was one of the most prosperous cattle ranches in northern Nevada.

She found Liam inside a birthing stall at the far end of the barn.

"What are you doing out here?" he asked.

"I was going to ask you the same question," she said.

"I just needed some air," he told her.

"You must have needed that air pretty desperately,"

she remarked. "You rushed out of the house without even grabbing a jacket."

He shrugged. "I knew I wasn't going very far."

"Who's this?" she asked, stroking the long nose of an obviously pregnant dappled mare who'd come over to greet her visitor.

"That's Mystery."

"You don't know her name?"

He managed a half smile. "Her name is Mystery," he clarified. "While we were growing up, all the kids took turns naming the foals that were born. This one came when it was Sky's turn, and she demanded to know if it was a boy or a girl. At that point, only her head and forelegs were out, so Grandad said it was a mystery, and Sky decided that was a good name."

"And when is Mystery going to have her own mystery foal?" Macy asked.

"Any day now," he said, stroking his hands over the mare's swollen flank. "But probably not today."

"That's too bad," she remarked. "I'm sure birthing a foal would be a welcome diversion—although checking on a pregnant horse serves the same purpose."

He didn't respond to that but gave the horse a last affectionate pat before he unlatched the gate and exited the stall.

Macy tried again. "Families are complicated, huh?"

"Yeah," he finally agreed.

"Anything you want to talk about?" she prompted.

"Nope."

She sighed. "It's obvious that there's some tension between you and your dad."

"And, like I said, it's not anything I want to talk about," he told her.

"I've been told that I'm a pretty good listener."

"You're also a really good kisser," he noted, tugging on the belt of her jacket to draw her toward him. "And I prefer kissing over conversation."

"Now you're trying to distract me," she accused, but even knowing it was true, she couldn't resist the temptation of his embrace.

"Is it working?"

Before she could respond to his question, his mouth was on hers.

And, yeah, it was working.

Very effectively.

And just like the first time he'd kissed her—or she'd kissed him—her mind went blank and her body came alive.

She lifted her hands to his shoulders, holding on to him as the world tilted and swayed beneath her feet. She'd almost managed to convince herself that the kiss they'd shared couldn't possibly have been as amazing as she remembered. That her body, long deprived of any adult male attention, had conspired with her overactive imagination to turn the memory of that kiss into more than it had been.

But his second kiss proved otherwise. If anything, her memory had not done the first one justice.

Was it Liam? Was this incredible chemistry specific to him? Or were her hormones overactive because of all the changes her body had been through, carrying and birthing three babies? She wanted to believe it was just hormones, and yet she suspected otherwise. She'd had plenty of male customers flirt with her at Diggers', and she'd received a few interesting propositions—but not one that had tempted her. No man she'd met had made her remember that she was a woman, with a woman's wants and needs. No one before Liam. Before now.

He banded an arm around her waist, gently drawing her closer. Even through her puffy coat, she could feel the heat emanating from his body—a heat that warmed the blood flowing through her veins. He skimmed his tongue over her lips, and they parted willingly for him. She wanted this—wanted *him*—with a desperation she couldn't remember experiencing in a very long time. Or maybe ever.

"Let's sneak up to the hayloft and pretend the rest of the world doesn't exist for an hour," he suggested against her lips.

Yes. Oh, please, yes.

But while her hormones were running rampant through her system, her brain was still in charge of her mouth, and she managed to hold that desperately needy response inside her head. She drew in a slow, steadying breath before responding lightly, "I've never had a literal roll in the hay."

"We could change that right now," he offered.

She laughed, a little weakly, and took a step back. A not-so-subtle retreat from the temptation he represented. "You're a dangerous man, Liam Gilmore."

His lips curved, but his gaze was serious. "I wouldn't hurt you, Macy."

She knew that wasn't a promise he could make. Oh, she trusted that he wouldn't want to hurt her, but she suspected that getting involved with "Love 'em and Leave 'em Liam" would inevitably result in a bruised heart.

Under other circumstances, she might have decided that the risk was worth it. Though she'd never had much success with relationships, she wasn't opposed to putting herself out there. But while she might be willing to risk her own heart, she had Ava, Max and Sam to think about now. She had to think not just about what she wanted, but what was best for her children.

And Liam had made it clear that he wasn't interested in a relationship with a single mom. If she gave in to the attraction between them, it wouldn't be anything more than a physical release. Of course, she was wound so tight right now she was almost ready to consider the benefits of a quick, no-strings affair to alleviate the sexual tension that simmered between them. But she'd never been the type to engage in casual sex, and she wasn't sure it was a habit she wanted to start now.

"I need to get back to—"

"Knock, knock," Skylar called out, as she pushed open the door, bringing a blast of cold air into the barn with her.

"Go away," Liam told his sister, his gaze never shifting from Macy's.

"I will," Sky promised. "But Kate wanted me to tell you that they're getting ready to bring out the cake, and she didn't want you to miss it."

"Well, you can tell Kate that her timing sucks," he said, because now that he had Macy in his arms, he didn't want to let her go. Then he sighed. "And that we'll be right in," he added, because he didn't want to miss Tessa's celebration, either.

"Will do," Sky said.

"Do I owe you another apology?" he asked when his sister had gone.

"Are you sorry?" Macy wondered.

His gaze dropped to her mouth and he shook his

head. "Not for kissing you. But I didn't give you a lot of choice in the matter."

"I wasn't an unwilling participant," she assured him.

"But that doesn't change the fact that this—" he gestured between them "—is a bad idea, does it?"

"A very bad idea," she confirmed.

He sighed and dropped his arms, letting her out of his embrace. "In that case, let's go get cake."

Chapter 8

So they went back to the house, where Reid carried out a stunning three-tiered cake. The bottom layer was decorated with pale pink fondant icing with polka dots of darker pink, lilac, purple and white; the middle layer was covered in lilac fondant with stripes of light and dark pink, purple and white; and the top was decorated to look like a crown. After the birthday song had been sung, the crown layer was removed and set on a plate for the birthday girl, who immediately dug into the confection with both hands.

Gifts followed the cake—because Macy wasn't the only one who had ignored the "best wishes only" instruction—and then the party guests began to make their way to the door. Macy started bundling up her kids at the same time that everyone else was putting on their coats and boots, and after calling the barn to enlist Wade's help with another matter, Liam gave her a hand.

It was harder work than he'd anticipated, because Sam stiffened up and refused to cooperate and Max kept trying to wriggle away, but eventually the triplets were bundled up against the cold.

He picked up either Max or Sam—he couldn't remember which one had been wrestled into the blue snowsuit with matching knit hat and gloves—and then his brother, who was clad in a similar green snowsuit with hat and gloves of the same color, leaving Macy to carry her daughter, in red outerwear, and the enormous diaper bag.

She halted at the edge of the porch, having finally noticed the vehicle he'd asked the foreman to ready and park near the house.

"It's a double seat cutter sleigh," he said, before she could ask. "I thought we could take a little ride, so you could see more of the ranch."

She nibbled on her bottom lip. "You can't really expect me to put my babies in that."

"Look in the back seat," he suggested, as he guided her down the steps.

"You just happened to have three extra car seats hanging around?"

"Four, actually," he said. "They belong to our foreman and his wife, for when their grandkids visit. Wade even installed proper child seat anchors, so you can rest assured that your babies will be snug and safe."

Still, she hesitated.

"It's a perfect day for a ride," he cajoled. "And Barney and Betty are already harnessed and ready show you around."

"Barney and Betty, huh?" Her lips twitched as she

fought a smile. "Well, the sleigh doesn't look like rubble, so let's give it a go."

He helped her buckle Ava, Max and Sam into the car seats, then Macy settled onto the velvet-tufted seat in front and he took his seat beside her and the reins in hand.

"It's so beautiful out here," she commented, as they glided over the snow-covered fields. "So peaceful."

"It is, isn't it?" he acknowledged.

She shifted a little in her seat, so that she could look at Ava, Max and Sam. He glanced over his shoulder to do the same, noting their wide eyes and happy smiles. Their cheeks were pink from the cold, but they were obviously having fun—as evidenced by the occasional giggles that punctuated the silence when the sleigh dipped or rose as the horses navigated the rolling hills.

But the motion must have simulated rocking—or maybe the triplets were just tired out from the party— because it didn't take long before their eyes grew heavy. The one in green drifted off first, he noted, but his brother and sister weren't far behind.

"Napping this late is going to wreak havoc on their bedtime," Macy noted.

"Did you want to head back?"

She shook her head. "There's no point now. And truthfully, as much as I like schedules and routines, having triplets has taught me that ideals don't always mesh with reality."

"It must be challenging, raising three babies on your own."

"It would be even more challenging if I was really on my own," she said. "Thankfully, my parents help out a lot."

"But not their dad?" he wondered.

"No."

The abrupt response didn't invite further questions, so Liam let the subject drop, though his curiosity remained unsatisfied.

"So why did you leave all this to become an innkeeper?" Macy asked, after several minutes had passed.

And now he was the one facing the question without a simple or straightforward answer.

"Growing up out here... I loved the ranch and everything about ranching," he confided. "I used to follow my dad around, wanting to do everything that he did. Wanting to be just like him when I grew up.

"Then my mom died...and everything changed."

Macy reached over and laid a mitten-clad hand on top of his, offering a gentle squeeze of encouragement.

"And after that, I hated the ranch," he admitted.

"Did it happen...did she die...on the ranch?"

He nodded.

"How old were you?" she asked.

"Not quite eleven."

She was silent for a minute, considering. "Loss is never easy," she finally said. "But for a young child to lose a parent... I can't imagine how difficult that must have been for you. It's understandable that you'd want to get away from where it happened, and you shouldn't be made to feel guilty about choosing your own path."

"But is it my own path?" he wondered aloud.

"What do you mean?"

"I'm not sure if I really wanted to go into the hospitality business or if I saw the For Sale sign and decided that reopening the old Stagecoach Inn would give me an opportunity to finally get away from the ranch.

"I'd always been fascinated by the old building and its history," he confided. "But I don't know that I would have taken the initiative to turn that interest into anything more if the pieces hadn't all fallen into place."

"Whatever your reasons, you've made something out of nothing," she told him. "You've created jobs for local people and, over the next few months, you'll get to watch the inn's success generate renewed interest in local tourism."

"And it only cost me all my savings and my relationship with my father."

"I noticed that he didn't show up for the grand opening," she said.

"He had more important things to do." Then he quoted his father: "Ranch business doesn't take vacations, you know."

"Your grandparents made the trip into town, though. Obviously they don't subscribe to the theory that Gilmores are ranchers."

"They want me to do whatever makes me happy, and they believe the inn is an investment in the community."

"They're right," she agreed.

"Right or wrong, my father isn't giving any indication that he'll ever forgive me for leaving the ranch."

"He'll come around," she said, speaking the words with such confidence that he almost believed they were true.

Or maybe it was simply that being with Macy made him want to believe in second chances.

Liam was in the barn at the Circle G, checking on Mystery and her newborn foal when Kate tracked him down Wednesday morning.

"What are you doing so far out of town so early on a weekday morning?"

"I've got a full-day trial in Winnemucca, so Martina's going to look after Tessa for me."

"You ever think about putting the kid in daycare instead of dropping her in the laps of friends and relatives?"

"Martina offered," she said, just a little defensively.

"As if that would matter."

"Be nice to me," his sister cautioned. "Or I might invite Caleb to dinner Friday night instead of you."

"Why are you inviting me to dinner Friday night?" he asked, a little warily. Because while he never turned down a free meal, he'd learned that nothing in life was ever really free. "What's the catch?"

"There's no catch," she denied.

"Okay, so maybe you don't think it's a catch, but there's something you're not telling me. What is it? Are you and Reid going to walk out the door as soon as I walk in?"

She sniffed indignantly. "If I wanted you to babysit, I'd ask you to babysit."

He waited.

"We're having a little dinner party and I need one more to round out the table," she finally told him.

"How big is this little dinner party?"

"Not very."

"You're being evasive."

"It's just me and Reid, Emerson and Mark, Em's cousin and you. And Tessa, Keegan and Karlee, of course," she said, adding her daughter and her friend's two little ones to the tally.

"Is this cousin of Emerson's female?" he asked suspiciously.

"As a matter of fact, she is," his sister admitted.

"It's not a dinner party—it's a setup," he accused.

"It's not a setup."

"Then invite Caleb."

"I was hoping to round out the table with someone actually interested in making conversation," she said, because they both knew their brother could be rather taciturn at times.

Liam shook his head. "Do you really think I'm incapable of finding my own dates?"

"You've been so busy with the hotel, you haven't had much time to go out, so I thought this would be fun. And Jenna is really sweet."

"It's a setup," he said again.

"It's an introduction." She tried another tack. "With two kids—and one of them still a baby, Emerson doesn't have much time to show Jenna around, so she asked if you might be willing to play tour guide."

"Is that all I'm supposed to play?" he challenged.

"Well, that would be for you and Jenna to figure out."

"While I appreciate your efforts, I don't need you to find me a date," he said firmly.

"Maybe not, but you do need to stop thinking that anything's going to happen with Macy."

He frowned. "I thought you liked Macy."

"I do like Macy, but I don't like to see you chasing after a woman you can't have."

"I'm not chasing anyone," he denied. And the truth was, he'd never had to chase a woman before—or maybe he'd never known another woman who was worth the effort. Macy was definitely worth the effort, but her children were a complication and he liked to keep his relationships simple.

"I'll admit that there seems to be some chemistry between you," Kate continued, ignoring his denial. "But you can't ever act on it."

"I know you're worried about a sexual harassment lawsuit—"

"As you should be," she interjected.

"But I would never take advantage of a woman," he assured his sister. "Whether she worked for me or not."

"I know," she acknowledged. "But your working relationship ensures an inherent power imbalance."

He frowned at that.

"You can scowl all you want, but that's not going to change the fact."

"You told me to hire her," he reminded his sister.

"Because she's the best person for the job."

"And now I have to fire her."

"You are *not* going to fire her," Katelyn told him. "That's pretty much the definition of unlawful dismissal."

"You haven't left me with any other choice," he said.

"You have all kinds of other choices, but sleeping with Macy isn't one of them." And apparently that was the end of that topic, because then she said, "Dinner's at seven. You can bring dessert."

"What am I bringing for dessert?" he asked. Because his sister had clearly mapped out every other detail of the evening, he had no doubt that she'd also decided what she wanted him to bring.

"Caramel fudge brownie cheesecake from Sweet Caroline's."

Her immediate reply confirmed his suspicion—and

aroused another one. His gaze narrowed. "Are you pregnant again?"

"No." She laughed. "Definitely no. We've got more than we can handle with Tessa right now."

"As I recall, you didn't exactly plan to get pregnant with her."

Her only reply to that was "Cheesecake. Seven o'clock."

"I'll be there," he promised.

Because although she hadn't told him what she'd be cooking, Sweet Caroline's made the best cheesecake in Haven.

A promise was a promise, but when Friday rolled around, Liam found himself wishing that he'd never agreed to attend the so-called dinner party at his sister's. But he picked up the cheesecake and pulled up in front of his sister and brother-in-law's at precisely 6:55 p.m., because Kate was a stickler for punctuality and he tried not to irritate her without good reason.

But he nearly turned around again when he walked up the steps to the door, through which he could hear a baby crying.

Right—the plan for the so-called dinner party was two couples, two singles and three kids.

"I should have brought alcohol instead of chocolate," he muttered.

"Don't worry," a female voice said from behind him. "I've got the alcohol covered."

He turned to discover a young woman standing on the edge of the step, a paper bag from The Trading Post tucked in the crook of one arm. She was tall—probably close to five-ten, he guessed—with the long, lean body of a dancer. She had pale blond hair, cool blue eyes, slashing cheekbones and full lips that a cover model would envy.

As a man who appreciated beautiful women, Liam had no trouble acknowledging that she was that. She was also young—*much* younger than he'd expected.

"Two bottles of red and two white," she said.

"That's a good start," he decided, then felt compelled to ask, "But are you old enough to drink it?"

She smiled, revealing even white teeth. "Unless the legal drinking age is twenty-five in Nevada, there's no danger of me breaking any laws."

"You must be Jenna," he said, shifting the bakery box to his left hand so that he could offer the right.

"And you must be Liam." She smiled. "You're every bit as cute as Emerson promised."

"Cute?" he echoed dubiously.

She laughed. "I meant it as a compliment—as did my cousin, who has no idea that I've been dating a security analyst for almost three months, so I apologize if anyone gave you the impression that I was looking for a setup or a hookup while I'm in town."

"No apology necessary," he told her. "As I wasn't looking for either but was encouraged to show you some of the sights while you're in town."

"I've already walked the whole length of Main Street," she noted.

"Then you've seen the sights," he said.

Jenna laughed and took a step toward the door. She hesitated, her hand poised to knock, as another wail sounded from within. "Maybe we should take the wine and dessert and have our own dinner party somewhere else."

"A tempting offer," he admitted. Especially since he

knew now that she had no illusions about a potential romance developing between them. "But Katelyn would hunt us down—or at least the caramel fudge brownie cheesecake."

"Cheesecake?" She laughed again. "Dinner is sounding a lot better already," she said, and rapped her knuckles against the wood.

Macy knew that Liam had hired her so that he didn't have to be on-site at the inn 24/7. Notwithstanding that fact, for the first few weeks, he'd rarely ventured any farther away than Jo's to pick up pizza. So she was understandably surprised when, on only the second weekend after opening, she didn't see him at all.

He did call to check in a few times, but their conversations were brief and to the point. He didn't offer any information about where he was, and she didn't ask. But she suspected she knew the reason for his sudden disappearing act when a woman stepped up to the desk around 10:00 a.m. Wednesday morning and said, "I'm looking for Liam."

She was young—early twenties, Macy guessed—blonde, built and stunningly beautiful.

"Liam?" Macy echoed, wondering why it bothered her that his name rolled so easily off the girl's tongue. As if she'd had plenty of practice saying it—and maybe had done so in a sleepy voice when she rolled over in bed that morning and saw him beside her in bed.

And how ridiculous—and inappropriate—a thought was that? It shouldn't—*didn't*—matter to Macy who Liam spent the night with or even if it was a different woman every night.

"Liam Gilmore," the girl clarified. "This is his hotel, isn't it?"

"I'll see if he's avail—"

"No need," the girl interrupted, a wide smile curving her glossy pink lips. "I've found him."

And she sashayed across the tile floor to greet the man who'd just exited his office.

Macy had never seen anyone sashay before. She hadn't been sure that type of movement ever happened outside of historical novels and romantic movies—until she saw Liam's visitor sashay toward him, her short skirt twirling around her thighs with every gliding step. The blonde gave him a quick hug and a peck on the cheek. He said something close to her ear, and she responded with a tinkle of laughter like a melodic wind chime dancing in the breeze.

Macy heard the murmur of their voices pitched low, but she couldn't make out any words of their conversation. Not that she was trying to eavesdrop, because that would be inexcusably rude. But she couldn't deny that she was curious about the woman—who she was, where Liam had met her, if he was sleeping with her.

He had a private suite of rooms on the third floor with a separate entrance, so it was entirely possible that he'd been curled up with his blonde bombshell all weekend while Macy had been greeting guests, setting up their activities and making their dining arrangements.

And so what if he had been?

That was his prerogative and absolutely none of her business.

But she couldn't tear her gaze away from them as they made their way toward the front door. They really did make a beautiful couple: Liam so dark and muscular; his female companion so slender and fair.

Macy wasn't jealous, she was just...surprised to realize that he was seeing someone. Especially when he'd been kissing her in the barn at the Circle G barely a week earlier. And even if those kisses had made her head spin and her toes curl, they'd agreed a relationship between them would not be a good idea. So there was absolutely no reason for him not to go out with other women. In fact, she should be relieved that he was dating, because now she could stop weaving inappropriate fantasies about any kind of romance developing with her boss.

But did he have to hook up with someone who was so young and so pretty? Face-to-face with the beautiful girl, Macy couldn't help but feel old and worn. Of course, she was a thirty-three-year-old mother of almost nine-month-old triplets, so if she looked tired it was because she *was* tired.

And wasn't this exactly why she'd decided to go ahead and have a baby without waiting to meet a man she might want to marry and have a baby with? Because men were fickle and untrustworthy. But being in Liam's arms had reminded her of all the reasons that a woman wanted a man, anyway.

She forced herself to watch them walk out together, and to acknowledge that whatever brief moment she'd shared with her boss had obviously passed. Now maybe she could focus on what was truly important: her family and her career. She didn't want or need a sexy cowboy messing with her head or her heart.

Not half an hour after Liam had gone, his sister came in with Tessa in her arms, looking frantic and stressed.

"Please tell me he's in his office," Katelyn implored.

Macy shook her head. "Sorry. He stepped out a little while ago."

"Where'd he go? When's he going to be back?"

"I don't know," she said. "He didn't share any of those details with me."

Katelyn muttered an expletive under her breath.

"Do you need someone to keep an eye on Tessa?" Macy asked her.

"Desperately," the other woman admitted. "I drew Judge Longo for a bail hearing, and he's generally pretty good about me bringing her into court when I have to, but she's a little out of sorts today. She's been fussing and squawking all morning, and I know that will not go over well."

"You can leave her with me."

"I'd feel too guilty asking," Kate protested. "I'm sure you come to work to get away from fussy babies."

"I come to work because I love my job," Macy said. "And you didn't ask—I offered. Plus, the Stagecoach Inn prides itself on being a full-service hotel."

"The best thing my brother ever did was hire you," Kate said. "You truly are a gem."

"Can you tell him that before my six-month performance review? And suggesting that I deserve a raise wouldn't hurt, either," she added.

"I will," Kate promised, already halfway out the door.

Chapter 9

Macy really didn't mind keeping an eye on Tessa while the little girl's mother was in court. In fact, she was happy to have her company. While there were always innumerable details to take care of at the inn, there were also quiet times, and right now was one of them.

She took Tessa into the library and let the little girl choose a book from the shelf. Although most of the rooms were designed for couples rather than families, they occasionally had younger guests, so Macy had ensured there was a modest selection of books for them in the library, too. They sat together on the sofa and Macy read the story aloud to Tessa.

As the little girl studied the colorful illustrations, Macy studied the child, noting that Tessa's delicate features favored her mother, but there were obvious hints of her father in the shape of her eyes, the color of her hair, the stubborn tilt of her chin. Tessa was obviously a mix of both her parents, as Macy suspected her own babies were. Everyone commented on the similarities between Ava and her mama but suggested that the boys favored their father.

Macy wasn't sure that "father" was an appropriate title for the man who had contributed to the triplets' DNA. Truthfully, Donor 6243 had done nothing more than deposit his specimen in a cup. She didn't even know if he knew that his donation had succeeded in mating with an egg and creating a child—or three.

Ava, Max and Sam weren't his babies—they were her own.

Tessa turned the page, drawing Macy's attention back to the book in her hands. When the story was done, the little girl decided that her mama had been gone long enough and called out for her. Of course, Macy's patient explanations about Katelyn's whereabouts and responsibilities did nothing to appease the child, who grew distressed when her increasingly insistent demands failed to result in her mother's appearance.

Thankfully, Macy had read a lot of parenting books, so she put on some music and began to dance, encouraging Tessa to move her body, too, hopeful that the activity would work to both distract the little girl and burn off some of her excessive energy. Since there were only a handful of guests staying at the inn and they'd all departed for their chosen activities, she cranked the volume a little and got into the groove. And when one of her all-time favorite songs came on, she added vocals to the dance routine.

She picked Tessa up and twirled her around, making

the little girl grin and giggle. So she twirled again, still singing, until the music abruptly shut off.

"Ma-ma!" Tessa announced.

Sure enough, the little girl's mother had returned and was standing in the doorway of the library, amusement in her eyes, her briefcase and a large take-out bag from Diggers' in her hands.

Macy was admittedly a little embarrassed to have been caught belting out tunes and shaking her booty—and relieved that it was Katelyn rather than Liam who had come in during the impromptu song-and-dance routine.

"How do you do it?" Kate wondered aloud.

"Are you referring to my complete and total lack of rhythm or my ability to sing so boldly off-key?" Macy asked her.

Tessa's mom laughed. "I was referring to your ability to effortlessly roll with the punches. I have honestly never seen you flustered by anything."

"Believe me, I get flustered," Macy said. "I just try not to show it when I'm at work."

"As a mom, you're always working," Kate said. "You're just not always getting paid."

"But there are other perks."

Kate's lips curved as she looked at her little girl. "You're right about that," she agreed. "And thank you, again, for watching Tessa for me."

"We had a good time, didn't we, Tessa?"

When the little girl nodded and leaned forward to plant a sloppy kiss on Macy's cheek, her heart melted just a little.

"Trade you," Kate said, offering the take-out bag in exchange for her daughter.

Macy handed over the child, who squealed as she reached for her mother. "How was the hearing?"

"My client was remanded in custody," Kate told her. "I figured she would be, but I wouldn't be doing my job if I didn't at least try to get her released. And since her fate was sealed before noon, I decided to pick up lunch for us."

"You didn't have to do that," Macy said, but she took the bag and followed the other woman into the kitchen.

"Are you kidding?" Kate set her briefcase on the floor and settled on a stool at the island with her daughter in her lap. "It's the very least I could do to thank you for bailing me out today."

"It's not easy, balancing a career and parenting, is it?" Macy remarked.

"It's not at all," the lawyer agreed. Then, as Macy began to unpack the bag: "There's a chicken Caesar wrap and fries for you." Because, of course, all the staff at Diggers' knew the usual orders of their regular patrons. "Cheeseburger and fries for me."

Macy distributed the food and Tessa immediately stretched her arms out, reaching for the fries.

"You have to wait a minute," her mother cautioned. "They're still hot."

The little girl pursed her lips and blew out puffs of air.

"That's right." Kate selected a fry and, following her daughter's example, blew on the hot potato to cool it.

"Reid keeps nudging me to register her for daycare," she confided, picking up the thread of her conversation with Macy. "But that seems too much like handing her over to someone else to raise. And Tessa is still so young—and vulnerable—that the idea of leaving her with strangers makes me shudder."

"Believe me, I know how fortunate I am that my parents stepped up to help out with the triplets," Macy acknowledged.

"You are lucky," the other woman said. "I lost my mom when I was twelve, and you'd think that seventeen years should be enough time to come to terms with her death, but it seems like I miss her even more now that I'm a mom myself."

"I can imagine. I'm constantly asking my mom for advice and reassurance. I don't always follow her advice," she admitted. "But it's nice to have somebody to talk to."

Kate nodded and chewed. "My grandmother stepped in to fill the void as much as she could, but as I'm the oldest sibling, my brothers more often confide in me—if they confide in anyone."

Macy smiled as she watched Tessa sneak another fry and carefully blow on it.

"As a result, I sometimes fall into the trap of thinking I know what's best for them when I don't," the other woman continued.

"Why do I get the feeling this is leading to some sort of confession?" Macy wondered aloud.

"Because you're both smart and astute—and because I saw Liam having lunch at Diggers'."

"There aren't many other places to eat in this town," she remarked, her tone deliberately casual.

"When I stopped by earlier, you didn't mention that he was with Jenna."

"I didn't know her name."

"She's Emerson's cousin, visiting from out of town,"

Kate said. "I asked Liam to show her around, as a favor to me."

"I'm sure he'll be a great tour guide," Macy said.

"But there's nothing else going on." Kate nibbled on the end of a fry. "Though, if I'm being perfectly honest, I'd hoped there might be."

"It's really no concern of mine," Macy told her.

"Are you sure about that?" the other woman asked. "Because I don't usually butt into things that aren't any of my business—at least, I try really hard not to," she allowed. "But when it comes to family, it's not always easy to know where to draw the line."

"I can understand that," Macy agreed cautiously.

"And I've been worried about Liam for a while now."

"I don't think there's any cause for concern—when he and Jenna walked out of here, they looked as if they were completely wrapped up in each other."

"She's a nice girl—and totally his type," Kate confided. "Or what I thought was his type."

"So what's the problem?" Macy wondered.

Tessa's mom pretended not to notice as the little girl stole another french fry. "The problem is that I tried to set him up with Jenna because I wanted him to forget about you."

"Me?" Macy echoed, stunned.

Kate seemed amused by her reaction. "You can't tell that my brother's completely smitten with you?"

She shook her head. "He's not. I mean, there was a moment…a kiss," she said, and that acknowledgment was enough to bring the memories of that first kiss rushing to the forefront of her mind—and heat rushing through her veins. And a few days after that first kiss, there'd been a second. "But then…nothing."

"Because I told him that if he pursued a relationship with you, he'd be opening himself up to a sexual harassment lawsuit," her boss's sister confided.

Macy was aghast. "You think I'd sue him?"

"My concern wasn't specifically about you," Kate explained. "I just think anyone in a position of power should be hypervigilant to ensure they don't abuse that power. And I wasn't just looking out for him—I was also looking out for you."

"Thank you," she said dubiously. "But I don't think you need to worry about your brother harboring any romantic feelings toward me—when I reminded him that I was a single mom, he was eager enough to back off. And even if that hadn't dissuaded him, my children are my priority, which means I'm not in any position to be thinking about a romantic relationship right now."

"That makes perfect sense," Kate decided. "But logic aside...how do you feel about him?"

Macy sighed. "Confused."

Kate's smile didn't completely erase the worry in her eyes. "Reid confused the hell out of me when I first met him. Four hours later, we were naked."

"Well, that's something I didn't know," she noted.

The other woman chuckled. "Yeah, it's not something many people do know, but since that's how we ended up with Tessa, I'm not ashamed to admit it."

"You lucked out," Macy said, a little enviously.

"I did," Kate agreed. And then, "I guess your situation was a little different?"

"My situation was *very* different."

"The dad didn't want to have anything to do with his kids?"

"His involvement began and ended with the donation of his sperm."

Of course, most people didn't take the words literally, so she wasn't surprised when Kate's follow-up question indicated that she hadn't, either.

"Any chance that he's going to change his mind about wanting to know his kids in the future?"

Macy shook her head. "Definitely not."

Kate opened her mouth, as if she wanted to say more, but she shoved a fry inside and closed it again.

Macy wished she could tell Liam's sister the truth about the father of her baby. She wasn't ashamed of the choice she'd made—how could she be when that choice had given her Ava, Max and Sam? But for all its recent growth and changes, Haven was still a small town where some old-fashioned beliefs were held dear. Proof of which was demonstrated by her own parents' shock and disapproval of her baby news.

She'd never meant for the paternity of her babies to be a big secret. But since coming back to Haven, she'd accepted that her actions were a reflection on her family. And though she was undeniably frustrated by their disapproval, she realized their attitudes were indicative of the larger community.

Maybe the residents would sympathize with and support a couple with fertility issues who opted for IVF or adoption in their desire to have a family, but she suspected they'd be less likely to understand or approve of a single woman choosing the same path. As a result, whenever Beverly was asked about the father of her grandbabies—because yes, there were people in town bold enough to ask the question—she was uncharacteristically cryptic.

"I don't know anything about Macy's relationship with him," she'd say. "She doesn't say much, and we never had the opportunity to meet him."

Of course, all those details were true—albeit deliberately misleading.

When Liam returned to the hotel following his lunch with Jenna, who was heading back to California later that day, he found Kyle Landry waiting in the library to see him.

"What can I do for you?" Liam asked, surprised by the unexpected visit of a man he knew only well enough to wave at in passing.

"Actually, I'm here because of what I can do for you."

Liam knew the beginning of a sales pitch when he heard one, and he was immediately wary. "Okay, what do you think you can do for me?"

"I can offer your guests a culinary experience that will be as unique and unforgettable as your inn," Kyle said.

"Thanks, but we already have a chef."

"You have someone who cooks breakfast," the young man acknowledged.

"That's all we need."

"You're doing your business a disservice by not offering dinner to your guests."

Liam's gaze narrowed suspiciously. "Have you been talking to Macy?"

"Not recently, but in the interest of full disclosure, we used to work together," Kyle said.

"Well, I'll tell you what I told her," Liam said. "There are other places in town where guests can get an evening meal."

"Diggers', Jo's Pizzeria or the Sunnyside Diner," Kyle said dismissively.

"I eat at those places frequently and have never had any complaints."

"But they hardly reflect the upscale image you're attempting to establish for your hotel."

"What do you know about what I'm trying to establish?" Liam challenged.

"The Dusty Boots Motel on the highway is never booked to capacity, so Haven didn't really need another hotel. Which suggests that you wanted to appeal to a different clientele. People who want to stay for a few days and not just sleep off their bachelor parties in Reno."

"How do you know about the hotel business?"

"Two years of restaurant and hotel management."

"Is that enough to get you a diploma?" Liam asked.

"No," Kyle admitted. "And then I went to England to get some practical experience."

The School of Artisan Food, he remembered Macy telling him. It didn't sound as fancy as Le Cordon Bleu in Paris, but Liam imagined the experience Kyle had gained there was still much more sophisticated than the palates of Haven's residents.

"And you think that qualifies you to run a hotel kitchen?"

"I think I'm more qualified than anyone else in this town," Kyle said. "I'd use locally sourced ingredients as much as possible—why truck ingredients in when we've got some of the finest dairy, beef and produce right here in Haven? The less we have to ship, the more we keep our food costs down. And I'd create hearty meals that would satisfy the hungry rancher and impress the sophisticated traveler."

Sure, the concept was appealing, but Liam still had reservations about venturing into the food service business—and especially about this particular chef. "Does your mom know you're here looking for a job?" he asked.

"No," Kyle said.

"Are you going to tell her?"

"When there's something to tell."

"I guess that's fair enough," Liam agreed.

"I could do a tasting menu for you," the chef suggested.

"What's that?" he asked, proving, no doubt, that he had no business in the restaurant business.

"Sample portions of appetizers, main courses and desserts," Kyle explained. "Do you have a girlfriend?"

Liam quirked a brow. "What does my relationship status have to do with your desire to work in my kitchen?"

"Nothing. I was only going to suggest that, if you do have a girlfriend—or any kind of significant other—I could do a formal meal presentation for both of you. A dinner for two slash job interview."

"You know what, Kyle? I think that sounds like a terrific idea."

"I was beginning to worry that you got lost on your way to the store," Macy's father commented when his wife came through the back door with the "few groceries" she'd gone out to get more than an hour earlier.

"You make me crazy sometimes, but I haven't completely lost my mind yet," Bev replied, setting her bags on the counter. "I guess I did lose track of time, though, chatting with Celeste Rousseau."

"What's the latest gossip from Miners' Pass?" Macy asked, referring to the name of the street where Ben and Margaret Channing had built the enormous home that Celeste took care of for them.

"The latest—and very exciting—*news*," her mother said, emphasizing the word because she did not approve of gossip, "is that the Channing family is going to grow by two."

Macy waved a hand dismissively. "That's old news. Deputy Neal told me weeks ago that Regan was expecting twins."

"Maybe I should have said *two more*," Bev clarified. "Because Jason's and Spencer's wives are both pregnant."

"That is exciting news," Macy agreed.

"I'd be more excited if I got to hear the news while I was enjoying the roast-beef-on-rye sandwich you promised would be my lunch," Norm said.

"Instead of just rummaging through the bags, you could actually put the groceries away," Bev remarked, gently lifting the carton of eggs that had been turned on its side by her husband's efforts.

"I just want the bread," he said. "Shouldn't bread be on top?" But he did as his wife had suggested—until he found the bread. Then he started pulling the other ingredients out of the fridge to make his sandwich.

Bev sighed. "Honest to goodness, you have the attention span of a gnat sometimes."

"My attention has been focused on a roast-beef-on-rye sandwich since you went out to get the bread."

"Sit." She pointed toward the table. "I'll make your sandwich."

"Horseradish and mustard," he reminded her.

"Because that's different than what I've been making for you for forty years," she muttered dryly.

Macy smiled at the familiar and affectionate bickering as she took over putting the groceries away.

When she was in high school—and helping a close friend deal with the fallout of her parents' divorce, she'd sometimes wondered what inspired one couple to weather the stormy seas of matrimony for a lifetime together while another might jump overboard when the first waves hit. She still didn't know the answer to that question, but she was grateful to her parents for providing her with an example of what a marriage could be. Bev and Norm's wasn't perfect, of course, but it was always a work in progress.

"When are the babies due?" Macy asked, when her father was happily chowing down on his coveted sandwich.

"Both in November, although Kenzie is due at the beginning of the month and Alyssa closer to the end."

"It's like there's suddenly a baby boom in this town," Norm chimed in, after gulping down half the glass of milk his wife had served with his sandwich.

Bev nodded. "And a sign that our young people are sticking around to help grow the community instead of running off to the cities, like they all used to do."

"You mean like I did?" Macy guessed.

"Like a lot of young people did," her mother said.

"And you're home now," her father pointed out. "Raising your babies where you were raised."

"And grateful to be here."

"Oh, don't start that again," Bev chided. "Tell me instead about your plans for tonight."

"My plans are to hang out with Ava, Max and Sam—reading stories, singing songs, rolling around on the floor and splashing in the tub." She grinned. "In other words, the usual."

"You should go out," her mother urged.

"Where would I go?" she asked, startled by the suggestion.

"To see a movie?"

"Or I could stay in and watch a movie," Macy suggested as an alternative. "There's got to be something new on Netflix."

Bev shook her head despairingly. "You really need to set the bar a little higher. Do something for yourself. Reconnect with old friends. Meet new people."

"Ahh. Now I see where you're going with this."

"What do you mean?" her mother asked, feigning innocence—albeit not very convincingly.

"You think if I put on some pretty clothes and high heels, I'll somehow manage to dazzle an unsuspecting cowboy who will then declare his undying love and desire to marry me and be a father to my three babies."

"A little lipstick wouldn't hurt, either," Bev said.

"While I appreciate your confidence in the power of painted lips, my days of dazzling anyone are long past. I don't have the time or the energy for any romantic entanglements right now."

"I don't want you to grow old alone," her mother admitted.

"I think I'm pretty much guaranteed not to be alone for the next eighteen years."

"And since you brought them into the conversation,

I'll say what I've been saying since they were born—those babies need a daddy."

"No," Macy denied, though perhaps not as vehemently as she had a few months earlier. "They need to grow up in a stable and loving environment, and I'm so grateful to both of you for helping to give them that."

"She gets that stubborn streak from you," Norm said to his wife.

"Whose side are you on here?" Bev asked him.

"Yours. Always yours," he placated her, rising from the table to put his plate and cup in the dishwasher. "But in this case, I think we all want the same thing—and that's what's best for Ava, Max and Sam."

"Of course, that's what we all want," Bev said.

"We just can't agree on what that is," Macy noted.

"I'm only suggesting that our daughter shouldn't close herself off to any possibilities," her mother said, refusing to let the issue drop.

"And I only wish—"

The ring of her cell phone cut off that thought.

Macy grabbed for the device, grateful for the interruption. But her finger hovered above the screen, hesitating to answer the call when she saw Liam Gilmore's name and number on the display.

"I'm going to hang out with my grandchildren," Norm announced, moving toward the living room.

"They're napping," Bev said.

"Then that's what I'm going to do, too."

His wife smiled as she shook her head.

"Are you going to answer that?" she asked Macy, when the second ring sounded.

"I probably should," she said.

Because while it wasn't often that her boss contacted

her when she was away from the inn, it wasn't out of the ordinary, either. He'd called her once because he couldn't remember the password for the computer— ST@G3_C0@CH_1NN—and another time to ask her where she'd hidden the laundry detergent—cleverly and deviously, in the cupboard beside the washing machine in the laundry room.

She didn't mind these harmless inquiries. What she minded was the way her heart inevitably skipped a beat when she saw his name on the display, and then another when she heard his voice. He'd made no more overtures since he'd kissed her in the barn the day of his niece's birthday party, but the memories of the kisses they'd shared continued to keep her awake at night— and tease her in explicit and erotic dreams when she finally did sleep.

Macy pushed those thoughts aside and connected the call.

Chapter 10

"Can you come in tonight?" Liam asked.

"Aside from the fact that today is one of my days off, I don't work nights," Macy reminded him.

"It's not work, really," he hedged. "More like a favor—with food."

"The last time you offered to feed me, I got pizza."

"Jo's pizza," he said, as if that somehow elevated the basic meal.

And, okay, Jo's pizza was the best she'd ever had. Vegas might have a lot more dining options, but she'd never found a pizzeria in Sin City to rival the local favorite.

"And tonight it will be Jo's son doing the cooking."

"You hired Kyle?" she asked, surprised and pleased to hear of this apparent change of heart.

"Not yet," he said. "I'm still not completely convinced

that there's a market for upscale dining in Haven. But as part of his interview, he's preparing a tasting menu."

"That sounds tempting, but—"

"Great. I'll pick you up at six," he interjected.

"I didn't say—"

But he'd already disconnected.

She huffed out a breath and scowled at the now silent phone.

"Is something wrong?" her mom asked.

"Liam wants me to have dinner with him tonight."

"A date?" Bev asked hopefully.

"No," she responded immediately. Firmly. "A working dinner."

"Regardless of what you call it, sharing a romantic meal with a handsome man sounds like a date to me," her mother remarked.

"I didn't say I'd go," she pointed out.

"I didn't hear you say no."

"Because he hung up before I could get the words out. But I'm going to call him back now and say it," she announced.

"Why?"

"Because I don't like being manipulated. And because I want to have dinner with you and Dad, Ava, Max and Sam."

"Honey, you have dinner with us every night."

"And I rely on you to look after my babies too much."

"Who says it's too much?" her mother demanded.

"I do."

"Well, I disagree."

Macy sighed and tried again, "I know they're a handful—"

"Actually, they're three handfuls," Bev interjected.

"But between your dad and me, we've got four hands and we love spending time with our grandbabies."

"Maybe you should check with Dad before you volunteer him for extra babysitting duties," Macy suggested.

Her mother immediately waved that suggestion away. "Now forget about making excuses not to have dinner with Liam and go downstairs to find something to wear."

"I really don't think this is a good idea," she hedged.

"Because you don't like Liam? Or because you do?" Bev wondered aloud.

"It doesn't matter whether I do or don't—I'm a single mother with three babies."

"But maybe you don't have to be a single mother forever."

She sighed. "Are we really back to this again?"

"I'm not telling you to marry the man," her mother said. Then she winked. "At least, not before you've had dinner with him."

It did take some time for Macy to figure out what she was going to wear. After a quick shower to ensure she didn't smell like baby spit—or worse—she stood in her undergarments in front of her open closet, surveying the contents.

She had work clothes: skirts and pants with matching jackets and an assortment of coordinating tops, and she had mom clothes: yoga pants and stretch leggings with oversized shirts and hoodies. She also had two pairs of pre-pregnancy jeans that she was able to squeeze into again, but she wouldn't count on the button holding through a meal. And tucked in the back of the closet were half a dozen dresses from her I'm-a-single-woman-in-Sin-City days, but as she rifled through them, she doubted there was even one that would accommodate the extra pounds she continued to carry, even eight and a half months after giving birth.

Although maybe…

She lifted the hanger holding a long-sleeved sheath-style dress off the rod. The fabric was a silky jersey knit in royal blue that had a fair amount of stretch and give and just might—if she crossed her fingers and held her breath—be suitable.

So she removed it from the hanger and wriggled into it. Smoothing down the skirt, she turned to check out her reflection in the mirror and decided that she didn't hate it. And if she put on a pair of Spanx—

No. She wasn't going to squeeze herself into Spanx for a dinner outing that wasn't even a date.

Then why the lacy underwear?

She ignored the taunting question from her subconscious. She'd selected her bra and matching underwear because they were comfortable, not because anyone else was going to see them—especially not her boss.

Although there wasn't a lot of snow on the ground, the frigid temperature had her opting for boots rather than shoes. Thankfully, she had a stylish knee-high pair with a chunky heel and silver buckles that worked with the short-skirted dress. She added silver earrings and a trio of bangle bracelets and decided she was good to go.

With her mother's earlier remarks still fresh in her mind, she almost ignored the makeup bag on the counter, but her vanity was apparently stronger than her obstinacy. And okay, even at her best she didn't look anything like a twenty-year-old Swedish model, but dinner with Liam wasn't anything like a real date, either.

"You look lovely," Bev said, when she came downstairs to check on her daughter's progress.

Macy glanced down. "I don't think my stomach is ever going to be flat again."

"You used to be too skinny—now you've got some curves."

"What I've got is ten pounds of baby fat."

"And it looks good on you," Bev insisted.

"Thanks, Mom. But it doesn't really matter how I look, because this isn't a date," she reminded her mother—and herself.

"I don't care what you call it—I just want you to relax and have a good time."

"I've got my phone," she said, tucking it into the outside pocket of her handbag. "Call me if you have any problems with the kids."

"You seem to forget that I raised three children of my own."

"I know you're more than capable of taking care of Ava, Max and Sam, but—"

"But you're looking for an excuse to weasel out of this da—dinner," Bev quickly amended.

The upstairs doorbell rang, and Macy sighed.

"And now it's too late," her mother pointed out unnecessarily.

Macy didn't stall any longer, because she knew that if she did, her father would answer the door, and she didn't want him to give Liam the same third-degree interrogation he'd given her boyfriends in high school.

But she was too late.

She reached the top of the stairs leading to the main foyer just as her father's fingers closed around the handle of the door.

"It's okay, Dad, I'll get…"

She was too late again. Her words trailed off as Norm opened the door—and were completely forgotten when she caught a glimpse of her boss. He was wearing his usual jeans and cowboy boots, but with a dress shirt, tie and jacket. He hadn't bothered to shave, and she itched to reach up and stroke the stubble that darkened his jaw. Looking at him, she knew why sexy cowboys remained a popular fantasy for many of her friends, and when his eyes locked on hers and his lips curved, her blood heated in her veins and pooled low in her belly.

Obviously this was a bad idea.

A very bad idea. Because her hormones were clamoring for her to forget about dinner and feast on *him*.

And the blatant appreciation in his gaze as it boldly skimmed over her made her suspect that he wouldn't object if she proposed such a change of plans. Or maybe that was just her own hormonally charged imagination running away with her.

"Good evening, Mr. Clayton." Liam offered his hand.

Norm shook it firmly. "You take care of my girl tonight," he instructed the younger man.

"I will, sir."

Macy could tell that the "sir" scored points with both of her parents, compelling her to interject.

"Your girl is thirty-three years old," she reminded her father. "And this dinner is for business, not pleasure."

"Why can't it be both?" Liam wondered aloud.

"Now that's a good question," Bev said, her remark earning a conspiratorial grin from her daughter's boss.

"Because it's not," Macy said firmly, before she brushed her lips against her mother's cheek. "Good night, Mom." Then she stopped by the playpen and bent down to drop kisses on top of each of the babies' heads and instruct them to be good for Gramma and Grampa.

"They're in good hands," Norm promised.

"I know they are," she said, and bussed his cheek, too.

Liam turned his head, a silent invitation for her to touch her lips to his cheek.

Macy rolled her eyes and shook her head.

He shrugged and helped her on with her coat. "I figured it was worth a try."

"I won't be late," she told her parents, as she knotted the belt at her waist.

"It doesn't matter if you are or aren't," Bev said. "We're not waiting up." Then, in case her point wasn't clear enough, she winked at Liam.

"Good night," Macy said firmly.

"Have a good time," her mother said.

She shoved Liam ahead of her out the door and closed it firmly at her back.

"Can I say now what I didn't dare say when your father was staring me down?" Liam asked, after Macy was buckled into the passenger seat of his truck and he'd taken his place behind the wheel.

"What's that?"

He looked at her and, even in the dim light of his truck cab, she could see the heat in his gaze. "Wow. Just…wow."

She felt her cheeks flush. She didn't know how to respond. She'd told her parents—and herself—that this wasn't a date, but the way Liam was looking at her, the way the butterflies were winging around in her stomach, she kind of wished that it was.

Or maybe she was just hungry.

"So what's on the menu tonight?" she asked when he'd backed out of the driveway and turned toward the inn.

"I have no idea. I told Kyle to put together the menu…and I didn't even think to ask if you had any food allergies."

"No allergies," she assured him.

"That's a relief," he said. "And while the chef didn't tell me what he was cooking, he did suggest that I could feature Circle G beef on the menu and highlight the connection between the ranch and the inn."

"What a great idea," Macy said.

"I thought so," he agreed. "Of course, I might need my manager to negotiate the terms of any supply agreement with the ranch's owner."

"Your father's still not happy about your career change?"

He shrugged. "I shouldn't have expected anything different. After all, Gilmores are ranchers."

Macy had heard the same refrain spoken by various people countless times, and she could only imagine how difficult it had been for Liam to buck that trend—and how much more difficult his father continued to make it by refusing to respect his son's choices.

The subject was abandoned when they arrived at the inn.

"Do you have a timeline for opening the restaurant?" Macy asked.

"*If* I open the restaurant," he clarified. "And no."

"I don't think you would have let Kyle prepare this tasting menu tonight if you weren't leaning in that direction."

"Leaning isn't the same as committed. And it usually takes more than a single meal to get me to make a commitment."

"I'll keep that in mind," she said. "But right now, I'm hungry, so lead the way to dinner, cowboy."

Kyle had enlisted help with the setting up and serving. He introduced Erin as a friend of his sister's—and also a part-time waitress at Jo's. The chef then proceeded to give them a preview of the menu.

White wines would be sampled with the starters— sweet potato soup garnished with Greek yogurt and toasted pumpkin seeds, arugula and pear salad with Gorgonzola dressing, goat cheese crostini with fig and olive tapenade, bacon-wrapped dates stuffed with blue cheese, and caramelized onion tart with a balsamic reduction; and red wines would be served with the mains—prime rib au jus accompanied by roasted fingerling potatoes and glazed baby carrots, chicken breast stuffed with spinach and mushrooms served on a bed of creamy risotto, and grilled salmon with couscous and a steamed vegetable medley.

Every detail of the meal was perfect. The presentation of each plate was as exquisite as its flavor. And sitting at a candlelit table across from a man whose smile was enough to make her blood hum in her veins was dangerously intoxicating.

"I'm trying to pace myself," Macy said, as she nibbled on a bite of salmon. "But it's not easy. Everything tastes so good."

"And nothing like what you'd find on the menu at Diggers'," Liam remarked.

"I didn't realize your reluctance to venture into the restaurant business was based, at least in part, on an unwillingness to step on the toes of the other dining establishments in town."

"Haven's a small town, and it's important that we support local businesses if we want them to stay here."

"And that's exactly why you need to offer fine dining," she told him. "To give people a reason to stay in Haven rather than trekking to Elko or Battle Mountain."

"With every bite, I'm growing more convinced," he admitted, reaching across the table to scoop up a forkful of the risotto on the plate in front of her.

"And when word gets out that there's a fancy new restaurant in Haven, you'll start to get people from Elko and Battle Mountain coming here for a meal."

"You think so?" he asked, still sounding dubious.

She tapped her fork on the edge of the plate with the prime rib. "I'd travel more than fifty miles for a bite of that flavorful, melt-in-your-mouth beef. Pair it with a glass—or a bottle—of that California cabernet sauvignon, and suddenly your diners are not only happy they made the trip but realizing that they can linger over dessert and another glass of wine and then check into one of the luxurious suites upstairs.

"And, of course, you could put together special dinner and room packages as part of your usual offerings or a special-occasion thing."

"Or *you* could," he suggested.

She smiled. "I'd be happy to."

"Did you have any questions, comments or concerns about anything on the menu?" Kyle asked, coming out of the kitchen after they'd had a chance to sample each of his offerings.

"I have one," Macy said, glancing at Liam across the table. "Who gets the doggy bag?"

The young chef smiled. "I'll let the two of you figure that out."

"Arm wrestle for it?" Liam suggested.

"Yeah, that would be fair," Macy noted dryly.

Liam grinned. "Why don't we put the leftovers in the fridge here? Then we can both enjoy them again for lunch tomorrow."

"I guess that would work," she agreed. And then, to Kyle, she said, "You must have been cooking all day."

"It's what I love to do," he told her.

"And your passion for food is evident in every bite," she assured him.

"It's only long-ingrained table manners that held me back from licking my plate," Liam said.

Kyle's smile grew. "Should I send out dessert now, then?"

"I don't know that I could eat another bite, but if your desserts are even half as good as everything else, I have to try," Macy said.

"Desserts aren't my specialty," the chef confessed. "But I have mango sorbet with fresh raspberries, a pecan tart with caramel sauce, and white chocolate mousse dusted with cocoa powder and garnished with sprigs of mint."

As he spoke, Erin set each of the referenced desserts on the table.

"If you wanted fancier options on the menu, you could consider partnering with Sweet Caroline's Sweets," he suggested.

"Another great idea," Macy agreed. "It would expand the options for your diners and support another local business."

"Did anyone want coffee? Tea?" Erin asked.

"Not for me, thanks," Liam said.

Macy shook her head. "I'm going to finish my wine," she decided.

"Then we'll leave you to enjoy your dessert while we clean up the kitchen," Kyle said.

Macy lifted a spoon and waved it over the three dishes, as if she didn't know where to begin. She decided on the tart, breaking off a piece with the side of her spoon, then sliding it between her lips.

"Oh. My. God." Her eyes closed in blissful pleasure. "Oh, yes."

The unintentionally provocative words combined with the expression of pure bliss on her face made Liam wonder if Macy would respond with the same passionate enthusiasm to the experience of other pleasures. No, not just wonder. Made him want to know.

Made him want.

He shifted in his chair as his body immediately began to respond to the contemplation of that possibility. He shoved a spoonful of sorbet into his mouth, as if the flavored ice might cool the heat rushing through his veins.

He cleared his throat. "It's good?" he asked.

She shook her head. "Good doesn't begin to describe it. It's—" she took another bite of the tart, sighed "—better than sex."

"Now *I* have to try it," Liam said, reaching across the table with his spoon.

She curled her hand protectively around the plate. "I don't want to share."

He chuckled. "Well, if you won't let me try the tart, then I'm not going to share the mango sorbet with fresh raspberries."

"Fresh raspberries in March?" Her tone was dubious, but her expression was interested.

"They might not be local produce, but they're delicious," he said, and nudged the glass dish toward the center of the table.

She spooned up another bite of the tart before reluctantly sliding the plate closer to his.

"Mmm...that's good, too," she said, after she'd sampled the frozen treat. "*Really* good."

"But is it better than sex?" he wanted to know.

"It might be," she decided. "The truth is, my memories of the event are a little foggy while this sweet taste of heaven is right here, right now."

"Dessert definitely satisfies a sweet tooth, but sex—" Now *he* sighed. "Sex done right satisfies the body *and* the soul."

She snorted at that.

His brows lifted. "You don't agree?"

"I probably shouldn't even express an opinion," she admitted. "Because I haven't had sex in...well, let's just say it's been a long time."

"How long?" he wondered.

She waved her spoon at him. "That's an inappropriate question to ask an employee."

"You're the one who brought up the subject of sex," he pointed out.

"You're right." She nodded. "But it's your fault."

"How is it my fault?"

"Because before you kissed me, I never thought about how much I missed sex."

"*You* kissed *me*," he reminded her.

"The first time," she acknowledged.

"You kissed me back the second time."

"Has any woman ever not kissed you back?" she wondered.

"I'm not interested in any other woman right now," he said. "I'm only interested in you."

The intensity of his gaze made her belly flutter. "I've got three kids," she reminded him.

"That's not what's been holding me back."

"What's holding you back?"

"I'm trying to respect our working relationship."

"Yeah, that complicates things," she agreed. Then she finished the wine in her glass and pushed away from the table. "Will you excuse me for a minute? I want to give my mom a call to check on Ava, Max and Sam."

"Of course," he agreed. "But I can't promise the rest of that tart will be there when you get back."

She gave one last, lingering glance at the pastry before she said, "You can finish the tart."

He was tempted by the dessert, but he managed to resist. He didn't know how much longer he could hold out against his attraction to Macy—or if she wanted him to.

Had he crossed a line by flirting with her? She hadn't reacted in a way that suggested she was upset or offended, but she hadn't exactly flirted back, either.

"Is everything okay?" he asked, when she returned to the table several minutes later.

She nodded. "I got caught in the middle of an argument."

"With your mom?"

"With myself."

His brows lifted. "Did you win?"

"I hope so," she said.

Then she set an antique key on the table and slid it toward him.

Chapter 11

Liam immediately recognized it as the key to the luxury suite on the top floor.

"You do know that I have an apartment upstairs?" he asked.

"Yeah, but it seemed presumptuous to invite you up to your own place," she said. "Plus, I've been dreaming about sleeping in that bed since the day you gave me the tour." Then she smiled and shrugged. "Or maybe not sleeping in it."

He wrapped his fingers around the key, gripping it so tightly that the cold metal bit into his palm.

"Are you sure, Macy?" Then, without pausing long enough to give her a chance to respond, he said, "Please say you're sure."

"I'm sure."

He exhaled a grateful sigh of relief.

But still, he had to ask one more question. "Should I worry that your decision is being influenced by the wine?"

"I've only drunk enough to lessen my inhibitions about letting you see me naked," she told him.

He abruptly pushed back his chair and stood up. "Then let's go upstairs so I can see you naked," he suggested.

"Are *you* sure?" she asked him. "On my way back from the desk, I started to wonder if maybe I was jumping the gun."

He drew her into his arms, felt her tremble a little as he pulled her close. Nerves? Anticipation? He was admittedly experiencing some of each.

He'd wanted her for so long but had managed to convince himself it couldn't happen and that, eventually, his feelings for her would go away. He'd been wrong. And now that he knew Macy wanted him, too, he wasn't going to deny those feelings any longer.

Instead, he lowered his head and covered her mouth with his own. It seemed like an eternity had passed since he'd tasted the flavor of her lips. They were as sweet as he remembered, her response as passionate as he recalled.

He slid his hands up her back, tracing the line of her spine. Then down again, cupping the curve of her bottom. She arched into him, her breasts crushed against his chest, her hips aligned with his so there was no way she could be unaware of his arousal.

"Does that answer your question?"

Macy blinked. "What was the question?"

He chuckled softly and lifted her into his arms.

She gasped. "What are you doing?"

"What I've wanted to do for months—I'm taking you to bed."

"Do you know how many stairs you have to climb to the top floor from here?"

"I've never actually counted them, so no," he told her. "But I'm pretty sure it's the same number to get to my apartment."

"And too many for you to carry me the whole way," she protested.

"Is that a challenge?" he asked, starting up the first flight.

"Of course it's not a challenge. It's a reasonable statement and a legitimate concern for your physical well-being."

"I promise, I won't be too tired when we reach the bed to remember why we're there."

"I wasn't—" She huffed out a breath. "Never mind."

If he was determined to carry her, why should she object to the ride? And truthfully, she quite enjoyed being held in strong arms, cradled against the hard muscles of his hot body.

Despite her extensive dating history, she'd never known another man who made her insides quiver with just a look. Who made her knees weak with the flash of a smile.

It had been a purely physical attraction in the beginning—she hadn't known Liam well enough for it to be anything more. But working in close proximity with him over the past few weeks, she'd been pleased to discover that she also liked and respected the man who was her boss.

"Fifty-two," he announced, as he unlocked the door. The room was dark, but he was familiar enough with the layout to navigate it without turning on a light. He carried her through the sitting room and past the bathroom to the bedroom before setting her on her feet. He bypassed the lamps in favor of the fireplace, creating light, heat and ambiance with the press of a button. Then he located the box of long wooden matches and turned his attention to the fat pillar candles lined up in a row along the mantel. Candles he'd bought when he went with her to the antique and craft market.

She wouldn't have thought he was the type to waste time with such romantic trappings. She certainly didn't want or need romance. She didn't want or need to pretend this night was anything more than two people succumbing to their long-denied attraction.

While he finished lighting the candles, she lowered herself onto the edge of the mattress, her hands folded in her lap. She was admittedly a little nervous and uncertain. Not about making love with Liam. She had no doubt that was what she wanted, but it was the details that eluded her.

What to do next.

Apparently he didn't suffer from the same uncertainty. He knelt on the floor between her knees and lifted one of her booted feet into his hands. "All night, I've been wondering what you'd look like wearing these boots and nothing else."

"I can't imagine how I'd look—"

"Sexy," he interjected.

"—but I'd probably feel ridiculous."

"We'll take them off, then," he decided, tugging on the zipper pull.

She was wearing tights, of course, because it was early spring in northern Nevada and the nights were still frigidly cold. But the slow, sensual glide of his knuckle along the inside of her calf as he dragged the pull downward made her skin heat, burn.

He drew the first boot off her foot and set it aside, then repeated the same shockingly sensuous process with the second. Then he lifted both feet into his hands. His thumbs stroked the sensitive inside arches, then skimmed over the tops to her ankles.

"Do you have a foot fetish?" she asked, a little breathlessly.

He chuckled softly. "I have a Macy fetish. I want to touch and see and taste every inch of you tonight."

While he spoke, those clever hands continued their exploration, over her knees and under her skirt, along the insides of her thighs.

He eased down the waistband of her tights. She lifted up off the bed to assist him, though her muscles, already quivering from his touch, trembled with the effort.

"Maybe I should help with some of your clothes," she offered.

"Let's just focus on you right now."

"As I recall, this was *my* idea," she pointed out to him. "So I don't see why you get to call all the shots."

"This might have seemed like your idea tonight," he acknowledged. "But it's been my fantasy for weeks, months. Since the first time I saw you."

"Maybe I've been fantasizing about this, too."

"Have you?"

She realized she'd backed herself into a corner. If she confessed that she had, he'd no doubt want to hear about her fantasies in explicit detail. If she denied that she had, he'd take that as justification to control every step of their lovemaking.

So she only responded by kissing him—long and slow and deep. Teasing him with her lips and tongue and teeth.

"You make me crazy." He muttered the confession into her mouth as his hands traced the curves of her body over her dress. "I want you naked, now, and I can't find a zipper anywhere on this damn dress."

She laughed softly, though the sound was a little strained by her own desperation. "There is no zipper."

"Then how the hell did you get it on? And, far more important right now, how the hell am I supposed to get it off?"

She stood up, praying that her wobbly legs would support her, and reached for the hem of her skirt.

"I wish I'd thought to put on music," Liam said. "Because watching you wiggle is just about the sexiest thing I've ever seen."

She finished drawing the garment over her head and let it fall to the floor.

"Correction," he said, his eyes moving over her body in a slow visual caress. "The second sexiest thing."

She blushed at the implication that *she* was the sexiest, grateful that the muted light from the fire didn't spotlight her stretchmarks or scar.

He finally yanked off his own boots and jacket, then added his jeans and shirt to the growing pile of discarded clothing on the floor. As they tumbled onto the mattress together, their mouths met, mated. Their bodies arched, yearned.

His hands stroked her skin, stoked her desire. He cupped her breasts in his palms, his thumbs circling the aching peaks through the silky fabric of her bra. She'd wondered if nursing her babies would decrease the sensitivity of her nipples. It appeared the answer was a clear and resounding *no*. Because, when he finally brushed his thumbs over the peaks, sharp, shocking arrows of pleasure speared from the tips to her core.

When he lowered his head to replace his hand with his mouth, suckling her through the fabric barrier, she nearly came apart right then and there. When he pushed the strap of her bra off her shoulder and freed her breast from the constraint, the sensation of his mouth, hot and wet, on her bare skin, did make her come apart.

As she continued to shudder with the aftershocks of her release, he made his way down her body. Kissing and licking, nibbling and sucking. He paused at her navel, his fingertip tracing along the horizontal line a few inches below it.

"My C-section scar," she confided.

"Does it hurt?"

She shook her head. "No."

He pressed his lips to her belly button, then the scar, then continued his downward trajectory.

She felt anticipation building inside her again, and when his tongue brushed against the ultrasensitive nub, she found herself teetering on the brink of another climax. But she wanted him with her this time, so she reached between their bodies and wrapped her hand around him. His groan vibrated through her.

"I'm not finished down here yet," he protested.

"I want you inside me."

He started to rise up, over her, then paused. "I didn't plan for this to happen tonight, so please tell me the basket of amenities in the bathroom has been checked and restocked."

"Every day," she assured him.

"In that case—" he pressed a quick kiss to her lips "—I'll be right back."

He slipped away, and Macy knew that if she was going to change her mind, this was her best chance to do it.

But she didn't want to change her mind.

She wanted this.

Wanted *him*.

Sure, she had some reservations, because she knew that once they were intimate, everything would change. Or maybe everything had already changed. Already she knew that she'd never felt about anyone the way she felt about Liam.

Working side by side with him over the past few weeks, her feelings had continued to deepen and grow. She'd observed many of his different moods: happy, annoyed, frustrated, amused. She'd seen him with his family, noted the obvious bond he shared with each of his siblings, the easy affection that characterized his relationship with his grandparents, his evident adoration of his young niece. And though he tried to pretend otherwise, she could tell that he was deeply troubled by the tension that had grown between him and his father. He was a man of many facets and every single one of them appealed to her.

"Now…where was I?" he asked, returning to the bedroom with two foil packets in hand.

"You were going to open one of those, put it on you and then put you in me."

His lips curved in response to her concise instructions. "So you want me to climb on top and get right to it?"

"Did you hear what I said downstairs? It's been a really long time for me, so there's no need to waste any more time on foreplay."

"Do you feel as if I've been wasting your time?" he asked, sounding more amused than insulted as his hands continued to move over her, making her sigh with pleasure, squirm with need. "Are you suggesting that you're not enjoying this?"

"You know I am."

"Then relax and let yourself enjoy," he suggested, just before he captured her nipple in his mouth again, swirling his tongue around the peak, making her moan.

He took her to the precipice again, and left her teetering on the edge while he rose up over her, spreading her knees farther apart and positioning himself between them. He nudged at her opening, testing, teasing. She lifted her hips, a wordless plea that he answered by burying himself deep inside her.

She gasped with shock, with pleasure, as the glorious friction of his invasion created a storm of sensation, enormous waves of pleasure crashing down on her again…and again…and again.

Finally, when she was certain she couldn't survive the barrage any longer, he linked their hands together and let the waves carry him away with her.

It was a long time later before she became aware of the weight of his body sprawled over hers, pinning her against the luxurious mattress. She knew her body would probably feel stiff and achy in the morning, but she didn't care. Because every muscle twinge tomorrow would be a reminder of the incredible pleasure he'd given her tonight.

Liam finally gathered up the strength to roll off her,

though he didn't move away. After another minute, he broke the silence to ask, "Are there any guests below this room?"

"Not tonight," she told him.

"That's good. I wouldn't want my manager to have to field noise complaints about the wild guests in Wild Bill's Suite."

Heat rose up her neck and into her cheeks. "I'm not usually… I mean, I never…well, not never but…okay, I'm going to shut up now."

He chuckled softly and brushed his lips against hers. "No, don't. I want to hear what you were going to say."

"I'll bet you do."

"You never…" he prompted.

"I've never…been particularly vocal before," she confided. "I've never…really lost control—certainly not like that—before."

His smile was satisfied. "I liked watching you lose control," he told her. "Whoever would have imagined that the tidy, efficient and organized Macy Clayton would be so uninhibited in the throes of passion?"

"Not me," she admitted. "I wasn't sure I believed the throes of passion even existed."

"Are you a believer now?"

"I think I might need just a little more convincing."

"Well, we do have one condom left," he said.

She felt a spark of arousal flicker through her body. "That would be a good start."

Macy knew she'd never be able to walk through the doors of this suite again without a smile curving her lips and erotic memories flooding her mind and teasing her body. The hours she'd spent here with Liam had been a perfect fantasy in so many ways, but now it was time to get back to reality—and her reality wasn't a sexy man and a luxurious hotel room but a basement apartment where three babies waited for her.

This brief interlude from the reality of her life had been fun, but it was only an interlude.

She nudged her elbow into Liam's ribs.

He grunted in protest.

"You can't fall asleep," she told him.

"I'm pretty sure I can," he countered in a drowsy voice.

"Let me rephrase," she said. "I don't want you to fall asleep."

"I'm flattered, but I'm definitely going to need some time to recuperate before we go another round."

She elbowed him again, a little harder this time.

His eyes stayed closed, but his lips curved as he wrapped his arm around her and drew her back against his body, nuzzling her throat, making her shiver.

"I can't stay," she told him, sincerely regretful.

"I know."

"And since Uber hasn't yet found its way to Haven, I'm going to need a ride home."

"I know," he said again. "But I'm not ready to let go of you just yet."

Whether she cuddled with him for another minute or two or ten, this night was only a stolen moment out of her ordinary life, and it was already over.

She hadn't expected that getting naked with him would magically transform their relationship. They were at completely different stages in their lives, looking for different things. Except that tonight they'd wanted the same thing. And that want had proven stronger than everything else.

She wouldn't trade Ava, Max and Sam for anything in the world, but she couldn't deny that she'd enjoyed feeling like a woman instead of a mom for a brief while. But she'd told her parents that she wouldn't be late, and she'd already been gone a lot longer than she'd intended. Plus, Max would inevitably be up early, wanting some cuddle time with his mom before his siblings woke up to demand their breakfast and—

"You're thinking about your kids, aren't you?" he guessed.

"Sorry. Occupational hazard."

"There's no need to apologize," he said, but he released her now to climb out of bed and gather up his clothes.

She did the same, more than a little sorry that the night was already at an end.

"How are we going to explain the tangled sheets to housekeeping?" he wondered aloud.

"I'm housekeeping tomorrow," she reminded him. "And I'll change the bed first thing."

"Or I could do it when I get back," he offered.

"You could try," she acknowledged. "But the result wouldn't fool anybody."

"True enough," he agreed.

Macy took a quick look around to ensure they hadn't left anything while he blew out the candles and turned off the fire.

They were mostly silent as they made their way down the stairs to the main lobby, where they'd left their coats. He held hers while she slid her arms into the sleeves.

When she lifted her hair to pull it out of the collar of her coat, he touched a hand to the side of her throat.

"You've got marks from my beard," he told her.

She suspected the marks weren't only on her throat, though she didn't worry that those other places would be visible to anyone else. "Hopefully they'll fade before morning."

"I'm hoping they don't," he said, as he led her out to his truck. "Then, when you see them in the mirror, you'll remember tonight."

"I don't think I'm going to forget anytime soon," she assured him.

The journey back to her parents' house was short and silent.

"Thanks for dinner," she said when he pulled into the driveway. "And…everything."

"Thank *you* for everything," he said, as he killed the engine.

"You don't have to walk me to the door," she told him.

"How else am I going to steal a goodbye kiss?"

She knew that she should protest, that despite Bev's assertion that she wouldn't wait up, it was entirely possible that her mother wasn't just awake but watching through her bedroom window. But if Liam walked her to the side door, no one would be able to see him kiss her—and just the thought of one more kiss was enough to make her insides quiver.

The kiss itself liquified her bones and turned her brain to mush. Even after making love with him twice already tonight, her body ached for more, yearned for the fulfillment only he could give her.

"Do me a favor?" He whispered the words close to her ear.

She had to moisten her lips with her tongue before she could respond. "What's that?"

He brushed his thumb over her bottom lip, tracing the plump curve. "Think about me."

Then he stepped back and waited for her to open the door.

As she slipped inside, Macy knew that she would.

She could hardly do anything else.

Chapter 12

Macy's former supervisor in Las Vegas had often commented on her professionalism. Even when she was confronted by unruly and obnoxious guests, she never lost her cool or raised her voice. She was always a consummate professional.

Until last night—when she'd slept with her boss.

That had been an admittedly *un*professional move, but she wasn't going to compound it by letting anyone at work know she'd slept with the boss.

Liam gave her a brief nod of acknowledgment when he walked through the door. She hadn't expected anything more, and yet she found herself wondering what his impersonal greeting meant. Of course, it was possible that it didn't mean anything, especially as she was busy with Mrs. Hemingway and her daughter, helping to plan their local activities for the day.

When the guests from Boulder City had gone on their way, he poked his head out of the library, which he used as an office when she was occupying the front desk. "Can you come in here for a minute?" he asked.

"Sure," she agreed, pausing on her way to peek into the solarium and ensure that everybody was being looked after.

Of course, it was a Wednesday morning, and aside from the Hemingways, who had already gone on their way, "everybody" consisted of a young couple who had booked the Bonnie Room and two middle-aged women—lifelong friends nearing the completion of a cross-country road trip—who were staying in the Clyde Room. At the moment, they were all digging into their cooked-to-order breakfasts, ensuring that she wouldn't be missed if she was away from the desk for a few minutes.

"What can I do for you?" she asked, stepping through the doors and into the library. It wasn't an unusual question but considering the things she'd done for him—and vice versa—the night before, the ordinary words suddenly took on a whole other layer of meaning.

Liam's gaze locked onto hers, his sparkling with heat and humor, and she knew that his mind had gone in the same direction. Then his expression sobered, and he said, "You can tell me if I crossed any lines last night."

"None that I didn't want crossed," she assured him.

He seemed visibly relieved by her response. "Good. But I realized this morning that we didn't talk about what was going to happen next."

"I didn't know that there was going to be a next... but I was hoping."

He smiled at that. "Me, too." Then he lowered his head and kissed her, slowly, deeply and very thoroughly.

"Next... I want to take you upstairs and pick up where we left off last night."

"Me, too," she admitted. "But my boss isn't paying me to lie down on the job."

"Is that your way of suggesting we should try it standing up?" he asked, and followed the question with a lascivious grin.

She shook her head. "It's my way of telling you that any extracurricular activities will occur outside of my working hours."

"You drive a hard bargain," he lamented.

But somehow, over the next few weeks, they made it work.

It wasn't easy, especially when The Home Station opened to offer evening dining. At first, it was only guests of the inn who showed any interest in eating at "that fancy new restaurant," but when those guests were overheard at The Daily Grind or The Trading Post talking about the fabulous meals they'd enjoyed, a few daring locals decided to give it a try. Then a few more.

The only downside was that Liam was no longer enjoying Jo's pizza two or three times a week—but not for lack of trying. He'd placed several orders that were somehow either lost or missed or made wrong, such as when he'd ordered a five-meat pizza and been given a vegetarian instead. He knew Jo was upset that Kyle was working at the inn now, but he hoped she wouldn't hold a grudge forever.

After only a few weeks, the restaurant was booked to capacity every night. Of course, the success of the restaurant meant longer hours for Liam at the hotel—and fewer trips out to the Circle G. But Caleb was right—

they didn't really need him there, so he stayed where he *was* needed.

And since Macy was usually at the inn, it was also where he wanted to be.

It took some creative juggling of other responsibilities for them to steal time alone together, and it was still easier for him than her, because he didn't have three babies depending on him. As a result, he found himself planning outings that were suitable for Ava, Max and Sam, too—even if that simply meant going to places where the triplets could ride around in their stroller and watch the scenery or other people passing by. And the more time he spent with all of them, the more he realized he was in serious danger of losing his heart to the single mom and her three adorable kids.

Liam was yawning when he walked into the inn's kitchen Wednesday morning, desperate for a hit of caffeine. He'd gone to bed after midnight and been up since dawn, and he wasn't sure how he was going to get through the day.

He halted in the entranceway, as if to remember why he was there. Macy came to the rescue, putting a mug of steaming coffee into his hands.

"Thank you."

"You looked like you needed it."

He swallowed a mouthful, willed the caffeine to jumpstart his brain.

"Is everything okay?"

He blinked. "What?"

"You seem really distracted this morning."

"I've just got a lot on my mind."

"Anything more than usual?"

"I went out to the ranch yesterday morning, to show my grandmother the updated menus for The Home Station," he confided. "And, not unexpectedly, crossed paths with my dad while I was there."

"Did you argue?"

He shook his head. "No. In fact, he was almost civil."

"Now I know why you look so worried."

When he didn't respond to her teasing tone, she realized that he really *was* worried.

"Maybe it's just that I haven't been out to the ranch in a few days, but he didn't look right."

"What do you mean?"

"I'm not sure," he admitted. "But he seemed pale, tired."

"Did you ask him how he was feeling? No," she answered her own question before he could. "Of course, you didn't. You don't communicate with your father."

"No more than he communicates with me."

"Did you say anything to your brother?"

He nodded. "Caleb didn't think there was any cause for concern."

"Then there probably isn't."

"You're right," he acknowledged. "I'm probably just feeling guilty that, as everything has amped up around here, I've been spending less time there."

"Is it only guilt?" she wondered. "Or is there maybe a little bit of second-guessing going on?"

"What do you mean?"

"You could have emailed the new menus to your grandmother instead of taking the time to drive all the way out to the Circle G," she pointed out. "Which makes me suspect that you wanted to make the trip—either to ensure ranch operations were running smoothly or to touch base with your family."

He scowled. "You sound like you've been reading my sister's psych textbooks."

"Or maybe just talking to your sister," she said.

"Why?"

"Because she stopped by yesterday morning when you were out at the ranch."

"Why?" he asked again.

"Because she wanted to know if we offered a family discount."

"For Sky? Yeah, she can pay a hundred and fifty percent of the usual rate."

"Even if the room is for your grandparents? For their sixtieth wedding anniversary?"

"I'm one step ahead of her," he said. "Wild Bill's Suite is already booked."

Macy smiled. "You're a good man, Liam Gilmore."

"Come back here later tonight, and I'll show you how good," he suggested.

Of course, she did.

Because even after more than a month together, the physical attraction between them showed no signs of abating.

She didn't have enough experience with relationships to know if this was normal, but she did know that she was well on her way to losing her heart to the sexy cowboy.

"Can you do me a favor?" Liam asked, a few days later.

Macy finished logging a new reservation into the system and clicked save. "Sure—what do you need?"

"Lunch."

She looked up from the computer, her expression quizzical. "You want me to make lunch for you?"

"No. I just want you to order it for me. And pick it up."

"I'm pretty sure running your personal errands isn't part of my job description."

"Not even if I offer to share my pizza with you?"

"Jo's still refusing to serve you?" she guessed.

His concern about backlash from the owner of the pizzeria had not been unfounded. Jo was furious with him for giving Kyle free rein in his fancy kitchen—a surefire guarantee that her son wasn't going to be tossing pizza dough anytime soon.

Liam nodded. "And I'm going through pizza withdrawal."

"What am I ordering on this pizza?"

"Pepperoni, Italian sausage and bacon crumble."

She wrinkled her nose. "And after lunch I'll make an appointment at the medical clinic in Battle Mountain so you can have your arteries cleaned out."

"My arteries are fine—and my stomach is empty."

"Okay," she relented. "Pepperoni, Italian sausage and bacon crumble on one half, ham, pineapple and black olives on the other. I'll order it in my name, but you're going to pick it up."

"Last time I went in there, she threw a ball of dough at my head."

"Which is why you need to go back and talk to her."

He grumbled, because he was certain that Jo wouldn't listen to him, but in the end, he walked over to the pizzeria.

The reception he got when he entered the restaurant was no less than he expected.

In response to the tinkle of the bell, Jo glanced up from the pie she was making, a sauce-filled ladle in hand. "You." She narrowed her gaze and lifted her other hand to point a bony finger at the door. "Get out of my restaurant."

He held up his own hands in a gesture of surrender. "I'm here to pick up a pizza for Macy."

"If she really wants her pizza, she's going to have to come and get it herself, because I'm not giving it to you."

"Come on, Jo," he cajoled. "Don't you think you're being a little unreasonable?"

"I don't have to sell my pizza to anybody I don't want to," she said stubbornly.

"That's not really true. A public business can't randomly refuse service to someone."

"Oh, don't worry. This isn't random at all."

"I've been buying pizza here for as long as I've had money to buy pizza," he pointed out to her.

"It's the only place in town to get pizza," she said, obviously unimpressed by his claim of loyalty.

"Exactly," he said. "And I have no intention of competing with your business. In fact, I've always encouraged my guests to come over here."

"Are you waiting for me to thank you for that?"

"I didn't do it for thanks, but I didn't expect to be punished, either."

"You hired my kid," she reminded him.

"Duke hired him first," Liam noted.

She waved a hand dismissively. "I knew he wouldn't be happy at Diggers' for long—and then he'd come back here."

"He came to me looking for a job," he said in his defense.

"He had a job here."

"You wouldn't let him make anything but pizza."

"The sign over the door says Jo's Pizza."

"A lot of pizza places do other things," he remarked.

"We do calzones, too."

Which was essentially folded-up pizza. "I was thinking more along the lines of wings or pasta."

"Folks want wings or pasta, they go to Diggers'."

"They might appreciate having another option."

"You plan on serving pizza in your fancy restaurant?"

"No," he immediately replied.

"Why not?"

"Because everyone in Haven knows that nobody does pizza better than Jo's."

"And you're not going to get around me by stating what everyone knows is a fact," she told him.

"I'm not trying to get around you."

"Then what do you want?"

"I want my pizza."

Her brows lifted.

"I mean, Macy's pizza." And then, since he knew she'd already seen through the ruse, he opted for honesty. "I also want you to stop canceling my orders—or deliberately screwing up my orders. And I want you to come to the inn one night to enjoy a meal prepared by my new chef."

"Unless your fancy new restaurant is somehow in a different time zone, dinner time there is dinner time here, which means I'm working."

"You could try leaving your daughter in charge for one night," he suggested. "Then maybe *she* won't be looking for a job somewhere else in a few years."

Jo's eyes narrowed dangerously, then she turned around and picked up a flat white box. An order slip with Macy's name on it was tucked into the end. "I think you should take your pizza and go now."

He didn't have to be told twice.

He picked up the box, dropped a twenty-dollar bill on the counter and left without waiting for his change.

"Do you think I've been spending too much time with Liam lately?"

"Why would you ask a question like that?" Bev wondered as she squeezed a rubber dolphin, squirting water onto Max's belly.

Her grandson giggled and kicked his feet in the water, splashing her back.

Macy shrugged as she rubbed a cloth gently over Sam's body. "Maybe because I'm feeling a little out of my element," she acknowledged. "I don't have a lot of experience with romantic relationships, and I can't remember ever feeling so much so soon."

Bev's sigh was both wistful and worried. "You're falling in love with him."

"Am I?" The panic that spurted inside of her at the thought must have been reflected in her tone, because her mother smiled and touched a hand to her arm.

"Love isn't anything to be afraid of," Bev assured her daughter.

Macy didn't think she was afraid of love—but she was afraid of offering Liam her heart and having it rejected.

"And if you had to fall, you could do a lot worse than Liam Gilmore," her mother continued.

"Why do you say that?"

"Because it's obvious the man is just as crazy about Ava, Max and Sam as he is about you."

"He's been great with them," Macy agreed, as she continued to wash her babies and her mother continued to distract them with play. "Of course, his sister has a little girl, so kids aren't a completely alien species to him." Despite his initial attempts to convince her otherwise.

"That's one child," her mother pointed out. "Three can be overwhelming for someone who doesn't have a lot of experience with kids."

"Believe me, I know."

"You caught on fast," Bev noted.

"As if I had a choice." She lifted Ava out of the bath and wrapped her in a thick, fluffy towel.

"The point is, he's caught on pretty fast, too. A lot of guys would have balked at the idea of dating a single mother with three kids."

Liam had, as well, Macy remembered. In fact, he'd taken a literal step back when he'd learned that she was a mom.

"Maybe I should take a step back," she mused.

"It's hard to make any progress when you're moving in reverse," her mother pointed out, with unerring logic, as she wrapped Sam in another towel.

"I thought I'd given up on having a traditional family," she admitted now. "But the more time I spend with Liam—especially with Liam and Ava, Max and Sam—the more I find those old dreams being resurrected."

"And what's wrong with that?"

"Maybe nothing—except that we haven't really talked about the future."

"So maybe you need to have this conversation with him," Bev suggested.

"You're right," Macy agreed, removing Max from the tub. "And I will. Tomorrow."

"Good. Because right now, we've got to get these munchkins into their jammies and into bed."

But their paths didn't cross until late the following morning, when Macy was on the phone with the wine merchant and Liam was on his way to a meeting with Kyle and a local organic wholesaler.

"Lunch?" he mouthed the request.

She nodded.

He glanced at his watch. "Twelve-thirty?"

She nodded again.

He returned to the inn at 12:25.

"You're early," she noted.

He leaned across the desk and kissed her. "I wanted to make sure I had time to do that."

She grabbed the collar of his jacket and brought his mouth back to hers. "You know, one-thirty is a pretty good time for lunch, too."

He drew away slowly, reluctantly. "It is—except when breakfast was a mere blueberry muffin more than five hours ago."

She pushed away from the desk and reached for her coat. "In that case, we better go get you fed."

"Over lunch, I thought we could review the website updates for the fall and winter—"

The ring of his cell phone cut through his words.

"Go ahead and take it," Macy encouraged.

"It's just my brother." He swiped the screen to send the call to voice mail. "Whatever he wants can wait."

But Macy had barely set the "Back at 2:00 p.m." sign on the desk when his phone rang again.

Liam frowned at the same name and number on the display.

"Obviously it can't wait," Macy said.

While he was talking to his brother, she tidied the brochures in the pockets of the wall display by the desk. The National Cowboy Poetry Gathering in Elko was long past, but she kept the flyers, in case they piqued the interest of anyone who might be planning a visit the following year.

She straightened the cards advertising the Basque Museum, replenished the Adventure Village brochures—and found a miniature Hulk action figure that she'd noticed a little boy playing with while his parents checked in the day before. Rick and Monica Wallace in the Clark Foss suite, she remembered now. They'd gone out to tour the town today, but she called up to their room and left a message that Harrison's action figure was at the front desk.

Though Liam was facing the front door, she read the tension in the line of his shoulders, heard it in his clipped tone. Obviously his brother had not called to share good news.

"What's wrong?" she asked, when he finally disconnected the call.

"I have to go. My dad—" He cleared his throat. "The ambulance is taking him to the hospital in Elko."

Chapter 13

"Give me your keys," Macy said.

Liam looked at her blankly. "What? Why?"

"So I can drive you to the hospital."

He immediately shook his head. "No, it's okay. I can drive."

Maybe he could, but she wasn't sure that he should. It was obvious that his brother's phone call had rocked him to the core. And understandable, considering that he'd already lost one parent and just learned that the other was in some kind of medical distress.

"Do you want me to go with you?" she suggested as an alternative.

"No," he said again.

"Okay." She understood that he was distracted and worried about his father, but she couldn't help feeling a little disappointed that he'd so quickly disregarded her offers to help. Maybe he didn't need her, but she thought that he'd appreciate having someone to lean on during a time of crisis.

"I need you here," he said now.

Which made sense and took a little bit of the sting out of his earlier rejection.

"Will you call me?" she asked, walking with him toward the door. "To tell me how he's doing. To let me know if there's anything I can do."

He looked at her, his gaze unfocused. "What? Oh. Yeah. Okay."

She gave him a quick hug. "He's going to be okay," she said, and fervently prayed that it was true.

While Liam was on his way to Elko, Macy called Rose to cover the desk at the inn. Then she went home to wait for Liam's call.

"You should go to the hospital," Bev urged, when Macy told her mother as much as she herself knew.

"He doesn't want me there," she reluctantly admitted.

"What are you talking about?" her mother demanded. "Why wouldn't he want you there?"

She shrugged. "Maybe because our relationship doesn't really mean anything to him?"

Beverly scowled. "That's ridiculous."

"Is it?" Macy wondered. Though she wouldn't put it in such blunt terms to her mother, she had to wonder if Liam preferred to keep her on the periphery of his world, as his inn manager and bed buddy, rather than let her be part of his life.

Thankfully her phone rang before her mother could question her further, and Macy immediately snatched it up.

"It was a heart attack," Liam said without preamble. "He had emergency bypass surgery and is in recovery now."

"So, he's going to be okay?" she prompted hesitantly.

"Apparently. We don't yet know how long he's going to be in the hospital, but the doctor made it clear that he's going to need time to rest and recuperate."

"Of course," she agreed.

"Which means that extra hands are going to be needed at the Circle G."

His hands, she realized.

"Well, you don't need to worry about the inn. Rose has already agreed to take additional and extended shifts, so the two of us can cover things for the short term. You might want to hire someone else for the longer term, but we can talk about that later."

"Yeah," he agreed. "My mind is spinning in circles right now."

"Understandable," she assured him. "You focus on your dad and let me know what you need."

"Thanks."

She'd hoped he might want to talk a little bit longer, and maybe open up about some of what he was feeling, but he told her that he had other calls to make, then said goodbye and disconnected.

The following night, she gave in to her mother's urging—and her own desire to see that Liam was holding up okay—and made a trip to the hospital. Anticipating that his grandparents and siblings would all be there, too, she took a couple of extra-large pizzas. Jo might still be mad at Liam, but when she realized who the pizzas were for, she refused to accept any payment for the pies.

Macy was greeted warmly by the family members gathered in the waiting room, and she felt confident that she'd made the right decision in coming. But while she was in the middle of a conversation with Jack and Evelyn, Liam drew her away from his grandparents.

"Let's take a walk," he said.

It was more a command than a request, but understanding how worried he'd been about his father, she decided to cut him some slack.

He fell silent again as they made their way down the brightly lit corridor, so she ventured to ask, "Did you have enough pizza? Because I think there were a couple of slices left."

He turned to face her then. "What are you really doing here, Macy?"

She blinked, startled by not just the question but the coldness of his tone. "I know hospital food isn't the best, and I thought you'd appreciate something different."

His expression was dubious. "You came all this way to deliver pizza?"

"And to be here for you," she said, wondering if he was really so thickheaded that he didn't know how much she cared about him.

"I didn't ask you to come."

"No, you didn't," she said, silently acknowledging that maybe she was the obtuse one. She'd assumed he hadn't asked because he didn't want to seem weak and needy. Apparently she'd been wrong.

"Because I can't let myself be distracted right now," he told her. "I need to focus on what matters."

Which clearly meant that she did not.

"You're right," she said, fighting against the tears that burned her eyes. "I shouldn't have come. I'm sorry."

She turned toward the elevators, but she could hardly

see through the sheen of moisture that blurred her vision. As a result, she nearly walked into someone approaching from the other direction.

"Macy?" It was Skylar. "Are you okay?"

She nodded. "Yeah. Sorry. I was a little distracted—not really watching where I was going."

"*Why* are you going? You only just got here."

"It's been a long day, and my babies are at home," she said.

"I don't doubt both of those statements are true," Sky said. "But I'm guessing my brother also said or did something to upset you."

"It doesn't matter. What matters is your dad and his recovery."

"So stick around a little while. They only let two visitors in at a time, but we could slot you into the rotation. I know he'd be happy to see you."

"I really need to get back," Macy said. "But please give your dad my best."

"And my brother a smack upside the head?" Sky prompted.

She shook her head. "Not necessary."

"Even when it's not, it's fun."

Macy managed a small smile at that.

"Seriously, though," Liam's sister said. "He doesn't mean to be an idiot. He just can't help himself sometimes."

"He's got a lot on his mind right now."

"I'm not sure he does, considering that he dumped all of the inn responsibilities on you."

"I'm happy to help," Macy assured her.

"I know you are." Sky gave her a quick hug. "And in case my brother didn't say it, thanks for the pizza."

* * *

"Ow." Liam frowned at his younger sister and rubbed the back of his head. "What was that for?"

She stood in front of him, her hands fisted on her hips. "I'm not entirely sure," she admitted. "But I know you're an idiot, so that was for Macy."

"Macy told you to hit me?"

"Of course not. She's far too sweet and compassionate to express her feelings through physical violence. She's also far too good for you."

He didn't doubt that was true.

But before he could respond, he saw someone exit his father's room and turn quickly to walk in the opposite direction.

"Did you see—"

"What?" she asked.

But Sky was facing him, so she wouldn't have seen anything.

"Someone just walked out of Dad's room."

"A doctor? A nurse?" she prompted, clearly unimpressed by his observation.

"A woman. She looked like—" He shook his head. "But it couldn't have been."

"Couldn't have been who?" his sister pressed.

"Valerie Blake," he finally confided.

Sky snorted. "I didn't hear any reports that hell has frozen over, so no, it couldn't have been Valerie Blake."

"You're right," he agreed. "Stress and fatigue must be playing tricks on my eyes."

"Obviously something is," his sister agreed.

"Well, let's go find out if the doctors have a plan for when they're going to release him," he decided.

Sky held up a hand, holding him in place. "You know

that even when they do let him go home, he's not going to be able to step right back into working the ranch."

"You think?" Liam asked dryly.

His sister's gaze narrowed. "I'm just saying, I know Caleb would appreciate it if you stepped up to help out."

"Six weeks ago, Caleb made it clear that they didn't need my help at the Circle G."

"Six weeks ago, Dad wasn't in the hospital and Wade wasn't on his way to Billings for his son's wedding."

He nodded. "You know I'll do whatever I can to help."

"What about the inn?"

"Macy can handle the inn," he said, because it was undoubtedly true.

It was equally true that he hadn't done a very good job handling Macy—or his growing feelings for her.

Macy didn't go back to the hospital, and Liam didn't come to the inn, so the next three days passed with only a handful of brief text messages exchanged between them. David Gilmore was sent home from the hospital on Sunday, which she knew had to be a relief to his family, but she was a little disappointed that she heard the news from Frieda Zimmerman who had run into the Circle G housekeeper at The Trading Post earlier that morning.

Monday came and went, again with no communication from him. Obviously he trusted her to do whatever needed doing at the inn. It was just as obvious to Macy that he didn't trust her as someone with whom to share his thoughts and feelings about what was going on with his father and, as a result, his own future.

She tried to be patient and understanding. His father's heart attack had been a shock to all of them; it was natural that Liam would be reeling. But it worried her that he seemed to be withdrawing from her. And she suspected that he didn't see any purpose in talking to her about his future because he didn't see her as part of that future.

"That looks good," Macy said, when she got home from work Wednesday afternoon and tracked her mother down in the kitchen.

"It's a teriyaki chicken casserole. This one's for us, for dinner tonight, but there's another one in the fridge for David Gilmore."

It didn't matter that the man had a housekeeper to prepare his meals; sending food was what the residents of Haven did when someone was sick or injured. It was their way of showing that they cared.

"Can you drop it off at the Circle G on your way home after work tomorrow?" Bev asked.

"The Circle G is hardly on my way home," she pointed out.

"Thank you," her mother said.

Macy didn't object to making the detour, but she was a little apprehensive about crossing paths with Liam.

Maybe he hadn't meant anything when he sent her away from the hospital, but she wanted *to* mean something to him, and it was becoming more and more apparent that she didn't. At least not beyond the limited section of his life that he'd opted to share with her.

Martina took the glass dish that Macy offered, then ushered her into the living room, where the family patriarch was reclined in his La-Z-Boy and scrolling through channels on the enormous television.

He pressed the power button to blank the screen and

give his full attention to his visitor. "A pretty face beats repeats on the Game Show Network any day," he told her.

"Yours looks pretty good, too, considering your recent ordeal."

He waved a hand dismissively. "Much ado about nothing—and now I've got all the neighbors sending casseroles and stews and whatnot."

"My mom sent a teriyaki chicken casserole," she told him.

He smiled again. "Your folks are good people."

"I think so," she said.

His smile faded and his gaze moved past her, as if looking for something—or someone—else. "You come by yourself?"

"I did," she confirmed, wondering who he expected would have accompanied her.

His next question answered her unspoken query. "Where are those babies of yours?"

"At home with the good people."

He chuckled at that, then grimaced and pressed a hand to his chest.

"Are you okay?" Macy asked worriedly.

"Yeah. I just forget sometimes that they had to crack my chest open to get at my ornery heart."

She winced sympathetically. "I can't imagine that was much fun."

"Not much," he agreed. "And now the doctor wants me to cut down on red meat." He shook his head, as if baffled that someone with a medical degree could offer such outrageous advice. Especially to a cattle rancher.

"I think that's standard protocol after a cardiac event," she noted. "Less red meat, salt and sugar. More fruits and vegetables. And exercise." Of course, she knew that Liam's father—like most other ranchers—did not lead a sedentary lifestyle.

"That's exactly what he said," David grumbled.

"My dad had a heart attack—" she paused to do a quick mental calculation "—eighteen years ago."

"Norm would have been quite young then," Liam's father noted.

"He was young," she confirmed. "And a smoker. But he followed the doctor's advice. He gave up the cigarettes, made some dietary changes to control his blood pressure and cholesterol, and started to take a walk after dinner every night."

"Maybe the doctor isn't completely full of crap, then," he mused. "And there is one good thing that came out of all of this."

"You're still alive?" she suggested.

"Besides that," he said. "My eldest son is back on the ranch, where he belongs."

Macy bit her tongue. She wasn't going to pick a fight with a man who was recovering from major surgery, but she was worried that David might take advantage of his condition to manipulate his son. She understood why Liam had abandoned his responsibilities at the inn to help out at the ranch, but she couldn't help but worry that this temporary solution would turn into a permanent arrangement.

And if it did, what would that mean for her and her future?

She pushed that admittedly selfish thought aside. Whatever happened with Liam and the inn, she knew she had the support of her family. She wished Liam could trust that he'd receive the same unconditional support from her.

"He's out in the east paddock supervising the calving, but I can call him in, if you wanted to see him," David offered.

She did want to see him, but she was apprehensive, too. And she knew that pulling calves—if assistance was required—was hard and messy work, and the crew on-site had likely settled into a rhythm that she was loathe to disrupt. Not to mention that she wasn't sure of the reception she'd get if she did.

"No, I don't want to disturb him," she said. "And I should be getting home, anyway. My mom and dad have had the kids all day."

"Sky tells me that you've been putting in extra hours at the inn so that Liam can be here."

"Lucky for me, I love my job," she told him sincerely.

"And you don't think Liam feels the same way about the ranch?" he guessed.

"I honestly don't know anything about his feelings." She was responding to his question about the Circle G, but realized the answer was equally applicable to Liam's feelings for her.

And perhaps that came through in subtext, because David shook his head. "In that case, my son's a damn fool."

"Don't worry about your son," Macy said. "You just concentrate on your recovery."

"I promise I will if you promise to bring those babies of yours to visit me soon. There's nothing like the laughter of young ones to soothe an old and aching heart."

She kissed his pale, weathered cheek. "I'll do that."

She was almost at her car when Liam came out of the barn, heading toward the house. Her heart bumped against her ribs when he spotted her and, after lifting a hand to wave, abruptly changed direction.

"Why didn't you call or text to let me know you were coming?" he asked, as he drew nearer.

"Because I didn't come to see you."

"Your mom sent food, didn't she?" he guessed.

"It's what people do in this town."

"Apparently," he noted. "Did you see my dad?"

Macy nodded. "He seems to be in pretty good spirits, considering."

"Considering," he agreed.

But she could tell that he was still worried. Of course, less than ten days had passed since he'd almost lost his father, and that was the kind of potentially life-changing event that made a person take stock and reevaluate.

"He looks as if he's aged ten years in the past ten days," he said to her now.

"He had a heart attack," she reminded him gently. "It's going to take him some time to recuperate."

"I know, but...he always seemed so strong, so powerful. Invincible."

"He's going to be okay," she told him, this time much more confident that it was true.

He nodded again, then surprised her by asking, "What about us? Are we going to be okay?"

"What do you mean?"

"I know we haven't talked much over the past few days, but whenever we did, I got the impression that you were pulling back."

"Really? Because I got the impression that I was pushed."

He winced. "Sky took me to task for my behavior at

the hospital. All I can say is that I was worried about my dad and—"

"And you needed to focus on what really mattered," she said, echoing the words he'd used.

"And you thought that didn't include you," he realized.

"It's okay," she said. "We didn't make any promises to one another."

"It's not okay," he said. "And you do matter to me, a lot more than you know. Maybe more than I wanted to admit."

She sighed. "Am I an idiot for wanting to believe that's true?"

"It *is* true." He dipped his head and brushed his lips lightly against hers. "I've missed you like crazy."

"I've missed you, too."

"I'm getting back into the routine here," he said. "Which means that I should be able to squeeze some time out for us—if you want."

"I want," she admitted.

He smiled, and she realized that he seemed genuinely happy.

She'd originally suspected that his return to the ranch was a form of penance—his effort to atone for the perceived sin of choosing a career and life away from the ranch. But though he was obviously sweaty and exhausted from the work he'd been doing, he also seemed entirely within his element in a way that he never had at the inn.

Oh, he did an admirable impression of an innkeeper, but she was beginning to suspect that, in his heart, he was a rancher.

But she wasn't getting into the middle of that mess— that was something he would have to figure out for himself.

Chapter 14

Over the next week, Liam did manage to sneak away from the ranch for a few hours now and again. Including Friday afternoon, when he found Macy in the kitchen arranging cheese cubes and crackers on a platter.

"What would you say to a movie?" he asked.

She tipped her head, considering. "Probably nothing, because I don't think the movie would talk back."

He rolled his eyes and tried again. "Okay, what would you say if I asked you to go to a movie with me?"

"If you're asking for tonight, I can't."

"Got a date with someone else?" he teased.

"Actually, three someone elses."

"I should have guessed."

She nodded and continued to prep for the guests' wine and cheese, starting a second plate with soft cheeses and pâtés, little bowls of olives and pickled onions.

He snagged a pimento-stuffed olive from a bowl and popped it into his mouth, earning a disapproving look.

He grinned, unrepentant, and chewed.

"You know, this is the point in our conversation where you could invite me to hang out with you, Ava, Max and Sam," he said, as she replenished the supply of olives.

"Is it?" she mused.

He folded his arms across his chest, waiting.

A smile tugged at the corners of her mouth. "If you really have nothing better to do, you're welcome to hang out with me, Ava, Max and Sam," she finally offered. "It's not Mann's Theater but we do have Netflix *and* popcorn."

"An irresistible combination," he said. Then, after looking around to ensure they were alone, he slid his arms around her middle and drew her into his embrace. "Or maybe it's just you who's irresistible."

He lowered his head to nibble on her lips—intending to keep the contact light and playful. But she closed her eyes and hummed low in her throat, and the sound stoked the fire that burned in his belly. The tenor of the kiss quickly shifted from casual affection to serious arousal. He captured her mouth and deepened the kiss; she pressed closer and kissed him back.

It had been a long time since he'd had his hands all over her, and he was tempted to lift her up onto the counter and—

"I'll have what she's having."

The dry remark was followed by giggles, and then two different female voices echoed in stereo: "Me, too."

Macy immediately pulled out of his arms, and though Liam could tell she was embarrassed to have been caught in a compromising position by a trio of guests, she responded without missing a beat. "Sorry, ladies, but this prime specimen is currently off the market."

"Damn." The first speaker, with bold purple streaks in her short dark hair, lamented.

Elaine, Liam remembered her name now.

The three women had checked in late the previous afternoon and boldly flirted with him throughout the process. He'd quickly determined that they were shameless but also harmless, and learned they were from nearby Elko and grateful that there were quality accommodations closer than Reno so they could enjoy a girls' weekend away.

The shorter of the two blondes—Serena—sighed. "I guess we'll have to settle for the wine and cheese."

"The wine's already set out in the library—and the cheese is on its way," Macy said, lifting a tray in each hand.

"We can take those through for you," Kelly—the taller blonde—offered, plucking one of the trays from Macy's hand, as Elaine took the other. She winked at the inn's manager. "I think you've got more important things to do."

"Enjoy your wine, ladies," Liam said, as the trio exited the room. Then to Macy, when they'd gone, "I think I'm the 'more important thing' you have to do."

"With laundry that needs to be transferred from the washing machine to the dryer, fresh flowers to be delivered to Wild Bill and fruit to be cut up for breakfast, you don't even crack the top three," she told him.

"I bet I could convince you to rearrange your priorities."

She quickly stepped to the other side of the island, putting the butcher block slab between them. "I'm not taking that sucker's bet," she told him.

He grinned at this confirmation that he only had to put his hands on her and she'd forget about everything else.

"You deal with the flowers and the fruit," he said, because she was a lot better with things like that, "and I'll take care of the laundry and see you later tonight."

"Thanks," she said. "The kids should be—" she held up her crossed fingers "—settled down by eight, so we can start a movie around then."

"I'd offer to come earlier and bring pizza for dinner but…" He let the sentence trail off on a sigh.

"But Jo's still messing with you?" Macy guessed.

"Worse," he said. "She's messing with my pizza."

"Well, I took lasagna out of the freezer this morning, so if you want to join me for that—and if you don't get waylaid by your guests at the wine and cheese—dinner will be on the table at six."

"I'll be there," he promised.

Liam arrived at 5:45.

Ava, Max and Sam had already been fed, but they stayed in their high chairs at the table while their mom and her guest dined on lasagna, warm bread and green salad. After dinner, Macy invited Liam to relax in the living room while she bathed the triplets and got them ready for bed, but he—after an almost imperceptible hesitation—insisted on helping.

An extra set of hands allowed the task to be completed more quickly and easily, and Max and Sam were soon clean and dry and zipped into their sleepers, ready for bed.

"Hey, Big Guy—is that a new tooth you've got?"

Macy glanced over her shoulder to see which "big guy" Liam was talking to as she wrestled her stubborn little girl into her pj's.

"Two new teeth," she confirmed. "The top ones broke through his gums yesterday morning."

"Good job, Sam," he said, lifting the baby's hand for a high five.

Macy was startled by his remark. "Why'd you call him Sam?"

His gaze shifted between the two boys. "Was I wrong?"

"No. But most people struggle to tell them apart. Even my dad calls them by the wrong names half the time."

"They do look a lot alike, but Sam's eyes have a little more grey mixed with the green, and Max's chin is a little more square."

"Good eye," she noted.

"Plus Max is a more introspective and Sam more demanding."

She couldn't disagree with those distinctions, either, but they were hardly apparent to anyone looking at the babies. That he'd obviously been paying close enough attention during his interactions with the boys tugged at something inside her.

You're falling in love with him.

Her mother's words echoed in the back of her mind, and she realized that they were true.

Liam, oblivious to the direction of her thoughts, turned his attention to Max. "How many have you got now?"

The baby smiled, revealing two pearly whites on the bottom.

"That's a good start, but you're going to need a few more than that to chomp on a Gilmore steak," he told the infant.

"Quite a few more," Macy agreed, pleased that her tone didn't give away anything of the emotions churning inside her. "Although Ava is well on her way to becoming a carnivore—she left six distinct tooth impressions in Gramma's finger yesterday."

"I'll bet that's the last time Gramma puts her finger in Ava's mouth," he remarked.

Macy's lips quirked. "That's what I said."

This is what it would be like to have a family, Liam thought, as he sat close to Macy on the sofa with her baby girl cuddled against his chest. The boys were both asleep in their cribs, but Ava had fought against gravity every time her eyelids started to close.

She'd eventually lost that fight, but she still looked ready to do battle, with her tiny hands curled into fists. Although her pose said warrior, her face was pure angel, with her little cupid's bow mouth slightly parted and her eyelashes—long and dark, like her mom's—fanned against the curve of her cheek. Beneath the now-closed lids, her eyes were blue like her mom's, too.

Of course, it was possible that her dad's eyes were also blue. Or maybe green, like Max's and Sam's. There were other features he noticed when he looked at the boys that he suspected had been inherited from the man who had contributed to their DNA. Of course, he didn't know for sure, because Macy remained frustratingly tight-lipped about the father of her children and her relationship with him.

Whenever he asked any questions, she just said that he wasn't part of their lives. The vague response was hardly reassuring. Did he still live in Las Vegas? She'd shrugged, claiming not to know. Was she still in love with him? She'd denied ever having been in love with him.

He wanted to believe her, but he couldn't shake the feeling that she was holding something back. And every time he tried to wrangle more details out of her, she sidestepped his queries. When he determinedly pressed for more information, she shut the subject down. And then she'd point out that she didn't ask him about his romantic history, the implication being that he shouldn't care about hers.

He wished she *would* ask about his past relationships, so that he could be open and honest and prove that he had nothing to hide. The fact that she didn't, that she was obviously wary of an expectation of reciprocity, made him wonder what she was hiding.

Or maybe she wasn't hiding anything.

Maybe he was making a whole lot of something out of nothing.

It was possible, he knew, that she didn't want to talk about her relationship with the babies' father because there really was nothing to talk about. It might have been a casual relationship that had run its course, or a short-term fling, or possibly even a one-night stand.

Certainly she'd given no indication that she was harboring any feelings for another man. And when they made love, she didn't hold anything back. But she had yet to give him a glimpse of what was in her heart and, as a result, his own remained wary.

"Do you want me to put her in her crib?" Macy asked now, her voice pitched low so as not to disturb the baby.

"Nah, she's okay where she is," he said.

"Let me rephrase," she suggested. "Why don't I put Ava in her crib so that we can make more effective use of the sofa?"

He immediately rose to his feet, careful not to jostle—and wake—the baby tucked close to his chest. "I know where her crib is."

"Then I'll wait for you here."

Later they moved to her bed.

She was sprawled half on top of him on the narrow mattress now, and sighed contentedly as he stroked a hand down the length of her naked back.

"I missed this," she said.

"I did, too," he told her. "But I didn't come over here tonight to get lucky—I figured I was lucky just to hang out with you and your kids."

"It was a good night, wasn't it?"

"It was," he agreed. "Although I have no idea how the movie ended."

"The way all good movies do," she assured him. "They fell in love and lived happily ever after."

"Good movies have bad guys chasing good guys and battles to the death," he said.

"And Rodents Of Unusual Size in the Fire Swamp?"

"Huh?"

"*The Princess Bride*. We'll watch that on our next movie night," she promised.

Then she fell asleep in his arms.

Our next movie night.

The words echoed in his mind, tempting him to believe that this could be a regular event for them. That they could be a real couple and do all the things that real couples did.

He liked to pretend he enjoyed his bachelor lifestyle, but the truth was, he wanted to find the right woman, get married, have a couple of kids. Or maybe three. Maybe even more.

That was when he realized he didn't just want *a* family, he wanted *this* family.

And the longing was so sharp and strong, it scared him.

Macy isn't Isabella.

He knew that, but the knowledge did little to alleviate his concerns.

Because what else did he really know?

Nothing about Ava, Max and Sam's father. Certainly not enough to be sure that the man wouldn't show up one day to lay claim to the children that were rightfully his and the woman who was their mother.

And then Liam would be shut out of their lives.

Alone.

Macy wasn't surprised when she woke up alone, but she was admittedly disappointed. She should have asked Liam to stay, so that she wouldn't now be missing the warmth and strength of his arms around her.

Still, she was sure that last night had marked a turning point in their relationship. And, in the interest of open and honest communication, she resolved that the next time they were together, she would share her feelings—she would tell him that she loved him.

The idea of saying the words aloud was a little daunting, but she felt confident they were the first step on the path of their future together.

Her conviction wavered a little when he didn't stop by the inn at all that day. And a little more when he failed to even call or text.

Late in the afternoon, she finally sent a brief message, just to check in.

Everything okay?

His response was equally brief: Fine.

It was late Sunday afternoon before he made another appearance at the hotel. Ordinarily she would have been gone by two, but she'd promised Rose that she could stay until four, so the other woman could attend her niece's bridal shower.

When Liam showed up, around 3:30, Macy couldn't help but wonder if he'd timed his arrival expecting that she would be gone. She wished she could dismiss the idea as paranoia, except that he looked so surprised to see her, she knew that was, in fact, what he'd done.

She continued to reply to email inquiries and, since she was working at the desk, he took the folder Kyle had left for him into the library.

After a few minutes of internal debate, she followed him. "Are you going to tell me what I did wrong?"

"You didn't do anything wrong."

"Really?" she challenged. "Because you didn't even look up from your file when you said that."

Liam lifted his head to meet her gaze. "You didn't do anything wrong," he said again.

"Okay, *now* I believe you," she said, though the sarcasm in her tone indicated otherwise.

But she turned back to the double doors, and he exhaled a silent sigh of relief.

A premature sigh, he realized, when she closed the doors instead of exiting through them.

"I'm busy here, Macy."

"I only want ten minutes of your time—and an explanation. I think you owe me that much."

She was right. He did owe her an explanation. But he didn't have one to give. Certainly not one that would satisfy her.

"What do you want me to say?" he asked wearily.

"I want you to tell me why, after a thoroughly enjoyable evening together, you disappeared in the middle of the night and have been incommunicado ever since."

"And what if you don't like the answer?"

"I want to hear it anyway."

"Fine," he relented. "The truth is that hanging out with you, Ava, Max and Sam the other night…it just got a little too real for me."

"I don't understand," she said. "It's not as if that's the first time we've hung out together. What changed all of a sudden?"

What changed was that he'd realized he was falling for her—and her kids. Why else would he have spent a Friday night sitting on an uncomfortable sofa in the basement apartment of her parents' house with her children sprawled around them? All the while basking in the feeling that he belonged there, with them.

And when Ava had climbed into his lap and laid her head against his chest, his heart had swelled so much that his ribs actually ached. It had been an exhilarating—and terrifying—feeling.

Because he knew that if he let himself get in any

deeper, he might not survive losing them. It would be smarter, easier, he'd decided, to walk away now.

"Being with your kids simply reminded me that I'm not daddy material," he said.

"Disregarding the blatant inaccuracy of that statement for a moment—have I asked you to step into the father role for my kids?" she challenged.

"No," he admitted. "But if we keep seeing each other, isn't that what you're going to expect? If I keep spending time with your kids, isn't that what *they're* going to expect?"

"They're nine months old," she pointed out. "I don't think you need to worry about their expectations. You definitely don't need to worry about mine."

"I never meant to hurt you, Macy."

She shook her head, her eyes glittering with moisture. "And I never meant to fall in love. In fact, I'd given up believing it would ever happen," she confided. "I thought maybe I didn't have it in me to give my heart to someone else. And then you came along."

Was she saying that she loved him?

Was it possible?

No, he didn't—wouldn't let himself—believe it. He wouldn't be led down that garden path again where poisonous weeds could wrap around his heart.

"You don't love me, Macy."

She lifted those tear-filled eyes to his. "You don't have to feel the same way—and you've made it perfectly clear that you don't," she said. "But don't you dare presume to tell me how *I* feel."

Then she exited the library, grabbed her coat off the hook and slammed the intricately engraved wood door she'd once admired behind her.

Chapter 15

Macy knew better than to go straight home.

She needed some time to bury her heartache before facing her mother's inquisition—and if she arrived home early in the day, Macy knew there would be an inquisition.

She also needed ice cream. Because nothing soothed a wounded soul like ice cream.

She left The Trading Post with two bags of groceries and a fresh perspective.

"I saw Alyssa Channing this afternoon," Macy said, setting her grocery bags on the counter. "She was on her way home from the hospital."

Bev reached into one of the bags for a familiar-looking box. "Regan had her babies?" she guessed.

Macy nodded as she opened the freezer to tuck away her stash of ice cream.

"What did she have?" her mother immediately wanted to know. "And how are they all doing?"

"Two girls, each just over five pounds, and everyone's doing fine. Although both the new mom and dad are exhausted after twenty-two hours of labor."

Bev winced sympathetically as she opened the flap of the box and pulled out the cellophane package inside. "Bet you're glad your doctor finally opted to do a C-section."

"Yeah, the sixteen hours of labor that preceded it only felt like forever," Macy remarked dryly.

"But Ava, Max and Sam are worth every minute, aren't they?"

Her gaze shifted from one to the next and the next, and her heart overflowed with so much love it almost filled the cracks caused by Liam's rejection. "They are," she agreed.

Bev distributed teething biscuits to her grandbabies as Macy continued to unpack the groceries.

"You should go see Regan and her twins," her mom suggested. "I don't mean now, but when she's home from the hospital. I'm sure she'd appreciate talking to someone who has experience with multiples."

"I will," she promised.

"Good. And now, you should scoop up two bowls of that ice cream and tell me why you're home in the middle of the day."

"I haven't seen you around here in a while," Sky remarked, when her brother settled onto a stool at the bar.

"I've been busy," Liam told her.

"And suddenly you're not?"

"I just needed a break."

She set his beer on a paper coaster in front of him. "Is that what you told Macy?"

He scowled at the amber liquid in his glass.

"Alyssa came by earlier and mentioned that she saw Macy at The Trading Post—and that she looked upset."

"Why would you immediately assume that has anything to do with me?"

"Because I know you," she said simply.

He lifted the glass to his mouth.

Sky picked up a towel and began wiping and shelving the rack of glasses the dishwasher had brought out to her. "Successful relationships require honesty and communication."

"Did I ask for any advice?" he challenged.

"No," she acknowledged. "But you're here."

"Only for the beer," he assured her.

"Did you tell her about Simon?"

Her gentle tone failed to soften the blow of the question. "There's nothing to tell."

"And maybe she'd say the same thing about the father of her babies."

"Except she doesn't say anything about him at all," he remarked.

"And that's what worries you."

"I'm not worried," he denied. "I just decided that I wasn't interested in taking our relationship any further."

"Really? Because if I had to guess, I'd say you're hurting just as much as she is right now."

Maybe he was, but he figured it was better than continuing along and hurting even more later.

"How'd the calving go today?" David asked his sons, as he poked at the grilled salmon on his plate.

Liam could tell by the disinterest on his face that his father was wishing he could be cutting into a juicy hunk of sirloin instead of heart-healthy fish.

"No major snags," Caleb said.

He nodded, confirming his brother's assessment. There had been a few scary moments when they'd had to turn a breech calf—a situation that could quickly turn fatal for both the mom and baby—but in the end, they'd got the job done and there was no reason to worry their father with the details now.

Of course, Caleb's response exhausted that topic of conversation, and with not much else to talk about, the rest of the meal passed in relative silence.

When he was finished eating, Caleb folded his napkin on the table and pushed his chair back. "We're starting early again tomorrow, so I'm heading up to bed now."

Liam should do the same, but there was a question that had been niggling at the back of his mind for some time now, and he knew that it wasn't going to go away. So he stayed where he was while Martina cleared the table.

"Can I ask you something?" he said, when the housekeeper had finished.

"Can I stop you?" his father grumbled.

It wasn't exactly an invitation, but Liam forged ahead anyway. "When you were in the hospital, did Valerie Blake stop by to see you?"

His father's gaze shifted away. "Where would you get a crazy idea like that?"

"At the hospital," he said. "When I saw a woman who looked a lot like Valerie Blake leaving your room."

David was quiet for a long minute, as if uncertain how to answer his son's question. "Yeah, she stopped by," he finally said.

Which, of course, led to Liam wanting to know: "Why?"

"She's a Blake. She probably wanted to know if I was going to kick the bucket."

"That's sounds like a credible explanation—except that she was wiping her eyes, as if she was crying, as she walked out."

"Mourning the fact I wasn't dead, I guess."

"I don't think that's why," Liam said.

"It doesn't matter what you think. Her visit didn't mean anything," his father insisted.

He should let it go. Everything about his father's body language and tone warned Liam to let it go—and that's why he couldn't. "Did you and Valerie Blake… were you ever…involved?"

"No," David denied, not looking at him. "We were never involved."

"But you slept with her," Liam guessed.

His father sighed wearily. "Once. A long time ago."

The reluctant admission made him feel both vindicated and sick. "You cheated on Mom?"

"No! Never." David scrubbed his hands over his face. "How could you possibly think…?" He shook his head. "Your mother was the love of my life," he said. "From the minute I set eyes on her, I didn't even see anyone else. She was it for me."

"Then it was after she died," he realized.

His father exhaled and slowly nodded. "Five years after. Five years to the day, in fact." And although he'd been reluctant to start talking, now he couldn't seem to stop. "Five years and I still missed your mom just as much as I had every single day since her passing. So I went into town and had a few too many drinks at Diggers'.

"Valerie was a waitress there at the time. Being a Monday, the bar was practically empty, so she sat with me and we talked. We talked until the bar closed—and then we went back to her place.

"She moved away to Washington shortly after that, and only returned to Haven three or four years ago. I've crossed paths with her in town a handful of times since then, rarely exchanging more than a nod of acknowledgment."

"She never stopped by the ranch?"

David shook his head. "Never."

"And yet, when she heard that you were in the hospital, she went all the way to Elko to see you?"

This time his dad nodded.

"Why?"

He sighed again. "Because she wanted to tell me that her daughter, Ashley, is my daughter, too."

Two weeks, Macy realized, noting the date on the computer screen.

Two weeks had passed since the last time she'd made love with Liam. Two weeks since she'd accepted that she was all the way in love with him. And twelve days since he'd made it clear he was never going to feel the same way.

But her heart, battered and bruised as it was, continued to beat inside her chest. And she continued to enjoy her job at the inn, even if she wasn't particularly fond of her boss right now.

"Jensen." The male voice broke through her reverie. "Gord and Isabella."

Macy offered a welcoming smile. She noted the couple's linked hands and the easy affection in the look they exchanged. She keyed in the name and quickly found the reservation—for Wild Bill's Getaway Suite.

"And Simon," a young boy piped up. "That's me."

"Hello, Simon." She smiled at him as she took the platinum credit card his father slid across the desk. "I'm Macy, and if you have any questions or need anything at all, you come to me and I'll see what I can do to help you."

"I'm thirsty," he announced.

"There are complimentary hot and cold beverages, and some light snacks, available in the solarium—" She pointed across the hall. "That's also where you'll have your breakfast in the morning."

"Can I have pancakes?"

"I'd guess that's up to your mom and dad," she said, looking to them for direction. "But there are pancakes on the menu."

The boy's mom smiled indulgently as she brushed a lock of hair away from his forehead. "You might want to try something else for a change," she suggested.

"Nuh-uh," Simon said. "I want pancakes."

"Then you can have pancakes," his dad confirmed.

"Yay!" He punched his fist in the air. "I'm gonna have pancakes."

"Are you in town for business or pleasure?" Macy asked the couple.

The wife spoke first. "Pleasure."

"Definitely pleasure," her husband agreed.

"Nuh-uh, Dad," Simon protested. "You said we're goin' to Adventure Village to ride the go-karts."

His dad chuckled. "And we will," he promised.

Macy handed over the key to the room and gave a brief summary of the inn's features. "And please, let me know if there's anything you need to enhance your enjoyment," she said again.

"Thank you," the husband said, reaching for his wife's hand again. "But I think we've got everything we need."

Liam's head was still reeling over the revelation that his father might have another child—and that he might have a twelve-year-old half sister he didn't know anything about—but he pushed that information to the back of his mind and focused on the ranch. Apparently his grandparents thought that focus translated into neglect of the inn. Although they trusted that Macy had everything running as smoothly and precisely as the gears of a Swiss watch, they reminded Liam that the inn was his investment and his responsibility.

And that was why, after breakfast Saturday morning, he found himself behind the wheel of his truck, driving into town.

He had mixed feelings as he walked through the doors of the inn. He was proud of the success the hotel had already achieved and grateful to Macy for all of her work. But he missed her—so damn much. And not just the warmth of her naked body tangled with his—though he definitely missed that, too—but working alongside her, talking to her, laughing with her.

But he still believed he'd done the right thing in ending their relationship before they got in too deep. Sure, he missed her sometimes—maybe even all the time— but he'd get over her. He just needed a little more time.

And he needed to live his own life separate from hers and her kids so that he didn't start to think of them as a family. He wasn't going to go through with her what he'd gone through with Isabella. He wasn't going to risk his heart that way again.

Maybe it was because he was thinking about her that he almost wasn't surprised when he walked into the solarium and saw Izzy there. Or maybe he was *so* surprised that it took him a moment to realize that she wasn't simply a figment of his imagination.

But she was obviously startled to see him, because her fork slipped from her fingers and clattered against her plate when her gaze locked with his. The man seated across from her—Gord, he guessed, though he'd never met her husband—said something, and she forced a smile in response as she picked up her fork again.

As if of their own volition, Liam's feet propelled him closer to their table, his gaze fixed on the boy seated between the adults.

"I had pancakes for breakfast," Simon announced, and his lightning-quick smile was like a sucker punch in Liam's gut. "And *four* strips of bacon."

"That's a lot of bacon," he remarked, pleased the even tenor of his response gave away nothing of the emotions churning inside him.

Simon's head bobbed as he nodded. "I like bacon."

"Extra crispy?"

The boy's eyes went wide, as if he couldn't imagine how Liam might possibly have guessed such a thing, and he nodded again.

Liam forced his attention to shift to the boy's parents. "And was your meal satisfactory this morning?"

"It was," Gord agreed, as he dumped a packet of sugar into his coffee.

"Delicious," Izzy said, a tentative smile playing around the corners of her mouth.

"That's good." He didn't smile back. "If you need anything at all during your stay, please don't hesitate to contact the front desk."

He started across the room, in the direction of a smaller table where a young couple was just being served. But his heart was heavy and his smile was stiff, and he knew he couldn't go through the motions. Not right now.

Instead, he turned and exited the solarium.

Of all the days to come into town, why had he chosen this day? And how soon could he make his escape without appearing to be doing exactly that? He decided that until then, he would take refuge in the library. He only wanted a moment alone to gather his thoughts and his composure. Of course, Isabella had never given him what he wanted.

"Please, Liam," she called out to him. "Don't walk away from me."

He turned to face her, his voice low and tightly controlled. "You're the one who walked—no, ran—back to your supposedly ex-husband."

She lifted her chin. "Because I owed it to him, and to Simon, to give our marriage another chance."

He hadn't been distressed by the sight of his ex-girlfriend with her husband, because he had no lingering romantic feelings for her. But seeing the little boy who'd once asked Liam if he could call him Daddy had cut to the quick.

"He doesn't even remember me," Liam said now.

"He's eight," Izzy pointed out, her stance and her tone noticeably softer. "And he hasn't seen you in more than four years."

He nodded. Four years was almost half of Simon's

lifetime, but the blink of an eye to the man who'd once thought he'd be part of the boy's life forever. Liam cleared his throat. "He's gotten so big."

She smiled at that. "Don't I know it? He outgrows new clothes almost as soon as I take the tags off them."

"I can imagine."

Her expression grew serious again. "I'm sorry, Liam. I didn't know… Gord booked the room. The weekend away was a surprise for me and Simon," she explained. "But if this is too weird, we can—"

"No, it's not too weird," he told her.

"Are you sure? Because it feels pretty weird to me."

"It's fine," he said. "I'm not going to be here most of the weekend, anyway, so you probably won't see me again."

"Well, I'm glad I saw you now," she said. "And I'm glad you finally got away from the ranch."

He just nodded and said, "You should get back to your breakfast—and your family."

After she'd done so, Liam remained where he was, a dull ache in the center of his chest. But that pain wasn't anything he couldn't handle. It sure as hell didn't compare to the gaping wound he'd been left with when Izzy took her son and walked out on him four years earlier.

Or the gut-wrenching emptiness that had nearly consumed him when he shut Macy out of his life.

Except that she was there now—and looking at him with sadness and sympathy in her beautiful blue eyes.

Chapter 16

"I didn't mean to eavesdrop," Macy said apologetically. "I came in to reshelve the books that housekeeping had retrieved from various rooms and King—" she pointed to the lowest shelf in the bookcase behind the sofa "—goes between Kellerman and Koontz."

"Or anywhere on the shelf, for those of us who don't have OCD," he noted dryly.

"Are you okay?" she asked, ignoring his remark.

"Of course."

"I checked them in yesterday," she said, and almost felt guilty for having done so.

She remembered thinking they were a beautiful family: Gord and Isabella Jensen, and their inquisitive son, Simon.

"Is the boy…is he…yours?"

Liam immediately shook his head. "I would never have let him go if he was mine."

Macy nodded, his words confirming everything she believed about the man she loved.

"But I dated his mom for eleven months," he confided now.

"Almost a year," she murmured.

A long time in the life of a child. She could only imagine how close the little boy and the man had grown in that time—and how hard it had been for both of them when the relationship between Liam and Isabella ended.

"I thought we were going to get married," he admitted.

"You were in love with her." Though Liam had never claimed to love Macy, the realization that he'd loved the other woman still hurt.

But he shook his head again. "No, but I was crazy about her kid. Not the best reason to get married, I know," he acknowledged. "But Simon really wanted a dad and I wanted to be his dad."

She hugged the books against her chest. "Why didn't you ever tell me about her? About him?"

He shrugged. "It was four years ago. Ancient history."

But she knew it wasn't. And she understood now why he'd tried so hard not to let himself get close to Ava, Max and Sam. It wasn't because he was incapable of letting them in, but because he didn't know how to keep them out. Because he was trying to protect his heart, which had been bruised and battered already by the loss of a child who wasn't his own.

She started toward him, then remembered the books

in her hand. Setting them on the edge of the closest shelf, she moved around the sofa.

He watched her progress, a little warily at first, but as she drew nearer, his expression changed. Heated.

Then she was in his arms and their mouths were fused together, their bodies straining to get closer as awareness gave way to want, want to need. Need to hunger—a desperate, aching hunger.

"Macy, I can't find—" The housekeeper's words halted as abruptly as her steps in the doorway of the library. "Oh."

Macy gave a vague thought to pulling out of Liam's arms, but they tightened around her, as if he wasn't going to let her go. And it felt so good—so right—to be in his embrace, that she didn't bother to pretend otherwise.

"What is it you can't find, Camille?" she asked.

"Nothing," the housekeeper decided. "I mean, it's nothing that can't wait."

And she turned on her heel and disappeared again.

"Now the staff are going to talk," Liam warned.

"I think *we* need to talk," she said. "Because there's something I've been holding back, too, about Ava, Max and Sam's father."

"You never wanted to talk about him," he noted.

"Because I didn't know what to say—how to explain."

He waited, silently, for her to find the words.

"Do you remember the first night we were together?"

"In clear and vivid detail," he assured her.

She smiled at that. "Then you must remember my blurted and awkward admission that it had been a long time since I was intimate with anyone?"

"It had been a long time for me, too."

"More than two years long?" she asked.

"Not quite."

Then his brow furrowed, and she knew he was realizing that the length of a standard pregnancy—nine months—added to the age of her kids—nine months again—came up well short of her two-year claim.

"How is that possible?" he wondered.

"It's possible because I never had sex with Ava, Max and Sam's father," she confided.

"You're not going to claim it was immaculate conception?"

She shook her head. "No. It was intrauterine insemination—or IUI."

His brows drew together. "They were test tube babies?"

"No, that's intro vitro fertilization—or IVF," she clarified. "IUI is what my friend Stacia refers to as the turkey baster method."

"So who is Ava, Max and Sam's father?" he wondered.

"He's a college professor of English and German heritage, six feet tall and 190 pounds with curly brown hair, green eyes and a dimple in his left cheek. He volunteers as a dog walker at his local SPCA, plays guitar, enjoys classic literature and contemporary art, and he likes to read and cook in his spare time."

"That's a pretty detailed description," he noted.

"But I don't know his name," she said. "I only know him as Donor 6243."

"Well, that clarifies some of your earlier and always abrupt responses to my inquiries," he decided. "But it doesn't tell me why."

"Because I wanted a family and my efforts to make that happen via more traditional routes were unsuccessful," she told him.

"So why didn't you just tell me that when I asked about their father?"

"I should have," she said. "But when I told my parents, they were so vocal...and harsh...in expressing their disapproval that I worried other people might react the same way. And I didn't want my parents—or my children—to be the subjects of gossip and ridicule because of the choices I'd made.

"But when I told you that Ava, Max and Sam didn't have a father, it was the truth. The man who contributed half of their DNA was literally nothing more to me than a sperm donor. And while I will admit to feelings of deep and sincere gratitude for that contribution, I'm not, and never have been, in love with him."

She lifted her hands to Liam's face, so that she could look him in the eye, so that he could see the truth in her own. "But I am in love with you. And at the risk of freaking you out again, I happen to think you'd make a pretty great dad to Ava, Max and Sam someday...if that idea appeals to you at all."

The idea appealed to him—a lot more than Liam was willing to admit. Even more appealing was the prospect of spending his life with Macy and her children.

But love?

That was more than he was capable of giving.

Nope. No, thank you. No way.

He drew back, and her hands dropped to her sides.

She tucked them into her pockets and worried her bottom lip. "You're not saying anything," she remarked quietly.

"It's a lot to take in."

She nodded.

He'd envisioned various scenarios to explain Macy's reluctance to share any information about the man who'd fathered Ava, Max and Sam, but none of them had included a sperm donor.

On the one hand, he no longer had to worry about Macy reconciling with the guy, because she'd never been with him. On the other, he had to wonder if she was really in love with him, as she claimed, or if she was looking for a father for her children who didn't have one. To give them a normal family and spare them from becoming the focus of small-town gossip as they grew up.

"I should probably get back to the desk," she said lightly. "I don't want my boss to catch me slacking off."

She was offering him an out, and he was only too eager to take it. "And I need to get back to the ranch."

She nodded again. "I didn't mean to put you on the spot or make you uncomfortable. I just wanted to clear up any miscommunication."

"I know," he said. "And you didn't. I just need some time…to process everything."

"Well, you know where to find me, if you want to talk."

"I do," he confirmed.

And then he fled, pretending he didn't see the tears that shimmered in her eyes.

When Liam returned to the Circle G, his jumbled thoughts and feelings were forced to refocus when he discovered his father in the barn, measuring out grain and feed.

"What are you doing?" he demanded.

"The doctor said I could do with some fresh air and exercise."

"And lots of rest."

"If I was any more rested, I'd be dead."

"A few weeks ago, you almost were," Liam felt compelled to remind his father.

"It'll take more than a heart attack to put me in the ground," David promised.

He didn't doubt it was true, but he didn't want to talk—or even think—about his father's mortality. Instead, he said, "Well, it's good to see you back on your feet."

"And now that I am, you can wash your hands of your responsibilities here?" his father guessed.

"I never washed my hands of anything," he pointed out. "Even when I was spending twelve and fifteen hours a day at the inn, I was here every morning to help with chores."

"We would have got along just fine without your help."

"I know you would have," he acknowledged. "But maybe I didn't want you to."

"You're not making a heckuva lot of sense," David said.

"It didn't make a lot of sense to me, either," Liam said. "Especially considering that, for so many years, I felt trapped here."

"You made that clear enough."

"When I bought the inn, I thought I was freeing myself of the responsibilities and expectations that weighed on me here."

"You didn't think running a hotel would come with

responsibilities and expectations?" his father challenged.

"Of course I did, but those were completely my own."

"You think I demanded too much of you?"

"Maybe I did," he allowed. "But I knew it wasn't any more than you demanded of anyone else—including yourself. And when Caleb called to tell me that you'd collapsed—"

"I staggered a little," David interjected. "It's not like I was lying in a boneless heap on the ground."

"You had a heart attack," Liam said again. "And it was scary as hell for all of us."

His father didn't dispute that.

"So I came back."

"We needed you here, Liam," David grudgingly admitted.

"Maybe. But more than that, I *wanted* to be here. Because Gilmores are ranchers."

"They have been for more than a hundred and fifty years," his father noted. "Because that was the choice Everett made when he bought this parcel of land. And then he built a modest home on that land and, with the help of his sons, they turned a small herd of cattle into one of the most successful ranches in the whole state."

"I know the history of the Circle G, Dad."

His father nodded. "But maybe you don't know that I'm trying to offer you an apology."

Liam was intrigued by this grudging admission. "I'm listening."

"Over the past few months, I've realized that I might've been wrong in trying to force you into a life you didn't want. Every time you tried to tell me that you wanted something different, I shut you down. I refused to consider the possibility that you might actually leave the Circle G because—" His gaze shifted away and he cleared his throat. "Because then I'd lose you, just like I lost your mom.

"It was your grandmother who helped me see that I was holding on too tight—to you and your brother and sisters—trying to hold on to the only part of Theresa that I had left."

Liam was stunned by this admission. He'd been working through his own demons over the loss of his mother, and though he knew how deeply his father had been affected by the tragic death of his wife, he hadn't considered how that loss might have impacted his subsequent actions.

"She also pointed out that your mom would be disappointed in me for driving you away—not from the ranch, but from the family. She had such grand dreams for all her children. She didn't care if any of you wanted to be doctors or lawyers or ranchers—she only wanted you to be happy. To find someone to love as we loved one another, to raise a family...

"So, with that thought in mind, I've decided to support you—and your siblings—in whatever you want to do with your lives. Because maybe Gilmores can be anything they want to be."

"For a man of few words, that was a helluva speech," Liam remarked.

"It was a long time in the making," his father said.

"Well, I've been doing a lot of thinking, too," he confided. "And it turns out that *this* Gilmore wants to be a rancher."

David was understandably taken aback by his eldest son's confession. "You really mean that?"

"I mean it," he confirmed. "Maybe I needed to take some time away from the ranch to appreciate what it means to me. To realize how much I enjoy working with you and Caleb and Wade and Uncle Chuck and Michael and Mitchell."

"You can't know how happy that makes me," his father said. "But…what about the hotel?"

"It's already proven to be a sound investment, and I'm confident that it will be in very capable hands under Macy's management."

"And since you mentioned her name," David prompted.

"I've still got some things to figure out there," he admitted.

"Well, don't take too long to figure them out," his father cautioned. "Because those babies of hers shouldn't have to grow up without a daddy."

He shook his head. "You're already looking for the next generation of ranchers, aren't you?"

"The next generation of Gilmores," David clarified.

Though he was pleased to know that his father would accept Macy, Ava, Max and Sam as part of the Gilmore family, Liam knew that wouldn't happen unless he found the courage to put his heart on the line again.

She thought about turning around.

As Macy drove toward the Circle G, her fingers wrapped tightly around the steering wheel, she couldn't help but wonder if she was making another mistake and worry that she was setting herself up for more heartache.

She'd told Liam to find her when he wanted to talk. Instead, he'd sent a text inviting her to come out to the

Circle G to see Mystery's new foal. She didn't know
if that was the real purpose of his message or merely
a pretext to get her out to the ranch, but, remembering
the promise she'd made to Liam's father the last time
she saw him, she went home first so that she could take
Ava, Max and Sam with her.

And maybe she was counting on the presence of
her precious babies to help her hold it together if Liam
told her that he had no interest in a future with her and
her family.

She didn't regret the things she'd said to him earlier.
He deserved to know the truth of her feelings and everything else. If, when he'd had his say, it turned out
that he didn't want what she was offering, at least she'd
know that she'd given it her best shot and not held anything back.

She strapped her little ones into their triple tandem
stroller and was making her way toward the house when
Caleb came out of the barn.

"Liam's in there," he said, jerking his thumb toward
the building he'd just exited.

"Actually, I thought we'd say 'hi' to your dad first,"
she said, because she didn't know that she'd want to
stick around after she'd talked to her boss.

He pointed a forefinger toward the house.

She took Ava, Max and Sam into the house. David
was genuinely pleased by their surprise visit and unhappy when she tried to cut it short. He insisted that she
could leave the babies with him while she went out to
the barn, and her protests were silenced by the housekeeper's assurance that she would keep an eye on Ava,
Max and Sam—and the recovering rancher.

Macy found Liam watching over the dappled mare

she recognized as Mystery, along with a chestnut foal she was nursing.

"Sky named him Enigma," Liam told her.

"Fitting," she remarked.

He fell silent again for a moment before confiding, "I've been waiting for you."

She knew he meant today, but she felt as if she'd been waiting for him forever—and she hoped that, after today, they could move toward a forever together.

"Have you had time…to process everything?" she asked him.

"I didn't really need time," he said, his voice raw with emotion. "I only needed to think about everything I could have with you, Ava, Max and Sam, and how empty my life would be without you in it." Finally, he drew her into his arms. "I don't know if there are any words to express how much I've missed you."

"I think I know," she said. "Because I've missed you just as much."

He kissed her then, with a hunger that bordered on desperation.

And she kissed him back the same way, expressing without words the truth and depth of her feelings.

And then, when the kiss finally ended and she managed to catch her breath again, with words: "I love you, Liam."

"You said that earlier," he reminded her.

"And you didn't trust my feelings."

"I didn't trust my own," he said. "And I didn't know if I was capable of being what you needed."

"You *are* everything that I need," she told him. "Everything that I want."

"I hope you mean that," he said. "Because I love you

and Ava, Max and Sam, too. When you asked me earlier if the idea of being their dad appealed to me at all, I didn't say anything because I was afraid to admit how much I wanted what you were offering. But I'm admitting it now. I'm putting my heart on the line—for you and our future together. Our family."

Tears filled her eyes and overflowed along with the joy in her heart.

"Please don't cry," he said. "You know I can't handle tears."

"You're going to have to get used to them," she warned. "Because I sometimes cry when I'm really happy, and I know we're going to be really happy together."

He lifted his hands to frame her face and gently brushed her tears away. "Happily ever after," he promised.

Epilogue

August 13th

"Okay, we've practiced and practiced, but this time it's for real, so I need you to stick to the script. Do you understand?"

His tone must have conveyed the seriousness of the situation, because Ava, Max and Sam—officially toddlers now—nodded solemnly.

They were dressed in coordinated outfits that their grandmother had picked out: Max and Sam in denim overalls and red T-shirts, Ava in a denim skirt and white shirt with a glittery red heart on it. They all wore cowboy boots and hats and held oversized cue cards in their hands. One by one, he lifted them up to sit on the hay bales he'd arranged for this moment.

It wouldn't be Valentine's Day again for another six

months, but that was exactly how long it had been since Liam and Macy had shared their first kiss, and he figured that was enough time to convince her he knew what he wanted.

"No, Ava, you're in the middle," he reminded her, pointing to the spot between Max and Sam.

She stubbornly stayed where she was, her legs stretched out in front of her, booted feet crossed at the ankles. He picked her up and settled her on the hay between her brothers. She gave him a mutinous look that he recognized all too well as a precursor to trouble.

"And if we get this right, we can go for ice cream later."

His promise seemed to placate the little girl—at least for the moment.

"You ready, Max?"

Max responded by extending both of his arms, proudly displaying the blank side of the card he held.

"That's good," Liam said. "But when Mommy comes out, you're going to turn the card over."

He turned the card, so the word was visible—albeit upside down.

Liam rotated the cardboard. "Just like that."

While he was getting Max organized, Sam dropped his card. Naturally, he leaned over to pick it up—and nearly toppled off the hay bale. He lost his hat in the process and cried out in distress.

"It's okay," Liam soothed, settling the hat back on top of the boy's head and placing the card back in his hands—and beginning to question the wisdom of his own plan.

He recognized the sound of Macy's SUV pulling up outside and breathed a sigh of relief that she was on time. Checking the kids again to ensure they were in position and ready, he pulled out his cell phone to send a quick text message asking Macy to meet them behind the barn.

Half a minute later, she came around the corner, a smile lighting her face when she saw them. "What are you guys doing out here?"

"We have an important question to ask you," Liam said, then turned to her children and prompted, "Max?"

The little boy turned over his card, his sister did the same with hers, his brother followed and then Liam showed his own.

Each card held a single word that, when put together, should have spelled out: WILL-YOU-MARRY-ME?

But when Sam dropped his card, Liam had mistakenly given the boy his, and Ava had turned hers over upside down so that what Macy saw was: ⅂⅂IM-YOU-ME?-MARRY

Thankfully, she was savvy enough to figure out what he was really trying to ask. Of course, the princess-cut diamond he pulled out of his pocket might have helped, too.

She laughed through her tears. "You once said a man would have to be crazy to want to marry a single mom with three babies," she said, reminding him of the words he'd spoken months ago.

"I am crazy," he confessed. "About you and about them. And there's nothing I want more than to make our crazy family official."

"In that case, yes," she said, then responded to his question the way he'd asked it: "I will you marry."

He slid the ring on the third finger of her left hand, then drew her into his arms for a long lingering kiss as Ava, Max and Sam clapped their hands in approval.

Then the clapping stopped and Ava demanded, "I-cweam!"

Liam broke the kiss on a sigh.

"You bribed them with ice cream, didn't you?" Macy asked, amusement in her tone.

"I wouldn't call it a bribe…it was offered as more of a performance bonus."

"And did they perform according to your expectations?"

"Well, my expectations were pretty low," he acknowledged. "But I'd say my mini cupids did their job."

"I love that you made them a part of this," she said.

"They are part of this—part of us. *Our family.*"

Fresh tears shimmered in her eyes. "And that's only one of the reasons I love you."

"And I love you right back."

"I-cweam!" Ava said again, stamping her booted foot for emphasis this time.

A stern look from her mother had her reconsidering her strategy.

She shuffled closer and looked at Liam with big blue eyes. "P'ease, Da."

She'd picked up the word from hanging out with Tessa, and though he doubted Ava understood the significance of it, she'd quickly discovered that using it often got her what she wanted. Because every time she uttered that single syllable, Liam's heart melted just like her ice cream would do in the summer heat.

He looked at Macy now. "What do you think?"

She smiled. "I think we're going for ice cream, Da."

And that's what they did.

* * * * *

**IF YOU ENJOYED THIS BOOK
WE THINK YOU WILL ALSO LOVE**

SPECIAL
EDITION

Believe in love. Overcome obstacles. Find happiness.

Relate to finding comfort and strength in the
support of loved ones and enjoy the journey
no matter what life throws your way.

6 NEW BOOKS AVAILABLE EVERY MONTH!

HSEXSERIES2020

SPECIAL EXCERPT FROM

H HARLEQUIN

SPECIAL EDITION

*When Chance Foley wished for a million dollars as a
teenager, he never expected it to come true—especially
not via his late brother's twins, who are now his
responsibility. Luckily, Poppy Digby has known the twins
all their lives and agrees to stay—just for a few days!—
but they each find themselves longing for more time…*

Read on for a sneak peek at
Be Careful What You Wish For,
the first book in New York Times *bestselling author
Elizabeth Bevarly's new Lucky Stars miniseries!*

"Wait, what?" he interrupted again. "Logan worked for a
tech firm?"

Although his brother had taught himself to code when he
was still in middle school, and he'd been a good hacker of
the dirty tricks variety when they were teenagers, Chance
couldn't see him ever living the cubicle lifestyle for a steady
paycheck.

"Yes," Poppy said. "And he developed a computer program
several years ago that allowed companies to legally plunder
and sell all kinds of personal information and online habits of
anyone who used their websites. It goes without saying that it
was worth a gold mine to corporate America. And corporate
America paid your brother a gold mine for it."

Okay, that did actually sound like something Logan would
have been able to do. Chance probably shouldn't be surprised
that his brother would turn his gift for hacking into making a
pile of money.

Poppy pulled another piece of paper from the collection in front of her. "I have another statement that's been prepared for your trust, Mr. Foley."

He started to correct Poppy's "Mr. Foley" again, but the other part of her statement sank in too quickly. "What do you mean my trust?"

"I mean your brother and sister-in-law have put funds into a trust for you, as well."

He didn't know what to say. So he said nothing, only gazed back at Poppy, confused as hell.

When he said nothing, she continued. "The children's trust will begin to gradually revert to them when they reach the age of twenty-two. That's when the funds in your trust will revert entirely to you."

Out of nowhere, a thought popped up in the back of Chance's brain, and he was reminded of something he hadn't thought about for a long time—a wish he'd made to a comet when he was fifteen years old. A wish, legend said, that should be coming true about now, since Endicott had been celebrating the "Welcome Back, Bob" comet festival for a few weeks. Something cool and unpleasant wedged into his throat at the memory.

He eyed Poppy warily. "H-how much money is in that trust?"

Her serious green eyes had never looked more serious. "A million dollars, Mr. Foley. Once the children have reached the age of twenty-two, that million dollars will be yours."

Don't miss
Be Careful What You Wish For *by Elizabeth Bevarly,*
available August 2022 wherever
Harlequin Special Edition books and ebooks are sold.

Harlequin.com

Copyright © 2022 by Elizabeth Bevarly

HSEEXP0622

Get 4 FREE REWARDS!

We'll send you 2 FREE Books plus 2 FREE Mystery Gifts.

The Charming Checklist
HEATHERLY BELL

A Rancher's Touch
ALLISON LEIGH

The Wrong Cowboy
Sasha Summers

Cowgirl's Secret
Melinda Curtis

FREE
Value Over
$20

Both the **Harlequin® Special Edition** and **Harlequin® Heartwarming™** series feature compelling novels filled with stories of love and strength where the bonds of friendship, family and community unite.

YES! Please send me 2 FREE novels from the Harlequin Special Edition or Harlequin Heartwarming series and my 2 FREE gifts (gifts are worth about $10 retail). After receiving them, if I don't wish to receive any more books, I can return the shipping statement marked "cancel." If I don't cancel, I will receive 6 brand-new Harlequin Special Edition books every month and be billed just $4.99 each in the U.S or $5.74 each in Canada, a savings of at least 17% off the cover price or 4 brand-new Harlequin Heartwarming Larger-Print books every month and be billed just $5.74 each in the U.S. and $6.24 each in Canada, a savings of at least 21% off the cover price. It's quite a bargain! Shipping and handling is just 50¢ per book in the U.S. and $1.25 per book in Canada.* I understand that accepting the 2 free books and gifts places me under no obligation to buy anything. I can always return a shipment and cancel at any time. The free books and gifts are mine to keep no matter what I decide.

Choose one: ☐ **Harlequin Special Edition**
(235/335 HDN GNMP)

☐ **Harlequin Heartwarming**
Larger-Print
(161/361 HDN GNPZ)

Name (please print)

Address
Apt. #

City
State/Province
Zip/Postal Code

Email: Please check this box ☐ if you would like to receive newsletters and promotional emails from Harlequin Enterprises ULC and its affiliates. You can unsubscribe anytime.

Mail to the **Harlequin Reader Service:**
IN U.S.A.: P.O. Box 1341, Buffalo, NY 14240-8531
IN CANADA: P.O. Box 603, Fort Erie, Ontario L2A 5X3

Want to try 2 free books from another series! Call 1-800-873-8635 or visit www.ReaderService.com.

*Terms and prices subject to change without notice. Prices do not include sales taxes, which will be charged (if applicable) based on your state or country of residence. Canadian residents will be charged applicable taxes. Offer not valid in Quebec. This offer is limited to one order per household. Books received may not be as shown. Not valid for current subscribers to the Harlequin Special Edition or Harlequin Heartwarming series. All orders subject to approval. Credit or debit balances in a customer's account(s) may be offset by any other outstanding balance owed by or to the customer. Please allow 4 to 6 weeks for delivery. Offer available while quantities last.

Your Privacy—Your information is being collected by Harlequin Enterprises ULC, operating as Harlequin Reader Service. For a complete summary of the information we collect, how we use this information and to whom it is disclosed, please visit our privacy notice located at corporate.harlequin.com/privacy-notice. From time to time we may also exchange your personal information with reputable third parties. If you wish to opt out of this sharing of your personal information, please visit readerservice.com/consumerchoice or call 1-800-873-8635. **Notice to California Residents**—Under California law, you have specific rights to control and access your data. For more information on these rights and how to exercise them, visit corporate.harlequin.com/california-privacy.

HSEHW22

Love Harlequin romance?

DISCOVER.

Be the first to find out about promotions, news and exclusive content!

Facebook.com/HarlequinBooks

Twitter.com/HarlequinBooks

Instagram.com/HarlequinBooks

Pinterest.com/HarlequinBooks

YouTube.com/HarlequinBooks

ReaderService.com

EXPLORE.

Sign up for the Harlequin e-newsletter and download a free book from any series at **TryHarlequin.com**

CONNECT.

Join our Harlequin community to share your thoughts and connect with other romance readers!
Facebook.com/groups/HarlequinConnection

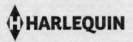

HSOCIAL2021